The JOURNEY of the FLAME

THE JOURNEY
OF THE FLAME

BY
WALTER NORDHOFF

FOREWORD BY
REBECCA SOLNIT

SANTA CLARA UNIVERSITY, SANTA CLARA, CALIFORNIA
HEYDAY BOOKS, BERKELEY, CALIFORNIA

Library of Congress Cataloging-in-Publication Data
Nordhoff, Walter, 1858-1937.
  The journey of the flame / Walter Nordhoff ; foreword by
Rebecca Solnit.
    p. cm.
  ISBN 1-890771-58-9 (pbk. : alk. paper)
  1. California–History–To 1846–Fiction. I. Solnit, Rebecca. II.
Title.
  PS3527.O438 J68 2002
  813'.52–dc21
                                        2002010026

Cover Illustration: Alfredo Ramos Martinez
Cover & Interior Design: Philip Krayna Design, Berkeley, CA
Printing and Binding: McNaughton & Gunn, Inc., Saline MI

Orders, inquiries, and correspondence should be addressed to:
    Heyday Books
    P. O. Box 9145, Berkeley, CA 94709
    (510) 549-3564, fax (510) 549-1889
    www.heydaybooks.com

Printed in the United States of America
10 9 8 7 6 5 4 3 2 1

RESPECTFULLY DEDICATED
TO THE MEMORY
of
La Señora Doña Ysabel
de la Cerda Sanhudo
BY COMMAND OF JUAN COLORADO,
WHO HAVING BEEN ONCE HER SERVANT
OF NECESSITY ALWAYS SO REMAINS

CONTENTS

Contents

FOREWORD

THE JOURNEY OF THE FLAME can be read as many things: as a coming-of-age story, as a picaresque tale in the vein of *Don Quixote* or *Candide*, as a travel narrative, as an Old California romance in the mode established by Helen Hunt Jackson's best-seller *Ramona*, or as a veiled self-portrait. For Walter Nordhoff (1855–1937), it was an occasion for exploring his real love, Baja California as he knew it during the decades it was his home. The book is lavish in details of desert plants, marine life, and mule psychology, of Mexican equestrian abilities, codes of honor, and customs, and Nordhoff, writing as Antonio de Fierro Blanco, stresses the accuracy of these descriptions in his introduction to the book:

> Every statement regarding Missions, roads, animals, fish, or plants is taken directly from histories, private letters of that time, or from conversations with descendants of those who then lived. I felt that accuracy was so much to be desired that I had a map drawn from old sources, giving each day's travel as that which a well-tended mule train could easily make. Mission conditions are as nearly those of 1810 as documents and histories, corrected by those who saw these Missions then or soon after, enable me to give. Mexican life at that date is, I think, correctly described, as my account comes from children of those who thus lived.

In Nordhoff's narrative, Baja California seems to have remained for many decades longer what Alta California ceased to be when American California swept aside its vaquero pastorale.

The romance of Mexican California is a complicated business, celebrating a relatively brief interval between the indigenous and Anglo phases of the state, an interval in which the ranchers in their extravagance of horsemanship, festivity, and courtesy seem to have paralleled another antebellum era, that of the Deep South. Indeed, both systems were propped up by ownership of huge tracts of land and, more or less, ownership of people to work that land—though the affectionately patronizing view of natives that Nordhoff describes and takes up as his own is far from southern attitudes about slaves, and he often disparages the efforts to civilize them too. (The "first boarding-school for girls in the Californias" taught its six hundred pupils "to wear clothes, cook Spanish food, and care for a house; after which they were turned loose to live without clothes, eat bugs, and dwell in the open.") Nordhoff is affectionate everywhere, from his descriptions of cactuses and pearls to those of cross-cultural confusion, and so this book is a love story, although this romantic love is for a place and a people. The way he came to that place is telling.

Walter Nordhoff's paternal grandparents emigrated from Germany in the 1830s, reputedly because of their politics rather than the poverty that drove most to cross the Atlantic. They took themselves and the family silver to the Mississippi Valley, then the western frontier of American settlement, where they sipped mineral water and died young anyway. Their son Charles (1830–1901) ran away to sea in 1844, a golden age in American sailing if for no other reason than that a lot of literary material washed up in that decade, including Richard Henry Dana's *Two Years Before the Mast* and Herman Melville's *Typee* and *Omoo*. Charles Nordhoff wrote a few sensational sea adventures himself before moving on to other subjects, including the evils of slavery and the merits of religion. Most notable among his many books of travel description, at least for its impact, was the 1873 *California for Health, Pleasure, and Residence.* Nordhoff had gone west and written about California extensively for *Harper's Magazine,* the *New York Tribune,* and other prominent journals; the expanded version that made up this book was intended as a lure to bring out more immigrants on the new railroad lines, and as such it was a tremendous success, helping to produce the biggest wave of immigration since the gold rush. The book was so helpful to the Southern Pacific, which was the transportation monopoly that ran California like a private kingdom into the twentieth century, that the corporation reprinted it in 1880. And because of it, Nordhoff père was offered another job in 1887, one that lies at the root of *The Journey of the Flame.*

Virtually the entire northern half of Baja California had come into the possession of the Mexican International Company of Hartford, Connecticut, and the principals of this Anglo-American real-estate investment firm wanted a book that would promote settlers and investors to purchase some of their eighteen million acres. Nordhoff produced a sort of extended prospectus and press release lacking the descriptive charms of *California for Health, Pleasure, and Residence* and was rewarded with a fifty-thousand-acre rancho a little south of the brand-new coastal town of Ensenada. ("I selected and bought a small tract on and near the bay of Todos Santos," he wrote.) He sent for his son, Walter, to manage this tract.

Walter Nordhoff had earned a degree in mining engineering from Yale's Sheffield School during the glory days when Louis Agassiz held court there, Clarence King would pass through between expeditions, and geology was the most exciting and controversial science of the day, but like his father he lived by his pen, advancing as a journalist until he was the European correspondent for the *New York Herald.* He had mastered several languages and acquired, said one literary historian, "a lifelong passion for all things Spanish." In 1890, when his father sent for him to come and manage the vast new Baja hacienda, he seems to have responded with alacrity. With Philadelphia society wife Sarah and three-year-old son Charles Bernard Nordhoff (1887–1947) in tow, he made the leap from London and Berlin to this little-populated coastal desert.

The Mexican International Company eventually collapsed and was replaced by new schemes, and Baja California never attracted settlers as Alta California had, but the Nordhoffs stayed on. The men hunted on land and on sea, sailed, fished, rode horses, and presumably participated in some activity to pay for all this, but when it came time to school the children, Sarah Nordhoff insisted they return to southern California. The extent to which Walter had embraced local ranchero culture is evident in a story about his son Charles's visit with school friends to the hacienda early in the twentieth century. The schoolboys had managed to catch a two-hundred-pound sea turtle the day before, but rather than turtle soup for breakfast, Walter had served a "typical Mexican dish" of a blackened steer's head. He popped out an eyeball from the seared sockets and, calling it the best part, put it on the plate of one of the visiting boys, winked at his son, and chewed and swallowed the other eyeball. It was an act that Don Juan Obrigón, the protagonist of *The Journey of the Flame,* would have appreciated—whimsical, bold, and challenging.

It is not hard to read Obrigón as a fantastic self-portrait of the blond outsider-aristocrat Walter Nordhoff. A redhead and eventually a great landowner and patron, Obrigón begins life in Mexico, the son of an Irishman named O'Brien and thereby an eternal outsider, though not an unfortunate one. This O'Brien seems to have been nothing more than a castaway sailor but left behind the impression that he was a king at home in Ireland. His son succeeds on his own merits of loyalty, bravery, resourcefulness, and aplomb to become something of a king himself. *The Journey of the Flame* tells us how he got there and, with its retrospective glance, a little of what "there" was like.

Nordhoff was in his late seventies when he published this tale of a hundred-and-four-year-old Obrigón looking back on his life. Though the book sets us up to expect a biography, the last eighty years or so of Obrigón's life are summed up quickly as the fruits of the youthful adventure the book describes. Nordhoff too seems to have had most of his adventures in the first half of his life, with his father in California, with the press in Europe, and with his family in Baja, where he lived on and off until the Mexican Revolution of 1910.

(The hacienda wasn't confiscated by the new government, but Nordhoff felt doubtful about the safety of outsiders and the strength of their title to the land.)

In late middle age, Nordhoff, with his son Charles Bernard and John H. McKnight, started the California China Products Company in San Diego, manufacturing dishes and the kind of ceramic tile that had become popular as part of the Mission Revival style—celebrating Hispanic California in another way. The enterprise lasted only six years. The First World War made the quantities of fuel needed to fire the kilns hard to come by, and Charles the Younger, whose own aristocratic sense of self had always scorned factory management, joined the army. After the war, this son launched a career as a writer that, after faltering beginnings, became a vast success. He moved to Tahiti in 1920 with a collaborator, James Norman Hall, and together they wrote adventure novels, culminating in the *Mutiny on the Bounty* trilogy, whose first volume was a huge publishing success the year before *The Journey of the Flame* appeared.

The Journey of the Flame is framed as a tale of youth told by an old man, written down by another, and translated by a third, and nowhere in its original publication was Nordhoff's name mentioned. Obrigón and Antonio de Fierro Blanco were fictions, but he who (as it says on the title page) "Englished" the book, Walter de Steiguer, was a real person, selected perhaps for friendship, perhaps because he shared the real author's first name. De Steiguer was a young man with a degree from MIT and a gift for ceramic glazes who had lived with Charles the Younger and his brother Franklin Nordhoff when all three worked at the dish and tile factory, and he remained friends with Walter Nordhoff and stayed in southern California long after Charles left.

The literary successes of his father and son suggest reasons for Walter Nordhoff's elaborate distancing and veils of pseudonyms; he may have wished to avoid comparisons and complications for both himself and them, and yet, as literature, his small offering far exceeds the promotional and journalistic work of the father, and it has wit and elegance not found in the earnest page-turners of the son. There is, for example, this "translator's" footnote: "El Camino del Rey: the King's Highway, now changed in California to Camino Real, in deference to the Monroe Doctrine." Or there is his long disquisition on dreaded nicknames, including a family called "Sabichi, because the grandfather had often used, and improperly pronounced, a very offensive American oath."

Although *The Journey of the Flame* is highly stylized, humorous, and self-consciously mannered, it does share elements of the literature of Walter Nordhoff's father and son: a preoccupation with the good place and the good life. Charles the Elder's most intriguing book has the unwieldy title of *The communistic societies of the United States; from personal visit and observation: including detailed accounts of the Economists, Zoarites, Shakers, the Amana, Oneida, Bethel, Aurora, Icarian and other existing societies; their religious creeds, social practices, numbers, industries, and present condition.* Taking a surprisingly evenhanded approach, he declines to call his unusual subjects fanatics and notices that they are for the most part better off than the laborers—industrial and agricultural—of the time. The book seems motivated by a sincere curiosity about how we might better live. And the *Mutiny on the Bounty* books are most memorable for their vision of a tropical paradise with its beautiful women, abundant foodstuffs, sensual lack of hurry, and balmy weather. Charles the Younger had in fact embraced this vision, marrying a Tahitian woman with whom he had four children, and not leaving Tahiti until after the outbreak of the Second World War.

A few years before Charles left for Tahiti, the factory had folded and Nordhoff had retired to Santa Barbara. He died there only four years after this book was published. It had been a long journey for the Nordhoffs, from Germany to Tahiti in under a century. Walter Nordhoff's vision of paradise, being in the middle generation of this journey, had less practical problem solving and more of the chivalric virtues than his father's, and less harmony and ease about it than his son's vision. It was a paradise of adventure and heroism, of the full development of the physical and moral man in the face of difficulties and dangers. And in this it also recalls the boys' adventure books that Walter Nordhoff's father and son wrote, but this is not a boy's book as boys would see it but as an old man did after the adventures were long over. It is as though something of late summer sunlight streams over it, gilding its subjects and giving them shadows that stretch far longer than they are tall, placing them in that magical moment just before darkness. This darkness is both the end of its author's life and of the way of life he knew in Baja California long before.

— REBECCA SOLNIT
San Francisco

THE JOURNEY
OF THE FLAME

BEING AN ACCOUNT OF ONE
YEAR IN THE LIFE
of
SEÑOR DON JUAN OBRIGÓN

KNOWN DURING PAST YEARS IN
THE THREE CALIFORNIAS
as
JUAN COLORADO

AND TO THE INDIADA OF THE SAME
as
THE FLAME

BORN AT SAN JOSÉ DEL ARROYO,
LOWER CALIFORNIA, MEXICO, IN 1798 AND,
HAVING SEEN THREE CENTURIES CHANGE CUSTOMS
AND MANNERS, DIED ALONE IN 1902 AT THE
GREAT CARDON, NEAR ROSARIO, MEXICO, WITH
HIS FACE TURNED TOWARD THE SOUTH

WRITTEN DOWN BY
ANTONIO DE FIERRO BLANCO

ENGLISHED BY
WALTER DE STEIGUER

For this autobiography I make no apology.

Those who know Mexico, and those who love the remnants of early California, will ask none.

For my part in catching the words of a rapid talker, who often used antique Spanish words, and was much given to idioms from a dozen Indian languages, I crave indulgence—especially from those who could have done better than I.

Beyond this nothing, except according to our ancient customs, when a worthy story-teller begins his tale:

—GENTE DE RAZÓN

THE JOURNEY
OF THE FLAME

JUANITO'S ROUTE ········

Scale of Miles

40 30 20 10 0   50   100   150

INTRODUCTION

I HAVE BEEN ASKED by readers of this book to give the early history of Jesuit Missions in Lower California, Mexico, and their fate after the Franciscans and Dominicans (who followed the Jesuits) took them over.

In 1697, the Jesuits landed near Loreto on the Lower California Peninsula, to which they had been ordered by the King of Spain. They came gladly to face the unknown but certain perils of a desert and barbarous land. They felt God had called them to save the souls of millions of Indians, who did not know they had souls, and always politely resented having souls forced upon them.

Hell caused the only great Indian rebellion of those days. A tactless missionary, preaching one freezing midwinter morning to houseless, unclothed Indians, represented Hell to his congregation as an eternally hot place, yet indignantly refused their request for immediate access to Hell. Religion at times makes these errors. In this case it cost some thousands of lives, but unfortunately not that of the preacher.

The two greatest Jesuits in Lower California were Salvatierra and Ugarte. Both were unceasing workers with hands and minds. Both had tact and knowledge of humanity. Salvatierra was that most unusual product of theology, a fanatic with a kindly soul and also a sense of humor. Moreover, he understood that the body must be fed before the soul can be saved. Though after an Indian's soul was saved, Salvatierra might be a bit careless about his body.

Ugarte can only be described as the highest type of missionary and of man. He was human in all ways except in weakness: over six feet high, heavily built, and of enormous strength and vitality, yet not without culture and learning. His exploits thrill me as I am seldom thrilled. But there was no heroine in his dreams. He planted, harvested, and cooked for his congregation. He built great stone churches with only Indians to help him. These Indians had never seen a house, and were by their own religion forbidden to build a wall over four feet high. Ugarte constructed the first grist mill in the Californias, and attempted a woolen mill while New England was still a wilderness. He hewed timber in high mountains and hauled it to the sea, where he built a ship. What he did not do would be easier to describe than what he did.

Above all, he clothed, fed, and civilized countless thousands of Indians so barbarous that they called his first house door "The House's Mouth," because all who went in were swallowed by it.

Under the Jesuits, the Indian population of the California would have increased had it not been for diseases brought into the country by an infected and filthy soldiery. In spite of such diseases, the Indian population of Lower California did not begin its great decrease until the Jesuits were expelled.

Among the noteworthy Jesuit accomplishments was a College for Indian Girls, which in 1771 housed and fed several hundred girls. No female college then existed within the limits of the United States.

Political intrigues at Madrid, Spain, drove the Jesuits from all Spanish dominions, seventy years after their arrival in Lower California, Mexico. These seventy years remain unexcelled anywhere for civilizing work done among savages. With their expulsion came that quick depopulation of Lower California, which everywhere marks the destruction of a Indian civilization (religion) before any other is completely substituted for it.

The Jesuit dream of a theocracy under their exclusive control would undoubtedly have produced in the Three Californias a vast Indian population, contented, hard-working, and happy in spite of intellectual and religious tyranny. But even the wisest Jesuit could not foresee what steam and money-lust were forcing upon the world.

Jesuits in Lower California, as elsewhere in the world, objected to having safety forced upon them by the presence of soldiers. They saw correctly, in troops and governors, only diseases, epidemics, and political corruption, which then everywhere followed Spanish soldiers and governors.

The Jesuits in Lower California were, with few exceptions, men of unusual force of character and intellect. Many of their priests had been leaders in their own countries. Some came of noble and rich families. All lived lives of poverty, loneliness, and the hardest of physical work. Nevertheless, their geodetic records of the rising coast of the Peninsula have not been equaled, for that district, down to our own time. Their botanical studies are well worth the attention of botanists. Their zoological work in Lower California has been excelled within the last forty years, but is still in some respects unique.

They believed in the Devil as firmly as in God. That, of course, in our time makes them ridiculous; than which nothing is more fatal.

By order of the King of Spain, Franciscans succeeded Jesuits in all the Californias as the Church Militant. Franciscans, under Serra, devoted themselves to Alta California, with disastrous results to Lower California. When Franciscans practically abandoned Lower California, the Dominicans replaced them and ruled the Coast nearly to San Diego.

I had the good fortune, as a young man, to hunt in Lower California when it was, in its northern part at least, almost devoid of Mexican control: no custom-houses: few officials: no taxes. The hawks were still called *"empleados"*[1] because they so deftly robbed the gulls and pelicans of their fish. To a horse-breaker who stuck tight to his mount they still called *'Qué abalón!'* (because an abalone needs a crowbar to pry it loose from its rock).

I talked much with the few remaining Indians, and had as servants half-breeds who personally remembered the arrival of Mission ships.

[1] *Empleados:* minor officials.

In the uneventful days of their far-off youth these were great events, and they still chuckled at the joy of Indian women given a few yards of bright calico from these ships.

I am convinced from these talks, and from books, that the population of Lower California was greater before a Spanish soldier set foot on that Peninsula than at any time since then. In 1696, before the Spanish landed, there were only Indians. Now there are men of all races and mixtures of races.

Civilization speaks for itself in Lower California.

THE JOURNEY OF THE FLAME is in fact an historical novel in which certain deviations from the truth are essential. In the main, every statement made therein is truthful, though some are founded on legends and family traditions. For instance, San José del Arroyo does not exist. Its prototype does, however, and I have given a fictitious name merely because I have used events at several Missions, condensed into one for simplicity's sake. The poisoning of Juanito by the church robber was as described. The Paso del Diablo was described to me by a man who had ascended it. The battle near San Vicente is a legend, but the digging up in that vicinity, from graves, of Spanish ironwork, seems to endorse the truth of that legend. I owned one of these pieces, the decoration of which implied its making several centuries before the Spaniards conquered Mexico.

Every statement regarding Missions, roads, animals, fish, or plants is taken directly from histories, private letters of that time, or from conversations with descendants of those who then lived. I felt that accuracy was so much to be desired that I had a map drawn from old sources, giving each day's travel as that which a well-tended mule train could easily make. Mission conditions are as nearly those of 1810 as documents and histories, corrected by those who saw these Missions then or soon after, enable me to give. Mexican life at that date is, I think, correctly described, as my account comes from children of those who thus lived.

Don Juan Obrigón, who, at a hundred years old, herein relates his childhood and (as a boy eleven to thirteen years old) his adventurous muleback trip from the south of Lower California to San Francisco Bay in the north, is called "Juanito" at first, later "Don Juanito." *Don* means practically "Honorable Sir" or "Master," and is applied to the first name of anyone respected or in authority. *Señor* means "Mister."

The Don Firmín Sanhudo of the story came to the Three Californias armed with the powers of the King of Spain, to decide whether Spain could retain its American colonies. All about him called him informally "Don Firmín."

La Señora Doña Ysabel de la Cerda Sanhudo, his wife, would not be alluded to by Don Firmín's men except in emergency. Then she would be called "La Señora de Sanhudo." Juanito, in his ignorance of etiquette, calls her "Doña Ysabel," but never to the men about him. By the monks, and at Monterey, she was called formally "Lady Ysabel," because of her title from the ancient De La Cerda family. Inocente is her son.

Of necessity some Spanish terms are left in this book, as there are no good English equivalents. The context explains them.

Human life was not of great value (except possibly to the owner) in Spanish America. The knife was the most highly prized weapon. To be a deadly fighter with a knife in each hand was to be the equivalent of a two-gun man on the American frontier. In this knife-fighting the feet were used more than the arms, but never to kick with. Fist-fighting was held in the greatest contempt. Even small boys fought with wooden knives or swords.

—*A. de F. B.*

PRELUDE

"D ON JUAN!" called a *vaquero*, dipping sideways on the saddle until his head was well within an open kitchen door. "The bulls are here."

"Shut thy mouth, gabbler! Let thy Patrón eat his *tortillas*," grumbled a woman's voice from inside the kitchen. "Finish thy coffee, Don Juan. It is well to be hot within when it is cold without." Her tone was gentle and wheedling, like that of a nurse talking to a fretful child.

"Am I then bedridden, that I cannot look at a cow before I am sodden with tepid drink?" growled an old man as he stepped from his door. He was tall and straight, with hair still flaming red. Though he shuffled his feet a trifle as he walked, and rested both hands for a moment on the door-frame, as he crossed the rough-hewn lintel, he still disdained a cane. He often said that a man who needed three legs to carry him was better underground.

"Go thy way as thou wilt," retorted his cook's voice within, "but tomorrow, when gentry come from all quarters to honor thy hundredth birthday, who will cook for them if I am sick with worry about thee? *María Santísima* guard thy stubborn throat! Who will tell them thy life-story, if thou art again ill with the grippe?" Her voice trailed off into mutterings and terminated in a crash of tin dishes.

Outside the kitchen door, *vaqueros* swept off their hats in morning greetings. A tenseness stiffened both riders and horses as the old man neared the herd of seven-year-old *mesteños*[1] were being held in front of the house that their owner might select, to his liking, three bulls to grace tomorrow's barbecue.

Don Juan Obrigón was of those men from the Old Days of the Three Californias who still believed bull's flesh the only fit food for man. He was strongly of the opinion that eternal disgrace would forever perch on his tombstone if he fed the crowd coming to honor his hundredth birthday with steer or cow's meat. He had even been heard to mutter, as he left the house of a distasteful American neighbor: "I complimented that *cabrón* by dining with him, for one must be most polite to those one most hates; and he fed me the tenderloin of a six-months'-old steer! As if I were a girl, or had no teeth. Bah! In the Old Times I would have known that his insult in offering me a tenderloin was intentional, and he would have had his knife ready to clash with mine when next we met. But now—there are no longer any manners. Perhaps he meant to compliment me by hinting I have no more teeth than a cow."

Each of these *vaqueros* knew his Patrón, Don Juan Obrigón, would take undue risks in examining these half-savage bulls, simply because his cook had again reminded him concerning an illness of ten years before, for which she still tried to nurse him. Likewise, they well knew they would all be eternally disgraced for five hundred miles north and south of his ranch if Don Juan were injured by one of these bulls.

"Who is this hag who worries our old man?" muttered a new *vaquero* to a neighbor.

"Where wast thou born, simpleton? Under a *cholla*[2] in Sonora deserts, perhaps, that thou callest her 'hag'? Guard well thy tongue, *Cholito*,[3] or Don Juan Obrigón will fasten a tin can to thy tail, and chase thee off his land. That old woman who growls at our Boss is the best cook in the Californias, and daughter of the girl Don Juan

[1] *Mesteño:* stronger than bronco. A mesteño has never felt riata or branding-iron.

[2] *Cholla:* the worst form of prickly cactus.

[3] *Cholito:* diminutive of cholo, a low class of laborer. A play on words.

would have married. If thou wert over seventy and had cared for thy Patrón for more than forty years, even thy gab might be endurable."

"Holy Mother of God!" sighed the cattle foreman. "Does our Patrón think these ill-tempered bulls respect his age or his past? Now he slaps the flank of that *orejón pinto prieto*[1] which, disputing passage of the Cliff Trail, killed both Manuel and his horse not a month ago! I dare not wound his pride by a word or an act. If his Saint brings him back alive from among these surly brutes, I'll stay drunk for a month to forget what worries he causes me."

Near the foreman was a *vaquero* dressed in leather from head to foot, as is the custom in the extreme south of the Lower California Peninsula. He suddenly swung his riata loop so that it gradually lengthened, and fast enough, in its semi-vertical circle, to create a low musical note as it tore through the air.

"The music of the bull-pens" that melody is called. All bulls in the waiting herd looked around, their attention momentarily distracted from the unusual sight of a man walking fearlessly among them.

"Well done, Pedro of San José del Arroyo!" exclaimed the foreman. "*Ojala!*[2] We may yet save our Old Man. See Don Juan's red hair rise as he hears thy riata-tune from his old village!"

Each *vaquero*, following Pedro's example, tuned his riata. Their horses, excited as always by this leathern melody, danced with nervous eagerness to be after the bulls; but as California riders habitually boast, so that a silver peso would cover the tracks of all four prancing hoofs.

In front of the kitchen door lounged a group of American tramps, mingled with Mexicans and Indians; all waiting for that indiscriminate Mexican hospitality which daily feeds all who need food. If American beggars, they are fed courteously, but with concealed contempt, because they give nothing in return; while Indians and Mexicans of the same class carry water, chop wood, or by some such service show gratitude for what they receive.

[1] *Orejon pinto prieto:* a black pinto bull without earmarks, and never having felt the riata, therefore, exceptionally dangerous.

[2] *Ojala:* God grant it.

"Who's that Antiquity among the bulls?" asked a ragged American tramp. He had started around the ancient adobe house, but at its corner met a stray bull, occupied in pawing the earth and at intervals lifting clods with its horns. Therefore, he retreated with great haste to the kitchen door, looking behind him so anxiously that he fell over a dog asleep in the sun.

"Shut up, Bonehead!" whispered his mate. "They'll think you locoed by the sun, and souse a bucket of water over your thick skull. It's Don Juan Obrigón—Juan Colorado! Or perhaps you've heard him called 'Red John.'"

"Or 'The Flame,'" suggested an aged Indian politely. "When I handled a bowstring,[1] he once destroyed the warriors of a wild tribe by fire, which sprang from the earth at his command. They perished in flame while he rode on, not even looking back to see whether any survived to chase him."

Meanwhile, within the kitchen, a dozen girls gossiped as they prepared breakfast for *vaqueros* and tramps.

"Will Don Juan recite his life-history to the gentry tomorrow, after the bulls are eaten?" asked a young girl. She was newly arrived from the south to be taught cooking in Doña Luz's famous kitchen, where the only degree given was a box on the ears, awarded by the old lady when her jealousy of a girl's success in cooking caused her to lose her temper. "The Priest waits" that accolade was called; since all whose ears were thus boxed obtained husbands within a month.

"Who knows?" two or three answered in chorus.

"Why is the Patrón only a hundred years old?" continued the newcomer. "When I left San José del Arroyo, my parents said he should be a hundred and four years old this year."

"So he is," assented the group of young cooks, laughing at her mystification. "It is an old custom that when one reaches a hundred years of age he must recite to his guests, on his birthday, all he remembers of his life. Our Patrón, at each birthday for the last three years, has refused his duty. Therefore, Doña Luz states privately at

[1] *When I handled a bowstring:* when I was young.

the end of each barbecue that he is but ninety-nine; and that next year, becoming a hundred, he will recite his life's history to all who are polite enough to be present."

"Will he, this year?" The newcomer seemed almost breathless with interest.

"*Ojala!* If so, I shall spend a hungry afternoon tomorrow," answered the oldest girl present. "I would not dare to eat a mouthful while he speaks, lest the grinding of my teeth cause me to lose a word!" And she opened her mouth to show a set of teeth splendidly equipped for food.

"Thou! Go hungry!" laughed the rest. "Thy teeth are always occupied and were so busy last night that all heard Miguel's whisper except the one he meant it for!"

NEXT DAY AT NOON, when first hunger had been appeased, the carcasses of three seven-year bulls still turned slowly on their spits above red-hot coals. But they were now mere bony remnants of the fat cattle they had been.

Within Don Juan Obrigón's house, guests overfilled his great room, so that only doors and windows were left for *vaqueros* and the serving people. Beside the old man sat the prettiest of the girl cooks. While Doña Luz and her bevy of girls had attended to the wants of all the others, this girl had watched the Patrón's feeding and kept his plate supplied with all he best liked. They were good chums, these two—one under twenty, and the other over a hundred.

"Do not disappoint me, Don Juan," she now whispered to him. "I live only for this day, and the story so long denied us."

"*Que beso su mano,*[1] Pretty One. Were I Panchito, it would not be thy hand I would kiss!"

A sudden silence fell over all present as Doña Luz, in the old way, called shrilly, "*Gente de razón!*"[2] Such were polite and silent. This is

[1] *Que beso su mano:* who kisses your hand. The formal ending of a letter, or among the very old and formal, the thanks for a compliment.

[2] *Gente de razón:* people with reason.

the ancient demand for silence while he of his hundredth birthday relates what he has seen and what he has learned from life. Of events and of people he may tell, but mainly he is expected to draw conclusions from his experience, that youths of from ninety-nine years down may benefit from his wisdom.

Don Juan turned toward his guests. "To begin is difficult," he said slowly, in that voice which had been deep, though now beginning to shrill. "But to end will be impossible, if I am to tell you of Mission times." And so began abruptly the story of his youth.

CHAPTER I. *How Juanito Stole Molasses Candy —The Wizard Gopher*

A N OLD WOMAN cooked *panocha*[1] in an earthen olla outside our hut, over a tiny fire of last year's corn cobs. When it was thick like *masa*,[2] she drew out great gobs with a wooden ladle. Then pulled it to a straw yellow color, using a dry oak limb to hold one end of the sweet paste as she doubled thin streamers over it.

Occasionally she gave me two of her sticky fingers to lick, and once I bit these fingers, not meaning to, but in fear lest some remnant of *alfinique*[3] escape my lips. Then she slapped my dirty face with her molasses-crusted palm, and I, retiring out of reach, tested the ability of my tongue to cover my whole face and leave no trace of candy upon it. Already I had learned that my fingers, no matter how carefully used, failed to convey to my mouth all that cane syrup left by the hag's hand; but that my tongue extracted the very last flavor of such sweetness from all parts it could reach. How I envied a lizard its ability to use a tongue so long, and so accurately aimed, that what it desired returned to an expectant mouth! I spent hours feeding flies to my pet cachora that I might learn its secret, but uselessly.

The old woman received brown *panocha* cakes from the padres of our Cathedral of San Borromeo, the Friend of Christ. This was

---

[1] *Panocha:* brown sugar. [2] *Masa:* common dough. [3] *Alfinique:* molasses candy.

weighed out to her, and she returned to them a fixed weight of sweet yellow candy, made up into cakes like a small palm leaf. These cakes were composed of twisted strings of *alfinique*, brittle when it is chilled, and delicious beyond dreams. Any devil could have bought my tiny soul for one of them; but until a child leaves his father's house, Satan may not tempt him.

A hard bargain our monks of San Borromeo drove with this old hag. If she delivered less than the weight they demanded, she lost much of that scanty dole on which she lived. I knew this, for children of the poor are born with their eyes open, and hearing much, know all things before they can walk. An advantage that is, if one has but the wit to emerge from poverty. This I knew, but a piece of *alfinique* on my forehead, left there by the old woman's palm when she slapped my face, tempted me. My tongue could not reach it, and I felt it to be so small that I could scarce taste it on my finger, if I thus removed it.

Therefore, I let it stick where it was, as something to dream of that night, and with my left hand snatched a cake of *alfinique* when the old woman's back was turned. She screamed like a hawk when she missed it, but as I was stark naked and had stuck her warm, gooey cake in the small of my back, she did not think evil of me. Rather, she looked toward my mother, just then stooping to enter our brush hut. Terror-stricken by a million fears, and scarce knowing what I did, I turned my thumb backward toward our hut, and the hag took this as a hint and poured abuse upon my mother. Then, emboldened because her curse received no answer, the candy-maker entered our hut; but in a moment she came out again, sobbing.

"It was as if I had accused the Holy Virgin of stealing," she said to me. "Mother of God! What a look your mother gave me!"

"Juanito!" called my mother. I knew I must obey the call, for my mother was not one to trifle with. Also, a thief must be bold, I had heard older boys say; so I went into our hut as if she had called for firewood.

"Turn about, little thief," she ordered, with that uncanny knowledge of hers; and pulling the cake of *alfinique* from my hips, she brushed it off and began to eat it.

My very soul melted within me while she crunched that molasses candy. Had I not been the son of an Irish King, I would have squirmed on the floor in an agony of grief. I knew then that all my life I had waited to steal that great treasure, and that never again could I hope for such a chance. I was but a little tad, pot-bellied, bow-legged, and naked as when born; but I learned quickly then what I have never forgotten since—that it is an error to allow fear to prevent thought. Had I not feared overmuch, I could have escaped with my treasure while the hag entered our hut.

"Feel what it is to steal and be caught," said my mother. "Honesty may go hungry, but a thief knows the gripings of Hell in his belly." Henceforth I thought carefully around all such adventures before I took the smallest chance. If, after this, any profited by an error of mine, it was without my knowledge then or later.

At this time of which I speak, I was coming four years old. We lived on corn *tortillas* and beans *puro*[1] so that I was hungry all day and most of the night. Had it not been for an old cow which had lost its calf, I might not have grown tall, strong, and wily, to enjoy life as God sends it, and to return to others as they gave to me, whether good or bad. To this cow, each morning, I crawled on all fours, blatting like her calf, before her owner was up. The rich morning's milk, sucked from her teats, carried me each day with new strength into further pastures, where food was to be had in exchange for guile.

I then owed but one grudge to God—that, if in the excitement of sucking warm creamy milk from this cow, I lifted my hands from the ground, the beast kicked me over and went off, lowing, with my breakfast. At four years old I was still so small, when on my hands and knees, that there were two of her teats I could never reach, despite endless tryings. These two, I dreamed at night, yielded liquid

[1] *Beans puro:* without fat.

alfinique, such as the old woman pulled in front of our door. What contortions of my body, what stretchings of my neck I made to reach those two short nipples, without taking my hands from the corral ground, and thus losing my cow! How often I pulled grass or leaves for this brute which ate without thanks! Yet never could I breakfast without pretense of having four legs, like her real calf.

I had quickly learned that she regarded me with suspicion and held her milk if I did not often push up violently against her udder with my stubby nose. A trial this was to me, until I found that the back of my head bumped upwards against her milk bag would answer as well as my soft nose to calm her suspicions. If I bumped too hard, a forward stroke of her hoof knocked me over; though little I minded this, as thereafter the cow, bending her neck, licked my bare back and seemed more content that I breakfast my fill. Only on one point was she adamant. No calf had ever stood on two legs. Nor could I, if I would satisfy my hunger.

But enough of hardship. Providence is kind to those she maltreats. Doubtless, but for suppleness of body thus learned from my cow, I had suffered more and done less in life. Moreover, from this cow I learned much as to the necessity of yielding when one would conquer circumstances. Many times in later life, when Fate blocked my path, I stood for a second thinking, "What would this cow have me to do?" Never have I failed to find a way. For the world has its prejudices as had my breakfast cow: and I have dined throughout life as I breakfasted in childhood—by regarding prejudices and disregarding circumstances. Thus it is with all who, having little, yet live well and do much.

There are some who say otherwise and preach morality. I have talked with them and assented politely, but all such are those who, born to land and cattle, yet leave neither to their children. One of this type I fed but yesterday, as, clothed in rags and leaning hard upon a crooked stick, he stopped my horse and asked for alms.

Of right and wrong I am no judge, having been born poor, but in no court have I ever appeared even as witness. I would any time rather privately stab a man who haled me to testify in court than so disgrace myself. A knife wound sullies no man's reputation, but to write what the tongue relates, in a book, may injure many. Says the proverb: "A judge and a lawyer drove Satan from Heaven. Without these two there could be no Hell."

My mother was a beautiful woman, nearly white, who in great poverty still refused all advances from men, whether for her right hand or for her left.

"I await my Irish King," she said, proudly. But having left us after I was born, he never again returned to care for us.

My father came from a great ship with three masts and many sails which the wind filled as it does the wings of the *quileli*.[1] On one tack this ship neared our river entrance, and while all its men worked with sails, my father jumped overboard and swam to land. There was a great commotion as he leaped into the sea. He had been steersman, and his ship hung in the wind when he sprang overboard, until we hoped that it might be wrecked on our rocks, which we called "Gifts of God." Many a ship had there yielded its treasures to us since these rocks are jagged teeth so well hidden that little foam shows except at low tide.

Because of danger from our rocks, this ship's men cursed violently and ran about shouting, but no one dared follow my father. When he had landed, he lay so long upon they beach asleep that Felipe, whose turn it was to have that which came ashore, pulled off his clothes without stabbing him, thinking him dead. But when Felipe would have jerked off a medal my father wore, my father struck him such a mighty blow with his clenched fist that thereafter we called him "Philip Flatnose."

My mother was the best-born as well as the most beautiful girl in our village of San José del Arroyo, and within a week after he landed, my father sat outside her house each evening, singing. He knew no

[1] *Quileli:* This has become a semi-mystical bird, and its cry foretells death, earthquakes, and great catastrophes. There are still a few very aged Indian wizards who can interpret its calls, but I have never been fortunate enough to hear its cry while in company with a wizard.—*A. de F. B.*

Spanish, but sang in Irish, so like a mating nightingale that all listened to him. Even our *cantina* was emptied that its drunkards might hear him; though not in sight, truly, for that is not etiquette when a girl is serenaded.

One night my grandfather, who hated all strangers, stood in his doorway and cursed my father. Thus should the serenade have ceased. But my father was ignorant of our customs, and cursed in his turn so loudly and with such strange words that my grandfather retired within doors, ashamed. What made it harder for those in the house was that they could not understand one word of what my father said. It might be, therefore, that he used words for which a knife is the only remedy.

My uncles then went out with daggers, but my father danced about in irregular fashion, twirling a heavy stick around his head. When each of my uncles in turn would have stabbed him, he tapped them one by one upon the head and they lay down to sleep for a while. A stick with dancing is not usual with us.

My mother, a girl of sixteen, watched from the doorway, and when her brothers lay upon the ground, drew her *mantilla* about her head and went away with my father. What else could she do? A girl must have some protector, and when father and brothers are helpless it must be a man who calls her. But my grandfather and grandmother cursed them both from the doorway, and when my father would have returned to quiet them, she held him back.

In the struggle her *mantilla* fell from her, and thereafter she was called "Bareface," for it is a disgrace that a girl goes to her husband with her head uncovered and unashamed. Nevertheless, no one so called her while my father remained with us, for he would then twirl his stick until all fled. He came from a great city called Ireland, where he had been King, but there was a *pronunciamento* while he slept. Therefore, he fled for a time to see the world. His hair was red as is my own, and he could sing a bird out of a tree. When he was drunk he staggered up our village street calling upon God and whirling his stick until all stayed within doors.

Of his Irish language my mother learned only two words, "spalpeen," which is a charm while you fight, and "Come-on-Pat," as the sailors of a great ship called to him perpetually, when a year later and after I was born, it came for him even into our own harbor.

Long he delayed, for he loved us; but a kingdom called him, so he said, and the sailors took him away while he was drunk. My mother wept, but she was proud that his country demanded him, and taught me to say "Come-on-Pat," that I might thus greet my father when he sent for me to succeed him in his kingdom. These are the only words of any language, except my own Spanish, I ever learned. Though Indian dialects I have learned by the score, but these have no words, being simply grunts.

To him who speaks Spanish, all other languages are fit only for slaves and Indians. Irish perhaps has a rude force, for when my father cursed his best, our whole village retired within doors. But to all except my mother it lacked that music of sound which also all Indian dialects I have learned so greatly lack. There is perhaps in the world only one language—Spanish. A very learned man, who could read, once told me all other languages came from monkeys which, hearing Adam in the Garden of Eden speak Spanish, thought by chattering to imitate him.

My father's name is O'Brien, as is my own: though O'Brien being a crude and unmusical sound at which Spanish ears rebel, it was quickly changed to O'Brion. To separate the *i* and the *o*, which should not meet, we added a *g,* so that I am Obrigón. Though perhaps better known as *Juan Colorado*[1] from my hair. In my time, when wild Indians still lived in the Californias, you had but to shout "Colorado" and a tribe would scatter, as do quail when a lion drops from some tree branch into a flock of those earth-scratchers.

Obrigón and *león.* There is a rhythm and a sympathy which connects us. Never in all my life have I killed a lion. Not fear, but respect, held my hand. Cowards they call lions, and yet each one drinks fresh, clean blood of its own killing nightly. Is it cowardice to

[1] *Juan Colorado:* Red John.

remain alive? We are born to kill, not to die; and he who lives longest, and takes most, is most man.

I remember, much later when I was a man, I one day tracked a deer, which was browsing and therefore moved slowly. I put up a wet finger to test the wind, and found it was from me to the deer. Therefore, that I should not be scented by the deer, which trusts its nose more than its eyes and ears, I went around and ahead of it to wait in a *portezuelo*[1] it must pass. Looking back from the hillock on which I waited, I saw a wild Indian following my deer, while a lion tracked this Indian. I took my deer, of course, and the lion, unabashed by my presence, carried off its Indian.

"Well done, *compañero*," I called to the lion; and baring its dripping fangs, it saluted me with hearty growls.

Search for food, for a little one like myself who must eat often and much, so overshadowed all else that I remember little of my childhood. Catching minnows with a horsehair loop in the stream by our hut furnished me many a meal. Where this stream broadened into our lagoon at the seacoast I also profited much, and perforce learned to swim while still scarcely able to walk. Seeing me in this water, little larger than a tadpole and already nicknamed "Frogling," passersby threw me bits of food. To keep from larger waders that part I could not bolt down at once, I must risk swimming.

Thus again came more food thrown to me, for swimming is unusual with us. Lumps of hard *panocha* tossed to me, which being heavy sank at once and could not be wasted, caused me to dive. All this gave me such strength that soon I headed a gang of rapscallions twice as tall as myself. Even those old enough to wear clothes respected me, for I struck and bit, and kicked like my breakfast cow with the heel of my foot. In youth, as in age, few offended me without regret. Only one bitterness then filled my heart—I could not dance and twirl a stick around my head as had my father. When I tried this, his club hit my head, and all laughed, even my mother.

[1]*Portezuelo:* a narrow passage between hills or mountains.

Chapter 1

About this time came a Mission galleon, and from what it brought my mother received, as a gift from the Mission fathers, enough patterned *indiana*[1] to form a skirt. With flushed face and sparkling eyes she sewed together its breadths, using a visnaga thorn for needle and thread from mescal leaves.

I, who paraded before our padres, heading my tribe of wild lads, received twice as much as they. Cloth for a breech-clout came to me, and to them nothing, but soon I taught my companions to sink envy in pride of their chief. When my mother and I were both dressed, we walked up and down one whole day in front of my grandfather's house, in order to show those rich people we also had clothes. I would have cursed them as my father had done, but my mother prevented, saying: "Blood is blood, even though we hate each other."

While the others within took their siesta, my grandmother came to the door and stood weeping. To her we kissed our hands, and went quickly home lest the men find her or neighbors report her tears. My grandmother was but little considered in my grandfather's house because she had borne many girls and but two boys. In the village she was called *"Cuatera"*[2] since of three pairs of twins, all were girls, and this was thought to have disgraced her. Therefore she dared make no protest, nor aid us when we starved. My grandfather also had his village nickname, which from respect for him I do not mention. Being of quick temper he had exclaimed, "Drown the least comely!" when a third pair of girl twins was announced to him.

These Mission ships[3] came once a year bringing Spanish and Philippine goods, but chiefly for our monks. From them we could buy privately, if there was money. But who had money? Therefore, such things as we raised, we traded to our padres for food which we had ourselves grown; and each year they gave us small presents of luxuries from their ships. A piece of calico, or a strip of cotton cloth, a mouth-organ, or a knife.

[1] *Indiana:* a special bright-colored calico greatly admired by Indians.
[2] *Cuatera:* twinner.
[3] *Mission ships:* Manila galleons.

Always there were bitter heart-burnings over these gifts. Without luxuries from such vessels we might have been happier, for the monks' presents were always to those they approved, or to those they feared. The year I received a mouth-organ, because my influence was great among our boys, I fought perpetually with ambitious ones who would have replaced me as leader and perhaps next year have had a present. As our monks did not discourage such *pronunciamentos* against me, I hated them; though without showing this feeling. Rather, of course, with greater deference to the priests and stronger flatteries. But from this policy of gifts to flatterers and to the strong, and the hatreds thus caused, came great evils. When at last the Missions fell, they therefore had no friends, and so a system perished which was perhaps the best for the Indians and for Mexico.

Soon after I got my mouth-organ—for of years I knew nothing, and now can only count by great events—our irrigation ditch broke and caused much damage. *La Topa Chisera,*[1] all said; and with reason, for that ground we found honeycombed with holes. This gopher was famous among us all, and many a night my mother stopped my hunger cries with "The Gopher will come for you, *niño!*"

It is said that when first Father Blood-of-Christ[2] came to San José del Arroyo, he found there a devil of such force that no Indian had ever lived in our valley. This devil had wings, great claws, a beak like an eagle, and eyes spitting fire. Holding Christ's Cross before him for protection, our padre cursed this devil, and they bargained as to where it should be allowed to live. He forbade it to live either in the air or on the earth, or elsewhere except in Hell. But Father Blood-of-Christ wearied of the Cross's weight, and this devil flew nearer and nearer to him, full of foul smells and fouler words. It became a rabid skunk, which crawled toward him gritting its hydrophobic teeth. It was a multitude of rattlesnakes, which surrounded him coiled to strike, and but one evil thought would have

[1] *La Topa Chisera:* the Wizard Gopher.
[2] *Father Blood-of-Christ:* a mythical character believed in locally.

ended his life. It changed into a beautiful girl, twining her arms and calling to Father Blood-of-Christ in pure Castilian: "Thou had come at last, dear one!"

Worn out, our padre commanded: "Into the ground, then, Foul Fiend!" And there it retired to live forever, and eternally to vent its spite upon our Mission and our people. When the ground closed over this foul devil there came a great earthquake, which hid the sun and moon in dust and split the vast domed mountain of San Pablo into two halves, which remain to our day as witnesses.

Many years later, by our priests' commands, Indians built that *ẓanja* which carries water from the Falls of Guatamote to the sea. High above our land it runs, always full of water from which each in turn takes as he may need for such irrigated land as he owns. From this ditch all live, for without it there could be no crops. Therefore, the Topa Chisera attacks our *ẓanja*.

There is but one of him, for having no mate he could not breed. For him traps or poison arrows or lead are useless. Could anyone kill him, that man might for life levy a tenth on all soil crops in our valley; but the Topa Chisera lives on. Once in so often he pierces our *ẓanja* walls, and we who cower in our huts hear a thundering rush of water, which tears out yards of ditch and destroys acres of our best land. Should any go out at night, or without a padre, to repair our ditch, he who first places foot in the mire is pulled down into a great cavern, where this devil sits smiling and hungry for men's souls and bodies.

Pablo Montero, in my grandfather's time, was venturesome; and as he owned land being destroyed by flood, he went too near a *ẓanja* break, and the Topa Chisera grasped one of his feet. Those nearest him threw their longest riata, but as its loop caught about his neck they hesitated, lest they choke him.

"Haul me out!" he cried. "Save at least my soul!" And pulling with the strength of six men they extracted him, but dead from a broken neck.

CHAPTER 2. *Sacrilege at San José del Arroyo* *—The Church Robber Poisons Me*

W HEN I WAS TALL ENOUGH to grasp a horse's belly with my legs, my mother said to me: "Go thou and work. Be such a *vaquero* as was thy grandfather. When thy father sends for thee, he need then fear no shame from thee."

Therefore I sought that rich man who owned the wildest horses in our district, and asked for work on horseback. He, smiling, answered: "Choose rather a donkey," for being poor I had owned no horse; but through all my life, in the early mornings while others slept, I had ridden every calf and all the colts I could catch.

His nickname was *Burrón*.[1] Therefore, I answered him: "I have chosen the most stubborn burro within a league." The man looked at me as if to strike me, for boys do not often jest with their elders in my part of Mexico; but I smiled up at him and said: "I am not your hireling. When I am, do what you will."

At this he laughed silently, as was his way; then swore by the soul of Barabbas, that Master Thief who would have saved our Lord Jesus Christ by stealing the Cross itself that he had lived eighty years of folly, and until now no one, to his face, had called him correctly by name. No donkey, he swore, had ever been more pig-headed than he. As Barabbas was not a stealer of piglings, I bore him no grudge for his favorite oath.

[1] *Burrón:* big donkey.

Chapter 2

In truth, Don Bonifacio was stubborn. He had promised on his eightieth Saint's Day to visit his mother, who lived across our river. There came a great flood on that day, but though wife and children and grandchildren knelt to him, he would not listen. When his favorite grandchild implored him, he merely answered him, "In thy time be also a man, my son," and clad in heavy *vaquero*'s armor as if for a day in our thorn forests, Don Bonifacio spurred his horse at a run into the torrent. When his stallion drowned, he swam on alone, grasping a tree trunk here, and there avoiding a wildcat which, sitting on a thatched rooftop, spat anger at him as they floated downstream together. At a bend he took land, and by midday ate with his mother. She was a very old woman who still threatened him with her cane if he did not at once agree with her in all her thoughts.

"Be a *caballero*,"[1] she would say to Don Bonifacio. "In Spain our people were not weak and foolish as all now become. By God's help, there we took what we wanted, where we could most easily obtain it. If any man objected, by God's Soul, we did the necessary."

I have often heard her say this. Being greatly afraid of this woman, we boys often listened at her windows and copied her oaths.

"And your pay for your work on horseback?" Don Bonifacio asked me, making amusement with me, for boys are not paid.

"Food, and armor for forest riding," I answered. Then, greatly daring, "And when your Señora Mother permits, a suit of clothes that I may sing to[2] some girl."

"Angels of Christ!" he swore. "This frogling should talk to my mother. Did he answer her as he has me, he would need no leather trappings to ride our worst thorn forests. The Topa Chisera itself could not scratch through a hide like his, once my mother had tanned it for him." To get rid of me Don Bonifacio set me to breaking wild horses.

When I had tamed a fierce gelding, biting a piece from its ear as it raised its head from bucking to see if I was still on its back, they prepared leather armor for me. Within, buckskin tanned in deers'

[1] *Caballero:* gentleman.
[2] Sing to: to court.

brains, against which rawhide outer armor could chafe without bringing blood from my skin. Outside, thick hide leggings covering even my feet. Above that a jacket still thicker, which stood on an *armazón,*[1] and into which I got by stooping and rising within. This covered me, front and back, to my hips. With arm pieces and a hat of hide covering my head, ears, and forehead, I was fully protected for our wildest cattle chases through even our thorniest brush.

Thus attired, I rode to my grandfather's house, and, entering unasked, requested his blessing. Kneeling, of course, and with my hat off, to show subjection to his will, in that with his cane he could strike me dead if he so willed. Was I not of his family? Could he not do to me what he wished?

Long I knelt, for the old man slept; but though my eyes were downcast, as is proper, I thought he blinked at me as if to see how long I could remain motionless.

"What wouldst thou?" he asked finally.

And I answered: "Your blessing!"

"This King's son takes that which is not given willingly," he mocked me, but gave his blessing. Then, as I did not rise, he asked: "What else?"

And I replied, "They still call my mother 'Bareface'!"

"Send her back to my house, and her brothers' bare knives shall answer for her!" he exclaimed in anger.

Thus my mother returned to her parents and was cared for by them. Ten years she had hungered. Ten years she had waited, wasting her youth and her beauty; but for all this I had never heard a word of complaint. Were all women like my mother, there were more men in this world.

Were my mother still here, as well she might be, the adversity and the prosperity of my life would seem less incredible. To you who have come to greet me on my hundredth birthday, and who listen to the story I am telling, it may seem impossible that I should ever have been a naked child crying for food, and sucking the teats

[1] *Armazón:* a trestle which fits to and holds armor—formerly used for chain armor.

of a neighbor's cow before dawn to fill my belly. Yet even though I now own a *rancho de verano*[1] at San Buena Ventura; a cattle range in the mountains back of San Diego; and best of all, one of the desert missions taken from the padres by Mexico and sold to me; nevertheless, each word I tell you today is true.

Times change. When I was the child of whom I now tell you, the bulls which roast near us would have been surrounded by naked, yelling children, licking up the melted fat as it dripped upon the ground. Indians clad only in breech-clouts would have turned the spits, and cracked for you, with smooth cobbles, the marrow bones. They would have sighed enviously as you ate that marrow, but would have contented themselves by licking the inner tubes of the bones cast aside by you. If young and with unbroken teeth, they would have chewed up all the smaller broken parts. Often I have heard my grandfather call: "Less noise of the teeth, there!" when a cluster of Indian servants behind him thus chewed bones too noisily.

In those days of my naked childhood, when you were through eating you would have turned over the remnants of the bulls to those Mexicans who served; and in polite thanks for excellence of the meat they would have smacked their lips so loudly, over its eating, that your siesta would have been difficult. For having eaten to satiety, you would have stretched yourselves upon the ground, about an open fire, to sleep.

"He who does not sleep has not honored his host's food!" was our motto.

Now, to please me, you sit upon a well-swept dirt floor around our fire, as in the shallow pits near us the bulls roast, and I tell my life story. Some of you who come from cities pull up your breeches as you sit down, lest creases flatten. Most of you, my guests, brush off your clothes as you rise to stretch your cramped legs while you walk about. Muscles unaccustomed to crouch, with body balanced upon bent knees, or to lie half reclining on the ground, find these positions difficult. Thus, also, the Californias have changed, and

[1] *Rancho de verano:* rich moist land where all crops can be grown during the summer dry season.

luxuries unknown to the rich in my childhood days have crept in. Chairs are now even offered to women, who in my day by preference crouched on the floor, thinking the exposure of legs when seated in a chair indecent. I also have changed, and only on my delightful Mexican deserts are all things as they were in my boyhood.

Soon after I gentled my first wild gelding came the great robbery of our Mission Church of San Borromeo, the Friend of Christ. This Cathedral was of adobe[1] and shabby, with much of the outer plastering fallen off; for Father Blood-of-Christ had taught from the beginning: "The exterior matters little. It is what lies within which God values."

Some said that this father spoke of the soul, but such were not in favor with our monks, and if too loud-mouthed risked what was not pleasant to think of.

Within our church was the richest shrine for a thousand miles. On our Gulf Coast the *mareas*[2] cast up great heaps of pearl oysters, which belonged, of course, to him who found them; but of all found, San Borromeo received his part. Therefore, in front of our Virgin were bowls full of the finest pearls. Before the Saints, also, were figures in silver and even in gold, with much jewelry from mothers who had sick children and from those who asked intercession for whatever cause. From all the coast north and south came gold and silver figures, or jewelry from those who were fortunate or unfortunate, needing protection for what they had, or help if in misery. San Borromeo refused no request, or, if he refused, then only because of fault in him who asked.

All these vast treasures lay in sight and unprotected, since the Cathedral's Founder had said: "God will protect that He values."

[1] *Adobe*. Mud bricks for building are made still in Mexico exactly as the Egyptians made them in Biblical times. The proper heavy clay is placed in a shallow pit, mixed with sand, and trodden out by foot until all is well mixed. Cut straw is then added, and trodden in after water has been added. The semi-wet mud is then trodden or hammered into moulds, and these bricks dried in the sun. It may interest readers to know that I still visit with pleasure a handsome house, furnished with abundant plush easy-chairs, but the women of the family sit on the floor when visitors are present.—*A. de F. B.*

2 *Mareas:* spring tides.

Therefore the doors of this church were never closed, and only God Himself, or perhaps those of His Saints deputed for such labor, watched all this wealth.

Three times had come robbers. First a Spaniard, whom, like all of the meaner class from Spain, we called "*Gachupín,*"[2] for they value money above honor, and life more than valor.

Entering at night, he filled a bag with pearls from the Virgin's altar. We found him the next morning, fallen on the Cathedral steps with an apoplexy. When he was taken up, he said the Virgin had placed the Infant Christ from her arms into those of San Borromeo, and, stepping from her Shrine, had followed him to the door. Laid by our priests before the High Altar, he died in a torment of shudders, and we, who had been called to watch, wondered at the power of God. Of all the pearls he had taken not one was lost. One great brilliant, the Madonna Charm, fallen from the bag this Spanish thief carried, had rolled behind a stone step. This step being displaced by one who trod upon it, the pearl was by the providence of God revealed to an honest man who returned it to our padres.

The second robbery was by a man who had dug a cellar in which to store yams. Since the Topa Chisera had been given by Father Blood-of-Christ the earth for its dwelling, all excavation for houses was forbidden lest it emerge and injure men. But this man dug his cellar secretly and, being found out, became sullen and resisted our church.

As he explained afterwards, he entered by the open front door since it could not but please our Saints to see a worshiper come at night, when the lazy sleep. Having asked intercession of Mary, Mother of God, for the success of his robbery—for being drowsy at this time she might promise aid for his purpose without investigation—he took no pearls from her altar.

"Regarding adornments a woman is merciless," this thief said. "Therefore perhaps it was that She abandoned Her Infant and followed to punish that Spanish robber. But San Borromeo was a man,

[2] *Gachupín:* pig.

a jolly old soul, who had also his weaknesses if the stories one hears be true. Little I thought he would grudge me a trifle of his wealth. Then, having taken what I needed of gold and silver, I went out the back door thinking: 'These Saints are great people. What do they know of back doors, even though perhaps the flatteries in my prayers have not dulled their watchfulness regarding the front door?'"

As this thief passed by the priests' path behind the church, a rabid skunk bit his ankle. He went to our padres for aid, and while they worked over him a golden figure of Saint Peter dropped from a hole in his pocket. The priests laid the thief before the High Altar, as was our custom for sacrilege, and he died in torment, refusing the Sacrament and spitting upon the Body of Christ offered him—since, as he said, "If these Saints have betrayed me in spite of my flatteries, why consider them more?"

The third robber was a sailor from our Mission galleon. He took all our silver and gold figures aboard this ship, and as it was sailing time he thought himself safe from pursuit. But his ship refused to move. It had grounded upon a sandbar, and a great storm arising, all were nearly drowned. Therefore another sailor, who had known of the theft, and had been refused a part, told the galleon's captain, and all church treasures were recovered.

As for the sacrilegious thief, they hoisted him by his left leg to the masthead, and there he hung until he died. The Saints could thus see that his pockets, being upside down, were empty; and by their permission the ship sailed off contentedly like a great bird. It was noted at that time that a land breeze carried the galleon out, as if our Saints were glad to be rid of its crew; for a wind from the land by day is most unusual with us.

Within my memory is the last great robbery of our shrine. He who stole had first prayed before the altars, since we found there mud from his feet. Then with pieces torn from the priests' vestments he had bound the eyes of all our Saints, even of the Infant Jesus in his Mother's arms. Thus having deceived the Virgin and Saints by praise, and blinded them with bandages, he took everything of value from them—pearls, jewelry, and figures, both silver and gold. We were like a swarm of bees deprived of their honey when, next morning, we heard of this sacrilege, but the padres soothed us, saying: "This robber will die as have all others. We must, therefore, intercede with the Virgin that she deliver his soiled soul from the Topa Chisera." This they said, but we knew they prayed God for vengeance both on his body and on his soul, since they held continuous Mass day and night.

On this morning I saddled a half-wild stallion, and after I had mounted my bit broke. This was the more curious because it was recently made by me of new iron; but we later found it had been so filed as to break easily. Nor could I, being still only half-grown, hold my great brute with his hackamore.[1] He began more in play than in viciousness, but having run a mile from our village, he put his nostrils to the ground for a moment and seemed to go crazy. At furious speed he charged up a narrow horse trail which rose rapidly along the slopes of San Pablo Mountain, and following the scent which excited him, plowed a way through thorn scrub to the ridge-top. Thence by goatlike leaps he bore me down into the chasm made by the great earthquake which had split San Pablo's dome, at the time Father Blood-of-Christ allotted to the Topa Chisera its earth dwelling.

Quickly, when my stallion came to a mare grazing on the small flat, I slipped off, leaving the enamored pair to their mating, and glad to escape unhurt from flying heels and savage teeth.

Then, wondering how a neighbor's mare could be so far from home, I glanced around; and never have I been more affrighted. In front of a small fire sat a man melting up silver figures from our shrine. Before melting, he had cut off their heads, which lay in a heap near him. Doubtless he had thought: "Who knows about these Saints? They may spy upon me even though their heads be melted. Better let their heads lie here."

[1] *Hackamore:* from *jaquima,* a nose-halter, usually of braided horsehair. Used on wild horses so as not to ruin their mouths by heavy pressure on the bit.

"Help yourself, Princeling," he called to me, pointing to the piles of heads. "Was it the Virgin called your stallion here?"

I went to him dragging my feet and covered with a cold sweat which ran down my body in streams. That he had lured me here through his brood mare I knew. That he would kill me was certain, and with these silver heads in my pockets our priests would condemn my soul to Hell forever. Was it not I who had led in all deviltry since I could walk? Was not the color of my hair an indication of my final resting place? Many a woman had so told me, for red hair is not a sign of grace. There is no Saint known having hair of that color.

I should have killed him where he sat, but was so paralyzed through fear that I forgot the dagger at my side, and its uses. When a boy is under twelve years old, he lacks vigor to attack a grown man. Moreover, at that time I had never killed anyone, and though carefully taught I lacked practice. Learning alone has little value. A man may know by heart the two hundred Spanish name-colors of horses and yet be easily tumbled off by any old brood mare.

Since that day I have always believed that, if a boy ever called me father, it would go hard with me if I could find no man upon whom that boy could practice his dagger thrusts. Many a boy of spirit and usefulness has died for lack of such practice. My master's mother was right. These are days of too much thought and too little action. It still angers me to think that I might have spent an eternity in Hell while this sacrilegious thief lived his life out in a house of three rooms, all with doors, because those who taught me my dagger stopped at theory.

"Hold the ladle, *cuñado*,"[1] he said to me; for so all church robbers call each other, being by marriage related to Satanna, the wife of Satan. The man smiled at me with that cold politeness with which the well-bred welcome one they are about to destroy. That smile, I learned as a boy, deceives only those who hope against hope and die a dozen deaths while waiting for their end. Thus he dallied with me, and had not Saints' heads lain heaped between us with their

[1] *Cuñado:* brother-in-law.

threat of Hell fires, I would have been but as an entrapped fly, to which the spider approaches ever stroking and petting its victim, but still a bloodsucker.

I poured the molten silver into dry clay moulds, with every drop damning my soul. Small bricks they were, such as fit easily into pack-bags. Even I pocketed, laughing, a great pearl flipped to me across our fire: "the Madonna's Charm," which had been set in the Virgin's hair.

"Did the Virgin weep much," the church robber asked, "when Father Talk-Much uncovered Her eyes?" And we chuckled finely together as I told him of the Virgin's frock wetted by tears She had shed over the loss of Her pearls. I was but a boy, yet I could then joke with death, as afterwards when grown up. A boy must die bravely, for he is a man, though only half-grown.

"Let the Virgin seek other pearls," he exclaimed, "and when you are older you may take them all yourself. As for me, I am not a Spaniard and know when I have enough. By tomorrow I shall be at La Paz, mourning deeply for the sacrilege at San José del Arroyo, and promising the Virgin a double portion of all pearls I may find in shell-heaps this winter.

"'By the Eyes of the Saints,' I shall swear hereafter," this vile thief continued. "No oath of that sort need be kept since I blinded them."

Thus we laughed and talked, I doing my share gaily while my hair was damp with fear-sweat and my buckskin underclothing drenched as well.

When our melting was done and dozens of small, easily carried bricks of gold and silver lay around us, the robber yawned, stretching his arms; and to taunt my helplessness with a dagger, said: "Were it not that I must reach La Paz tomorrow, I would sleep for an hour before eating."

And I, not to be shamed, answered: "A boy is always hungry; and I must be returning, or they may come for me, since I left without orders. Let us eat at once."

Over the cooking he wasted much time to torment me, concealing what he fried from my sight and keeping the boiling olla hidden by his body so I might imagine all things unsafe. Then, without shame, when all was ready, he poured into my earthen cup from his palm a handful of poison powder and, breaking a twig, said:

"Stir it well. This sugar dissolves slowly but is none the less sweet."

I tasted it, and bitter as death though the tea was, I answered gaily: "You found then also the priests' sugar loaf. Little chance they give us poor devils to taste white sugar!"

Though my throat was parched almost beyond swallowing, I ate heartily to hold back the poison and entertained this thief with stories of my adventures so that, as I had hoped, he lost caution in laughter. Therefore I got a chance to pour half of my cup contents down my chest armor, where it trickled from chest to legs and ran down even into my foot protectors. In those days we wore *guaraches*,[1] not shoes, and in driving wild cattle put on overshoes which covered our legs to the knees.

"How your gang of young *cabrones*[2] will miss you!" he exclaimed, holding his fat paunch with one hand in order to laugh more easily, and with his left rolling a long cigarette of corn husk and tobacco coyote. Thus he kept his right hand always free and near a knife handle, in case I attempted resistance. Both to take his eyes off me at moments and to ensure his death should he repeat these stories to others, I had told him of the adventures of Padre Anselmo and the Virgin's frock, which I had watched, but never dared even to hint at before, since this padre was of high repute and not given to forgiveness. Also concerning an adventure of the tenth son of our Governor Verdugo. There was little I did not know of our great people, and much aids have I derived from such knowledge; though chiefly from a reputation thus gained for holding my tongue.

[1] *Guaraches:* sandals made of leather or rawhide and held on by a thong over the big toe. Old automobile tires are now exported from the United States in quantity for use as *guaraches*. —*A. de F. B.*

[2] *Cabrones:* literally, "sons of goats"; the worst name possible, but as applied to boys, "hellions." If applied to a man, knives are drawn at once.—*A. de F. B.*

With the first poison pang—since, not knowing what he had given me, I dared not stimulate its pains earlier—I rose, staggering and holding my belly.

"I am ill!" I cried, weeping like a baby. "Take me to my mother!"

"So soon?" he asked, puzzled; but as I began to bellow loudly, he led up both horses, saying: "These foreigners lack endurance for poisons, it seems."

Princeling and foreigner they called me because my father was an Irish King. This poisoner knew he must get me away from his melting-place before the venom he had given me rendered me unconscious. Otherwise, searching the hills for me, men might trail me to his den, and by our tracks understand his part in my death and thus locate the real church robber.

With one foot in my saddle stirrup and my left hand on my stallion's hackamore, I pretended to swoon, calling loudly, "I cannot mount!" so that he might boost me up. Then, while both his hands were occupied in lifting me, I struck him full in his throat, back of the windpipe, turning my knife so as to open the wound, that his life-blood might find no impediment.

Never in my whole life have I seen such surprise in any man's face. In spite of my poison pains I laughed.

"Princeling yourself!" I called to him, for he knew this nickname was one I hated. Had not his poison been griping me, I would have stayed to watch his death. A full-blooded man dies slowly, and to have taunted him would have eased my own passing; but it best suited me to reach our village alive, and thus save my soul, which otherwise the Madonna's Charm I carried in my pocket would cost me.

While I mounted my stallion, the church robber's mare was loose and restless, being fed full of corn in readiness for the long ride to La Paz. Terrified by the blood and her master's sudden fall to the ground, she started for San José del Arroyo on full gallop. My stallion, seeing his whole *manada*[1] vanishing, gave chase with equal spirit, and conscious or unconscious I still clung to my saddle.

[1] *Manada.* Each stallion on range has a harem of mares.

Passing my grandfather's house, I fell off by choice; and, spurned by my horse's heels, shot in through the open doorway and landed at my mother's feet, calling as I lost my senses:

"The church treasure! The robber poisoned me and I killed him!"

Then, content to die, I dropped my hold on life and knew no more except pain, until I was past danger.

They drenched me with more milk than any twin calves ever sucked, and our padres prayed over me. One, indeed, who was learned in such things, and possibly practiced them, gave me a cure which helped. Though as always it was chiefly that I was tough and too young for dissipations to have weakened me.

Over my buckskin underwear, drenched with fear-sweat and the tea I had poured down my chest armor, my mother worked all that night long to prevent stiffening of the deer hide, doubling the *gamuza*[1] and pulling it this way and that to keep it from hardening. So women must do when their men hunt wild cattle or are hunted.

The church treasure they recovered without loss of a pearl. Truly God protects that He values. But the church robber's body had been privately removed. His family was influential, and none dared to disgrace it or risk his nine brothers' daggers.

[1] *Gamuza.* Tanned buckskin which has been wetted must be worked by hand until it dries. Otherwise it stiffens and hardens. Tanned in deers' brains it stands wet better than as ordinarily prepared.

CHAPTER 3. *My Grandfather Gives Me a Cigarette and a Toledo Dagger—A Hinny Has but One Vice— "A Woman's Smile is the Devil's Wile"—The Time of Pitahayas—How to Steal Piglets from a Wild Sow*

WHILE I RECOVERED, which took much time, I noticed some man was always with me; and when I was able to walk, one uncle was at my right and one at my left on our *paseos*. My grandfather said to me privately: "Those who recover too quickly sometimes have but short lives"—meaning that, though I had killed the tenth, nine brothers still survived to avenge him. Thinking over this hint, I complained and tottered about, declaring myself destined to die, until I felt complete strength both in body and mind. Certain it is that those hours in the Topa Chisera Chasm had for a time taken from me some quality, lack of which left me limp and easily depressed. My grandfather watched over me closely, though never so that I felt his care, and one day he called me to him and I knelt at his feet.

"Sit," he said, and offered me a cigarette. Then my whole body swelled with pride. No boy sits in his father's presence. Therefore, he recognized me as a man. Beyond this, no unmarried man ever smokes in his father's sight until he has accomplished some notable deed. To be ennobled twice in a moment by my grandfather, and he one who thought much of old customs, shook me from head to foot.

"What are your plans?" he asked; and I answered deferentially: "To serve you."

But I saw in a moment I had struck a jarring chord. The guitar has its uses in life as well as its pleasures, for it teaches the inutility of discords.

My grandfather was a man of great wisdom who planned for all, but gave no hint of his wishes, saying: "That colt which needs a whip to direct it is not worth the trouble breaking."

Therefore, sitting bolt upright on my wooden bench, and barely touching the cigarette which I had not dared to light, I added: "He, of the stolen treasure, has nine brothers."

"All well grown, and trained robbers of all things—even life," he added, smiling slightly.

"And I too young to live long in such company." By his face I saw I had hit the right trail.

"Your uncles will be always with you."

"But if steel finds a way, it is then a blood feud; and I being dead leaves us only two against nine." I almost whispered for I saw where all this led. I was but a boy, and each night my mother still drew up my bedcover, and, whispering a word of advice, stroked my forehead. These things count much in the life of a child and, half-grown, to leave his mother racks a boy's soul.

"With your permission I leave tonight for the north," I said mournfully, and if my eyes filled and my mouth twisted, he was too considerate to notice this weakness.

"Run away?" he asked.

"They would follow me and, truthfully or not, boast they had killed me. Thus again a blood feud with two of us against nine. Help me with your great wisdom, Grandfather," I asked.

He sat long in thought, till I fancied him asleep; for thus it happens at times to aged men. But who, more than he, had a right to sleep when he would and where?

"Had I a dozen boys instead of a gross of useless girls," he began fiercely, "I would wipe these *cuñados* from this earth. But we are two and they nine. Nevertheless, each of my two shall increase to a dozen men in time. If not, then their wives shall not grow old. This bearing of girls is a vice for which a woman should suffer, as men for cowardice. God grant I may live to see twenty-four knives ceaselessly destroying those who now threaten us! For the present it shall be courtesy from us in all things toward them, so that they may suspect nothing. Honesty to a friend but courtesy to an enemy, until God opens a way for our knives.

"As for you, tomorrow the Sanhudos leave for Alta California. It is a great and numerous family, and even these shameless church robbers dare not attack you while you are with them. Be prepared."

I left him, first kissing his hand, which pleased him. To me he gave that day a pacing hinny, black as the soul of the man I had killed, and trained to perfection. Of these things only was she afraid: of a bear or a dark stump or a deep shadow. These being black, as is the color of mules' ghosts, caused her those same fears which white figures, strolling by moonlight in our Campo Santo, gave me. I have seen these Returners, for as a boy nothing daunted me.

To this hinny my grandfather added a saddle and a Toledo dagger, at sight of which my soul was filled with delight. A blade which, unnicked, would cut iron, and all so balanced for throwing or striking that one could depend upon it as on an arm. Never has it failed me, and in my life, when knives clashed, mine was always first to draw blood.

Standing before the hinny, my grandfather said, "She has but one vice," and taking out his tobacco pouch of buckskin, with its drawstring of rolled silk which had come from Spain, he put in my palm a handful of coarse tobacco leaves. The mule's limpid eye watched every motion, and extending her neck with lips open, she begged for her treat.

"Thus she knows her new master," said he, and in her glance from one to the other I saw a puzzled brain.

"Never feed her tobacco in public," he said, "but remember she misses what she chews, as you your cigarette. Do not forget her and she will never forget you. How many are your pleasures and excitements, and this poor brute has but one."

The hinny glanced from my grandfather to my extended palm as if in doubt, but at his permissive word she browsed the tobacco from my hand. While she chewed it with half-closed, dreaming eyes, I handled her all over, stroking her legs to feel for bruises or thorn wounds, and lifting her hoofs to search for aught that might injure her.

"Save her from drowning, should flood ever reach you," advised my grandfather. "This alone is the weakness of mules, that quicksand below water causes them to lose their reason. When bearing the Virgin and the Infant Jesus in the Holy Land, one of the donkey tribe walked into quicksand. San Gabriel, watching from above, noted his danger and pulled him out by his ears, which then stretched to such length as all burros now have.

"The poor brute's fear, lest Jesus and the Virgin on his back be drowned, was so great that in water all its descendants lose their courage. Depending entirely upon heavenly aid to extract them from quicksand, they do not exert themselves, but rather drown helplessly. You have seen a burro in our river? His ears are thrown back and together, waiting for San Gabriel to gather them in his hands, as when he thus saved the Infant Jesus and the *Santísima* from drowning."

My hinny was trained in useful ways. She traveled at a tireless running walk which yielded six miles an hour all day. If an unknown man or an enemy of mine came to her head, she would strike with both forefeet, and then, seizing him with her teeth, shake him until he lay limp. The same if one approached her from the rear; except that both hind legs, hitting like flails, left no need for shaking. Yet to those she knew she was all gentleness.

If a child fell between her four legs, all she did was to push it to one side or lift it by its hair and deposit it in a doorway. As all children were then naked, she could only move them to safety by their hair. When a man rode close beside me, as was not courteous, and I doubted him, I had but to touch my hinny's hipbone and she would jump sideways so violently as to overturn that man and his horse. Nor could the man take offense, for a mule is always skittish. Thus we trained a riding hinny in my country, where he who trusted a stranger seldom lived to explain his folly.

From the horse, its father, a hinny gets courage, size, and docility. From its mother, the donkey, comes great wisdom, endurance, and love for all foods. It will not starve as do horses with food all about them, simply because they demand grass. Dry mescal leaves, bits of bark, and desert growth all suit a mule's belly. Beyond this is its instinct against poisoned spring water, which the Topa Chisera has caused to issue in various places from the ground, and which kills man and beast.

"Drink, Pretty One," you say to your hinny when you come to a new spring; and if she backs away snorting, it is safer to die of thirst in the desert than to touch such water. Some say that beside each such poison spring stands a devil to seize the souls of those who die drinking, and that the mule, through the tribe of its mother the donkey which Christ rode, inherits capacity to see such evil ones. Certain it is that all donkeys also refuse to drink poisoned water.

My mother gave me that small medal my father had worn about his neck, and which she had taken from him while he lay drunk and the sailors were about to carry him to the ship his country had sent for him. There is writing upon it, but what it says I do not know, never having learned to read. I suppose "Come-on-Pat," which my mother taught me as the motto of my family, that being what the sailors who took him away called to him. Lest the rival to his throne should stab me, if he found me, I showed this medal to no man, but kept it in case my father sent for me.

Concerning reading, as has been said to me in later life, I have no doubt it might help me to locate my father could I but read what this medal says. Nevertheless, I fear learning my letters, though in these times many of our oldest families permit their children to be so taught. When these learned children have become of such age as decides their character, I may study if it then appears that reading does not make them lazy, treacherous, or worthless.

For the present, as in the past, it suffices for me as for all the best of my time to sign, when this is necessary, by *rubrica*[1]. My rubric is so finely penned, both involuted and convoluted, and with so many curves and flourishes that no man can forge it, and not a schoolteacher I have ever known can even imitate it. That is perhaps as well for them, since I have little patience with teachers, and if I suspected one of them in any way I might be unduly tempted to do him injury.

It is true that all *empleados*[2] must read and write, though very little suffices most of them. The question is, therefore, does learning make them lazy and dishonest, or do only those born crafty learn to read? It is also true that priests and governors read and write, and that therefore wealth and power may come from learning. As for me, I would rather be honest and well thought of by my neighbors than have aught that reading could give me.

That some read for pleasure I have been told, but scarce believe. Man can write only what he has seen, and to gossip what one knows must be of more interest than to look at dots and dashes such as writing is. Were all writing like my rubric, a pleasure simply to gaze upon, I might be more ready to learn it; but written words are ugly as an Indian squaw at twenty years old. Over writing, even the squaw has this advantage: that she had an earlier youth when she may have had some beauty.

Business, they say, demands learning. Yet give me rather a man's word than his bond, for if he break his word no man thereafter trusts him, and he can neither buy nor sell nor live. But if he refuses his bond the law deals with him, and most men have such contempt for law and lawyers that whether he is punished legally does not con-

---

[1] *Rubrica:* a curved and convoluted line peculiar to each man, literate or illiterate, and essential to his legal signature in Spanish America.

[2] *Empleados:* the lesser Government employees; held in the greatest contempt because so poorly paid as to be forced to illegal exactions.

cern them. For my part, I trust a man regardless of his law dealings, until he breaks his word. If then he runs away faster than I can follow, it remains only for me to confess myself a fool without judgment of men or power to enforce my bargain. If he remains within reach he pays, for when I deal with a man I touch my knife, saying: "This blade shall be lawyer, judge, and executioner."

Few, therefore, deny me justice; nor am I hard upon debtors. No one leaves my door naked or hungry.

But I must halt my wandering tongue and return to my departure from San José del Arroyo. All gave me something for my departure with the Sanhudos, so that I was ready for travel with better equipage than had ever left the south. The Governor came to look over what I had received and added thereto, rather than carried away with him as was his usual custom. The padres I watched carefully, for of all things they claim a tenth, and I had no mind to yield to them of what I had; but they made no demand. Rather, they promised a daily Mass for me until I safely reached San Francisco Bay in Alta California. What one receives without cost is not to be despised. Therefore I thanked them, and set one of my chums to inform me in how far they kept their promises.

The nine brothers of the man I had killed each came with a present to me—of a knife of some kind. These knives I traded to Indians—or gave to certain ones of them who might thereafter be useful to me. Church robbers deceive the Saints, and these nine brothers, therefore, might have had spells and charms at command which would have caused their knives to turn back upon me in battle and so injure me. To their inquiries and goodwill I answered as one does when an enemy is within one's own house: politely, and with such courtesy as would have chilled them to the bone had I then been the man I was later.

The last evening I was at home, my grandfather called me, and I knelt to him that he might advise me from what life had taught him.

"A knife is for self-defense only," he said, "but over the gambling-table or over wine-skins do not disgrace it.

"Debt is slavery. It is equally bad to be or to have a slave.

"In gambling you lose what you have or gain that which ruins others.

"When drunk, you threaten your enemies. Therefore they kill you; or having shown your mind, you lose power to injure them.

"A woman's smile is the Devil's wile.

"Never buy a horse from an enemy. Who knows what tricks may have been taught it?

"Be courteous to all, but to those you hate be most courteous. Nevertheless, not so they recognize your mind.

"Never forget a benefit nor an injury. Even a dog does as much.

"Youth does not last forever. Therefore conserve it."

Which having said, his head fell forward a little as if he would sleep, and I turned away not to see those tears which ran down his cheeks. The old man felt disgraced to have so few sons as to be forced to avoid feuds by sending even a daughter's boy from his house.

"A dozen illegitimate sons," I heard him murmur to himself, "would have saved me this shame; but all my life I have been full of hopes and heedless for the future. Better a brood of illegitimates with keen knives than that which has happened to me. A wife who does not yield sons, and yet is jealous, destroys her family."

I kissed the old man's hand as I left him: an antique custom and passing into disuse, but it pleased him. I knew I left him dreaming that each of his sons might raise a dozen men of his name, so that these church robbers could be met on equal terms when knives clashed. As for me, I vowed to the Topa Chisera, as my most sacred oath, that with God's help I alone would cause each of his tears to be covered with a smile, when age permitted me to meet these *cuñados*.

It greatly pleased me that the boy I had appointed as chief of my band of *cabrones* came to me early on the day I left and whispered in my right ear: "We shall remember!"

Since my feud with these nine brothers of the church robber was a private one, I would not have asked this courtesy; but being offered, I accepted it, certain that the sons of these nine brothers would not greatly increase in number during my absence.

To the boy I had appointed chief of my *cabrones,* I suggested, as likely to maintain his authority, that he recover from the Topa Chisera what I had lost when it destroyed our cave. Being anxious to show contempt for all law, I had dug years before, in a high bank below our irrigation ditch, a great cavern; and here, while my gang stood about the entrance, I had cursed the Topa Chisera and defied it. Though cracks and earth-falls came from the Topa's rage while I dared this beast, yet not until night did my cave ceiling fall in. Thus proving that for the brave there is no danger.

Being then only six years old, I had braved the Topa Chisera with my only weapon, a wooden sword. When clods began to fall, I rushed out in a panic, forgetting my sword, and leaving it behind to be covered up in my cave's destruction by this foul beast. My wooden sword was a boyish toy, truly, since all my *cabrones* now wore knives; but to regain it would prove that their new chief feared not to break church law, which forbade all excavation lest the Topa Chisera be set loose. Also their new chief would thus prove that of the Topa he had no dread.

On my last night at San José del Arroyo I slept in our corral with my hinny, that on our long journey she might learn to feel security during the night by nuzzling my hand. At earliest dawn I was waked by my grandfather, who, motioning me to remain quiet, sat beside me and told me of the Sanhudos, with whom that day I was to start for Monterey in Northern California. I knew at a glance that he had spent a sleepless night of doubt whether I could be trusted with what he had to tell me.

"We come of an old Spanish family," my grandfather began, "which is connected with the great and ancient De la Cerdas. Doña Ysabel, Don Firmín Sanhudo's wife, is the last representative of that famous race. Therefore, Don Firmín came to see me as soon as he had landed at our port, from Sinaloa.

"Finding me what I am, one with a closed mouth *(boca cerrada)*, he told me what I now tell you. But remember, neither to him nor to others can you show your knowledge. To speak of what I tell you now would mean your death, for Don Firmín is a hard man who never forgives foolishness and regards carelessness as worse than crime.

"Don Firmín Sanhudo comes to the Three Californias as Inspector-General of Colonies, but also as the King's personal representative, with all the powers our King has. To hang a governor or send a viceroy back to Spain are as nothing to him. He is one of the wealthiest men in the Spanish colonies. He and his family control events in the Americas to a great extent and have much influence in Spain, where his father lives. His marriage to Doña Ysabel added vastly to his powers.

"Mexico is on the verge of rebellion. It has been corruptly mismanaged despite Don Firmín's influence. He tells me a rebellion will break out while you are on this trip (1810), but that it will be suppressed without difficulty. He fears that the next attempt may succeed and drive the Spaniards from Mexico.

"Don Firmín Sanhudo comes here to decide whether Spain can and will retain its Californian colonies despite a successful revolution in Mexico; so it will rest upon his decision whether you die a Spaniard or a Mexican. God grant you remain a Spaniard.

"Don Firmín sails again from Monterey for Spain, having decided your fate and that of the Three Californias, but saying nothing to any man of his decision." My grandfather hesitated for a moment, and then went on: "See that no flies alight within thy mouth on this trip to Monterey. An open mouth and a riata loop around thy neck are twins, where the Sanhudos rule."

The old man returned to his house, still doubtful as to his wisdom in telling me so much, and wondering whether he had thus signed my death warrant. Had he known how much I already knew and of which I had never spoken to anyone, he would have been more at ease.

Chapter 3

That morning, before I began our fifteen-hundred-mile journey through deserts and hostile Indians, I loitered through all those places I most loved in our delightful valley of San José del Arroyo. I visited again that river-crossing where once, to prove myself the most hopelessly wicked boys in our village, I had placed rollers under the flattened tree trunk which served as a bridge over our irrigation ditch. Then I and my *cabrones,* from a clump of bushes near at hand, had watched that padre whom we called "Tamale," from his fondness for chicken *tamales,* fall into the stream as the flat leg rolled beneath him. Ordinarily I could still have laughed at remembering the outraged dignity on Padre Tamale's face, but now I saw God driving me relentlessly from all I loved because I had then persecuted His Saints.

"Holy Virgin! Mother of our Patient Jesus!" I cried. "Make me worthy of return to this Thy home!" As if in answer to my prayer came memories of "The Time of Pitahayas"—those three months during which life was one continuous pleasure. Then there was no hunger and little work. Young and old thronged our thorny forests, eating juicy, ripe, red pitahayas as large as a horse's hoof; eating and drinking continually; sleeping when tired of dancing, and eating again as the languor of sleep passed.

This was the mating season when young men, seeing for the first time the charm of some slim girl, would select for her the ripest and best pitahaya, and at night would sing for her. If two followed the same *enamorada,* and she, not loath to be fought over, encouraged both, older men intervened between drawn knives, exclaiming: "While the pitahaya ripens, eat, dance, and be mirthful. He insults 'The Time of Pitahaya' who does aught else." Thereafter, both suitors followed her laughing and singing, without thought of what must happen later. Thus it is that youth slips into age with no preparation for quick coming death.

Even the birds respected our pitahaya: for when this fruit first set, great flocks of the beautiful *guacamaya* flew from Sinaloa across our

Vermilion Sea and held loud debates as to quantity and quality of the coming crop.

If all was to their liking, these *guacamaya* birds returned when the fruit was ripe and feasted for a month with us; but if these birds foresaw rains destructive to this fruit, or otherwise misliked crop prospects, they flew away and were not seen again for a full year.

Our local Indian *guamas*[1] pretended that by conversation with these *guacamaya* birds they could predict an abundant crop, without that rain which destroys the fruit. The truth of this matter remains to this day doubtful in my mind. The padres forbade as devil's magic all those predictions of distant events in which our *guamas* excelled.

One such wizard—very secretly, from fear of our monks, and only, as he said, because I had devil's red hair and must go to Hell in any event—always predicted for me, two days in advance, the arrival of our Mission ship.[2] This annual arrival was the greatest event of our whole year, except, of course, Pitahaya Time. By knowledge of when this ship was to arrive, I cemented my control of my *cabrones*. They went about for two days carrying this great secret to be hinted at to all but not told to any. Than this, nothing is more pleasing to boys, as we then all were.

Through the "Time of Pitahayas," Father Salvatierra had converted all our *Indiada* by preaching that Heaven was a great plain filled with thornless bushes always full of ripe, red fruit, and that in Heaven it never rained. Therefore the pitahaya crop never rotted in Heaven.

The Indians followed him everywhere, crying: "Father, take us there."

"Work," Padre Salvatierra urged; and the Indians, full of this hope of year-long seasons of juicy pitahaya fruit, built for him great stone missions and long irrigating ditches. Our Indians could never understand a future life and thought our Great Padre promised a Heaven in this life.

[1] *Guamas:* sorcerers.

[2] This power of predicting the arrival of ships existed from Alaska to Yucatan among Indians of all tribes and is mentioned repeatedly in Mission chronicles. Being from the Devil, such information was severely punished by the padres.

Chapter 3

Then came Father Tamarel, preaching, in our coolest weather, Hell fires for those who would not listen to him. But our Indians lived without roofs or houses. In our winter rains they sheltered themselves only by mortarless stone walls a yard high. Frequent earthquakes had taught them the folly of roofs which fell upon them or high walls which tumbled inwards. Religion is only a sanctification of useful habit, and their religion threatened them with "no bugs to eat" in this life if they built houses.

"Father, lead us to that eternally warm place," the Indians cried as, unclothed, they shivered in chill north winds. But Father Tamarel, incensed by the demand of his Indian flock for Hell fires, curtly refused them the warmth they thought he controlled. Whereupon, rising in rebellion, they killed him and others, saying:

"For the Heaven of pitahayas we worked, and it has not come. Now they refuse us also their comfortable Hell of warmth. Why should we serve these cruel foreigners?"

Remembering these things as I wandered among the places I loved, I thought; "Thus I also, like these padres, have deserved through my heedless misunderstanding all that has befallen me in being driven away from my mother and home by a church robber." And I made up my mind to die as quickly as might be and thus avoid further vengeance of those worthy Saints I had offended.

Cheered by this thought of a quick death, and by the hope these Saints would then regret me, seeing when too late how much good I had in me, I turned my mule for a last quiet look at San José del Arroyo. It was in those times a small village of under three hundred souls, and so near the ocean as our *chubascos* permitted—for at times these winter storms lifted the sea and thrust it bodily over dry land. But to shelter our church, God had placed a great mountain flank, jutting out into our valley and half-closing it; so that in the flat beyond stood both church and village, with a thousand-foot shoulder of hard rock between them and the sea storms.

Through our valley murmured a little stream, which ended in a half-salt lagoon held back by sandbanks which only great floods or more resistless tornadoes could tear away. On one side, above all cultivated land, lay our *ȝanja*, full always with clean, warm water of a bathing temperature; ready, as the padres had taught us, to baptize the soil and bring forth proper harvests, God willing, in their season. Below, fertile acres covered with fruit trees and with that sweet cane from which *panocha* was made.

As I looked long on all these things, striving to fix them forever on my memory, I could even see my old friend, a half-wild hog which bedded in our stream nearer to me than our village. Many of its piglets had I roasted secretly. To rule animals by guile was amusing and of much value for later practice with men. This sow taught me much, as I shall pause for a moment to tell you.

The suspicions of a sow are what those of every man should be. They do not diminish digestion, and interfere little with sleep, but leave few possibilities unconsidered. To acquire this sow's piglets, and that without conflict, was necessary for my leadership with my *cabrones*. To that end, I learned first quick control of that muscle in a shoat's throat which stops its voice without cutting off its breath; for a sow is a dangerous devil when its young squeal. Many a dog has found this out, nor are two lessons needed. Thereafter does one but grunt like an enraged hog, the fiercest dog turns tail as if instinct and flight were one. One thing further was necessary for me—to learn how far a pig can count. But this is knowledge not to be confided even now to others; since I own hogs, and doubtless there are still those who would eat suckling pigs if obtainable.

These things being learned, the rest was simple. I had but to choose from a neighbor's brood some likely and venturesome piglet, of which its owner had said to his pigherder: "Guard well that shoat, *mi hijo*.[1] It seeks to feed a coyote with its sleek sides." Such venturesome ones exist in all broods, and on them boys and other wild animals fatten. Extracting from its companions such a one with care, at the proper time I played with it until hunger made it musical, and then, rubbing it all over in the mire bed of my sow, I turned it loose

[1] *Mi hijo:* my son.

where my fat friend slept. My pigling would rush like a whirlwind to eat, and the hog, waked by its hungry punchings at her belly, was filled with suspicions of such untimely starvation; but by its smell thought it her own. While she hesitated in doubt, I extracted her fattest offspring, and when she called her brood for counting the number proved correct.

Thus the owner of my pet hog never objected to my friendship with it, and those who lost piglets blamed others, for the pigs I cared for never lost their count. Thus also my wages increased, since they said of me, "This *cabron* keeps his tribe from stealing what he cares for."

It was a profitable game, but must be played by rule. One of my lieutenants thought to outdo me, in early days before my mastery had been learned, and spent a night in a thorn bush, while my enraged friend the hog waited below, anxious to eat him. At intervals she shook this bush with renewed hopes of tumbling the fruit, and to be at least certain, from his cries, that he had not escaped. Like all mankind, a brood hog must be taught confidence before it can be safely deceived, and the lazy, therefore, make poor pig thieves.

As I gazed for the last time over our Valley of San José del Arroyo, cattle everywhere dotting hills on both sides of its fertile expanse reminded me of wild rides on bronco calves and meals of warm, stolen milk. And I thought: "If Heaven is like this village, I can but say with our Indians, 'Lead me there, Father.'" In one house, I knew, my mother lay on my couch face down, shrouding herself with her mantilla, silent among chattering aunts. In another doorway stood a girl, indifferent to tears which wet her face. Thus I shall always see San José del Arroyo. Possibly this memory has made me a wanderer, but I had rather remember than be content elsewhere.

How often, in later years, some man passing me at a gallop in our deserts has called: "Where from, *paisano?*"

And when I answered him: "San José!" there would come into his voice a something nothing else calls forth, as he demanded: "Not San José del Arroyo?"

Then, though horses might have wandered or cattle stampeded—though water might be a hundred burning desert miles away, or death tracking us—we stopped. When two who love this Arroyo meet, all else is forgotten.

CHAPTER 4. *The Sanhudo Family
and Why the Best Knives in Mexico Serve It—
"A Silk Dress for Every Tear"—How a Gentleman
Traveled in 1810—Some Reflections on Mules and
Other Animals—Our First Camp at Santa Anita,
and How the Mayas Played Ball There*

D ON FIRMÍN SANHUDO, our leader, was of that great family of
Sanhudos of whom I have heard my grandfather relate:
"The Twelve Apostles are all cousins or related by marriage, and
Satan a half-brother: or some say, a left-handed son. If there are any
notables in Heaven or Spain who are not Sanhudo's cousins, they at
least have furnished a wife to, or taken one from, this family. Certain
it is that all who dispense justice or control office have an 'S'
engraved on their hearts, as we brand cattle to show we own them.
Their horse-brand is 'N,'[1] and Mexico begins with an 'M.' Nearer
than this to placing their brand on Mexico would be too ostentatious
for their good breeding. They know it is better to own New Spain
than to govern it."

Like all of his family, Don Firmín Sanhudo was a man of detail,
and nothing was left to chance. "Accident," he was accustomed to say,
"is folly, and only a fool loses." If a cow in Mexico dropped twins, his

[1] *Nuestros:* ours.

men bought it, and thus each year more and more of his cows yielded two calves. Thin cows were sold in springtime when all should be
fat, and cows still fat at the end of our dry season his men never sold.

Accepting my services for his trip, he had walked to the end of
our village street, holding my arm; and meeting the nine brothers of
my church robber emerging from their house, he stopped to explain
his journey, saying: "They tell me there is danger to life, since the
Indians of San Vicente are risen: but what Indian does not know the
left ear of a Sanhudo calf is worth a hundred lives?"

Thus he warned them of his care for me. Seeing myself surrounded by these nine enemies, boylike I held my hand on my knife-
hilt. Therefore he advised me: "Bide your time, *hijo mio.* There are
many days in ten years, and if your arm strengthens each hour, the
point of your Toledo dagger will then be more feared than now."

Whenever the Sanhudo family traveled they went surrounded on
all sides by a dozen of the best knives in Mexico. Wild men these
attendants looked, clothed in leather, and with thin, bronzed faces
resembling Spanish tan. If one had a spare ounce of fat upon him,
Don Firmín Sanhudo perhaps smiled when he saw him, and that day
the poor devil trotted on foot. Or, if in good humor, the master, seeing his resolve to keep in good condition, said: "Push your mule by
its tail, my friend."

Thereafter the man, though still on foot, had help in that day's
travel; since all mules were taught to pull their riders by the tail.
This was essential, because in case a mule died two men could not
ride one mule; but one man could ride and the other run a long distance if thus pulled by a mule's tail.

All these Wild Men worshiped the Sanhudo family. It had happened in much earlier days that a Sanhudo was ambushed by one of
the proud Zamorras, who, lolling on horseback, idly looked on,
smiling and twirling his mustache, while his hireling assassins killed
all the Sanhudo escort. Don Gabriel Sanhudo's knife-men perished
around him, for this family has always been faithfully served.
When the last of his escort lay dead on the ground, Don Gabriel,

unwounded and active, since he had disdained to soil his daggers with the blood of paid assassins, jumped the wall of dead around him and killed the Zamorra.

The assassins, filled with admiration for a man who had stood fearlessly while a score attacked a dozen, and who finally, on foot and using only his *misericordia,* had killed a fully armed man on horseback, threw down their knives and on their knees to him begged to serve him. Don Gabriel, accepting their offer, married them to the wives of those they had killed, that none might suffer because of what had happened. Then, while all Mexico waited in suspense, uncertain as to the result of this feud, Don Gabriel found opportunity to attack and destroy that branch of the Zamorras, so that no male remained alive. He used for this attack the same men formerly hired by the Zamorras to destroy him.

Therefore the best fighting men in Mexico sought service with the Sanhudos, saying: "The Sanhudos fear no man and are merciless, yet trust those who serve them. Did not Don Gabriel kill all the Zamorras' sons, using those assassins the Zamorras hired to kill him? The Sanhudo family has great men in it. *Ojala!*"

WE BEGAN OUR LONG JOURNEY by midday, and to all I showed a stolid face; though the night before, when my mother covered me and blessed me, I had wet the saddle on which my head lay with more tears than even a child should shed. Of that departure morning I saw little and remember less, my mind being clouded by grief. But in the doorway of our last village hut stood a girl older than I, whom I had teased, and who in years past had often smarted my cheeks with her bare hands. More grown than I, and verging on womanhood, she now wept as she watched me pass.

While with her I had never thought of her as more than shrill-voiced and stopping our best plays by her tattling. Now my very soul went out to her. Love is the greatest of all beautifiers. Doubtless every house in our village had a girl as perfect as this one. Yet, as she stood in the doorway, clothed only in a short smock of buckskin, and with her shoulders and arms bare, I thought her handsomer than even our Governor's mistress. That famous beauty, accepting the Governor's left hand, lived in greatest luxury, with powder for her face, shoes brought from Spain, and even, some said, a dress of silk. Not being interested in girls' folderols, I had never investigated this question, as was my habit concerning matters of which a boy should know.

Seeing a girl thus weeping for me, I determined to buy or in some way acquire for her a dress of silk, if she wanted it. Or a dozen silk dresses, I silently vowed, and each of her tears should be a wish granted. As I passed, she lifted her foot to scratch a flea which had hopped from the earthen floor, and I can still see her perfect grace of movement. For others there may be others, but for me no other than this girl. As I watched her, I would willingly have waited at home, risking life and feud, but was now too shamefaced to say so. My hinny, *simpático* always, turned her head to look at me, and there were tears in her eyes or in my own. In my hundred years, many a man has said to me, "God is good," as some woman passed whom earlier he would have married; but to me this feeling has never come.

We traveled in this wise: First, the Sanhudo family, surrounded by guards. All of our company rode upon mules since in our intolerably heated and grassless deserts a horse is but an encumbrance which inconveniences its rider by dying when most needed. For protection against sun-glare all wore tall-crowned, wide-brimmed straw hats decorated in silver according to their place in life, even the small Sanhudo children. With such hats, eye-guards of wood with narrow slits for sight are little needed, except where salt covers the ground, and by its reflection of sun rays cripples the strongest vision.

In later life I myself have found that, in following an ancient trail nearly destroyed by time, these wooden eye-covers concentrate sight; so that what is imperceptible to the eye near at hand can be plainly seen on the next hillside, even though some miles away. Thus locating such an antique trail from hillside to hillslope, I have found my way where others were lost and died of thirst. Nevertheless, these slotted eye-guards are now little used, desirable as they are on saline deserts or in locating ancient trails.

Behind the Sanhudo family and their guards followed pack-mules loaded to three hundred pounds each, and with an *arriero*[1] to each of the four animals. Thus we carried in leathern *aparejos*[2] food, clothing, and seed. It was Don Firmín Sanhudo's purpose to pass in camp one whole rainy season, during which travel would be difficult and dangerous, while we were en route to Monterey and California. Therefore he planned to sow grain seed as hay for our animals, as ground and rains permitted.

Pack-saddles are now much used but *aparejos* are always better. Despite the best care, some hard-gaited pack-animal scars its back through heat scalds or a crumpled pack-blanket. To cure such a wound the *arriero* need only relieve pressure upon the injured part by hollowing out the grass filling inside this leather pack-sack. Hide wounds are thus cured while the mule continues working. This is difficult with a pack-saddle. Besides, these *aparejos* are our banks, inside which is carried the gold and silver money we may need in travel.

Close behind this pack-train followed twenty unladen mules, to replace those we must lose over cliffs or from thirst in the desert. To lose less than twenty on such a trip would have made us famous in all the Three Californias. Were there not rattlesnakes and lions, and in some *ciénagas* poison weed, as well as meat-loving Indians who ate mules by preference? Scarce had our march begun before I heard our mule-guards and *arrieros* selecting those animals which would die on our journey.

"To bring a white mule on such a trip!" exclaimed one. "What son of Judas selected it? No lion or Indian needs a moon to see it at night—and the sun on its hide! San Gabriel himself could not keep it alive, nor make a pack-rope of its brittle hide when it dies."

[1] *Arriero:* mule-driver.

[2] *Aparejo:* a leather or rawhide sack fitting on both sides of the mule's back, and filled with grass.

"See that *alizan* stumble on a plain trail of round cobbles!" growled another. "Mother of God! If that mule had six legs, it would still tumble a thousand *varas* over the first ten-foot cliff we pass. Let Pedro ride it! He will not be missed."

"Notice!" broke in a third, pointing to a pinto mule. "That *cabrona* has its mouth on every water-weed we pass. At Mulege the *yedra* will poison it. Muzzle a mule? Muzzle thyself, son of a donkey!"

Behind our mule herd I followed, with a dozen milch cows all having three-months-old calves; and at the head of my herd two young bulls. Being the youngest of our party, and perhaps because they pitied my homesickness, I was given these cows to drive. This was an easy job, as all these animals had been herded together for a month and were little inclined to stray. Also, my hinny understood her business, and if a cow lagged behind, she bit the root of its tail as warning. Or if a lively calf kicked up its heels and with a defiant blatt started back for its San José corral, she wheeled automatically and blocked its path. Hardly had we started when an active three-months-old bull calf ran under her and between her legs. This was contrary to the rules of our game, as being likely to upset my mule and perhaps cripple the calf. Therefore, as it emerged, I swung the loop of my rawhide riata and hit it a stunning blow upon its forehead with the heavy running eye through which the loop slides. The runaway shook its head thoughtfully, staggered for a moment, and then returned sedately to its mother. This beast caused me some trouble later, but its meat was excellent when we ate it. Intelligence in all animals except mules and dogs leads to a quick death.

With cattle as with men, much trouble is saved by wise management. Consider the calves. Like children, they mean no wrong, but need discipline at the right times. The cook, knife, or a lion's teeth await all which are badly trained.

As for the bulls, let them alone. That is what their dignity demands, and to infringe this self-respect means useless and dangerous battles. In springtime, perhaps, when their blood boils, it may be difficult to avoid conflict with them. But a bull, being masculine, reasons; and force is needed only for unreason.

These three meats are also of their kind. That of the cow tough, stringy, and producing nerves in those who eat it. What fighting man eats cow meat without protest?

Calf beef is delicious, but lacks strength. On our last night at San José I heard one of Don Firmín's *soldados de cuero* shout to the cook: "Bring me an *arroba*[1] of dried bull's beef, thou washer of fry-pans! Must I lose my strength and rot my teeth eating this calf jelly? Beef must have horns before it is fit food for a fighting man."

Had I a boy to bring up as a boy should be brought up, I would kill a seven-year bull weekly, and if the child, from six months old, ate aught else than bull's flesh, I would dress him in skirts and set him to growing greens in a garden. Bull's beef is man's food. Half that I am comes from borrowing a chunk of the round from every bull our village killed.

Of other meats much might be said. The lion and the skunk are not savory, but with care in cleansing can be eaten when one would otherwise starve. A rattlesnake is strong food and needs a steady stomach. Also, it is well to kill both of the pair or else the living snake, seeking its dead mate, may resent your meal.

Mule meat and horse meat are not bad, and the donkey excellent, were it not that Christ's cross upon its shoulders forbids it as food to all Christians, except in extremity. Bear's meat is not to be despised, though antelope is too dry for pleasure in eating. Of all wild game the best is a six-months-old mountain-sheep ram broiled on oak coals and with quail's fat melted over it. If any man deny this, set him down as a liar or one who talks of what he does not know. But my tongue runs on at every cross-trail, and I am perpetually telling you what I did not know when I left home.

Few of these cows could be expected to live through deserts to come on our trip, but the Sanhudo children would need milk. Also

[1] *Arroba:* twenty-five pounds.

this stock being, as we said, "Sanhudo"—which meant the finest in our south—what we did not eat on our road would improve the herds of Alta California, then said to be more noted for horns than meat.

Back of me dawdled heavily armed men. These were to stop all stragglers, and if we fell into an ambuscade would gallop forward at the first sign of danger, and by their weight and valor decide the matter. Not that we dreaded such a happening; but since we could make only twelve to fifteen miles a day, and must often travel spread out for a league so our poor brutes might graze where food was to be had, anything was possible. Especially to a party encumbered with women and children.

When the padres first taught me of the Garden of Eden, my thought was of Adam and his woman and two children, driven out among wild beasts and the *Indiada* of those parts. A man of courage Adam must have been, and probably with a reputation for handling his knife. Otherwise God alone knows how he saved his family.

Knowledge is much when one works for others. Had I not stolen milk for food from my earliest youth, our rear guard had been swearing at me half the time for having lost cows on the road. One must know how animals think to manage them easily. If I saw some cow looking this way and that, intent upon hiding in thick bush or making off at a gallop up some side trail, I rode to her and brought down my riata loop on her back; and with a deep sigh she felt herself hopeless of escape. One slashing blow on such a cow's back saved me perhaps five galloping miles and, more important, prevented insubordination.

The padres taught me "Rule by Kindness," but by the cock which crew for our Holy Apostle Saint Peter, kindness may follow a blow but never precede it where a blow is needed. Force and guile and justice rule this world, in that order. Strike a cow when she is restless. She is feminine, and unless ruled by force will destroy herself and the herd; and being feminine, is curious by nature, of bad judgment, and despising all rule except force.

Chapter 4

That first night we camped at Santa Anita: a long ride for a late start, but pleasant since it was through a land filled with cotton, sugar cane, and all fruits. Above us on our right was the mountain range of San Lázaro, towering a mile high. To its summit it is filled with the most beautiful valleys covered with bunch grass, and with heavy oak and pine timber on its peaks and ridges. In no country is there such land for cattle and for people.

We camped in this wise: When our packs were down and placed in a circle for easy defense by those who slept within, six of Don Firmín's *muleros* slowly drove our *mulada* and cattle to some little valley, after allowing them to drink and roll to their satisfaction. Rolling on dusty ground is for mules like a night's sleep to Christians. Each evening our *muleros* watched our mules, and if any did not roll in the dust, or failed to roll completely over, it was certain that such were ill or overtired.

During each night six men took turns, two by two on muleback, to guard our animals against theft or wandering. The remaining four did not sleep, but rested their mules. It is a fact without explanation that many an honest man will steal a mule he greatly fancies, although with money or goods he may be trustworthy.

Ground was first of all selected for Doña Ysabel Sanhudo's tent, which contained a floor of canvas sewed so high on its walls that no snake could get within. These tent walls were only two varas (six feet) high, but above, in wet weather, we placed a peaked roof which shed rain. For coolness on our deserts this roof was never used. Within was protection from sight. About her tent at a proper distance six of the Wild Men slept, but of them two were always awake and walking restlessly around the circle they guarded.

These Wild Men came from the far south and could understand no language except their own. Later, when I spoke to them, they shook their heads, but pointing to themselves said *"Maya, Maya."* They were not tall, but had such narrow hips and broad shoulders that they seemed like triangles walking. At first I thought of them as monkeys, but later as cats, for only great cats have such slender muscles combined with enormous and tireless strength.

Once when one of our *arrieros* found difficulty in raising *alforjas*[1] with one hundred and fifty pounds in each, these Wild Men laughed, and using our *alforjas* as balls, threw them from one to the other, and having passed them around their circle lifted them like feathers to the mules' backs. A Mexican is proud and not to be outdone by any Indian. Therefore, afterwards, that *mulero* who found packages heavy was not well thought of by his chums, and we had no more grumbling.

A small fire served our cook, while around a larger one—for our nights are chilly in winter even on deserts—those who rested lay and talked of days past and those to come. We ate chiefly meat, fresh when it was to be had, or otherwise dried bull's beef, which tests the teeth but fills the belly with sustenance. Fruits when we were in their vicinity, or sugar cane peeled and chewed. Afterwards on our trip, when all else failed, the cook gave us dry, hard, white cheese to be eaten with lumps of *panocha*,[2] of which we carried many crates in our mule cargoes. Our cook's work was trifling, as most of us preferred to roast our own meat on a stick till the fat dripped. There was naught else needing heat except coffee, when that was to be had. For this each man carried a cup slung to his belt, just as his own knife cut such meat as politeness demanded his teeth should not touch. Not even a savage uses his teeth to sever a string of dried meat from that other portion of which his neighbor must eat.

Doña Ysabel Sanhudo and her children were more delicately served, but always by her own women, from a fire before her tent. Being of breeding, we never looked that way, so I know not how they fed. Between this fire and the always-open door of his wife's tent, Don Firmín slept upon the ground; and his fire being made of logs set point to point in a circle, it was the duty of his wild men to

[1] *Alforjas:* large hide bags fitting one on each side of a mule's *aparejos.*

[2] *Panocha:* small round cakes of hard brown sugar formed in moulds, and packed in stick crates of about two hundred pounds.

push in at intervals one or the other log, so there was always light before that door until dawn.

Of Doña Ysabel I saw little and heard less, since we Mexicans do not discuss those women who belong to others. Concerning widows, *solteras,*[1] and those who have soiled their lips, it is different. Of them there is always much discussion.

[1] *Solteras:* spinsters of uncertain age, distinct from girls of marriageable age, who are not discussed.

CHAPTER 5. *How We Traveled and Where We Camped—Miraflores and Its Flowers— Polite Adieus to a Spanish Gentlewoman— "Am I Not a De la Cerda?"—The Coyote Rabiosa*

Each morning of our desrt journey the *mulada* and our cattle were driven into camp at earliest dawn, and while for a half-hour they drank and rolled and played in the chill of daybreak, I chewed my dried meat and cheese. Then I started the cattle upon our trail, urging them forward while coolness helped their way, but easing our speed as the sun rose and with its fiery rays rendered travel difficult for all animals which did not sweat freely or were too well fed.

Fat, as I learned on this long journey, is the one great obstacle for desert travel; since, yielding easily to heat, fat melts within all animals and they die. So also men die, and for this reason a fleshy man on a desert is like a whale on dry land. There are those who claim a hog suffocates when urged beyond reason in heat, but this is nonsense. Its fat melts within and, running, clogs all the body exits, and it dies. Concerning such matters it wearies me in my old age to hear much discussion among those who know least; though it is not for me to correct them.

How am I to teach those who know little and who can teach those who already know too much? Of all wisdom, only that of the

Ancients is of value, since it is founded upon observation. Now that I am old, all men study in books. And who make books? Only those who are too lazy to rise before dawn and see for themselves how night and day meet in twilight. Then, for one short moment of least light, those who have gone before and those who are to follow us converse together, giving of their knowledge some slight hint to him who rises betimes and waits with open mind. But as with all old men, my tongue perpetually takes side trails of little interest except to myself.

Behind me followed six of our heavily armed guards. The pack-train came as fast as loaded, there being much competition in loading among our *arrieros*. Don Firmín Sanhudo and his party took their time and often passed at a gallop with a soughing of their Wild Men's leather armor and a call to me from the children. Even the two little girls waved to me in passing, though they were guarded as closely as lambs when lions howl, and could only notice me when their elders were otherwise closely occupied.

For Doña Ysabel's convenience two of our best packers and two pacing mules remained behind. Her tent, with its food service, followed her on these two pack-mules at such pace as her party made, and was ready for immediate use when she signified her will to camp. This was easy since these mules, lightly loaded and carefully packed, could pace six miles an hour with no disarrangement of their packs; though the rest of us made only three miles an hour and did well at that.

Following them slowly, as was necessary with cattle, I often rebelled at the dust and heat in which I always rode; but being cautious, said never a word to others, and was then unashamed when the fit of discontent passed. Besides, each night I talked with him who had arranged our route, and by day amused myself by guessing in advance where we would camp. Always Doña Ysabel selected a place where wild flowers grew, and it was our pleasure to climb hills or search valleys for the rarer blooms which, given to her women, might please her.

When flower time passed and grim deserts replaced our fertile southern mountains, she chose curious views: camps where distant ranges of hills turned purple at sunset, or by day shimmered in heat rays and seemed to move from place to place. There mirage turned sand into water, and we saw great ships sailing a heaving ocean and men loosening their sails: phantoms, perhaps, of those who in former times had roamed our seas, and who now, in expiation of some sacrilege, forever floated over burning sands. English we thought them, and cursed them for our Philippine galleons robbed and sunk, and for towns sacked by these British pirates.

Once near Magdalena Bay we saw, in a waterless desert thirty miles across, a whaling ship with all its tiny boats capture a great whale. While we watched with open mouths, and wondered whether we dared face such enchantments, there came a light wind which blew away both boat and whale. Instead, a great herd of antelope ran across that barren waste where a whale had spouted and died. Our Indians have many legends concerning these mirages; all interesting to hear, but gross, and not appealing to a good Christian like myself.

The padres preach they are enchantments seeking to entice us, but for my part I give devils credit for more ability. A horse perhaps might perish thus, but no man nor any beast with sense. Satan is no such fool as to set horse traps for men.

Often we camped among date palms or pitahaya scrub, or where giant *cardones*,[1] spreading out for miles, made us, by moonlight, imagine a great host of Titans surrounding us. Such colossi they seemed as that twelve-foot Indian dug from his stone grave by Father José Robea at San Ygnacio Mission and, so he said, one of those pagans who by God's order drove Adam from the Garden of Eden.

We consulted every whim of Doña Ysabel Sanhudo because one of her women told us she prayed nightly that the next "Time of Pitahayas" might not bring rain as had the last. One shower destroys our whole crop, and there is hunger and gloom over our south. The

[1] *Cardones:* columnar cactus.

pitahaya bush thrives only on dryness. If rained upon while fruiting, it produces so much sap that its sweet fruit swells too suddenly; and the skin breaking, mildew enters and the whole crop rots. In this way also, in our dry climate, the fig tree, if water falls upon it, loses its two crops: both the *brevas* and the *higos*.

I remember as a boy of ten lying upon the ground during heavy rain, clenching my fists in the mud, and swearing to tear down our whole Church of San Borromeo, the Friend of Christ. Being sleepy, or idle, or full of gabble to other Saints, this lazy one had not looked down from Heaven in time to prevent a storm which destroyed our pitahaya crop. But it was a large church, and I was so delighted with a single ripe pitahaya which had escaped destruction that I forgot my vow.

Not that I habitually disregarded oaths. Sometimes, having in a moment of anger vowed to kill a man, I have later fulfilled my vow unwillingly, and only because I feared the vengeance of the Saint by whom I had sworn. Yet in such cases I have found the relations of the man I killed unlikely to forgive my act. This is not reasonable, for it is certain that an oath to kill, if sworn by a powerful Saint, must be carried out even though sworn in anger and later regretted. The man you fail to kill will later certainly find a way to insert the point of his knife in you where you would rather not have it. Undoubtedly the forsworn Saint must instigate his knife-thrust. I have never been badly wounded from this cause, for certainty of the forsworn Saints' vengeance has always made me squeamish about forgetting such oaths to kill.

Nevertheless, such oaths become at times inconvenient, and since I have grown older and wiser, and have acquired property too valuable to risk passing into other hands, I have in anger sworn only by Saint Anthony of Padua, who for his foolishness concerning women can be but little regarded in Heaven. If I insult him by neglecting such vows to kill, he must make the best of it; and I doubt his power for vengeance, since I have never suffered from his rage.

We traveled so slowly that at Miraflores[1] we also passed a night, and here I could have spent my life, for it was even more beautiful than San José del Arroyo. The very names defined the charms of this land—Miraflores; La Laguna de los Flores;[2] La Floreada,[3] which was a great hill on our right with rounded top from which burst forth myriad-colored bloom; La Pintada, like a blood-red gash in the mountains because here God has painted this hillside with red flowers only; La Florada;[4] La Florida;[5] and a hundred other such, showing how we Spaniards love that which God gives and can express our love in our language.

Truly we have over-many Saints' names fastened upon our land, since our religious are great explorers and claim their right to name for their profession that which they discover. A Saint's name is no disgrace, but I prefer names with less religion and more grace. *San Juan Capistrano* does not fit itself to a broad and fertile valley. Nor is *La Reina de Los Angeles*[6] fitting for a secular village which, when they named it, contained but one white man, the rest being Negroes and Indian half-breeds. At least so the monks of San Fernando told me as we camped there on our way north. But again I am like a grazing cow which follows its tongue without regard to where it should go. From Miraflores I have wandered to Alta California, and passed over eighteen months of time.

We spent one night at the terraced hills of San Bartolo because this was a great curiosity and its owner one to whom it was not wise to give offense. A tall man of great age I found him, and dressed, Don Firmín Sanhudo told me, as if for attendance at Court. At his breast a jeweled order with a golden sheep hanging below it: his manner stately and cold. While he welcomed Señor Sanhudo, the rest of us shrank away, glad to escape from his sight. Having heard much of him, I made pretense of an errand, though when he glanced my way I also hurried from his house.

---

[1] "Behold the Wild Flowers."   [2] "Lake of Blossoms."   [3] "Crowned with Flowers."

[4] A bee ranch; i.e., where bloom lingers.   [5] "Bursting with Blossoms."

[6] "The Queen of the Angels."

Chapter 5

This man's eyes were large and noble, being wide apart; but a single look from them chilled me to the bone, and I knew that my life was to him of no more value than those blades of grass his cows ate that he might drink cream. If my death could benefit him or my life inconvenience him, I felt myself already dead. Indeed, quickly as I left his house, I yet took time to glance each side of the doorway as I went out, lest someone with an axe await me.

Who he was, or why here, no man knew, but it was said he terraced these hills at vast expense for irrigation and tree planting, because thus his home in Spain had been. Of his many wives all were Indians. His rule was that but two wives speaking the same dialect could live in his house. This was because his wives might forget jealousy of each other and become friends if all used the same language. Then, as intimates with the same grievances against him, they would be more likely to avenge themselves on him who tyrannized over them.

Nor was it wise for any one of them to learn a second tongue, since if so, he dismissed them with their youngest child at breast, escorting them himself to the gateway with ceremonial courtesy. But there, for them, life ended: since no man, whether Spaniard or Indian, dared feed them.

The whole place displeased me, especially as a hundred dirty half-breed children lounged insolently about, knowing as well as I that I dared not bleed them into courtesy. Even Don Firmín Sanhudo breathed a sigh of relief when next morning, with minutest ceremonial, we went our way.

The old man escorted us to the end of his estate, sitting his horse as master of it, and when leaving us near the top of a hill, backing his pinto stallion until a hundred yards behind us. Then Doña Ysabel Sanhudo turned her mule about, and bowing, waved her gloves. At which his horse shot forward as if from a bow and, coming at racing speed, was pulled up when another foot would have overturned her. His rider, with plumed hat swung at arm's length, sprang to the ground, and with one knee touching the dust kissed her hand. Again he backed his stallion a hundred yards, and I envied his horsemanship; for the beast he rode, excited beyond endurance, had seldom more than one hoof to the ground. Yet his head was always toward us. When the Señora de Sanhudo turned to wave her gloves in farewell, each time the rider with doffed hat bowed to his saddlebow, while his stallion, struggling viciously, reluctantly bent his head in salutation and touched his fore-knees to the ground. A dozen times Doña Ysabel turned her mule to bow and wave her gloves to him, and he a dozen times repeated his salutation.

As for me, I crossed myself, and swore to kill a crook-eyed son of his as soon as the old noble died: that is, waiting long enough to be certain he would not come to life again, nor haunt the road to Miraflores. There are those who say this old man died and is buried in a tomb with two doors, and there lies until something on earth angers him. Then he emerges by the second door, young and active for a new life, and places within his tomb that one who has enraged him.

Before now I had begun to teach Inocente, the son of Don Firmín, to handle my bow. Also such details of arrow wizardry as fascinate a boy, from those which an old Indian sorcerer had taught me. Therefore he clamored to have me about him, and I rode always with their party.

"A page," his mother called me, as I helped her to mount and to alight. But Don Firmín made more of me.

"As to my son," he said, "so to you."

And I, placing my right hand grasping my knife-hilt between his two, repeated: "As it happens to Inocente, so also shall it happen to me," which was an oath and meant that, as I received the boy each morning from his mother, so also must I again deliver him safe and sound. If not, then honor demanded that I die as he had died. Therefore I rode with them, surrounded always on all sides by our wild men, and listened to the Sanhudo conversation.

"I do not trust him," exclaimed Don Firmín, referring to our host of last night, now hill-down behind us.

"Who does?" scoffed Doña Ysabel. "Did not my second dagger dangle always by its golden chain from my left wrist, and he, knowing why, watch it smiling? But he plays the game as we are taught in Spain. It refreshed my soul to find in these deserts one to whom courtliness is a science. As the breaking of a wild horse to you, so to a woman is the control of such as he. At times dangerous, perhaps; but without danger there is no thrill to life."

"He is mad."

"Truly," and she shrugged her shoulders, "but so are his line."

"Why is he here?" Don Firmín spoke hesitatingly as if he had thought much of this question.

"While our bastard King lives, would this man be alive elsewhere?" suggested Doña Ysabel.

"God in Heaven!" Don Firmín stopped her with finger on his lip, and glancing anxiously at me; but his eyes found me lolling carelessly in my saddle and talking to Inocente about the wizardry of arrows.

"Am I not a De la Cerda?" she exclaimed, drawing herself up proudly on her saddle. "Our motto since Spain began has been, 'We fear no King, nor any devil; only God when He is just.' Dispose of this boy as may suit you, but he has learned caution and silence by hard lessons. Otherwise, I had not trusted him with Inocente."

"You married a Sanhudo," he replied, with some humility.

"What is there in Spain for that man?" she continued. "For generations all his ancestors daily risked their lives. Do you think danger does not become a part of our blood, so that at last there is no other thrill in life? He is here because his family must always so rule as to be hated by all. In Spain remains only etiquette and obedience to his supplanter, the King. Here he sees no one who does not hate and fear him. Yet he lives. *Alma de mi corazón,* is not that a triumphant life for such as he? Not a morsel of food which does not yield its thrill of possible death. Not a doorway he passes which may not hide an axe man. And yet he lives on! Angels of God, what a life! Not a dull moment, not a second awake or asleep in which he does not earn life by fear, by guile, by knowledge of that human nature which he daily outrages!

"What am I, *esposo mio?* I live for your pleasure and for our children. But at times—*bien,* but at times I lack that charm of life which my grandmothers in olden days had. That love of danger bred into us by generations of war does not quickly leave our souls. Therefore, all highly bred women flirt with viciously strong men, leading them on, only to control them. If by chance such a woman loses her all, the merciful God may pity her, but not we of her own class. Has she not had weeks or months of fear, furnishing pleasure to her life?

"My grandmother of old, when her castle was about to yield to Moors, cast herself headlong from its tallest battlement, and falling, crushed their leader. Another of our women, watching our castle gateway, herself loosed a great vat of molten lead, and standing in the fiery bath, laughed because this boiling metal swallowed in its path a host of her bravest enemies. Of all my quarterings that is the one I love: a Moor's skull, and a laughing woman's head.

"In these hard years of travel I shall be happy if I can but see thee in one great feat of arms, and if it fails to save us, do not think me regretful. My dagger lies between my breasts ready, for such an ending, and I shall die happy because I have thrilled with fear. To die in bed! God's Angels! Firminito—what an ending! When my grandmother died, and I knelt while the passing bell tolled, a greasy priest whispered to another kneeling beside him: 'The old lady dies hard—'"

"And the cactus barbs must be laid for three nights on a graveyard fence to fatten in the moon's sweat," droned Inocente, speaking of the wizardry of bows and arrows. Thus I lost what followed, for it is well to hear, but bad breeding to listen; and a reputation for curiosity keeps away much information. Of all winged things the mockingbird hears most, since he sings eternally, but never closes his ears.

Soon we began to leave our pleasant land of afternoon, beautiful beyond the dreams of men, with its rounded mountains clothed in verdure and shade to their mile-high tops, and its valleys filled with fruit and sugar cane. For the rich all things which can be desired are always here. For the poorest comes once each year the "Time of Pitahayas" when for three months there is a delirium of abundance and the whole world eats and dances. Beyond this, two more months of sour pitahayas which are not to be neglected, being full of sustenance, though not sweet.

Around us now began to appear barren hills clothed in cacti of a thousand types, all guarded by barbed thorns. In dry years, which come once in a generation, we burn off these thorns, and our cattle *aguantarselo*[1] on woody stalks and watery leaves. Many a calf has suffered from hunger in such rainless years; but having horns and will, he is the better for what he thus learns.

On the rolling cactus-covered hills toward La Paz, with Inocente, I hunted hares for food and skins. There I met that which caused me for a moment to wonder whether the church-robber who poisoned me had so destroyed my nerves as to make the bow better fitted for me than my knife. But I must explain why I used my bow so expertly.

When I was six years old, I was much abused because always ready to fight. Being a King's son, could I help fighting? Therefore, great bullies of eight and ten years old would taunt me until I butted them in the belly. Then they would so beat me that often I have crawled home irrigating our dusty road with my tears.

Once an old Indian servant found me thus, and said in his dialect:

"Little-Fool-Who-Fights, come to me tomorrow and I will teach you."

As this Indian was reputed a great wizard, I went gladly to him, stealing away after my mother had bedded me where he sat within our *campo santo*[2] fence, while overhead vagrant clouds wandered uncertainly across a waning moon.

"Sit outside," he ordered in a tone quite new to me. Now he was Master of Spirits, and I was glad to be without; though I would have followed him within the graveyard had he so ordered. I am so made as to be always afraid, yet always ashamed to acknowledge fear.

[1]*Aguantarselo:* suffer the dry year through.

[2] *Campo santo:* graveyard.

From under his left arm the Indian drew a small bag formed of the tanned skin of an enemy, and from it took various precious things, such as the toe joint of his grandmother, who had been a famous witch. By blowing through this he could summon her spirit.

Having warned me to close my eyes, he called her. Though I heard nothing, her message was clear, and she brought me a bow and arrows with blunt ends, curiously cleft.

"First practice," the wizard ordered, "until a wasp on the wing is not safe from you."

Then he showed me the secret of these cleft arrows, and said:

"Place in each cleft such and such a cactus barb, hardened for three nights in the moon's sweat on this tombstone, where I now sit. Then, when thy enemy leans over to pick up cobblestones to use against thee, shoot but one arrow, hitting him exactly where I have shown thee, and calling loudly as thy arrow flies, 'Go thou upon thy belly for a week.' So it shall be if thy eye is as thy tongue, and as thy knife shall be. But shoot only at bullies, or thy arrow shall turn back upon thee for thy suffering."

According to his orders, so I used my arrows; and the cactus barb, penetrating a certain muscle, left my enemy in such misery that if he would watch us play, he must crawl upon his belly to where we were. Whereupon we ran away, and he followed weeping as I had wept. By the week's end the barb within my enemy's muscle had rotted, and we were again good friends; as are always those who fear one another.

Being inordinately proud of my skill, I practiced until I taught my bow as much as it had taught me. When leaving home with the Sanhudos after I had been poisoned, I was minded to abandon my bow as a boyish toy, but my mother said to me: "You will need rabbit skins where you go. It is cold there."

And while I hesitated, the old Indian wizard who had taught me whispered in my right ear: "Little-Fool-Who-Fights, there was once a lion which, parting with his mother to hunt alone, left behind all his claws because he had claws when a kitten."

Therefore, I carried with me my bow and arrows, and cared for them well, keeping them from the moon's sweat and the sun's anger, and greasing them in the desert.

One day, having wandered with Inocente through the wild cactus-clothed hills west of La Paz, and killed such hares as we could carry, I sat in the shade of a bush to clean them; since in desert heat game must be quickly cleansed if one would preserve it.

Being wary by training—for as a small boy at home older ones had often hunted me to my damage—I stood up often to look about me for enemies. It is a great help to be distrustful, for distrust is the parent of long life. As I thus looked about me, I noticed a pair of ears rise from the bushes a long way off, as if a dog jumped aloft the better to scent food.

This did not please me, as when with Inocente I needed greater care, having two lives then to protect. Therefore, with caution, and standing in the center of a great bush to hide my red hair, I watched. It was a coyote which, following our tracks, jumped in air in order to locate us. Now, the coyote is an animal full of curiosity and a camp-robber which follows tracks for what he may find, but does not hunt men. Therefore I settled down to my rabbit-skinning without anxiety.

But in a moment it occurred to me that a coyote thus jumps only when he seeks hares, to locate them as they run and dodge about. When he follows a man's track, seeking camp refuse or leather to chew up, he slinks along, belly almost touching the ground, and taking advantage of every bush for shelter against sight. Therefore, I knew it must be a *coyote rabiosa*,[1] since being already too insane for thought, he followed only by habit what instinct taught him to destroy. Fearing man no more than he fears a rabbit, the hydrophobic coyote hunts both in the same way.

"Run straight ahead," I ordered Inocente, "and passing through that bush turn back abruptly on thy trail, and at the clump nearer to us jump as far toward it as you can, and there cower until this business is finished. Thus this coyote will pass you by."

[1] *Coyote rabiosa:* a coyote afflicted with rabies.

But the boy refused, and when I pressed him only said:

"My mother teaches me that no one of my race ever ran away or hid."

Seeing him set, and in not a bad road, I could only advise: "Hold then thy daggers ready, fool. One in each hand, and guard well thy throat, for this is not child's play. Pray your very best to Saint Hubert who protects against dog-bite, and who, if now awake, may help us with this mad coyote."

Then, watching for the mad beast as every few paces he leaped in air to locate us, I selected a bush ten yards away which he must pass. I planned, when I saw him there, to whistle, so that my first arrow might be aimed before his last quick rush at us came. A mad coyote which hunts men treats them as he does rabbits, at first moving slowly and tactfully so as not to excite his prey. Then, when within striking distance, he gives such a burst of speed as makes him seem like a streak of lightning which arrives at the horizon almost before it has left the zenith.

Thus we waited, seeing a nose and a pair of ears appear at intervals above the bushes which hid the beast. Each time we saw the coyote's ears they were nearer to us. Inocente, at my elbow, did not once whimper; though I, under stress of my great fear of hydrophobia, kept my nerve only by saying aloud while the beast approached: "Here comes Tomása's Pedrillo,"[1] that being the boy I most hated, and in years gone by the first victim of my bow.

Soon we saw the great beast more plainly. Almost bare of hair he was, as the fires of madness had roasted his body; his eyes blurs of blood, while from his open mouth hung a dry and swollen tongue. When he had reached the bush I had chosen, I whistled sharply, throwing the sound a little to one side to puzzle him. For an instant he stopped; and shouting without knowing what I said, "Go thou upon thy belly for a week!" I drove a war arrow into his left side, so that, as he bent his neck to bite off the arrow's shaft, his throat might be exposed. Swiftly I sent another arrow into his throat, and no

[1] Thomasina's little Peter.

longer filled with foolish fears, took my time in driving a third arrow lengthwise into his body.

The strain being over, Inocente made me laugh more than I otherwise would have done by asking me: "Why did you want the coyote to go upon his belly for a week?"

Had I been alone, I would have gone to see the writhing body, but having the Sanhudo boy to care for, I made a long detour around the coyote and thus back to camp. There are certain animals impossible to kill, and which pretend death only to decoy their hunter to destruction. Such a risk I could not take while Doña Ysabel's son was in my charge. Neither of us remembered, until next day, that all the hares I had killed for food were left behind to rot in the desert.

That night, not being sleepy, I heard through their tent canvas— for as Inocente's guard I slept near by—Doña Ysabel whisper to him several times as he woke with a start after dreaming of our *maldito* coyote.

Doubtless also she put her hand upon his forehead to calm him. So my mother had often done to me when, as a child, I slept beside her and had been unduly excited by my day's sports. Now, nearing twelve, I had become too old for such care; and yet at times one regrets age and its loneliness.

But I am not the kind which ever hid behind his mother's skirts, nor even before I could walk did I cry "Mama! Mama!" when older boys beat me. This perhaps was only because of my red hair, which urged me to strike back when struck. Red hair does not carry its owner to Heaven, but as a help through life few things are better.

CHAPTER 6. *The First Four-Wheeled Vehicle in the Three Californias—"My She-Devil Planted Two Hoofs in My Belly, and I Wait for Them to Sprout"—Inocente is Lost—"Come and Drink Chocolate"*

NEVER HAD I BEEN IN LA PAZ, though during my whole childhood I had dreamed of it more than of Heaven, and feared it far more than Hell. This is why. To San José del Arroyo came continually pearl-divers from La Paz to be cured of knife wounds or to recover from illnesses; but most of all to forget those dangers from voracious sea animals to which, in our Vermilion Sea, they were continually exposed.

From the time I had first learned to deceive my mother by stealing away from my bed after she had stroked my forehead and said, "Be a good boy, Juanito," I had listened nightly to those pearl-divers' tales: of the manta, which is wily and without mercy; of sharks; of that burro-shell, which lives upon men; of the one-eyed *ojón*, which controls whirlwinds; of the octopus; of mermaids, and of the Seri Indians.

That I have no white hair from fright at these stories is due solely to the color I was born with, which refuses to yield a shade of its red to age or to fear. Therefore, the day we journeyed to La Paz was as long as that week before the pitahaya fruit ripens, which we of the south call the thirteenth month. But all days have an end, and when within a mile of La Paz I thought my longest day ended, though for me it had hardly begun.

Just when all the men of our party had relaxed their vigilance, and were heaving sighs of contentment at the prospects of food and cool sea water, we met suddenly a four-wheeled wagon drawn by six mules at a gallop, and within its high sideboards men shouting and women calling upon God with tears.

We learned later that a pearl-diver, Domingo Melendres, having found that great pearl which is still among the Spanish crown jewels, and being able, therefore, to seek the favor of a La Paz beauty, had bought this wagon for his *enamorada*. This was the first four-wheeled vehicle ever seen in the Three Californias. And why anyone, in those days, should have brought it there is beyond understanding except by pearl-divers, who know only their trade, and how foolishly to spend what they earn with so much danger. Of the four hundred leagues between San José del Arroyo and Monterey Bay, little then permitted more than two riders abreast, and much of it with difficulty but one horseman. Now that I am old, they call "road" that which is for wagons; but when I was a boy, *"El Camino del Rey"*[1] was for a King where he should be—on the back of a serviceable mule. While we had, of course, two-wheeled ox carts with solid wheels to bring in our sugar cane, we respected mules too much to use them in wagons and ourselves beyond being willing to ride in such contraptions.

There happened to be at La Paz then no one who had ever driven a team of horses. The problem of the wagon having been laid before the Company of Manta-Feeders,[2] they had decided first of all to fill it with the girl the giver sought and her relations, since after the unbroken mules were attached it would be difficult to load in women. Six riding mules were then harnessed, but as they had never before worn harness, they had bucked it off several times before

[1] *El Camino del Rey:* the King's Highway, now changed in California to *Camino Real*, in deference to the Monroe Doctrine.—*A. de F. B.*

[2] The La Paz Pearl-Divers' Association was generally known as "The Manta-Feeders" because so many pearl-divers were eaten by mantas.

being fully convinced that it could only be some new and foolish form of saddle. They had finally been completely blindfolded in place, and the wagon with its load rolled up behind them.

Seated on each mule was a pearl-diver's apprentice, not over-pleased with his job, but ready to guide his mount by bridle reins, since no other method of driving was known to any of them.

All being ready, the Admiral of Pearl-Divers had fired a gun so that all the postillions might pull off the mules' blinders at the same instant, thus ensuring that all animals would start at the same time.

They were off at the shot like a cannon ball. Mules wearing harness blinders for the first time, and unable to look about them, could only surmise from the noise and confusion that a herd of hungry lions, seeking mule flesh, was approaching. Therefore a quick start was their only hope of life.

Not having been allowed to see the wagon behind them, the terror of these six mules was infinite when it rushed after them, with screechings and groanings due to the lack of a road and to ungreased axles. Instant death which they could not even look behind to avoid, this team thought, must be about to destroy them, and flight their only hope of escape. The shootings of all La Paz behind them and the loud wailings of terrified women in the wagon did not discourage this hideous idea.

Therefore, these six mules had been violently running away from their following wagon; but now, meeting the Sanhudo pack-train, they stopped suddenly so that all were hopelessly tangled in their harness. In their terror and distress they brayed as if being tortured to death. Our own animals, both riding and pack-train, startled at seeing several of their kind pursued by a four-wheeled devil filled with yelling men and weeping women, volte-faced on one leg and scattered over the plain.

When my hinny saw this runaway wagon, she stopped, trembling all over. Yet such was her confidence in me that when I patted her neck and spoke to her, she advanced snorting with distended nostrils, ready in a second to turn about and fly; but nevertheless curious to know what this thing might be which chased mules. Had a wheel turned, she would have been a mile away, with confidence in me gone forever.

Doña Ysabel sat her mount like a *vaquero* of the first, using her spurs to keep her mule from dropping to the ground to roll her off. This is the primary idea of all mules when in danger. In any emergency they imagine a lion leaping from a tree branch upon their flanks. Only by rolling on him instantly, before the great cat's claws reach from above around the mane, to tear open the jugular vein, can they crush him.

Unable to roll, her mount reared in an effort to fall backward upon her, and seeing her danger I yelled, like a fool. But such as she need neither warning nor advice. When she shook her head at me, my face flamed to my hair color.

As her mule rose on his hind legs, she struck him heavily between the ears with her loaded riding-crop, carried for this purpose. Stunned, he dropped forward, and yielding to her horsemanship advanced by short, high bounds toward the wagon. A dozen times he wheeled suddenly to run away, but each time surrendered his will; and stood at last gasping for breath and expecting instant death, but with his bit-chains touching a wagon wheel.

"A charming day for a drive," she said, in her soft, low voice, to those who, watching this struggle, had not yet alighted. We of New Spain know horses and are joyed to watch such a rider subdue her mount. Only one man, perhaps dazed by excitement of his wagon trip, put out a hand to hold her reins.

"*Tonto!*"[1] she exclaimed, drawing her whiplash sharply across his arm. And "*Tonto*" became thereafter his name. Ten years later I saw him, and he answered to "*Tonto*" as does a dog. In fact, his real name had been forgotten, and his grandchildren were called "*Tontitos.*"[2] With us, nicknames, if given for cause, are greatly dreaded. Years after I knew a family named "*Sabichi*" because the grandfather had often used, and improperly pronounced, a very offensive American

[1] *Tonto:* fool.   [2] *Tontitos:* little fools.

oath. It is curious that we Mexicans so often swear with foreign curses which we cannot pronounce. Spanish is the richest language on earth in oaths, as it is also otherwise. How much better is *"cabrón"* than *"sabichi!"*

Seeing the wagon before me and the damage it had caused us, I then made an oath, which at a hundred years old I have not broken, never to enter a four-wheeled vehicle. Where a horse cannot carry me nor a mule take me, there I do not go. Simplicity of life vanishes when goods can be brought cheaply in wagons for long distances. When a store is less than a hundred miles away, it is impossible to restrain women, who by perpetual weeping obtain that which is unnecessary. They buy thus merely to boast of riches above their neighbors, who in turn must do the same. In the olden days, when a Jewish peddler came too often and tempted women with his pack, we set Indians upon him and later covered their tracks, saying to the women, "A lion scared him." Where a storekeeper houses his goods, this is difficult.

Any Spaniard knows that it is impossible to take one's eyes from a beautiful woman who subdues properly a wild mount; but as I now looked around me and could not see Inocente, I knew Don Firmín would feel that my eyes should have been upon the boy. To explain why, in our first emergency, I had forgotten his son's danger, would be beyond me—and I was not bad at explanations when such were necessary.

Inocente was nowhere within sight. So tense was my anxiety that my eyes responded beyond their normal power, and far distant as some were, scattered everywhere on the plain behind us, yet instantly I knew each mule and rider within view.

Not far off stood a pack-animal, with his cargo fallen between his legs. At times he tried to buck, which is difficult with three hundred pounds dangling below the belly. Bray he could, and did, until not a chum within hearing but imagined that the four-wheeled devil which chased mules had caught one and was eating him. A little farther on a Wild Man argued with his mule, which stood stubbornly with legs apart, refusing to move. To any *vaquero* his language was plain.

"I trusted you, in part," the mule was saying, "and you permitted this devil almost to kill me. Go your way, idiot, and I will go mine, but your way never, lest I be not so lucky next time. Just hear that poor chum of mine bray as it is being eaten!"

To pass this man I went a little around, and with head averted as if following a track, for these Mayas have a dignity which does not permit laughter. On such a trip as ours there are many opportunities for stabbing, if one gives them offense. His mule tried to follow me, but as the man's duty was to guard Doña Ysabel, and his mule objected to going in that direction, they continued their argument. As he spoke only Maya, his mount, yearning for good Spanish oaths, held him every moment in greater contempt. As I looked back I saw that the mule tried at intervals to bite pieces from his legs and thus get rid of him.

Ahead were a few riderless animals, but this was not such a great disgrace, as all our mules were new and first ridden at five years old. Good riders were needed for such selected half-wild beasts. Especially when the seventh vial of the Wrath of God, of which Padre Talk-Much so often preached, was opened suddenly before their eyes, and a wheeled terror appeared from it madly chasing six mules as if to swallow them at one gulp.

Ahead of me one pack-mule had bucked off his crate of *panocha*, and three hundred pounds of these round brown-sugar cakes were scattered for a mile over the plain. Here collected a string of mules placidly eating this delicacy. "Not to eat is to die," a mule argues, "and to die with a full belly is not such a bad death." For variety and charm of curses this spot was perhaps the best of our whole trip. What *panocha* these mules ate, our packers would not eat, and these hard lumps of brown sugar, with hard white cheese, are their delight on a journey. Therefore came paths which caused all mules to switch their tails. One knew by watching these tails which packer swore most to their liking, and that only Spanish is really effective with animals.

At this place the runaways had fanned out, and I set myself to select Inocente's track. On our first day I had learned the footprints of Inocente's mule, and later those of Doña Ysabel's and Don

Firmín's mounts. In fact, by now I could have given a fair guess at the track of any of our mules, just as any *rancho* milker must learn the hoofprints of his hundred milch cows. In these later days of schools, when even a Mexican can walk a road and know little of what has happened thereon, I am asked how I know this track from that. In fact, no two hoofprints are alike. Nor two beasts throw their feet in the same way. So simple is this knowledge that only two eyes are needed. Every piece of land over which animals have passed gossips to me as I walk. Books! Lord of Heaven! What book can tell half of what the earth relates to me?

All of life is passed upon the earth, and for such life's actions are recorded on it. As I ride or walk, I know without pause what has been done thereabouts since I last passed. To follow a trail without seeing who has preceded you or where he turned aside to ambush you; to pass under a tree without knowing whether a hungry lion there awaits his meal; to trace a deer unknowing what wild men also hunt him—all these things shorten life unduly.

With little difficulty I picked out the tracks of Inocente's mule, and here met from my hinny that aid I might have expected. The two animals had been so much together that they had become great friends, and now she missed the other. My pet jerked at her reins and looked around at me impatiently until I gave her full freedom of head. Then, smelling carefully to be certain this track was what we sought, she followed the trail at a fast rack. This she increased at times to a lope on sand where prints were deep, or slowed to a walk on rocky soil or where other animals blurred those tracks we followed.

I had only to be certain from time to time that she made no error, by noting those hoofprints of Inocente's mule I knew so well: his left fore foot striking not quite so deeply as the right; the left rear hoof overreaching a trifle less the right, while this right foot threw more sand ahead of it, in its fall, than the other. Such are a few of trackers' signs, but only those all eyes can see. Finer sight determines easily an animal's age and whether his paces are natural or taught. Also the weight and size of the rider.

Before me as I galloped after Inocente lay a *soldado de cuero,* and I whistled like a hunting lion. At this sound he sat up so freely that I had no more fear regarding damage to him from his fall.

"*Hi, chungo!*"[1] he called to me. "Where did you fall from? What happened back there? I was behind, and saw nothing until the whole train of crazy brutes, men and mules, overran me and carried me away with them. Had the wild beast I rode thrown me off then, a hundred hoofs would have carried away bits of my bones; but *gracias á Dios,* we were so packed together that had I wanted to fall, I must have climbed over a dozen riders. In the name of Satan's daughter, what happened back there, *chungito?*

"One wagon, you say! And in the town where I was born there are six. Holy San Miguel! How I would like to drive our pack-train through my birth town! Where did Don Firmín Sanhudo get these mad devils with four legs, and wrapped in mule hide, which he gives us to ride? Madre Santísima, now I am happy again! I lay here planning to cut my throat as soon as it became too dark to see the blood, because I had run away from a great battle. I, who have fought all my life, and never yet shown my back to an enemy! Even they say I battled with my mother before she bore me. Now I have run away from a wagon and been tumbled off by a devil, improperly wrapped in mule hide."

He rose reluctantly, feeling of every bone in his body and exclaiming "*Ojala! Ojala!*" as he found each whole. I caught his mule for him, and they went their way, occasionally disputing the direction of travel.

A mile or two farther on sat a packer, by name Heraclio, bowed with his head almost to the ground and clutching his belly with both hands.

"*Qué hay, mulero?*"[2] I called, and he groaned loudly, but did not change his position.

"My she-devil," he gasped, "planted two hoofs in my belly as she rolled me off, and I am waiting to feel if they sprout properly. If

[1] *Chungo:* monkey. Applied to an active boy.

[2] *Qué hay, mulero:* "What has happened, mule-packer?"

Satan has hoofs like that brute of mine, I must turn monk and earn a passport to Heaven." Then, glancing sideways at me: "But thy boy, fool?"

"Ahead of me," I answered, trotting on.

"Water?" he implored.

"Mine was all spilled when this thing I ride tumbled me," I replied, for it was miles to any spring, and the quart I carried little enough for Inocente, if I had to search long for him.

"Mother of God!" he called after me. "How easily this child lies! But go thy way, liar, and if thou findest not Inocente, I will groan for water behind thy back all thy life both day and night." Nor was this a jest, for so it happened to an Indian I knew, who drained his companion's canteen in the desert. Day and night the dead man groaned continually into his left ear.

My hinny halted, and I could see that the boy I sought had been tugging at one rein, in an effort to stop his mule. Therefore, their tracks led to the right; but our trail back to San José turned toward the left. Certain that Inocente's mount meant to return to San José, I struck across the desert to shorten my trip, feeling sure that when the child tired pulling at the right rein his mule would turn to the left, and I thus meet them by cutting across their circle.

My hinny carried me to the San José del Arroyo Trail, where it leaves these eternal rolling hills and follows a box cañon difficult to enter except at this place. Having cut all tracks on this box cañon trail thoroughly, to be certain Inocente had not passed, I halted. I was reassured by my hinny, as she stood facing the direction from which we had come, with nostrils distended, the better to scent her chum's approach. I turned her head toward San José, and waited an hour with ever-increasing anxiety. He who leaves a track to pick it up later, when he seeks the track's maker, is a boy or a fool: and in my case both, I thought.

Nevertheless, I held my face resolutely south, so that if Inocente cried, as he came from the north, he might have time to compose his features. A child so young and tenderly nurtured, alone in wild deserts after such a stampede, might weep as he pleased without injury to his courage. But to be met when crying would permanently destroy his self-respect.

At last, from behind a northern hill, came a mule's mournful bray.

"I am lost," it recited. "A Thing attacked me, and I ran away. My chum has been eaten by lions, and the White Mare which mothers me has left me to suffer alone."

My hinny put back her ears, for mules tell all their many hysterical fears in brays, and others of their kind within hearing believe them and are also terrified. But I tickled her flank as I do when we play, and she reached back to nip my leg, kicking upward with both hind legs to catch my boot soles a rap. So, when the next wail of woe sounded, she answered with a contemptuous bray of: "Keep closed thy lying flytrap, misbegotten fool born of a mare! This is a merry world."

"Must a cemetery be newly filled to be useful for curing wizards' cactus thorns?" asked Inocente when he met me; and I knew he thought himself unsuspected of weeping, though tears had plowed deep furrows in the desert dust of his cheeks.

"Drink!" I said, offering my canteen.

"Why? I have saved all my own canteen, lest tomorrow's sun be more scorching than today's."

We rode to La Paz almost in silence, both being over wearied; and I considered, as my hinny led the way, why a party so well managed as ours should suffer so much from such a trifling cause. A dozen San José *vaqueros* would have stopped all our trouble before it began. But to manage animals one must ride before one walks, and few of the men we had with us on this trip were experienced riders. In fact, if the mother herself does not come from a family *vaquerista*,[1] what hope is there for her sons? To ride is not merely to throw your saddle on a mule. One must know what these beasts think, and what they are going to fear by the preliminary note of the first one which brays.

[1] *Vaquerista:* born on horseback, as the saying goes.

What a rider feels, that his mount knows; for all four-footed animals are unreasoning and depend upon instinct, which misleads them in emergency. Let a *soldado de cuero* permit fear to enter his head, and instantly his mule will be ready to stampede. So, also, what his mount is about to feel, a rider must know, and divert the animal's mind.

Certainly in this world there are no *vaqueros* except those of the Californias, and of these the best are those of San José del Arroyo. Miraflores also may perhaps have its horsemen. They do what they can with what God in His wisdom has granted them. The good points of a neighbor one can recognize without losing respect for one's own superiority.

I delivered Inocente to Doña Ysabel, standing with hat off before her, but as far as I could from the light of their tent fire. Her eyes danced with amusement as she noted my precaution, but she smiled graciously and motioned me away without a word to draw attention to me. Thus always was this lady considerate of those who served her.

Had Don Firmín seen me then, he would have discharged me, or worse. He was never a man who pardoned a stupidity or a careless-ness. While he controlled his temper as a gentleman must, neverthe-less his orders, though given in apparent cold blood, were feared by all; and not infrequently they were harsh, and at times cruel. He pre-sented death to a man wrapped up in a smile, and always with a word of praise for some past deed well done. Thus the condemned man, from pride at unaccustomed praise, died happily and without protest.

Therefore, it was with gratitude to Doña Ysabel that I escaped unseen and, foodless, hunted a corral in which I might feed and shelter my hinny. Tomorrow, I reflected, would come with the next sunrise, and I should be stupid beyond my wont if I could not then placate Don Firmín until his first anger at my carelessness should have passed.

That night I strayed watchfully through La Paz, avoiding all who might have been sent to call me to Don Firmín Sanhudo; and I found

I had many friends among those who served him. One motioned me away, lest I be seen by his messengers. Another whispered a kindly word, and two or three handed me odds and ends of food, well knowing I dared not go near our cooks.

At moonrise I met a cousin, and he stood so long and so awkwardly on one leg that, had I had my bow, I would have planted an arrow behind his left wing, as one kills a wild goose.

At last he said, after many mouthings: "Come and drink chocolate with me."

By this I understood, of course, that he was to be married; for chocolate is our luxury at weddings, and so they are often announced. He was, like all bashful boys, too shy to say "marriage" aloud; so to tease him, I began: "Is the girl then so ugly that you avoid mention of weddings?"

At which he fingered his knife-hilt until I laughed.

"Listen, thou Laugher," he broke out. "This girl is the greatest beauty in our district. Were I not reasonably quick with sharp steel, every booby about here would court her. As for singing to her, or standing by her window for hours on the chance of a word through iron bars, all that is the custom and easy. But this thing of weddings affronts me. If she love me as I her, is not that enough? Why should our whole town come to see a fat priest mouth a few words over us? Once I said to her, "Come with me without fuss, or—"

"She threw up her shoulders and scorned me, remarking, politely: 'There is the daughter of Julano de Tal, who admires thee. Seek her, my friend.' And yawning—for I stood in the street and she behind iron window bars, so that she feared me not at all—she added: "Mention to the *Almirante*[1] of Pearl-Fishers, as you pass him, that my window is vacant."

"What could I do but swear and pray to her until she relented, and promise her a dozen weddings if she chose? It is not a girl one wants, but *the* girl; and she knows it."

[1] *Almirante:* Admiral. He then governed the Pearl-Fishers' Guild, which yielded to no other authority.

I left him to his days of misery, pending his marriage, and made up my mind, when the time came, to carry off the girl who wept as I left San José, and see the priest with her after I owned her. Using such precautions, a man may marry with self-respect. I am not one who believes in our old proverb: "Why marry a girl who loves thee? It is not necessary." Yet I would not willingly lose my self-respect to marry any girl.

To be near my hinny, who would be nervous after our experience with that runaway wagon, I spread my blankets in the corral beside her so that she might nuzzle my hand occasionally during the night. Also I fed her well on green corn suckers, which I borrowed from a pile I had noticed in the corner near the owner's house. Being thus fed and kept from nervousness by my presence, she got that hour's sleep just before dawn which is all a mule needs, but without which it loses flesh.

As for me, being exhausted by sixteen hours in the saddle and by anxiety regarding Inocente, I rolled myself in my blankets. As I lay looking up at the sky for a few moments before sleeping, I thought it easy to know that Heaven must be well lighted at night, and that God thus forgets our needs on this earth. Had He ever traveled or made camp in a cactus desert filled with rattlers and barbed spines, He would have provided at least seven moons, always full, so that between night and day would be only the difference of heat.

I once asked our padres about this, and by their faces one would have thought I proposed stealing that great pearl, the Madonna's Charm. But doubtless they had never heard anyone swear as did Tomasito, one black night, after he had tied his mule to a *cholla* stem, thinking it a bush. Nor was it safe for me to laugh while he thus conversed; which nearly injured me within.

Santísima Virgen! The things that man said as he plucked barbed spines from his hide—and then, nearly asleep, rolled over on several he had missed and now remembered! I learned much in that hour which has been useful to me ever since, as language for mules. Also, how not to laugh.

CHAPTER 7. *The Tailless Chickens of La Paz—*
The Mysteries of the Vermilion Sea Which Pearl-
Divers Taught Juanito—The Manta with Fifteen-Foot
Wings—The Burro-Shell Which Sucks Men's Blood
—Sharks, the Octopus, and the Ojón, Which
Demands Politeness at Sea

AT THE BREAK OF DAWN next morning, a fluttering of wings waked me. Near me was a chicken-house, without roof or sides, of course, as always with us, to prevent disease and start the hens early at eating and laying. It was composed of four posts stuck deep in the ground and eight feet high to prevent raids by flesh-eaters. Joining these posts, at their tops, round poles were tied with lashings of rawhide, and, extending across, still others on which the fowls perched.

All night cockerels from these roosts had lied in predicting dawn, but now the pullets were first awake, trying their wings, preening their feathers, and cackling like ten-year-old girls in pitahaya time. When an aged hen reached her bill so far back in flattening a dis-arranged feather as nearly to lose her balance, one would have thought squawking a remedy for all ills, so much of it there was.

Wide awake from necessity—for who can sleep while a bevy of females gossip?—I watched each bird cast her eyes about the corral, when preparing to fly down, as if expecting danger from coyotes or skunks. Looking up at them toward the dimly lighted east, I could see that not one of the chickens had a tail, and remembered that so were all desert fowls. In San José del Arroyo we had specimens of this breed, but as curiosities only. Our coyotes were better fed and were not those gaunt, sly, dry-land beasts, whose perpetual depredations perhaps caused tailless hens: through the survival for breeding, during two centuries, of only those birds with fewest tail plumes, who were least likely to be grabbed by the stern and held by such flesh-eaters. Or it may be because of continual extraction of their tail feathers by hungry jaws as the birds flew upward to avoid death. But certain it is that from La Paz northward, while deserts lasted, a hen's rump with plumes did not then exist. These chickens were good in all ways, and perhaps even better layers than our tailed birds.

We Mexicans work willingly and hard so long as heat maintains our energies, but rise unwillingly before the sun. Therefore I continued to lounge between blankets, waiting for sunshine to remove last night's chill; though I marked well, as I watched, where these chickens laid six eggs, planning to breakfast well thereon. Not to eat an egg I have seen laid has been difficult for me since I can remember.

When at last the first heat rays reached me from the far-off horizon of Sinaloa, I glanced that way and saw what checked my yawning and bounced me from my blanket. Before my eyes lay the Vermilion Sea.[1]

People think that because a child closes its eyes and is silent, it takes no interest in what is said by its elders. On the contrary, half a man's knowledge of life comes before he can speak, and learning ceases as his tongue accustoms itself to wagging. My understanding of women came to me from female tongues as I lay on my mother's lap and suckled at her breast, or soon after. "How easily he sleeps," they would say; and I listened none the less well because my eyes were closed.

Half the dreams of my childhood had centered about this Vermilion Sea. Each evening at San José del Arroyo, while yet I was scarce knee-high, men gathered about an open fire a little way from

[1] *The Vermilion Sea:* the sea of Cortés, now called the Gulf of California.

our village, where women could not interrupt with their calls. There newcomers related their tales of ocean and desert, but chiefly regarding our Scarlet Gulf.

Pushing and squirming until within hearing of that one who for the night was center of that charmed circle about our fire, I lay with eyes shut while some pearl-diver from La Paz told one of the many tales which still linger in my memory. About the manta, perhaps— that great flat sunfish, thirty feet across, and with a vast toothed bill, unseen until protruded from its belly to hold its prey.

Lazily swimming—nay, almost floating on the surface—the manta selects for its breakfast that pearl-diver most to its liking. The victim, deep beneath in the sea, is busy raking pearl oysters into a sack, quite unconscious that he has been chosen from among all his comrades to feed the great fish above him. The manta, grown expert by practice—for it has not grown so large without having previously breakfasted on divers—keeps at the surface just above its coming meal until the wretched man below must ascend for air or die. Thus, rising for air, the poor fellow perishes, hugged between this beast's two wings, which it brings together downward.

With gluttonous voracity this vast sea-devil tears and devours its victim, regardless of his comrades all around it: grinding its flat teeth as it eats, half in rage that it cannot consume all the pearler's crew at one breakfast, and half with joy at its meal. Meanwhile, the dead man's comrades, safe for that day, rise all about this crunching monster and, expelling used air from their lungs, swim to their boat; so rejoiced at their own escape as scarcely to mourn the dead companion, though bearing always with them the vision of greedy, merciless eyes and the sound of flat teeth grinding their friend's bones.

"All of us know"—the story-teller would drop his voice almost to a whisper, while my backbone quivered like pitahaya jelly when the spoon cuts it—"that the manta, while eating today's victim, selects its next day's meal from among those who swim back in terror to their boats. But that dull glare gives no sign of its choice, and thus the appointed one goes tomorrow to certain death."

I still know a score of names, each of which kept me in thrills for a week, since each was a new victim of the manta. The mere fact that it crunched these men's bones so terrified me that I cried at night: a delicious fear, since I would not have so much enjoyed these tales had the beast not eaten men bones and all.

Regarding the burro-shell, these divers often quarreled among themselves, some claiming this shell to be a blessing, since it kept sharks away from the pearling grounds; others denying this, and cursing it as having killed some old friend.

"Watch your feet as you work at sea bottom, *amigo*," one diver would growl to another as they thus disputed. "Some day Polycarpio will have you for lunch before you know it!"

"Did you see him snap at me, that day I wiggled my toes at him?" another would ask.

These great burro-shells lie half-buried in the sea bottom, waiting with wide-open jaws for the diver's foot. When the shell has caught its victim, it holds him until some watching shark, rushing in, bites the man in two and takes its half. Then the burro opens and greedily absorbs his blood. Thereafter that shell grows to such size as to dwarf the less well-fed of its kind, and, being easily recognized, it is called by the dead man's name. Some claimed each shell had a favorite shark which it called for the feast. Nearly all insisted it to be bad luck to kill any burro-shell, even had it caught several divers, since sharks then at once became active in the pearling bottoms.

From October to May these divers also had their stories, even though pearls are not then taken. They related that the manta, enraged at absence of its daily food, then attacks even boats; and that by its strength and ferocity, using its fin flaps and beak, it has sunk more than one, thus filling its belly.

"But the manta is a gentleman, after all," some old diver would say. "It eats only one of us at once." And the rest, shrugging their shoulders, would assent.

At times there come great sea battles, when the manta meets some unknown but more powerful enemy. Then, despite its horribly rapid progress by skimming over the sea surface with its two vast fifteen-foot fins flapping like a bird's wings, it is itself partly eaten and floats ashore. Delicious meat, say those who have tried it—like the breast of chicken with a flavor of clam. But in after years, when I had the chance, I could never eat it or watch it eaten. Even rattlesnakes I have eaten, and all other meat-eater's flesh as necessity forced, but the manta nauseates me.

Sailors, about our campfire, talked much of the octopus of this Vermilion Sea, which have arms twenty feet long with suckers of the roundness of a silver dollar for holding their prey. These suckers are spaced every six inches the length of the arms. These rulers of the surf hide in seaweed at the entrance of harbors, or rivers, or any place frequented by men. There they wait like monstrous sea spiders, ready to throw out an arm at their prey, as we cast a riata at a cow. Where this arm catches, there it holds, since the suckers, once fastened, never relax their grip except by the animal's will.

The octopus is lead-colored, smooth and slippery as an eel, with a hide like a bull's for strength and arms strong enough to throttle a whale, as our pearl-fishers have seen it do. Its enormous red, greedy eyes are all which can be easily seen in the sea, and then probably too late to ensure safety from its tentacles.

When the octopus is in the mood, or hungry, it rises from our Vermilion Sea below a small boat and fastens its body to the keel, thus holding the vessel against motion by oarsmen or sails. While some of the crew of such a captured boat trim sails or make frantic efforts with oars, the rest pray or, cursing, draw their knives. One snaky arm seizes an oar, another fastens on the mast; while others, rising stealthily from the sea on all sides, seem to warn the prey against jumping into the water with any hope of thus avoiding death. These arms progress like giant inchworms, never releasing their grasp, but ever extending their reach.

Crew and passengers fight as Spaniards ever battle against death, but knives are of little use against cork-like flesh, and blows rebound from the octopus as from rubber. No sooner is an oar freed for use as a weapon than another arm rises and takes it from the man who struck.

Except for the greater fear of stopping his story, I would have shrieked aloud as some sailor thus told how an unseeing tentacle at last touches a man, and how his comrades shrink from the cowering victim as from the living dead. Other tentacles instantly tie the man's struggling arms and jerking legs. Then, its victim being well trussed for delivery, a great round body rises from the sea. With dull, piggish eyes the monster approves its arms' selection, and, gazing into its vast, champing parrot's beak, the condemned man sees his fate.

Those left in the boat, exhausted by fear, without oars, their sails in shreds, are fearful to risk their arms in water; for at times such octopuses run in pairs. Nevertheless, so eager are those sailors left alive to be elsewhere that they paddle themselves to shore with their bare hands.

Happy were those days at San José del Arroyo, when I sailed with sailors, dived with pearl-divers, was eaten by mantas, and carried off by cuttlefish. So filled with sea lore and sailors' tales was I that I dreamed half the day of what last night I had heard, and the other half waited expectantly for what I might hear that evening. It was well, indeed, that I had red hair and a tongue to provoke combats, or I might have dreamed my life away.

Yet, until a batch of old hens waked me at La Paz, discussing precedence in flying to the ground, I had never seen my Vermilion Sea, that vast Gulf of Cortés which rises in a still greater river[1] called by the Indians of those parts *"Hawheelchawot."*[2]

At each tide this river thrusts up a curling wave twenty feet high, to drown man or boat which, seeking to explore its unknown reaches, offends its virginity. On its banks are springs of cold crimson water, burning the flesh it touches; and from this coloring comes that name I love—the Vermilion Sea. Poor Padre Consag, thinking these evil

[1] Formerly believed to be the Strait of Anian, uniting the Pacific and Atlantic Oceans.

[2] The Colorado.

fountains a deception of Satan, exorcised them in the name of Our Redeemer, and then, with perfect faith wading into them, nearly lost all the flesh on his legs.

Over these silent, unknown waters wander irresistible whirlwinds, often of such violence as to suck pearl oysters from sea bottom and transport them inland. These shells dropped in piles, as if God meant them to feed Indians or provide pearls for our shrines. Caught up by the rapidly revolving tornado spout, with its funnel dragging the earth and marking its path on the ground as a pencil marks paper, the salt vapor which carries these shells is finally abruptly loosed, as if some gigantic devil's whim had passed. Thus a million tons of salt water, suddenly falling on our mountains in a mile-high cloudburst, rushes seaward again, gouging out our desert soil to bedrock and leaving on square miles of land surface only polished rock.

The Vermilion Sea warns us of earthquakes, for its waters, quivering, rise and fall before great shocks come. Those of us on the shore then rush for high land to avoid tidal waves. Those on our hills, seeing the Vermilion Sea troubled, lie down flat, for when its surface vibrates the land as well may be tossed up and down.

This Vermilion Sea, which I love because to think of it fills my soul with its mysteries, contains also that Island of the *Seris*,[1] of which every sailor talks, but with voice lowered. When the name *Seri* was mentioned, I, as a child, crept closer to him who spoke, and the rest, listening eagerly, disregarded all else and leaned toward the speaker. Then wood was piled upon red coals, and in spite of its flame we drew closer to our neighbors. If a stick crackled or a leaf rustled in some vagrant wind, we drew our knives and then looked behind us.

Those *Seri* cannibals, never yet seen by man, seize from ambush such as venture too far, or without sufficient numbers, upon their island. Then, having devoured them, the *Seris* lay out their victims' skeletons where they landed, to welcome their Spanish comrades. These skeletons are neatly pieced together and subject to *guamas'*

[1] *Seri:* Tiburon.

commands. More than one of my chums has seen, from his ship, these horrid forms of bone rise up at midnight of full moon and beckon their live comrades on shipboard to join them.

When *soldados de cuero* land in numbers to punish these cannibals, *Seri* magicians raise by magic a causeway to the mainland of Sonora. Dim multitudes can then be seen through sea fog, like spirits, passing over the water dry shod to Sonora, whence they return unharmed when their island is again free from intruders. But behind them, when they abandon their homes, poison thorns remain set in all paths and near the harbors. He who steps on even the smallest of these poisoned points goes mad and, running from his friends, remains to furnish food for the *Seris* when they return to their homes.

Around this island play innumerable fearless sharks large as whales, which, when hungry, attack even boats, or if blood has been spilled in fights among ship's crews, or when sheep are killed to furnish food for those on board. To land on this island of the *Seris* unharmed by giant man-eaters, one must avoid placing foot in the water; for these sharks follow as far as the surf goes, snapping at all meat within reach. Unharmed by these sharks, doree fish eagerly chase multitudes of little spawn which rise from the sea to avoid one pursuer, only to fall back into the next one's open mouth. So, the padres taught me as a boy, devils chase men's souls. But when in later years I saw for myself how few of these small sardines escape these doree fish, I thought it scarcely worth while for a child to endure the inconvenience of virtue with such a trifling hope of evading Hell.

Swordfish of great size race through my Vermilion Sea, so careless or so enraged that they pierce the sides even of ships with two masts. One sailor I knew when I was but six years old had just sworn at his guardian Saint as a useless encumbrance to an honest man's life when a swordfish pierced his leg, having passed its bone sword through the side of his boat.

"Be polite to these Saints," he warned me as he limped about San José del Arroyo. "Often they are asleep, or in dalliance, or quarreling with their like; but when one least thinks, they extend an ear earthward; and if what goes on mislikes them, they strike at once. It costs nothing to be polite to them, and then it will not happen to you as to me"—and he extended his leg for me to see how deep and ragged the swordfish wound was.

The boton, from the liver of which a deadly poison is made, hangs about every boat till the captain scarcely dares eat or drink from fear someone of his crew may bear him a grudge and use the boton to pay it.

Then, worst of all, is the mermaid, which swims vertically in my Vermilion Sea, so that its scaly end from the waist down may not be seen. From the waist up, though only three feet long, it is as a woman without scales, but having soft flesh with breasts and a not uncomely head. Its eyes are large, sweet, and timid, forever enticing men to their ruin. He who once gazes into those melancholy, lonely eyes must follow them where they go, and, unless his chums kill the mermaid which has charmed him, he rests neither night nor day until he is in the sea seeking it.

"You forget the *ojón,*" calls a voice across our dimming fire, as all my tiny toes curl with dread of mermaids' charms. "What is worse than to be obliged to politeness toward a flat fish with a single foolish, big ox's eye in the center of its ridged back? By the hands of Barabbas! I have come home from a Gulf trip so weak with suppressed rage at enforced politeness to an *ojón,* that I nearly died before I could pick a fight with some land dawdler or beat my wife about a trifle!"

"Better that than offend an *ojón,*" all his sailor friends concede, nodding their heads emphatically.

They say this flat fish is like San Pedro at Heaven's Gate in its dignity, and if one swears in its presence or gives it the least offense, it swims off seeking a manta or swordfish or octopus, as it may happen to have friendships among these tribes of flesh-eaters. Having found them, it mentions to such hungry ones a small boat it has just seen, with desirable meat therein.

But treat this one-eyed fish respectfully, calling it *Don Ojón,* or perhaps *Señor Gobernador,* as our great pilots do, and it ensures you calm weather with proper winds. If a good voice will sing to it the charms of its eye—for having but one it values that one exceedingly—such a boat can have what it will of quick trips. But let anyone smile in derision, or mention anything with two eyes, and the *ojón,* suddenly sinking in the Gulf, leaves a whirlpool in the water. This whirlpool, growing redder and redder, breeds a whirlwind while you watch, and that increases to a great *chubasco.* So when a vessel is lost during a tornado in these parts, we know some sailor has forgotten his good breeding in treatment of an *ojón.*

From such firesides tales as these the listeners went home in couples, talking loudly of nothing and once at their huts dropping hurriedly behind them the sacking which served for a door. I, who lived in the outermost *jacal* [1] of our village, feared even to whimper as the last man disappeared into his house, lest next night some tattler might warn my mother to keep me at home. I walked with my short six-year legs so boneless from fear that I staggered at every step. Nor would I have reached home at all had not those terrors which flitted just ahead of me been so much less horrible than those I could not see behind me. On each side of me for a half-mile stalked unseen things, frightful even beyond a mule's fears. Yet I must creep to bed in the dark, noiselessly, or tomorrow night's joys would be denied me.

To fear vividly is perhaps the greatest joy of life, but had I a boy of six years to raise into a brave man, he should be carried home nightly from such feasts of fear. Those midnight walks back to my mother's hut, always so silent at midnight that the scamper of a mouse disturbed at its feast chilled my blood, left on me a mark I still feel. Even when finally safe in bed, I knew that but one weak woman lay between me and such grisly horrors, and that my mother slept unconscious of dim shapes and dreadful forms which lurked around me just out of touch. What hope, I thought, that a single thickness of blanket, no matter how well tucked in over my head, could save me?

[1] *Jacal:* a brush hut roofed with palm leaves or rushes.

CHAPTER 8. *The Snake-Trap*—*"If so be There are Kidneys in Heaven"*—*The Admiral of Pearl-Divers Gives Me a Spanish Machete with a Blood Pearl in its Handle*—*"Watch Me Cozen This King's Viceroy"*—*Don Juan Ocio and His Unwelcome Domestic Improvements*—*The Company of Manta-Feeders*—*There was a Pirate Named Drake After a Male Duck, but Why I Know Not*

THUS LOST IN TOUGHT over all those mysteries of my beloved Vermilion Sea, I was suddenly recalled by a man's voice.

"Come hither, *Don Sin Agua*,"[1] it said, and since he who spoke held his belly tenderly, while leaning against my corral gate, I recognized him as yesterday's packer, Heraclio of the mule's hoofs, to whom I had refused my canteen.

"*Que hay, mulero?*"[2] I answered. "Have those two she-devil's hoofs sprouted yet within thee? Those which thy mule planted in thy belly yesterday?"

"Lacking water, how could they?" he reproached me loudly. "By thy fault in refusing to irrigate me yesterday, I must now wait for our first rains, and then they will grow with the grass.

[1] *Don Sin Agua:* excellency, without water.

[2] *Que hay, mulero:* What luck, mule-driver?

"Tell me, child, is it wise to eat eggs where thou sleepest? Were it not safer to sleep in one place and steal in another? I have watched thee guzzle a half-dozen, and by the yellow on thy chin, the woman who lives here may suspect thee and set a snake-trap for thee."

"A snake-trap?" I queried, being anxious to draw his brazen voice away from the subject of hens, as from within the house came noises of children waking.

He winked at me as the owner of this corral opened his wooden door, and continued: "They set upright a ring of iron or of wood, suited to the snake's girth, with an egg on each side; and, swallowing one, the serpent crawls through the circlet of iron to gulp the other. The ring, thus caught between two eggs, brands that snake a thief beyond possibility of lying.

"While on this subject, *hijo mio,* thou shouldst be more adroit in thy lies. Thy tongue is ready enough, God knows, but why not tell the truth when, as yesterday, that would suffice? Or if a lie, then arrange it well, for an untruth is of value only when it is believed. Wishing thy canteen yesterday, I had but to cast my knife where thy lie issued. Had there been dust on thy coat as from a fall, thy throat would have been safer."

"Try a cast," I answered, boasting, "and my mule will be chewing thy arm before thy knife is free from its case."

"*Ojala! Ojala!*" he answered derisively. "I have heard of such mules, and may borrow thine when I need a protector. Adieu, egg-eater, I must seek a henyard not yet robbed."

At a narrow place in La Paz I met the Admiral of Pearl-Divers, and knew at once I had the wherewithal to make my peace with Don Firmín Sanhudo. I well knew I needed a very influential friend to apologize for my carelessness in losing Inocente the day before, at the time of our great stampede when we met the runaway mule team. This Admiral was a very great man, who decided all matters in his district, and while he was respectful to our governor, would laugh to himself if given orders by him. Here, and at San Antonio Rial, two thousand people obeyed him, and all of a type so rough that he who ordered them must be better than they in strength and brain and daring. As for morals, none of them had any. Neither he nor they.

This Admiral was close to seven feet high and boasted of killing two steers by knocking their heads together, though he had held but one horn of each in his hand. He was such a man as I might have been had Fate fed me only bull's beef when I was young. He wore flat leather sandals held on by a thong over a big toe, and a woolen band over his belly to prevent chills. These all of his trade feared, since from chills came cramps, and a cramp meant death to a diver at sea bottom. Over this band he wore a pair of cotton drawers midway from his waist to his knees. Above these cotton drawers a loose cotton shirt, worn outside his drawers, flapped in the wind; and with all cut away which might in the least impede action. No arms: simply a narrow band above each shoulder to hold it up, with breast and back bare. He bought shirts only to prove his wealth, and that no man might accuse him of being a miser.

His long black hair, on which he prided himself, was held back by a band of leather an inch wide. This held his wealth of pearls, and when he gambled he loosed these pearls on the table, as if to dare all venturesome ones who might long for that they might not touch. His head was topped by a wide-brimmed, tall-peaked straw hat, heavily weighted with the silver insignia of his rank. Completely around its crown, next the brim, stood a row of silver Saints, each one holding a pearl in its small clenched hand. By the size of each pearl I knew at a glance which of these Saints the Admiral most depended upon for security. He who protected from the manta held in his fist a jewel almost as large as the Madonna's Charm at San José del Arroyo.

While I longed for this pearl to give to Doña Ysabel as return for the anxiety I had yesterday caused her concerning the lost Inocente, yet most of all I envied the Admiral's muscles, which swelled his arms and legs to the size of mescal kegs. Also I longed for his skin, which, tanned by our torrid sun as exposed alternately to sun and water in diving, had become like ebony in coloring: nevertheless not hard or stiff, for as he moved his muscles rippled beneath, as all muscles accustomed to emergencies must move if their owner is to be without anxiety when attacked.

"Come with me, Don Juanito of the Red Hair," he said in passing; and when we had reached a lonely spot: "Did that church-robber you killed say the sacrilege at San José must be divided between you and our Society of Pearl-Divers?"

I nodded my head, adding: "Since all the treasure was to have disappeared and I had but one pearl, the blame must be placed on others than I." Which was quite true, though I had not thought of it before.

"So I was told. So I inferred. Because we are a rough lot and live knowing each day may be our last, such smooth scoundrels plan to father on us all this country's deviltry. Steal we do not. That is forbidden. If we kill, then only among ourselves, and what harm in that? The Gulf receives, dead, what it would otherwise slaughter next day, and hungry sea beasts accept their meat pickled in brine as eagerly as when fresh. Perhaps we carry off a girl now and then, but only when her screams are for propriety's sake and to convince the neighbors she goes unwillingly.

"Make your journey in peace, *hijo mio*. If the shadow of a *cuñado's* knife falls within a yard of your family, each relation of that church-robber shall feed a burro-shell. Here is for your trip."

What he gave me was a Spanish *machete*[1] of Toledo steel, with a great blood pearl set at the end of its handle; its belt and scabbard of finest Spanish leather.

I wore this with joy on our whole trip, and if at San Buena Ventura, south of Santa Barbara, any of you have heard old men call to me in passing: *"Qué hay, Perlón?"*[2] it was because of the great size of the pearl in that *machete* handle. I wore this *machete* so jauntily during the week Don Firmín camped there that all at San Buena

---

[1] *Machete:* a long knife of steel about two-and-a-half-feet in length, and sharply curved at its point.

[2] *Que hay, Perlón:* how goes it, Big-Pearl?

Ventura Mission remembered me thus. A few ill-bred and ignorant *Yanquis* think these old friends called *"Pelón"* after me, but all my hair remains on my head, and its bright color is little dulled by a hundred years of use.

This *machete* I gave to Doña Ysabel when we parted at Monterey, and she was almost in tears at taking it from me, knowing how much I valued it. But I said to her, "The two best in this world should not part," and she, therefore, accepted my gift, laughing and exclaiming that could she but take me back to Spain with her, my tongue would make me a courtier.

When the Admiral of Pearl-Divers had shown approval of me by giving me his best *machete*, I felt emboldened to ask his aid, and I said with the greatest humility: *"Señor Almirante,* I am in a scrape."

He interrupted me with his great laugh, which was more like a bull's bellow than human laughter.

"Only one scrape?" he asked. "And you several days away from San José del Arroyo!"

"But," I implored him, "this is serious." And I told him that I had lost Inocente while watching Doña Ysabel control her mount during our great stampede.

"So young," he replied, with mock seriousness, "and already a woman betrays him!"

"Come with me to Don Firmín Sanhudo," I begged, "and say that for me which will secure my pardon."

"Bien," he answered. "I know these merchant princes. Do I not sell pearls to them? Lead me to him." And, laughing at me, he held out his great paw which I could not have grasped in two of mine. "These merchants value only that which others long for. Hence their greed for gold. Watch me cozen this King's Viceroy."

We went to Don Firmín Sanhudo's tent, and one of his Wild Men on guard there said a few words in Maya to the King's Inspector-General of Colonies within the tent.

1 *Pelón:* bald head.

Don Firmín Sanhudo, the King's Viceroy, Lord-Lieutenant, and much else I cannot remember, came out to greet us. He was dressed as if at Court, for so he did when we halted on our trip for him to receive officials. He well understood the importance of uniforms and carried on his chest a Golden Sheep like that worn by the Spaniard at San Bartolo. Also several other gewgaws, at sight of which every official who saw him bent the back until nose and the earth met. When we left a town, every official nose was at least an inch shorter than when we arrived, because each nose had been filed short by the ground it had grazed upon daily during our stay.

The look in my Patron's eyes as he first glanced at me so startled me that without thought I stepped behind the Admiral of Pearl-Divers, and thence explained:

"I ventured to spend the morning from dawn seeking the *Almirante,* because I thought the two greatest men in California should meet at once."

This I said almost in tears, for I was but a boy and knew not how properly to lie to such very great people. But it so happened that Don Firmín Sanhudo, in spite of all his offices and powers, somewhat feared this Admiral who held two thousand ruffians in the hollow of his hand. This I knew as soon as I saw them together, because I had studied Don Firmín on our trip from San José del Arroyo, as one studies every man of great importance who can make or mar one's career.

These two great officials bowed to each other with hats raised as if to the Virgin, and the Admiral, turning to drag me from behind him, winked at me. This somewhat calmed my heart, which was beating as never before. It was not that I was terrorized, for I was even then of stuff to die bravely when essential; but I had learned to love Doña Ysabel and Inocente. To part from them and lose my trip north to Monterey would have broken my heart as well as destroyed my reputation.

"I have a favor to ask of thee, Don Firmín Sanhudo," said the Admiral; and he gave the King's Viceroy all those titles which he knew from a printed paper posted everywhere as we traveled. This was signed by the King of Spain, and gave Don Firmín's titles and honors, with our King's orders that he hang without trial all defaulting or in any way objectionable officials. Also that he hang, shoot, or in any way pleasing to him kill any person or persons who might in any way impede his progress or his researches.

Don Firmín Sanhudo bowed to the Admiral graciously, though to me, who already knew him well, his mind was anxious.

"If consistent with my King's wishes and my powers," he said to the Admiral, "I grant in advance that you wish."

"If our King knew thee as I do, Juanito," the Admiral said to me as he pushed me forward a pace by a slap of his hand on my back, "he would permit me to take thee. I lacked a half-dozen eggs for my breakfast this morning because thou slept in Zarabia's corral last night. Zarabia knew not why his hens were barren today. Nor did I until I met thee this morning."

Then, turning to Don Firmín, he went on:

"This child saved me and my two thousand men from a great disgrace when he killed the church-robber at San José del Arroyo. Never have I known a boy who could see and hear so much, yet thereafter hold his tongue; nor a child so quick of brain and ready of hand. I am not one to rob the King's service of anything of great value, but if thou art willing, give this boy to me. In ten years he shall be my left hand."

"Let the boy decide between King and Admiral," replied Don Firmín.

My giant friend, pleased with himself at having thus deceived Don Firmín into pardoning me, let out one of his great bellows of laughter and good-naturedly patted my head. I did not wince, though that downward pat cost me a year's growth since it shortened my neck. Men said that in moments of excitement the Admiral's love-pats had crippled many a woman; but they still flocked after him. A woman's life is so eventless that she loves to think of danger, though she can only shriek when it comes.

At this moment Inocente, loosed by his mother, Doña Ysabel, ran to me, and the Admiral stooped to pat him; but I snatched him away lest one so tender might be the worse all his life for such petting. I raised Inocente's hand in mine as a sign that I chose the King's service.

"Come hither, Juanito," called Doña Ysabel—anxious, as I knew, to save me from a personal interview with her husband. Bowing deeply to both the great men, and walking a little space backward to show that I had noticed how officials retired from Don Firmín's presence, and with a *"con permiso"* of politeness to him, Inocente and I obeyed his mother's call.

When the Admiral, with all the bows and politenesses imaginable, had gone away, Doña Ysabel said in a loud and rather shrill voice, new to me:

"In this hell of La Paz, are they all giants ten feet high? God in Heaven! Do all here laugh as my wildest fighting bulls bellow when they enter the arena ready and willing to fight for their lives? Holy Virgin! Tonight not one of my serving-women will sleep, from fear lest they be carried off by one of these great animals."

She spoke as if afraid, but by the sparkle in her eyes I knew she so spoke only to prevent her husband calling me. In a lower voice she added: "Inocente is to be page in the King's Palace when we return to Spain. I would that he should know what manner of men these pearler giants are. Take him with you for the whole day. Let him see all you see and meet all your friends." She motioned us away by a back path, so that I might not pass in front of Don Firmín's tent, lest he call me to him.

She trusted me again! I, who by my carelessness had lost Inocente the day before; I, who never before had been completely trusted by anyone. "With my life," I said to Doña Ysabel. She merely nodded, well knowing that I thus pledged my life for Inocente's safe return.

Doña Ysabel was a natural ruler. Any or all of our company would have died for her with pleasure. Her husband, Don Firmín

Sanhudo, had learned to govern men. We would all have died for him, but as a duty only.

That which chiefly interested me in the town of La Paz was to see Don Juan Ocio, who was the richest man in all the Californias. At the time of the Great Whirlwind he was a Mission guard at Loreto, and when the tornado was past he found multitudes of Indians stripping meat from pearl oysters along the course of this terrific *chubasco*.

Never had so many shells been sucked up from sea bottom and carried inland before, and these Indians were preparing a great feast of oyster meat. The pearls, however, were cast aside with other refuse. This man, being a Spaniard and miserly, offered them old clothes and a little lard if they brought him three five-gallon pails full of brilliants. They did so, and he, hiding them, sold one pearl here and another there until he could buy his discharge from the army. Then, turning his pearls into silver, he settled down in La Paz to astonish its people by his luxury.

To his house he brought water through logs split in half and hollowed out, then bound together again with rawhide. Needing water for cooking or cleansing, his women had but to pull out a wooden plug. Did they like this? Not one of them. They complained bitterly because other women could walk half a mile to the stream with empty buckets on their heads and there gossip. While going and coming, the young girls could meet those they wished to flirt with. Carrying a full bucket of water on their heads, they must, of course, stop and set the bucket down, before *mantillas* could be drawn across faces not over-anxious to be hidden if a young man passed.

"Her *mantilla* moves slowly," we say, when we mean a girl is beautiful. "Thy *mantilla* reluctantly covers thy face," sings a young man before the iron bars of his *enamorada's* window.

Or if the older woman, guarding these flighty and daring young beauties, could be engaged in some gossip and allowed to go slightly ahead, there might be glances and sighs. The youth, forbidden by fear of disgrace to speak a word, could nevertheless pretend to be stricken blind as well as dumb by these half-concealed faces. When a girl has small feet and shapely legs, such a chance to shorten a skirt or extend a foot it were folly to miss.

"She is dressed to carry water," girls in La Paz said, when meaning praise for another's good taste, even though the costume was so daring in shortness as to expose the ankles.

In other ways this rich pearl-buyer offended his household. For himself was a great padded chair, which swung backward and forward when he pushed with his toes. This was his right. When a man is rich he may waste as he will, no matter how great his folly. But when he provided chairs for his household, there was outcry.

"The floor is so comfortable to sit upon," his women moaned. "One works so conveniently there. But these chairs! They are not decent for a woman who respects herself. Any man can see under them—and if one's skirt be disarranged? They are worse than the tortures of Santa Gertrudis, who dreamed each night that through Eternity she sat upon a cloud with her legs hanging over. Thus every devil from the Bottomless Pit might feast his eyes.

"Besides, these chairs he forces upon us have but four slender pieces of wood to support them. There is some reason in benches. At least they are strong. But to be always ready to jump up suddenly, if these slim legs break, is most tiresome."

"And if one weighs three hundred pounds, as does my mother!" a visitor might exclaim. "If my husband bought chairs, I would go home to my father."

The glass windows of Don Juan Ocio's house must have cost him an *almud*[1] of pearls, at least, and most of his comfort. Every newcomer in town must gaze through them and punch their panes with a finger to see how strong they might be. Below every window were streams of dried blood where over-curiosity had broken the glass and cut its hand at the same time. Others equally curious, but less bold, picking up broken glass to test its thickness and edge, contributed still more blood from their cuts.

[1] *Almud:* fifty pounds.

I myself still have a scar on one finger where I broke a pane, and my hinny's upper lip was marked by her curiosity in examining the piece which cut me. These luxuries of the rich, I thought, were doubtless good in their way, but I preferred rather a brush *jacal* with sacking for doors and open spaces for windows. A wooden door might bind and shut one within at the first earthquake shock. As for glass windows! How could a child escape from his bed for an outing at night if glass barred the opening?

Doubtless, I muttered half aloud to myself as I sucked my cut finger, Satan had rebelled and sunk into Hell because he had demanded such foolish luxuries. Better for me, therefore, to be always on God's side. What greater Heaven could there be than that preached by Padre Salvatierra: of great plains with dry, torrid heat, and full of pitahaya bushes yielding their fruit at all times of the year to those who, like myself, had deserved reward?

For me, I grumbled, there must be a Heaven with no folderols and rich man's fixings. True, if I tired of pitahayas—as never yet had I, but Eternity was longer than yesterday—I might send for some *arrobas* of seven-year bull beef. This, of course, must have been well dried in desert sun, where wasps could not destroy it. Such meat cooked with kidney fat, if so be there were kidneys in Heaven, should satisfy every honest man who had reached Paradise by rights.

Inocente, with ill-concealed amusement, had watched while I examined each of those great curiosities: glass, running water, and chairs, in Don Juan Ocio's house. With little understanding he had also listened to my musings on Satan and Heaven, pitahayas and bull's beef. But from a child of his age, knowledge of the really important things of life could hardly be expected.

Therefore I turned to him, saying: "Let us eat *dulce de leche.*[1] I ate six raw eggs this morning and already I begin to dream of food. It must be that all things liquid, like water itself, quickly evaporate in this desert climate. I can remember when a half-dozen eggs would

[1] *Dulce de leche:* milk boiled to a stiff paste with tequila.

have satisfied me for the day, provided no fat piglet ran by me squealing to be eaten."

Inocente thought little of Don Juan Ocio's improvements, saying he had seen a mile of glass windows in the King's Palace at Madrid. Also, that there no one carried water in buckets from an irrigating ditch, but rather had water from pipes. I replied nothing, for a little boy's eyes are frequently larger than his mouth, not only as regards the amount of food he thinks he can eat, but equally as to what he thinks he has seen. Therefore, that he might be amused and have stories to interest his mother Doña Ysabel that evening, I took him to the seashore where pearl-divers awaited their boats, in order to learn which of their friends had been eaten that day and by what.

At La Paz I knew nearly all the pearlers. Why should I not? Since my ears could hear, they had come to my village of San José del Arroyo for *alfinique*, sugar cane, and fruit. Or, if sick, wounded, or terrorized in their pearl-fishing, through too great destruction of their friends by manta, cuttlefish, sharks, or the burro-shell.

Therefore it amused Inocente and pleased me when some pearler called to me, *"Hi, chungo!"* because he had seen me as a child climbing trees; or when another yelled, "Come hither, *Armador de Perlas!*"[1] because I could swim when but four years old. What pleased me less, but amused Inocente so much that he politely retired behind a beached boat to laugh, was when an old man shouted after me, "How goes it, Knock-Knees?"

That name came to me because when I was six years old I must walk home alone at midnight after listening to pearl-divers' stories of ghosts, mermaids, and sea serpents. One very dark night while I thus hurried back, watching all about me lest something pounce upon me, a great choke owl flew from a fruit tree at my right hand. As it flew, it made that sound of a hanged man dying slowly, as he clutches the rope above him to ease lack of breath in his throat. Fright caused me then to scream, and my bare knees knocked together so loudly that in our alley an old woman woke and called:

[1] *Armador de Perlas:* Master of Pearl-Fishers.

"Holy Virgin! What a noise! It must be midnight, and that Irish King's son on his way to bed."

Because I had Inocente with me I could not sail upon our Vermilion Sea, though many invited us. He could not swim, and, besides, who knew what manta or cuttlefish waited, anxious to test the flesh of the Viceroy of the Three Californias? Such sea beasts learn, they say, from birds or from little fish listening beneath boats, who goes to sea, and whether fat or lean, or excellent for food.

We sat for hours upon the beach, and at first that which most interested us was a man with almost naked body covered with scarce-healed knife wounds, not deep, yet gashed well into the flesh. His name, he told us, was *"El Cuchillo,"*[1] and he esteemed the knife as the only arm with which gentlemen could quarrel. He had an enemy who preferred the *machete* and ventured always so to say. They met on the sea bottom while gathering pearl oysters, and he of the *machete* pushed *El Cuchillo* toward a burro-shell, named Ignacio because of the last diver it had closed its shell upon.

These two enemies fought at arm's length until, strangled for lack of breath, they rose to the surface in each other's arms, still slashing with their knives. *El Cuchillo* first drew in a mouthful of air and, thus gaining strength, was able to cut his adversary's throat. *El Cuchillo* bitterly lamented the difficulty of fighting with knives under salt water, saying:

"Surrounded by burros with shells wide open and longing for a meal, yet often so covered with slime as to be invisible, one must watch his feet as well as the weapons. Who can make his best knife-play thus? Besides, the weight of salt water at such depths slows up both thrust and defense, even though the slime stirred up by dancing feet has not hidden the one you seek. But he of the *machete* was a gentleman. We held hands as we fought, and he did not relax his hold until my knife edge struck his neck bone."

While we lounged on the beach I tried to teach Inocente to sit as Indians do, with haunches bent, but only their feet touching earth.

[1] *El Cuchillo:* The Knife.

Thus they rest for hours, and as a child, from shame that an Indian without soul should do aught I could not do, I also so trained my muscles.

But Inocente could only thus sit for a few moments, and then fell backwards from cramped legs. Each time the child fell, he laughed so heartily that he quickly had half the pearl-divers on the beach laughing at him. Soon also they tried their luck at this game. As all the others yelled with laughter as each fell backward, the Admiral came running, thinking it a battle he must umpire.

At first he bellowed with laughter like the rest, but declared he could thus sit longer than any other; as being always the best man of his company in all ways. I challenged him, and being trained, of course out-sat him, which caused great laughter not relished by him. He chased me to smack my face as an impudent boy deserves and could outrun me, of course, being fleet as a deer. But at San José del Arroyo, when barely able to walk, I had learned to avoid my many older enemies by dodging as a rabbit avoids a coyote.

Carried on by his weight of over two hundred and fifty pounds, the Admiral lost many yards each time I dodged him. At last, good-humored through weariness, he pardoned me, and sat down by us to tell us of that vast Bay before us. Since Cortés had discovered it, nearly three centuries before I saw the Vermilion Sea, it had been the safest harbor in my country, though truly it once had sheltered an English pirate,[1] who a hundred years before my time had captured our Manilla galleon, the *Nuestra Señora de la Encarnación de Sigano,* and taken from it two million silver pesos.

How the Admiral of Pearl-Divers swore as he told us of this galleon captured!

"Had my Company of Manta-Feeders been in power then," he said, "we would have chased those English pirates away with one of our pet cuttlefish. They are not fighters! One of them came here a prisoner ten years ago and wanted a battle with fists!" He spat in contempt. "These English fight for amusement, it seems."

[1] Captain Woodes-Rodgers, with the ships *Duke* and *Duchess.*

Chapter 8

At my humble petition, and to please Inocente, who had caused all of us so much laughter by falling backwards when he tried to sit as Indians do, the Admiral gave us a guide to the cave of the Indian Emperor of California.

"This guide," the Admiral said, "is the safest leader I could give you. He can quarrel with no one on the trail by which you go. Two weeks ago he, when drunk, tried to lead his mule backwards by its tail, claiming you can teach a mule anything, which is why he now carries a crutch. Last week he thought another lame man mocked him because that one also carried a crutch, and he now therefore wears his arm in a sling. Being crippled thus, he will live until both arm and leg are mended."

The present Indian Emperor was a mere youth, but so fat he could only eat and sleep. As he slept when we arrived, his attendants refused to wake him for us, saying, "To slumber between meals is the right of Kings." He was a descendant of that Indian child which, nearly three hundred years before I was born, sat upon this La Paz beach playing marbles with such an enormous black pearl that Cortés, perceiving it, swore to make La Paz the treasury for Spain's crown jewels.

The first Spaniard in the Californias gave that ancestor of the present Emperor a lump of sweet *panocha* for this pearl, and he, trading eagerly, led them to a hole where he had gathered a dozen smaller ones.

When later the Company of Manta-Feeders, which preceded the Pearl-Divers' Association, was formed, they looked for this child and found him bent nearly double with age, close to a hundred years old, and eating bugs for food. Being a jolly set, they elected him Emperor of Pearl-Fishers, and levied a tax of one bug for each pearl taken by them on our coast, so that he might be properly fed. They thus had their fun, for the rule was that each pearl-getter should also himself find the bug to pay his tax to their Emperor. When their Admiral or other notable crawled about on hands and knees looking for tax bugs, all the camp went along to jeer and taunt.

The aged Indian Emperor, seeing better food about him, tired of bugs and suggested payment in various edibles. Therefore, they compromised on a rial's[1] worth of food to him for each pearl above a certain size taken by them. When he asked that this right might descend to his son, they cheered him loudly, saying their Emperor should have the same prerogative as others of his title.

Because Don Firmín did not like the looseness of life in this pearlers' camp, and Doña Ysabel was revolted by what she saw there, we stayed at La Paz only long enough to get our pack-train in order again.

In leaving La Paz we passed its cemetery, which was small, since those divers who were not killed by sea beasts died by knives and were thrown into the Gulf. They considered it a disgrace to leave their bones on dry land. In passing I pointed out to Don Firmín the grave of Manuel Osio, who in one season had fished three bushels of pearls, and being avid for wealth had attempted to work the gold mines at San Antonio; and losing all there, had died. This story pleased Don Firmín, since he despised all eagerness for money, and with a certain bitterness he told Doña Ysabel various histories of pirates, old and new, concerning whom he had read and heard.

He told of one vile thief, called Drake, after a male duck, but why I do not know; who, in a boat called the *Golden Deer,* captured our Manila galleon with two millions in coined silver. And of Sir Thomas Cavendish, with the ships *Desire* and *Content,* who seized our galleon the *Santa Ana* and took from Don Tomás de Alzola three millions in silver pesos and forty tons of silks and other treasures from China.

"There is your chance," Don Firmín said to me. "All this great treasure the English pirate placed in his ship, the *Content,* which was lost in a Lower California bay, where they went seeking water. Indians found his men's bones where they had dug in dry sand for water; and at last came upon the ship anchored in that bay, but with only dried-up dead men upon it. Attempting to cook upon its deck,

[1] *Rial:* ten cents.

as they would on earth, such food as they found in its lazaret, they burned the vessel until it sank. But this was two hundred years ago,[1] and our coasts are rising fast both on Gulf and ocean. For ten leagues in width, sandy beaches now show before earth hills are reached, and this pirate ship *Content* must have risen with these beaches.

"Not that I have seen all this, but so Jesuits report to me, and they are able scientists who have accurately measured our rising coasts. Somewhere, therefore, toward the north, but near the ocean, lie five million pesos in this rotting hulk, waiting for him who examines hillock by hillock all this waste; or who, arriving when high winds have blown the sandy covering from this old ship, can tell its English oak ribs from native roots; for in our dry sands wood rots so slowly that much of its oak must still exist."

Then, turning from me to Doña Ysabel, he told her things of which I remember little, being hampered by Inocente, who was of an age which demands continual exercise of the tongue. I remember Don Firmín Sanhudo complained because, ten years before, a single Boston ship[2] had taken in two years from these poverty-stricken deserts twelve hundred thousand pesos in coined silver. Also forty thousand pesos in old Spanish silver plate valued as bullion, but worth, he said, its weight in gold. With over a hundred thousand pesos in pearls, and five thousand sea otter and seal skins worth a million pesos at least. All of which they stole from our King.

"Were the English as well-bred as the worst of my men, I would become English," he swore. "Could these *Yanquis* from Boston be reasonably honest one day in each week, I would go there. But because of self-respect I must remain Spanish and watch pirates and thieves take from us all we have, because we will not attend to details.

"No other nation except Spain ever has, or ever could have, carried on a line of passenger boats for two and a half centuries, sailing without seeing land for seven thousand miles, during eight months over tempestuous oceans. For nearly three centuries we have done

[1] In 1586. [2] *The Dromio.*

this; but how do we manage this longest and most dreadful sea voyage in the world? For food the crew depends largely on shark's meat, killed as they sail. Passengers and crew drink rainwater caught from passing showers, and when rain clouds fail, die of thirst. Our galleons, sailing for eight months through an ocean dotted with islands, and at times so far off course as to make this coast a thousand miles too far north, yet never see land from the Philippines to the Californias!

"*Madre de Dios!* Ysabel, do you know how many perish on each voyage of these Manilla galleons? By the King's order I have received in Mexico this list for two centuries. Seldom less than forty per cent of the passengers and crew die to their eight months' trip from the Philippines to Mexico. I have lists running as high as three quarters of all on board, dead of thirst, hunger, and disease before they saw New Spain.

"What heroism! What bravery! What folly! Is there any hope for a nation which combines these three qualities so completely that, in its third century of galleon sailing, as many brave men die on each trip as when in 1582 Don Francisco de Galie first voyaged from Manilla to this coast? It sickens me to think—"

But here Inocente drew me into talk concerning my pet hog at San José, and I lost the remainder of their conversation.

Leaving La Paz, we settled quickly into that patient endurance which desert travel demands. Don Firmín Sanhudo was curious to see each Mission, whether abandoned, as were many, in decay, as were most, or with a pretense of life such as a few showed. We traveled as water demanded, twelve to fifteen miles a day, if thus we could camp at springs or streams. Otherwise, when springs were lacking, we drove fast from earliest dawn until sun heat began to oppress our stock. Then all rested and slept, as the animals browsed, and with the first coolness of evening we urged all forward again: for a few hours, perhaps, or all night, if necessary.

Our poor beasts lagged and complained if the journey were long, but earlier or later in the night smelled water; and then our work was to hold them back, lest they kill themselves by too fast running. Arrived at the water-hole, those men sent ahead and on guard there held back our animals with difficulty and at times danger, since a thirsty animal lacks all self-control.

Rawhide troughs, kept filled with hide buckets, gave each beast a hurried gasping drink of five gallons at most. Then they were driven on for a half-mile, and detained there until all had had their first drink. Later, they were all again driven past the spring, and having drunk ten gallons each, again forced away. In another hour our herders allowed them to return as they would and drink as they wished, merely preventing too great crowding about our *canoas*[1] of water. Thus no animal so swelled its paunch with water as to lie down and die, though with less care a pack-train loses many mules from over-drinking.

After a night drive such as I have described, we rested for several days, since a day without water in our torrid deserts is equal to at least forty miles of rapid travel in the weariness it causes. With our mules one trick always amused me. After our first day without water, each mule accustomed itself to drink deeply before being saddled or *aparejado,* and when saddled, breaking away from its packer, returned to the spring and drank what it could, ending with a deep sigh of vain regret that it could hold no more liquid.

As with mules so with men. Years after this trip with Don Firmín, I took from our deserts an Indian, as packer, on a bear-hunting trip into the wilds of Northern California. I noticed that at each river and each stream and each spring he drank, but from an Indian one does not ask why lest pride of knowledge render him useless for work. Finally, he came to me, saying: "I must return."

And I answered him only: "Stop soaking up so much water, fool!"

"Since the sun shone and sand blew, my people have drunk their fill each time they came to water," he replied. "If not, they died. But in this foolish land where water is as sunshine with us, I must either kill myself by overfilling my belly, or, becoming careless here, die

[1] *Canoas:* rawhide or leather folding drinking-troughs carried to water animals.

when I return to our delightful deserts. Let me go back, Patron, and I will await you where springs and tanks are far enough apart to make drinking both pleasant and safe. Of what use is a waterlogged man?"

To show how these desert Indians are, I offered him food for his trip home, and he took what dried beef he could eat that night.

"More!" I urged.

"Why more?" he asked, astonished. "I am alone. If I travel sixty miles a day, finding my food as I run, is that not better than to lie and rest for a week while I eat this food you foolishly urge upon me? Why should I waste my strength in carrying food except in my belly?"

From La Paz north I found most useful that knowledge of Indian dialects I had acquired while a boy. These languages I had not learned willingly, but only because in San José del Arroyo were many Indian servants from all parts of my country. There were *Coras* from the extreme south, *Chokimas* from San Ignacio, *Guaicuras* and *Cochimics* from our great deserts, and *Icas* from the far north at San Vicente. All of these servants were old men, and all had been *hechiseros*[1] or *guamas*[2] deported by force from their own tribes. They loved me for my red hair, since that was the color with which our great volcano of the Virgin clothed its head when angry and about to cast out vast stones at those crows which tormented it by pretending to be also gods.

But much as these sorcerers loved me, none would teach me their wizardry except each in his own tongue. Therefore, I learned their languages quickly, and now found this knowledge most useful to me. When we met an Indian, I spoke to him; and he, being often lonely or oppressed, talked to me eagerly, and told me much I would not otherwise have known.

Another thing also helped me. These Indian conjurers never repeated what they told to anyone. Therefore, each night, when a child and learning their magic, I must retell exactly all that had previously been told me or hear nothing more. Thus I soon trained my

[1] Wizards. [2] Sorcerers.

memory never to forget. Then, finding this an error, since there is much which is trivial or unpleasant, I divided my remembrance into two parts: facts which were never to be forgotten, and doubtful statements which I could erase if false, or make indelible if true.

Thus, for example, as a child I heard our padres, talking among themselves, say this world is round; which does not seem probable. Anyone not blind knows it is flat, but, as I could not see why they should lie to one another, I put this statement aside for later determination.

Our Indians claim the sun sinks in the ocean, and a god, seizing it, runs with it underground and at the proper time pushes it up again through the Vermilion Sea, to make day for us. How much of this is true I do not know. Yet, having watched sun fires extinguished in the ocean each night, and at times, when overheated in hot weather, raising brilliant clouds of boiling red vapor, I think the old sun does not reappear, but rather a new fire is kindled in the heavens each day, and each day extinguished when it is soused in the ocean.

Once I questioned Don Firmín concerning our earth, and he replied: "The earth is round."

Since then, when asked, I say: "This earth is round. So wise men have told me and it must be true; but I do not believe it, nor need anyone."

While my memory has never failed me, there is one point in which a book, during my later years, has an advantage over me. When children bring in their lessons and I ask them, concerning geography, "Show me Mexico," they do not hunt through their book, but turn to a thing called an index, and thence direct to the page on which Mexico is printed; and flat, of course. My mind lacks this index, which seems a simple thing and easily added to any memory, yet it was not born with me. I had it neither when as a boy I traveled with Don Firmín Sanhudo from San José del Arroyo to Yerba Buena on San Francisco del Norte Bay, nor in later life when a mind index would have been most useful to me. Therefore, perhaps, I wander so much as I relate to you the tale of my hundred years of life.

CHAPTER 9. *The Mission of Dolores del Sur—*
How the Greatest Official in All the Californias Lost
His Dinner—Padre Ugarte's Method of Converting
Wizards—The Mission of San Luis Gonzaga, Where
Padre Ugarte Outdanced All His Converts—Felipe
Romero's Eight Months' Voyage from the Philippines
to La Paz—The Great Stone-Arched Church of
San Francisco Xavier de Vigge

THE MISSION OF DOLORES DEL SUR is the first north of La Paz. After a hundred years of prosperity, it was abandoned forty years before my trip north, and its eight hundred Indian converts moved to Todos Santos. There, a year after their arrival, homesickness, measles, a pestilential fever, and the plague killed all except a few house servants.

Don Firmín shook his head when he saw this Mission, thinking it too limited in resources to be useful; but I found there a man named Barco Victoriano, a half-breed Indian, who was interesting. He came from Todos Santos del Sur, where forty years before he had helped steal the dinner of Visitador-General Galvez. That great man, then absolute ruler of the Three Californias, was fond of eating, and also much feared. To please him, the monks of Todos Santos del Sur Mission had prepared for him a famous dinner. To the last mouthful this dinner was stolen and eaten by Indians, who hated Galvez because at Loreto he had publicly ordered that any Indian could be forced to work the salt mines of Carmen Island without wages; since, so he said: "All subjects of our King who are truly such have the obligation to serve their King, when and as he may desire."

As those who worked these salt mines died quickly from excessive heat, with salt dust floating everywhere and penetrating their lungs, it seemed to the Indians that such workers should be well paid to compensate them for short lives.

This Galvez, who is known historically for the trouble he caused in Alta California as well as here, waited impatiently for his dinner, since no one dared to tell him it had been eaten by others. Being extremely hungry, he was so overcome by rage when he found no cooked provisions remained, that he ordered immediate execution of every Indian[1] at this Mission; shouting loudly: "Hang those who stole my dinner, and put the rest of them to the sword, lest these infamous wretches contaminate and pervert all other *Indiada* of this country!" But as there were many Indians and few soldiers, all these villains escaped unpunished.

At Dolores del Sur I found that here as elsewhere each Mission had its special hero, though Padre Ugarte was thought by all to be the greatest priest known to the Californias. The very old men said of Junípero Serra, shrugging their shoulders: "He was a great walker."

Concerning Salvatierra, these old men discussed his miracle of the sea-gulls, and various trials of skill with native wizards. Remember that for twenty-five years after Padre Salvatierra arrived in Lower California there were no grasshoppers, and for twenty years no damage was done by cloudbursts or cyclones. Since such freedom from these scourges was unexampled, and therefore miraculous, the Indian *guamas* lost their influence. Some even were converted; especially by Father Ugarte, who was Salvatierra's right hand, and whose habit it was to seize a wizard in each hand by their long hair and knock their heads together until they begged humbly for baptism: declaring themselves long Christian by conviction but kept

[1] About 1,500.

from the church by humility. Once baptized, he retained them so near him that they could not safely backslide. Indeed, until this Padre Ugarte died of smallpox at seventy years old, it was not safe for his converts to renounce Christianity.

"Those I convert go to Heaven as Christians," he said grimly.

When, after a quarter of a century of immunity from grasshoppers, great swarms of locusts devastated our Missions, these native wizards were much encouraged, and pointed out to converted Indians the superiority of their old religion. These locust swarms destroyed all Mission crops of the new religion, and even ate the roots of what the priests had planted. Of the old religion crops these hoppers only devoured mescal tips, which Indians did not eat. So that to those Indians living in the old, age-hallowed way, no hunger followed when locusts came; whereas baptized Indians died everywhere of starvation.

All that I have just said relates to the long past before I was born. The hero of Dolores del Sur was Padre Guillen, than whom none could have been more patient and kind. When seventy years old, he found an aged Indian woman who spoke no known dialect, and whose soul therefore could not be saved through knowledge of the holy mysteries of our religion. Though infirm and old, this priest set himself to learn from her own language. At seventy-one years Padre Guillen died in misery because God, as punishment for some long past evil thoughts, took him to Heaven before he could learn enough of her tongue to warrant this woman's baptism.

"This God of theirs," said Barco Victoriano to me, as he told me this story, "must have curious ideas, so to reward a good man who needed but three months more to save a woman's soul and content his own." But even as a boy I have never been easily drawn into theology. There is little nourishment in it, and much anger comes from its discussion.

San Luis Gonzaga, our next stop on this long trip, was also an abandoned Mission, but like most of those founded by Padre Ugarte it had a stone church. This Fraile Ugarte was a really great man. He understood Indians and was not himself lazy. At San Luis Gonzaga, in clearing land for planting, he made wagers with his congregation as to who could pull up the most mesquite bushes, he or they. In making adobe brick for houses, the material for which must be thoroughly mixed by treading it, he laughed at his Christian natives because they tired of working this stiff mud, saying: "This is merely dancing in stiff clay. You boasters have told me you could *fandango*[1] all night. Come, I will outcaper you all." And lifting up his priestly habit he danced with bare feet, treading out the sticky brick kaolin until it was fit for forming into moulds.

All that Indian tribe danced with him, ashamed to be outdone by one who had never before been known even to shuffle his feet to music.

In such ways he led rather than ordered and for this reason is remembered where Junípero Serra, who arrived a hundred years after Ugarte, is forgotten or held in slight esteem. Salvatierra is also less thought of, and when[2] Padre Ugarte succeeded him as Chief of Missions, there was great rejoicing among all our Indians.

Some say that Salvatierra was more full of guile in dealing with Indians, but I have heard such stories of Ugarte also. When a revolting tribe threatened to kill him, he said, sneering: "Certainly, you have that power, but I will destroy all of you first." After much discussion, while Padre Ugarte went through the motions of Mass, native wizards decided it would be unsafe to murder him.

The Indians of San Luis Gonzaga, from superstition, would not kill mountain lions, thinking their spirits more dangerous than live lions, which, nevertheless, ate our *Indiada* as they did deer. Ugarte, therefore, went out with a stone in his hand, saying to the tribe he was with: "Let us test carefully this matter. Perhaps it is true."

Then, killing a lion with the stone, he carried the body across his shoulders weary miles back to the Indians' village. This whole tribe, at a great distance, watched and followed him. Dropping the dead animal outside his house, he took care to kick it each time he passed.

[1] *Fandango:* dance.   [2] In 1717.

Then toward evening, skinning it, he cut out a part, saying to the Indians: "This part which I have cut out is what caused your fear. Burn this part and the lion has no ghost." Roasting a hind quarter, he let its fumes tempt the *Indiada,* who loved meat, but seldom got it. Later he ate the flesh in public, smacking his lips in the Indian way while he chewed. He left what remained of the lion cooked on the carcass, and that night it was stolen by Indians and eaten. As he had hoped, thenceforth the native wizards of San Luis Gonzaga could only say to their people: "Kill lions and eat them. This man Ugarte is more powerful than lions."

But I could tell you stories of Padre Ugarte by the hour. He was a man, and while a boy at this Mission, I would rather have lived with Ugarte than have made my trip to Alta California. It seemed to me then that in my time no men existed, except perhaps the Admiral of Pearl-Fishers.

At the time of our trip, Felipe Romero owned this Mission of San Luis Gonzaga, with official obligation to feed Government travelers; though unless one paid for more and better than he gave, it would have been hard to live on official rations. Don Felipe Romero had come from the Philippines in one of our regular trade galleons, and what he told me of the frightful hardships suffered on this trip caused me to swear never to enter an ocean vessel.

Consider how the experiences of youth control the habits of age. Because of what Romero told me ninety years ago, of his galleon trip, I have always made on horseback my trips to visit my mother. Each ten years, therefore, I have ridden five hundred desert miles astride one mule and leading another rather than make the trip in a ship.

When I was eighty, which is seventy years ahead of my story, my servants in Alta California whined, saying: "Don Juan Obrigón, this five-hundred-mile trip is not too hard for you. You are still a young man. But at least permit one of us to go with you. Suppose an accident—or some thief, since all know you carry ten years' allowance of silver money to your respected mother when you go south."

But I answered them only: "When my head and hands cannot protect my life, why should I live longer?"

At ninety and a hundred I would also have made this trip if my mother had lived to old age, but her ten years of hardship, after my father deserted us, caused her to die prematurely at a hundred and one years.

To be honest, I must confess that at eighty years old I began to tire in the saddle on my quick trip south. The country and people interested me less. Even I sometimes permitted attentive friends to unsaddle and saddle for me, which no man who respects his mules should ever allow. Also I noticed, when I took my siesta—which had formerly been of only two hours—that three hours were required to rest me.

Yet what can be expected of one like myself, who starved as a child? Had I been fed on bull's meat from a year old, all I wanted and more, I would have been in my early youth at eighty. But now I have wandered again from my youth to my age, as hens in my yard run from one corn grain to another and thus lose both.

Don Felipe Romero of San Luis Gonzaga Mission told me that as a young man, strong and vigorous, he made the trip from Manila to California on one of the passenger galleons which have made this trip regularly for two hundred and fifty years. Being too poor to buy chocolate, he suffered always from hunger, except at such times as extreme thirst prevented the thought of food. Rich passengers embarking on such trips spent, he said, many pieces of eight on chocolate to bring with them and thus keep themselves alive. Yet on his trip half of the passengers and crew died from hunger, thirst, and knives, and were buried at sea.

The galleon on which he came to California had so crowded its decks with freight that exercise of any kind was impossible. A raging itch afflicted everyone. To sleep by day or by night was difficult. Blood-sucking vermin of all kinds, and flies, were everywhere. Food and soup were full of them. The biscuits yielded more worms than flour, but for this the passengers were thankful, as all other meat was rotten. One could not tell on Friday whether the fish served was fish or flesh. Therefore, on that day, many good Christians ate nothing, fearing the cooks were in league with Satan to cost them their souls.

Worst of all was the lack of water, for to save cargo space no water was carried. Both passengers and sailors depended entirely on water caught during rains in a large sail and badly apportioned by favor. At all times everyone on board was thirsty. Don Felipe Romero left Manila at the end of June, since thus they try to avoid those terrific hurricanes which rage later; but his galleon, owing to calms, was six weeks getting away from the Philippines. They had incessant storms between the Ladrones and Northern Japan.

"You can imagine," Don Felipe said to me, "the condition of a ship so crowded for our eight months' voyage that no one could even walk about. There were no lavatories or latrines of any kind. The vessel was full of the seasick and of the dying. Everywhere and at all times, all cried for water as if it were gold. I saved myself only by securing a place where fog-drip from a sail fell into my mouth. At night and in rains I drank perpetually and soaked my body in this water; because as the body sweats, so also can it absorb water. Before a rain I was mere skin and bone; but after it had rained for twelve hours, my belly was like a hogs-head, and my skin full and round.

"God save the soul of him who first found this sail-drip under which I lay, for I might have died had I not seen him lapping fog-trickle like a sick hound! Thanks to our Saviour, he was a weakling with little knowledge of knife-play and so light from hunger that I heaved him overboard easily.

"They say those English pirates who rob our galleons are great fighters. But our ship got into La Paz Bay with crew and passengers all so far gone with scurvy, hunger, and thirst that we could not drop our anchor or launch a boat. Had not help come from shore we had all died there. What merit is there in robbing a vessel so manned? Those English pirates would steal from a blind child and boast it as a deed of valor.

"As for me, I had meant to go to Mexico and make sugar and brandy; but by hard begging they sent me ashore, and I chose a place to live where not even a mirage can show me a ship. Now that I have talked with you about my galleon trip, I shall have nightmares for a week, and my wife, poor woman, must stay awake while darkness lasts to rouse me as soon as my dreams begin. I am no longer young, and to go through again, even in visions, what this galleon passage cost me, would kill me."

Therefore, we ceased to talk of ships, and I allowed him to tell me of how official travelers guzzled good food and wine for which they would not pay and, if not served enough, even hunted for it. Therefore, all his provisions Don Felipe had to keep in a rock cave a mile from his house, guarded by an Indian who ate what he pleased.

"But, thank God!" he exclaimed, "one thieving Indian is better than the officials. He, at least, does not waste food as do the others."

At San Francisco Xavier de Vigge,[1] where we next arrived, we saw the most beautiful stone church in my country, having eight bells. It was then two hundred years old, and in size one hundred and twenty-three feet long by thirty broad, with a vaulted stone roof and a cupola. I paced it then myself, because it was difficult for me to believe that Indians could do such cut-stone work. Any man can lay mud adobes and place a thatched roof over such walls, but only Padre Ugarte could make, of wild natives, mechanics capable of laying an arched stone roof of such width and length. Near here he died,[2] and though seventy years old, resisting smallpox as he had so long resisted hardship and disease.

Padre Gerónimo Soldevilla, aged and infirm from twenty-six years' lonely and hard work here, with only Indians as companions, was still alive when we arrived. We were the last white people to whom he spoke, as he died tended by Indians within a few weeks of our departure.

The day after our arrival, he came out, leaning upon Don Firmín Sanhudo's arm and supported on the other side by Doña Ysabel, to

[1] Of the mountains. [2] In 1730.

whom every moment he apologized for the trouble given her. Saying that to see her and realize her care for him made him think of those white-robed angels, who, God willing, he hoped might soon welcome him elsewhere as eagerly as he welcomed her here.

He was tremulous with an old man's pride in his life-work, and pointed out the church, which, he said, had cost two hundred thousand pesos and had an arched ceiling built by Padre Barco using Indian mechanics Ugarte had taught. But with even more joy he talked of the springs, gifts of God, led through an aqueduct cut in solid rock into two stone reservoirs. Thence irrigating small pieces of land neatly fenced with stone, and containing fruit and vines as well as gardens and grain.

"When the Jesuits left here,[1] he said, "this Mission supported five hundred Indians; but Captain Portola took from here, by order of his chief, Junípero Serra, 2,250 pounds of dried meat, 500 pounds of flour, 100 pounds of corn meal, 500 pounds of dried figs, and 300 pounds of sugar, with such else as best suited him, for use in starting Franciscan Missions in Alta California. Our baptized Indians, for lack of the provisions thus taken from us, must be dismissed to the hills, where they died of starvation or lost their souls among barbarians." At each item the old man shed a tear, and wrung his hands at mention of this dispersion of his Mission congregation.

"We Dominicans worked hard to bring the Indians back, though slowly, as we had first to accumulate provisions. After I had been here ten years,[2] smallpox destroyed almost all Indians south of San Ygnacio. Almost alone for sixteen years, I have labored to attract such of these kindly natives as, hearing of this home for them, came asking aid and teaching.

"Our cattle are wild, but we have a few milch cows. Our sheep still live, and I will walk with you to show you our sixty *tinajas* of wine, each holding seventy *cuartillos*. It is now made by Indians alone, since I am become infirm; but still not bad." One could see by

[1] In 1768. [2] In 1794.

the way he dwelt on these figures that he came from a wine district and knew good wine from bad. Then, brightening up, he glanced along this valley twelve miles long, but narrow and hemmed in by precipitous mountains of solid, barren rock, saying: "Short of Heaven, was there ever such a lovely view? It has sustained me through many weary hours of discouragement. When devils tempted me, I had but to glance at the Lord's handwork before me. Even when, in the smallpox year, I buried my last penitent, I knew that, while alone, I was alone with God."

Doña Ysabel turned her head to hide tears as the old priest talked, but he was too blind to see her face; and, so his majordomo told me, had not seen the view he spoke of for a year, though always he turned his face toward it. To me it seemed a prospect so unutterably sterile and dead that a week here alone would send me naked and mad to seek associates among coyotes and lions, if indeed such existed in this shameless land of stone. But where a man has worked and helped others, that is home; and than home there is no other place with such beautiful views.

CHAPTER 10. *Loreto[1] Capital of Lower California— Why an Official Swallowed His Teeth at Loreto—How Valuable Grants of Land are Obtained—An Island of Salt from Which All the Oceans Could be Resalted —The First Boarding-School for Girls in the Three Californias—The Library of Five Hundred Volumes*

F ROM SAN FRANCISCO XAVIER DE VIGGE we turned toward the Gulf; going by the Las Parras Trail, which in the San Xavier, Las Palmas, and Santa Cruz cañons gave us a way more rocky and frightfully precipitous than I hope to see again. On a narrow trail, worn by animals' hoofs six feet into a side hill, one of our pack-mules reached upward for a bunch of grass on a hillside above him. A snake sleeping uncoiled in this grass, for protection against heat greater than even its cold blood could endure, rattled as the animal's teeth neared it, but could not coil in time to strike.

The mule swung back his head too quickly and, over-balanced, rolled down the steep, long hillside, heels over head. He landed pack down, with his legs waving frantically in air. Two *arrieros,* jumping off their mounts instantly, rushed down the hill to cut pack-ropes and release the animal. Inocente, riding beside me, began to laugh at

---

[1] *Loreto:* a corruption from loretium, laurel, or a laurel thicket. When the Virgin's house was brought by angels from the Holy Land to Italy, it was set down in a laurel thicket. Thence came the great Shrine of Loreto.

the sight of four long legs fanning the air, while a neck curved first one way and then another, as when any four-footed animal on its back tries to rise.

I stopped the laughter at once, saying: "Do not hurt the feelings of those beasts we ride. This is a disgrace for every mule of our outfit. They all pride themselves on being surefooted. Until our mules can abuse that poor animal tonight as they feed, all will be so bad-tempered that, hearing you laugh, some one of them may do you an injury by kicking or biting you. Treat your mules as you would a Spanish gentleman."

Once the leather braided pack-ropes were cut and the tie-rope uncoiled from about his neck to prevent escape, the fallen mule rolled over, and rising, stood trembling. He tested his legs and breathed hard to know whether his ribs had caved in. Fortunately, a mule is almost indestructible, being compounded of all that is tough in a donkey and all that is enduring in a horse, with the weaknesses of both left out. Giving him time to adjust his nerves, the *arrieros* went over the mule bone by bone. Finding him unhurt, they shook their heads at a *mulero,* who back of us on the hillside held ready a spare pack-animal, and we went on.

The trail made two or three turns to reach the cañon bottom, and came out near where the *arrieros* stood reloading the fallen beast. "Watch," I called to Inocente. "Notice how our animals treat their unfortunate chum." Each of our mules, as he faced the fallen one in crossing the cañon, set back his ears and crunched his teeth. Then, when their backs were turned as they started up the other mountainside, each tail was switched and each nearest hind leg lifted as if anxious to kick.

"Holy San Gabriel of the Archangels!" whispered Inocente, so his riding mule could not understand, "will they all bite and kick that poor brute tonight?"

"So I have seen them do," I answered, "but all of us will be so tired this evening that perhaps even you may forget to kick me as you sleep under my blanket tonight. Observe these two *arrieros,* how they place the fallen mule between them to prevent his being abused on our road. See them gash their mounts with spurs to occupy their minds, and prevent them biting or kicking the poor brute which rolled down the hillside."

Thus we spent an afternoon so torrid that I watched my hinny carefully lest she become overtired; but a black pacing hinny feels nothing except love for her master and hunger for tobacco, of which I gave my hinny a double portion that evening as reward for a hard day's work.

We arrived in Loreto fairly early, but so exhausted by heat and difficult trails that even I could see nothing of the town that night. Next day, having finished what was given me to do and delivered Inocente to his mother that he might sleep during the hot hours of the day, I sought amusement and information in the town.

"I have been here many years," sighed an old *escribante*[1] for our Government, as we loafed in the shade of a building during siesta hours, "yet never have I seen an honest official."

I smiled, for a man who expects to find an uncorrupted Spanish official lacks judgment to know one if seen. "One of your men is within that store," continued the copyist, "and will have his throat cut soon if he is not more lucky than I. To that store go only those who pander in all ways to our Governor."

At that moment there came from the store opposite us many loud words followed by a crash, as if a man fell his full length on the floor, and, by the following silence, did not rise again. The copyist and I looked at each other for a moment. He was timid and I was only brave when I must be. Nevertheless, I rushed across the street to look on or take part, as the quarrel might be among local people or include one of Don Firmín Sanhudo's men.

Entering, I thought myself a fool for interfering in a quarrel, since the bright sunlight without and the darkness of this heavily shaded store made my eyes useless for a moment. In that moment

[1] *Escribante:* a copyist.

anyone might have knifed me. Getting my sight, I saw a crowd of officials gathered about a fallen man, who was spitting out his teeth. Heraclio, our *mulero*, had struck an official with the hilt of his knife, knocking out most of the man's teeth.

"One of the Governor's secretaries cursed Don Firmín," explained Heraclio, calmly wiping his knife-handle. "We are forbidden to use knife-blades unless attacked. I must have my dagger-hilt widened. It is too narrow for the mouths of these mad dogs who curse our King's Viceroy, and it therefore left some of this *cabron*'s back teeth unloosened."

"Cursed Don Firmín Sanhudo, the King's personal representative!" I blustered loudly so that all within the store might hear, but privately motioning the *mulero* to go outside. "Do you remember how many of these pen-drivers we hung in Sinaloa merely for scowling as they worked?"

Heraclio winked at me as we safely passed the score door, saying: "If I had thy ready tongue or thou my right hand, what a man one of us would then be!"

But I answered Heraclio in the same tone, that it might seem to those within that we quarreled: "Grant me only a year or two, and I will risk my left hand against thy right."

"God permit it," he replied, smiling pleasantly, "if thou then hast aught on thee I could use."

We walked rapidly to the custom-house, where Don Firmín worked over figures even during siesta hours. Standing near the high, doorlike windows of the Governor's office until Don Firmín Sanhudo noticed me, I said, neither loudly enough to attract attention nor so low as not to be heard by all who would: "Doña Ysabel asks your attention for a message from her."

He nodded and, stepping out, stopped next to the thick adobe wall so those within could not hear. I told him hastily what had occurred and the sullen feelings of all officials toward his men. He, frowning, listened, but said nothing. Going again within, he sat playing idly with the Governor's report on the financial and political conditions of the Californias, while all stood about him, pressing on his consideration one thing or another regarding government. Meanwhile, many of our men had joined Heraclio at the windows, for they flock to danger as flies to fresh meat. I left them there and stood in the doorway ready to take part in what might happen.

"Gentlemen," began Don Firmín at last to the officials all about him, "by the King's orders I have hanged at the capital cities of Mexico each official responsible for a false report to me, and through me to our King. Here I have been so charmingly received that I hesitate to read your report, knowing as I do that it is untrue. I beg of you, *caballeros*, to have ready for me a new statement by tomorrow forenoon so that I may not be forced to part with friends I so greatly value."

Bowing to right and left, he passed among a score of men who made no concealment of their hands upon knife-hilts, and went out the front door merely because it was a longer and more dangerous passage than the low window.

We had by now enough of our men at windows to prevent any trouble there, and as some hot-headed *empleados* eager to please their Governor moved to follow Don Firmín, I entered, deliberately blocking their way and intent on changing their thoughts. I was only a boy, but having been much with the Sanhudos had given me a certain reputation. Perhaps also these officials felt that, as I was known to have killed a church robber, I might be equally dangerous to those who steal from our King.

"*Caballeros!*" I called loudly, as the room had become like a buzzing hornet's nest. "For a consideration which each shall himself set as the value of his life, I will agree to save your lives. But give me security before I explain how, lest some, seeing me young and helpless, without ability in this matter to ask my master's aid, should refuse to pay me; and I have my treachery for my only reward." When I mentioned "treachery," the room stilled at once. That they understood; but had I said "honor," they would have tossed me out of a window leaking from as many holes as a sieve.

Lies were necessary, since I had little foundation of truth to go upon, but I trusted their knowledge of Don Firmín Sanhudo might be even less than my own. Therefore, I spoke boldly about him, ready to back each untruth with a knife thrust.

"You know the Sanhudos," I said, "and that, a foolish mouse having gnawed one of their cheeses in a market-place, they exterminated all rodents throughout that whole city." One or two nodded, for that is a story widely told, and even believed by some. "How, therefore, venture to touch a knife-hilt when one of this family is in your room? Moreover, this man is a duke and a grandee of Spain, who doffs his hat to no king on earth. No! Not even to our Admiral of Pearl-Divers!" This I said to make them laugh, for we were still near to tragedy, and it is well to divert attention a little at times. While they laughed at mention of our Admiral, they forgot to question my statements.

"Inocente, Don Firmín Sanhudo's son, has shown me his collar of the Golden Fleece and a dozen other such pretty baubles. One of his relations leads our King by her little finger—"

"Rather by her—" sneered a tall, sallow man, brother of the one Heraclio had deprived of his teeth.

"Do not finish, I beg!" I interrupted the sallow official with that honeyed politeness which causes even a dyspeptic to pause and think, lest he be killed with his mouth open. "I may betray my master for money which I lack, but abuse him in any way, or his family, and I die for him; also taking with me several neighbors as witnesses, so that Saint Peter at the Gateway of Heaven may not doubt I come honestly asking passage. I am not one to curse a Governor and then curry favor with him."

At this the tall official stepped backward and closed his mouth. This Governor, who watched all of us with a smile upon his lips, had a crude way with minor officials; and the man understood that to reply to me would only confirm the Governor's suspicions. Not that I knew he had cursed his Governor; but so everyone did, for this petty tyrant wished himself to profit by all graft and left little upon which his underlings might fatten. Also, he was not averse to daughters of minor officials. Having a wife weighing three hundred pounds, he naturally sought those lithe young damsels who by prettiness and grace were especially dear to their families. Therefore, not every father approved his ruler's good taste, nor liked him the better because protest against the taking of a daughter was dangerously impossible.

"If His Excellency the Governor permits," I continued, "here is good advice: a drunken pen-pusher today cursed the King's Viceroy, Don Firmín Sanhudo, and swallowed most of his teeth while still swearing. Had we been permitted by our master, Don Firmín, to strike with knife-points before being attacked, that official had had more teeth now and less blood.

"Take this toothless official, as if banishing him from California, and once on the boat throw him into our Gulf. Then kill him for having tried to escape. When returning to land with his body, let His Excellency, Don Bartolo, the Governor, go to the beach and angrily order the corpse towed to sea again. I would advise that His Excellency the Governor swear publicly that not even when dead may one who has cursed the King's *Visitador-General* remain in this loyal country. I understand Don Firmín, and know that thus you avoid great trouble."

"So be it," assented the Governor, and, taking off my hat, I backed out of the room, more than content to go. I had stood with my hat on because I dared not encumber my hands with it, and backed to the wall so none could thrust at me from behind; not to mention one of my hands on each knife-hilt. I was by nature too cautious for such a troubled life. Cow's meat, fed to the young, tends to deprive them of courage, and for ten years at San José del Arroyo we had been so poor that I cried even for pieces of udder.

Next day Don Firmín Sanhudo received the report he had asked for; and seated, while all stood about him, read and approved it. The tall, sallow official I had yesterday threatened, worried by the suspicion I had created against him in the Governor's mind, had been drinking heavily. Now he thought it proper to say from the back of the room: "Leads the King by her little finger? What nonsense! Who does not know what part of her leads our King?"

Don Firmín glanced at the Governor, who answered, "Perhaps your men are more expert than mine," which was a foolish insult; but my master calmly said a word or two in Maya. A single one of his guards, advancing with a catlike rush through the passage opened for him as all shrank away from him who libeled our King, bound the tall official's arms with his *facha*[1] and carried him out under an arm as one does a child. In a moment we heard through a window the official's struggles as first the tips of his toes pushed the ground and then his head struck that beam from which he hung.

Turning with courtesy to the Governor, Don Firmín explained politely: "Possibly you do not understand Maya, but my guards speak only that language, so it was necessary for me to use it. I merely told them we would hang but one, today."

The Governor went white to his hair roots. At first I thought in anger, but soon saw it was cowardice; for only a timid man plays with fate by using his tongue.

Turning to his *Secretario*,[2] the Governor ordered: "See that the beam on which he who insulted our King hangs is raised a foot today."

But Don Firmín, speaking with kindliest courtesy to the *Secretario,* said: "Do me the favor to leave this beam as it is. Your Governor is a foot shorter than the official I have just hanged. What need, therefore, to heighten the beam?"

By this order my master, Don Firmín Sanhudo, affirmed his authority as greatest in the Californias, since our King spoke through him. Moreover, as he had no wish for further executions, he thus prevented it being whispered about, for a thousand miles north and south, that he had raised a gallows he dared not use.

Then, as he rose to leave the room, and all stood with their hats off before him, Don Firmín added: "I am not here to remedy abuses but to inform my King why Spain loses all its American colonies.

[1] *Facha:* belt.   [2] *Secretario:* Vice-Governor.

Nevertheless, beware of injuring any of my party. If so happens, I shall strike less at the murderers than at those who countenance such murders."

Thus by the great wisdom and tact of Don Firmín Sanhudo we avoided serious danger, and a scandal as well. It was unusual to hang governors; and a governor, moreover, always divided his stealings with some higher official in the City of Mexico. Such a one, God knew who, might have been able to resent the loss of a part of his income.

Much of a governor's revenue, in those days, came from such *rancheros* as wished to buy more land from the King. Or rather, since much land was still to be had for the asking, from those who sought to buy officials, and thus secure a grant with seals covering an unlawful amount of exceptionally fertile land. As a boy at San José del Arroyo, still too young to be considered dangerous, I have watched through windows such land-buyings; and if you will pardon a wandering tongue, I will tell you how in olden days we acquired our titles.

The *ranchero*, having ridden in to our village, accompanied perhaps by a dozen sons and grandsons, seeks our Governor.

"Good morning, Excellency!" the buyer of land says to him; and there is much bowing and scraping. If the desired *rancho* be large, the purchaser and the Governor perhaps even kiss each other on both cheeks and, embracing, pat each other on the back, as our high officials do when they meet.

Not for me this kissing and patting, since once from my hiding place I saw an official so embrace his successor, patting him on the back with both arms around his neck. Then from his sleeve the superseded official drove a thin stiletto into the new Governor's back.

How they all mourned for him who thus died of a sudden apoplexy, and buried him with all imaginable pomp! He who had used the stiletto wrote to the City of Mexico, respectfully urging that delay in his successor's arrival, occasioned by the new Governor's death, would greatly inconvenience him during the three years needed for another of the Viceroy's favorites to be appointed and arrive. "Stilettoplexy," we *cabrones* called it, but to be clever with words in public was never my way. It is unprofitable and leads to inconvenience.

When the many preliminaries of this land purchase are past, a map is brought out by the purchaser, often with a haystack for its chief corner. This is easily rebuilt in another place if the *rancho* selected needs extension. A small bag of silver lies upon the table as legal payment to our King for such land, while a much larger purse passes beneath the table top. This having been weighed by hand and found reasonable, the grant is made. Or, if the buyer be thought niggardly, it is returned, under the table, of course, and next day the solemn farce begins again. Then, when all is finished, and a title with seals has been given, they say to each other:

"With deep regrets for your going."

"Which are equally mine, my dear Governor."

"And the hope of soon seeing again your charming sons and yourself."

"Who are all, Excellency, like myself, always at your honorable disposal."

Thus, with vast politeness,[1] they part as if they were enemies regretting each moment their knives were dry.

Afterward the Governor says to his *Secretario:* "Not so bad! But that old cowherd's belly is too fat. Find a way to thin it."

And the *Secretario* shakes his head, advising: "Fat accumulates when one has twelve sons and a host of grandsons already wearing knife-belts."

Outside the house, as the buyers of title emerge, a grandson perhaps fingers a knife half-drawn from its sheath, complaining loudly: "My knife across his throat would save many pesos."

[1] *Vast politeness:* Over-politeness was a delicate warning on both sides. The *rancheros* thus intimated: "Don't press us too hard, you thieving scoundrel, or we'll take the trouble to kill you as a warning to other officials." The Governor on his part conveyed: "I have the power of the Central Government. I have the troops. I'll put a ring in your noses and lead you around, if I choose." Had they been avowed enemies the politeness would not have been emphasized until they were ready to fight.—*A. de F. B.*

And the oldest son, sighing, exclaims: "It is much money for the Governor's Rosa to spend on silk dresses and face powder! One cannot blame that he-goat for his pleasures, but why should he tax us to support his joy-maiden?"

But the old father, with more wisdom than they, answers: "Close your mouths, foolish ones. Law is necessary, and officials are useful. If there were no formalities and no titles with seals, we should soon all be *empeonado*[1] to these Sanhudos. When we tire of money to support our Governor's Rosa, there are ways; but against a great family like the Sanhudos neither revolutions nor knives prevail. Observe always the law, my children."

In such fashion we of New Spain were governed by Spanish officials, and so it was when as a boy I left home for this trip to Alta California.

Loreto—as everyone knows who had been there, since every *viejito*[2] you meet will tell you so at least once—is the oldest town[3] in the Three Californias, and was founded by the Virgin's direct order. Her statue fell from a stumbling mule, led by Padre José María Salvatierra, en route to San Juan Londa. Seeing Her image thus refuse to pass Loreto, he realized at once her wishes must be obeyed, and where She fell, there was built our Capital.[4]

It is a beautiful and extensive plain on San Dionisio Bay, which is protected by the Islands of Coronado and Carmen. The latter island is formed almost entirely of rock salt from which our whole world could eat and then enough be left to resalt all oceans. But there is little fresh water, and this is much needed, since at Loreto less rain falls than elsewhere on our Peninsula. Indeed, when people complained to Padre Salvatierra that the Virgin was no judge of localities for a city, he answered: "Heaven is always brilliant with the sunshine of our Lord's presence. Therefore She selected this barren place for her Shrine, as the brightest spot on our earth."

Here are raised—*Loretistos* boast—the best mandarin oranges in the world, and all Mexico sighs for them, as having eaten them I am

[1] *Empeonado:* enslaved.   [2] *Viejito:* old man.   [3] October, 1697.   [4] 1697 to 1835.

ready to believe. Olives and vines also do well, but have been forbidden lest Spanish commerce be injured, though thereby every man in California was taught to hate Spain.

Pearl oysters exist here in great abundance, as you will see when I tell you of my adventure with these jewels. The most curious fossils are also found, such as only Satan when crazy with brandy could have invented. Of these some are vast stone heads having two great tusks growing out of their mouths, while others show only one massive curved horn projecting from the nose-tip. Of such I know little, and would willingly remember less, since when tired I still dream of the cave in which a *Concha guama*[1] showed me these fantasies sticking out on all sides and from the black roof as well.

Two things here seemed to me almost as fantastic as these Devil's cave cattle. At Loreto they boasted of having had the first boarding-school for girls in the Californias,[2] caring for six hundred Indian girls. They were taught to wear clothes, cook Spanish food, and care for a house; after which they were turned loose to live without clothes, eat bugs, and dwell in the open without roof through summer and winter.

The second was that I counted in their library five hundred books, though there were then but four hundred souls in Loreto, including all bloods, of whom only priests and *empleados* could read. What was in these volumes I do not know, as they had few pictures, and these generally of Saints expiring in various cruel ways such as our Indians would be ashamed to practice.

The Loreto Church was of stone and small, but richly decorated, and even the priest's house was of rock and with tiled roof. That the churchyard should be paved with cobbles astonished me, as I had never seen this luxury before. Perhaps it had its uses even in so dry a climate, since hogs will not bed upon stone and, therefore, one need not kick them aside and be snarled at when passing into the church. Of gnats there were multitudes, and so small one must squint to see them, but their bite produced a most intolerable burning sensation.

---

[1] *Concha guama:* Loreto Indian sorcerer. [2] Established in 1771.

CHAPTER 11. *Hidden in Dry Sand—*
Merely the Twanging of a Bowstring and Silence—
Living Eyes of Dead Beasts—I Fill One Pocket
with Enormous Pearls

ORETO OFFENDED MORE than La Paz had Doña Ysabel, though
for a different reason. La Paz was rough but honest. Loreto
was a city, and, like all cities, filled with dishonesty and abominations.
The Governor's mistresses dressed in silk truly, and it was fair to
see, but none of its people carried their hands in their own pockets.

While walking north of Loreto, I gave thanks to God as never
before, for that ground was covered with vast quantities of small,
round rocks exactly fitted to a child's hand. Had our kindly Lord
permitted Satan to scatter such cobbles about San José del Arroyo, it
is doubtful whether I would now be alive. No boy with independ-
ence of thought and using his tongue cleverly could long endure
those showers of such stones his older enemies would cast at him.

In looking about for Indians from whom I could learn local
traditions, I was astonished to find less than thirty in this district.
I knew from our San José del Arroyo padres, who frequently
lamented the decadence of all our Missions, that in Jesuit times two
hundred Indian children had been baptized here annually.

"By what do you swear?" suddenly asked an aged voice behind
me as I wandered by the Bay side, thus thinking.

"By the Bones of Loreto," I answered as soon as I could control my tongue; for I had seen no one and supposed myself alone. Nothing so violently discomposes me as to have a man speak before I know he is near me. This implies a carelessness or dullness of perception on my part which desert gods will not often pardon, and which they rebuke through poison snakes, lion's claws, or men's knives.

"By the Bones of Loreto," I exclaimed again, forgetting I had once answered the questioner. Thus the *Concha*[1] Loreto wizard at San José del Arroyo had taught me to reply when a *Concha* Indian should ask me. This was a password, or rather a religious oath, known to none except this tribe and their pupils.

"It is difficult to find you alone," grumbled the aged Indian, throwing off sand in which he had been completely buried for warmth's sake and to hide himself from my companions had such come with me. This trick of concealing one's self in sand and breathing through a hollow mescal stalk pleased me more than any I had learned for years. Next day I thus hid while the Governor and a crony of his discussed plans which were neither legal nor loyal to our King. Also thus in our sandy deserts, choosing places near trodden paths, I have killed antelopes when meat was hard to come by.

"And where are these bones of Loreto?" asked the Indian suspiciously.

"In the Cave of Dead Beasts," I answered.

"Why, then, seek those dead bones?" he continued, and with difficulty I kept from laughter; for this cave, while of vast importance to him, was the least of many things I had learned of when a boy, from those old servants who, because of my flaming red hair, had taught me the incantations and mysteries of a dozen tribes.

"I seek the Living Eyes of Dead Beasts," I answered. These *Concha* Indians believed that pearls were the eyes from the heads of those dead stone animals in their cave. These eyes, washed into the sea by rain, they thought to have been swallowed by oysters and thus revivified.

[1] *Concha*. The Loreto Indians belonged to a tribe called *Concha,* or "shell."

"Follow me, then," he ordered, "and step heavily on my foot-prints, that he who is always behind thee may think thou art alone. Thus, at a proper place I can drop back of a bush and close accounts with this dangerous half-breed who suspects thy errand."

Thus I did, so that he who followed found only my tracks, and thus it happened. Merely the twanging of a bowstring and silence, until the old man caught up with me. Nor did I ask questions.

Into his cave I went from shame, not from any wish to see that which might be there. To me, at that time, all caves were dens of the Wizard Gopher of San José del Arroyo. I greatly feared that terrible Gopher might lie in wait for me now, since he probably remembered how I had cursed him when a foolish child. But where an Indian led, there my father's son must follow.

We crawled through a hole, not difficult for me, but which by pressure on his belly made the old Indian grunt, as a hog does when too full for more food and yet fearful some rival pig may find and consume what remains. For my part, I was pleased the aged man went first; for it was dark beyond hope of sight, and I heard rattles which sickened me each time I put a hand down to help my squirming progress. I have no antipathy to rattlesnakes, but I could not help hoping these cave-dwelling crawlers would respect my youth and promise, and, if needing a victim, choose him who was teaching me to parody serpents in my manner of progression.

However, later I found this rattling came from dead snakes' buttons so deftly hung that a touch, or even my breath, started a buzzing which fairly stopped my heart's beating at each movement I made. Thus they discouraged entrance by chance comers. Why the *guama* at San José, or this *hechicero*[1] could not have saved me much misery by explaining these snakes' rattles before we entered, is beyond thought; but so are Indians. Had I shown fear, I would thereafter have been more useful with a hoe than as free man on our deserts.

Once inside the *Concha* cave of dead beasts and buzzing rattles, and my nerves a bit quieted after I had touched one of these rattles

[1] *Hechicero:* enchanter.

and found no snake attached to it, my guide lighted pitahaya candles.[2] I found myself in a low cavern. In part it had been shaped by hand, for where a dead brute's stone head had been seen, the Indians had slowly worked about it in the black rock, until its grotesque bulk was fully exposed at least up to its eyes. Into these empty jet sockets pearls had been placed according to the fancy of their keepers, past or present.

If the radiance of these creatures' real eyes contrasted as strongly with their ugly snouts and fierce teeth as did these mild pearls, they must have appeared most polite brutes, apologizing with gentle glances for their unseemly fangs. Of them all, only one seemed to me real enough, possibly, ever to have existed. This was a coyote in shape of skull; but that of the size of a mule's head, and with teeth twice the length of my thumb. Possibly, I thought, the Topa Chisera had died since I left San José, and this was his head. What other animal it could have been, Satanna alone might guess.

The *Concha hechicero* allowed me ample time to fill my eyes and my memory. When he thought my mind sufficiently stuffed with nightmares of Devil-invented beasts, he dipped his hands in deerskin buckets and let jewels shimmer in candlelight through his fingers. Those who owned this cave had for centuries saved all great pearls and those of curious colors, throwing away, after each great whirlwind which brought pearl oysters from the Vermilion Sea, only those small or ordinary pearls not worthy of a place in this cave.

"To each one who comes here belong such pearls as he may wish to carry away, but only once," he said; and I took in moderation, as was seemly, well knowing this to be a test for pupils, and that, did I take too many, a bowstring would twang behind me as we walked homeward. But picking and choosing among them, I took only those which spoke most clearly of abysses in the Vermilion Sea, unknown to man and unknowable, or which had retained in their pearly depths memories of tremendous battles between manta and cuttlefish, or

---

[1] *Pitahaya candles:* dry pitahaya branches contain so much fat that they burn readily, and are everywhere used for lights.

had seen a mermaid enticing some Indian chief to his end. Perhaps even had watched bathing in San Dionisio Bay all those impossible animals which, preserved by Indian magic, looked down upon me from the walls of this cave. Glowing from invisible centers of these pearls, it seemed to me that all knowledge shone, if one's eyes could but read what their constantly changing reflections implied.

I had been jarred almost beyond endurance by fear of rattle-snakes as I crawled into this cave, and filled with dreamy wonder at its strange animals; but in bright sunlight again, with familiar desert scenery about me, all things became immediately normal. In free air a pearl is a pearl, no matter how or where found; and I was glad to be rid of those thoughts which tickle the brain when one has been overcome by new and unexpected sights.

CHAPTER 12. *Cabeza de Vaca Misdirects Those Who Would do Us Harm—The Black Figs of the Mission of Comondu, and the Hog Which Distrusted Me There—"From These Vines and Fruit Trees Come All Those in the Three Californias"—Padre Salvatierra's Miracle of the Sea-Gulls*

T O LEAVE A TOWN by dawn is the greatest test of discipline when a pack-train is long and heavily loaded. In the country it is easy, but in a city all things are scattered and all in confusion, so that ordinarily it is noon before pack *alforjas* are loaded and mules *aparejado*. Then all must eat, so it is at least two o'clock before the start is finally made. Even then a man is missing, or some forgotten goods turn up, and packs must be disarranged to make all loads equal.

Here again I saw the greatness of Don Firmín Sanhudo. In the corral of the house where he slept, we spent the day before arranging our equipage, and each mule's load was laid out next its pack outfit, while *muleros* and *arrieros* slept in place as if we were journeying. Our mules and cattle ate hay in the next corral, guarded by heavily armed *soldados de cuero*. Doña Ysabel's special outfit, not being in use, was also packed ready to start.

The day before Don Firmín had called me to him, saying: "Tell the least trustworthy of our men we travel by the Mulege Road."

I smiled, for my grandfather had told me this is the method of wise travelers, who thus avoid ambushes laid or waterholes poisoned. Therefore I whispered confidentially to Cabeza de Vaca[1] what before night all the town knew; for this man was little thought of, and a secret well told lent him an importance he craved. Only Heraclio, my pet *mulero*, winked at me as he passed, but as at once I asked him loudly, "Why?" he went on confused and uncertain.

"Trust all or trust nobody" is the motto of my people, and a very wise one.

Never have I been more glad to leave a place than when saying goodbye to Loreto. As a town it was endurable, but capitals of countries accumulate a multitude of idlers who, thinking they must live, but despising labor of any kind, set their minds on all sorts of corruption. One kills for hire, and another steals for some greater rascal who protects him. A pretty daughter supports a third, and fraudulent deeds or forged seals a score more.

Then, the children of these vices know their parents' lives and are brought up in idleness, but taught to read and write. Or become self-taught because they have seen their fathers employ learning as a tool, by using which they are able to live dishonestly. They thus are more acute in evil than their elders, and with greater contempt for all work. What, then, must any capital be after two hundred years of such debasement?

Starting north by the Mulege Road, we followed it until in an *arroyo* we found solid stone upon which hoofprints did not show; and there we turned west toward San José, Commander of Comondu. Not that this precaution would long detain trained trackers, but it would delay them and, if they followed by night with evil intent, perhaps deceive them. Also, it was wise to teach a pack-outfit such knowledge. It would give them confidence in their Patron and perhaps help the men, when in trouble, to judge for themselves rightly and quickly.

[1] *Cabeʒa de Vaca:* Cow's Head.

From Loreto, Comondu is forty miles, but we made sixty as giving better water and less frequented trails. Cresta Blanca and Mercenarios Point are curious landmarks near the road we took.

Of the whole south, Comondu is perhaps best known, except, of course, San José del Arroyo; to which all except fools come once in their lives, and having been there, never cease to talk of its beauty. Here at Comondu, Ugarte, Salvatierra, and Mayorga worked together, so Doña Ysabel taught her children as we traveled. These three great Jesuit civilizers built a stone church with three naves and a vaulted cut-stone roof, which was the wonder of our country, being ninety feet long by forty wide. What an arch, to be built by soulless Indians who had never before seen even a roofed house! In all the Californias there was no other stone roof with such width of arch span.

When we entered the long, narrow, restful Valley of Comondu, full of vineyards, fruit trees, and sugar cane, with enough cotton for clothing and a thousand sheep grazing on hillsides for wool, Doña Ysabel drew a long breath. She said the atmosphere of Loreto had poisoned her soul, but with few people and clean air we might here regain what peace of mind we had lost there.

"Go find me some *higos*," she ordered me, for the ground below the Mission fig trees near Comondu was black with fallen fruit, juicy, sweet, and unbroken. I had the wide brim of my hat well filled when a sow which harbored under a tree there woke, and, being suspicious regarding her litter, chased me up to my very mule. Had she not been too fat from eating ripe, sugary figs to run fast, it might have gone badly with me; for in sight of our whole pack-train I could not throw away those figs I had selected for Doña Ysabel. To get away without spilling the rim contents of my broad hat, which flopped as I ran under its load of figs, implied care as well as great agility.

That night in camp, half the *muleros* and *arrieros* grunted like savage pigs if I passed them, and the very Mayas amused themselves with me, gnashing their teeth at me as the sow had. A boy has much to endure, and above all needs the most serene of tempers, for if he shows anger men never cease to tease him. Sometimes I think hogs have an instinct regarding me, and know that their shoats are unsafe where I am.

Here at Comondu was the largest herd of pigs I had ever seen: over forty of good size, not counting their litters. When hogs were first introduced into my country, Indian women objected violently to them because babies were left on the ground, as was Indian custom, while their mothers sought food. Many Indian babies were thus eaten by swine. Padre Salvatierra, therefore, forbade keeping of pigs at any Mission, and so strong is habit among us that even a hundred years had not made hogs numerous, except perhaps at Loreto among officials.

At the Mission a priest met and welcomed us with an excellent wine, of which they are always inordinately proud.

"We made this year," I heard him tell Don Firmín Sanhudo, "Seventy *tinajas* of a hundred *cuartillos* each, besides raisins and two tons of dried figs. Later you shall try a brandy we make of these dried black figs; but drink lightly, for it is the strongest liquor in this world, and deceitful, since its flavor is mild."

A dozen times a day this priest tried to get rid of me as I followed him about, for I was determined to hear from his lips the true account of Padre Salvatierra's miracle of the sea-gulls. Besides, this Mission of Comondu was Ugarte land, and every story of that great Jesuit padre interested me as few other things did.

At last he began his story to Doña Ysabel, and she, having seen and smiled at my efforts to remain near them, called me to her, saying:

"Hold this shawl. The sun begins to sink, and when evening coldness comes, throw it over me, for I shall be too much interested in this great miracle to remember that sunset chill is more dangerous here than even in Spain."

"First came Cortés'[1]—and the old priest took off his cap as they all do at mention of this great man's name. Then Salvatierra,[2] and

[1] In 1534. [2] In 1697.

the Jesuits ruled us for seventy years. With him came their great man Ugarte, who was of noble family, and a giant over six feet tall and strong in proportion. God's kindness sent very heavy rains in July, August, September, and October of their first year, causing all to think this country a paradise; as it is when the skies help us.

"The Jesuits began by founding Missions, and learning Indian languages that souls might be saved. Here in this place where we stand, our greatest man, Padre Ugarte, taught classes of Indians in a brush *jacal*. Being ignorant heathen, his pupils at first laughed at him, and then deliberately taught him obscene words for such holy things as God, the Trinity, and everything needed in saying Mass.

"Then, when Padre Ugarte thought he had learned enough of their language to serve Mass in their dialect, the whole sacred place was filled with Indian cackling. Not understanding why they laughed, he asked an Indian child the meaning of a sentence he had used, and found it foul beyond belief. Again the padre said Mass, and the *Indiada* for miles around came to laugh at this holy man's filthy tongue. The padre used the worst of these words as if in good faith, and an Indian chief standing just below the altar laughed as a mule brays. The enormously strong Ugarte, leaning downward, seized that chief by his long hair and swinging him lengthwise about his head, explained to all his congregation how the brute he now punished had deceived him.

"Then, taking children for teachers, he learned their language correctly, and these lessons were popular, as he fed his young teachers hot *pezole*.[1] Remember that to learn their dialect he must feed his class. That to feed his class he must first grow the corn himself, since none was produced in this country. Then he must burn limestone, for without lime he could not hull the corn. Finally, he must hull the corn and cook it himself. Until he had trained his congregation to work, he could get no help from any Indian. They were ready enough to eat, but never having worked they could not understand why anyone should work."

[1] *Pezole:* whole corn hominy.

The aged Comondu priest, in relating these early troubles of Padre Ugarte, raised his arms in wonder at the patience of our great missionary, and at his tremendous capacity for work; then continued the story:

"Having raised crops enough—for he said, 'To convert Indians you must first feed them'—he even sent corn to the Missions of Sonora and Sinaloa in their great famine. Then he brought sheep from Mexico and himself made distaffs, spinning-wheels, and looms, with which he taught Indian women to card and spin. Later he brought from Sinaloa a master weaver, Antonio Moran, and for two years paid him five hundred pesos annually, to weave clothes and blankets for natives, and to teach them such work in cotton and wool.

"Thus Padre Ugarte fed, clothed, and saved Indian bodies and souls until no longer, when he gave a penance for sin, the Indians answered him, 'This is pitahaya season and we can do nothing except eat.' He then had time to think of himself and his own wishes, so he brought from Sinaloa vines and fruit trees of all kinds, planting them here and at San Francisco Xavier. Remember, Lady Ysabel, that every vine and every fruit tree you will see from San José del Arroyo to San Francisco Bay in Alta California, which is over a thousand miles, comes from cuttings or seeds taken from those vines and trees Father Ugarte planted with his own hands and cared for as well."

"But," laughed Doña Ysabel, "you are telling me stories of giant monks who with one hand swing Indian chiefs about their heads while they preach and with the other plant trees. Such tales interest men, but for my part I came to hear of miracles. In my family we have been cardinals or warriors since Time was. Yet never has anything miraculous happened, unless perchance one of our cardinals went to Heaven."

The priest looked at her reproachfully and sighed, for to him a cardinal was a great and holy man. I also looked my reproaches, perhaps, for Padre Ugarte is to me the greatest man the world has ever known, and I could listen to stories about him forever.

"The miracle! The miracle!" she exclaimed, and put up a hand, half to shield her eyes from the setting sun and half to hide the color which had come into her face at our reproaches.

"*Bien*," said the priest. "I obey your wish, Madame. From 1697, when the Jesuits landed at Loreto, until 1722, there were no great grasshopper flights. The Lord had promised Father Salvatierra that while he remained in Lower California, no harm should come to his Missions. But when Ugarte began to plant trees and vines, Indian sorcerers feared our religion might triumph, and prayed to their gods for help.

"Let me explain to you first how locusts breed and feed. In June the old hoppers lay eggs like a reddish silk cord, which they place in earth cracks, for the ground is then dry and fractured in all directions as the sun has baked it. In July or August, with the first rain, these eggs hatch into wingless insects with very long legs, and dark gray in color. Such small herbage as there is supports them. Satan, who created them, ordered those from one mother to keep always together, and appointed for each such family a leader at whose command, during life, they fly or alight, just as a regiment obeys its colonel.

"When half-grown the locusts shed their skins and become perfectly green, being able then to take longer leaps, and uniting their regiments to form brigades under a general's command. In a few days their skins are again shed, and their uniform is dark gray, but now they have four wings. At three months locusts are mature, and are red with black spots. By summer they change color again to a yellow, having thus shed their skins twice and changed color five times, though why no one understands. How their leaders are selected Satanna alone knows, but their generals and their emperor are always the strongest and most malignant of all.

"Now these grasshoppers form into a great army under an emperor, and fly like birds, clouding the sky and darkening the sun with their numbers. The noise of their wings is like a great wind, and when they alight they break down all trees. The very air is corrupt from those millions which die while flying. A single such army contained, the Jesuits, who were great scientists, computed, fifty-five million locusts; and in a grasshopper year army follows army as ocean wave follows ocean wave, all intent on reaching the Vermilion Sea and there perishing.

"The Devil lacks originality, Madame. In the Holy Land he drove herds of swine down a steep place into the sea; while in these deserts billions of locusts obey his command and rush violently down into the Gulf of Cortés.

"Those three famous *frailes* who founded Comondu, long ago stood together in the garden you see before you, examining Ugarte's fruit trees, which in their second year had grown well, and even produced a few fruit blossoms. They still, alas, lacked strength of root to endure an attack by grasshoppers, which not only devour leaves and stem tips, but as well eat off all tree bark from the ground up. Only in the third year, on healthy trees, is bark hard enough to withstand the gnawing of locusts. Father Ugarte was then no believer in modern miracles, saying always:

"'Man is truly a miracle, and all that he does miraculous. Beyond that, who knows?' Therefore, he glanced with amusement at Padre Salvatierra, who had dreamed God's promise, that neither whirlwinds, waterspouts, hurricanes, nor locusts should be allowed to do damage in Lower California while he remained in charge of these Missions.

"'These trees shall carry fruit to those who live a hundred years from now, and your black figs shall enrich the Three Californias for a thousand years,' Salvatierra promised Ugarte, and he raised his arms in blessing over these trees which now you see before you.

"'*Ojala!*' exclaimed Ugarte, for he loved all those things with which he worked; but, nevertheless, he turned his face away. He was not a visionary, and, dreaming only of practical things, had little faith in visions; though he and Salvatierra were as brothers, being counterparts."

"My shawl, Juanito," called Doña Ysabel, for sunset chill had come into the air and I had forgotten her orders to cover her with that shawl. For the first time in my life I now helped dress a woman, and I was more awkward than a fish on dry land.

Her shawl showed four corners, though when I received it there were but three. In listening, I had disarranged it somehow, and which point was up and which down was quite beyond reason, especially as I, of course, could not touch her nor interrupt the priest's narrative.

She did more by hunching her shoulders than I with my hands, in settling this *malvado*[1] garment; for without taking her eyes from the priest, every bit of her seemed to know by instinct where a corresponding piece of her shawl should fit. When at last it was properly draped about her, I was more tired than after any forty-mile desert drive.

"As the padres gazed at these trees," continued the priest, "from the fruit of which you have already eaten, Ugarte's hopes were of food for his Indian converts, while Salvatierra dreamed of unborn generations, which for a millennium would bless Spain and the Jesuits for this planting.

"Then an Indian runner came panting from the north, and stood with bowed head before them. In answer to Ugarte's hand raised to bless his news, he said:

"'A single army of grasshoppers has taken wing south of San Ygnacio Kadakaaman, and without resting or eating, and borne by strong wind, comes this way.'

"'What is their color?' asked Ugarte quickly, for if natural they would be yellow, but if product of enchantments by *guamas* endeavoring to destroy confidence in our priests and the religion, they might be otherwise.

"'They are red with black spots,' answered the Indian. 'Their emperor, under whose command they fly so continuously that thousands drop dead from fatigue, is a four-year-old locust of great size.'

"Ugarte, always practical, walked to his trees to test their bark, hoping that red and black three-month-old hoppers might not be able to tear it off; but Padre Mayorga sank upon his knees in prayer,

[1] *Malvado:* malicious.

and Salvatierra, standing erect, raised his arms to Heaven, exclaiming: "Father! For what sin am I thus punished! Allow not Thy Holy Religion to suffer because I am guilty in Thy sight!" As the sainted *fraile* raised his arms, the sun in the east—for it was early morning—was darkened by great flocks of birds, and Ugarte called eagerly to the Indian:

"'Run! Run quickly and bring me word whether these birds are *gaviotas*[1] or *grullas*![2] For if they were *grullas,* which fly a hundred miles inland at times, it was natural, as they feed upon locusts. If *gaviotas,* which seldom leave their ocean, then God had wrought a great miracle, and they might hope.

"'They are *grullas,*' answered the Indian, gasping out his words, for he had run a league and back again. Mayorga continued upon his knees in prayer, and Salvatierra, as if built of stone, held out his arms imploringly toward Heaven, while Ugarte examined each of his loved trees, estimating which of them might survive these locusts.

"From the great ocean began to appear vast migrations of birds, and Ugarte's quick eyes noted their coming.

"'Run,' he ordered the Indian. 'Run quickly and bring me word whether these newcomers are *grullas* or *gaviotas!*'

"'They are the ocean birds—the *gaviotas,*' answered the Indian as he returned.

"The grasshopper army was now only a mile away, but the runner had over-exerted himself and fell forward dead from exhaustion as he spoke. Ugarte knelt before Salvatierra with face hidden in his hands, asking pardon for lack of belief in modern miracles. The Head of our Missions touched Ugarte's massive shoulders lightly in forgiveness; then, seeing the fallen Indian, ran to him.

"'Was his soul saved?' asked Salvatierra, for his knowledge of Indians was less than Ugarte's.

"'I baptized him myself,' answered Ugarte, 'and the Devil within him was so strong that I had to hold him under water until it ceased to struggle. For most, sprinkling with water suffices in this dry land,

[1] *Gaviotas:* sea-gulls.   [2] *Grullas:* cranes.

but this Indian was a *guama*'s son and needed strong measures. Yes, he was saved.'

"Indians, who watched this locust flight as a test of those faiths which then fought for mastery all about this Mission, brought word that all these vast multitudes of gulls stationed themselves on the west side of this grasshopper army, eating infinite numbers of them, but also pushing them gradually toward the east. A remnant of these Devil-born locusts which did not become food for birds passed into the Vermilion Sea, northeastward of Comondu and all other Missions, thus doing no harm whatever.

"Where this horde of locusts fell into our Gulf of Cortés is still called Mercenarios Point, since these grasshoppers were mercenary soldiers, brought by Satan to fight our Lord. Also, these Indians related that numbers of ravens, which are Indian gods, flew from the Wizards' Den at Mulege. In attempting to alight on the ground east of the grasshopper army, in order to drive them toward Comondu and its vineyards and orchards, these ravens were themselves crushed by those multitudes of insects which dropped, exhausted from their flight upon them. One of our Indian deacons saw the emperor of locusts, as large as a humming-bird, perch upon the back of a raven, which flew off with it toward the wizards' den near Mulege.

"Father Ugarte, walking over that ground which had been a battle-field between God's birds and native wizards' hordes of insects, found many gulls dead. These gulls having eaten live locusts until over-full, the last grasshoppers eaten had gnawed holes in their throats, and thus killed many of these God-sent birds.

"Ugarte himself, to commemorate this miracle, painted a picture which long hung at San Francisco Xavier de Vigge. Perhaps, Madame, you saw it there. Clouds of locusts darken the earth, while above them it is bright sunlight; and from all quarters multitudes of birds, both *grullas* and *gaviotas*, hasten to save this Mission of Comondu. All this, Madame, has been preserved, both orally and in writing, by those who since Salvatierra's time have served our Mission.

"Doubtless you already know, Señora, that until 1717, when Padre Salvatierra resigned his place as Head of Missions, no hurricanes, whirlwinds, or waterspouts ever damaged these Missions. But in that year after Father Salvatierra had left here occurred the most frightful hurricane ever known. Satan thoroughly avenged himself for his long self-restraint, imposed by God's will according to our Saint's petition.

"In answer to the padre's prayers, God forbade locust armies to march until 1722, so that his friend Ugarte might have time to control the *Indiada;* making twenty-five years without these destructive pests. This had much to do with conversion of natives, as before the Jesuits arrived there had been long periods of rainless years with locust flights and terrible *chubascos.*

"It was not until 1769, when Franciscans replaced Jesuits, that neglect, robbery, and evil years caused quick depopulation of all these Missions; but then, Madame, their souls had been saved, and for the body, whether Indian or Spanish, what matters after its soul is secure of Heaven?"

"I believe it! I believe it all!" exclaimed Doña Ysabel. "Never had I thought to accept any miracle from this new world, so given over to grasping for money and power; but these priests were great men and good Christians. What will not God do for such?"

I thought by a look in her eyes that she exaggerated her belief to please the priest, offended by her doubt of the sanctity of cardinals. If so, she had her will, for he now ceased to call her "Lady Ysabel" and "Madame."

"Tell me now," she went on, "some small miracle which I can relate to the King when I return; and if that pleases him, then I can go on with your story of these sea-gulls. Poor King, he longs for a miracle in his favor." She stopped suddenly and sighed, but later I knew that the King of Spain then still hoped to preserve Mexico for his Spanish Empire.

"That is not difficult," answered the priest. "Our *Indiada* always consume grasshoppers in great quantities during these army flights.

Also, drying them, they roast and grind them into flour. But this army of red and black locusts being Satan's offspring, Padre Salvatierra forbade all Indians to use them as food. For generations, natives, unharmed, had eaten and fattened on these grasshopper hosts, which did them no damage since Indians planted nothing. On the contrary, locusts furnished them with desirable food.

"Now, when an Indian ate of this red and black flight, contrary to Salvatierra's orders, he sickened and continued troubled until so completely sprinkled with Holy Water that Satan's essence, which the eater had absorbed, was driven out."

"Never have I had a more interesting afternoon!" exclaimed Doña Ysabel. "Tomorrow, Father, would you tell me of your Indians? I like them. Their life is simple."

As we walked from the orchard to that house in which the Sanhudos lived, I said: "Lady Ysabel."

She bowed to me in a curious way, holding her skirts on each side with one hand and sliding one foot behind the other. "What is your will, Don Juan?"

I stared, with mouth and eyes both wide open, but soon seeing she amused herself with me, and perhaps objected to titles, I began again: "Señora, may I suggest to you—"

"What you wish," she answered.

"Do not ask about Indians. It will only pain and shock you."

"A woman must then be kept in ignorance?" she questioned.

"Certainly; and a man also, for that matter, if he be so lucky. Cattle must be killed, but those who kill become callous. The last gurgling sigh of a steer almost stopped my heart when I first heard it. The eyes which roll and glaze; the steaming blood which pours forth, and gasping breath, all left me in rebellion against death. That first day I went hungry to bed. Now I am hardened, and from the still warm flesh of such dying beasts I eat raw tidbits without qualms. Believe me, Señora, those are indeed fortunate who can avoid too great knowledge, whether of death or of Indians, or whatever else is so unpleasant as to make one unfeeling."

"Perhaps! Perhaps!' she murmured. "God alone knows."

"May I ask a favor, Señora?"

"Of a certainty," she replied, and with no explanation of my purpose, I said:

"Would you request Don Firmín to permit me all day tomorrow for my own affairs?"

CHAPTER 13. *The Rock Aljibe of "Hell Awaits Thee"—I See the Skeleton of Don Sturgo Nacimbin—Its Eyes Move and Its Arm Beckons—"Never Again Will I Sleep in a House"—My Hinny Prays for Me*

NEXT MORNING, being called to Don Firmín Sanhudo, I asked for twelve hours of holiday and stood with my hat off waiting for his answer.

"Take Inocente with you, then," he said.

"But—" I hesitated.

"Where do you go?" His defect of breeding is that, feeling suspicion, he shows it. That is when mistrust should be most carefully concealed. It warns if just, and irritates if unjust.

"To the water-tank of *El Diablo Te Espera*."[1]

"Leave the boy with me," he ordered; and as if to make amends for injustice, "But why go to that horrible place?" And, smiling, "How your hinny would suffer if you did not return! There are responsibilities as one grows older."

"Don Sturgo Nacimbin died there," I explained.

"Did you know Sturgo Nacimbin?" Don Firmín asked, startled for a moment, it seemed to me, from his ever-present self-restraint into a flame of interest. "Impossible, he died while you were a child!"

1 *El Diablo Te Espera:* Hell Awaits Thee.

"At six years old," I answered, "he stroked my head and said, 'You would be a great man if you could be a good man, but this world has been difficult for you, my boy. Be of good cheer, God values effort, not result!' I repelled his blessing because my chums called 'loco' after him on the street. Then, having denied him, I spent two whole days alone with my pet hog. Señor Nacimbin is the only man I ever trusted—except yourself, sir!" I added hurriedly, for I had nearly forgotten politeness. "It seemed to me that after he had touched me I could not stand any other human being near me, and that hogs were better than humans.

"When my chums found my nest and called 'loco' to me also, I sicked my pet hog at them. She could run like a deer, and she trusted me, that Fat One. I had deceived her completely and eaten most of her brood, but I had only to say 'Sick,' and that hog would chase an angel from Heaven, and eat it, too, if caught. *Santísima María!* How those boys ran! I laughed so much at their fear of stumbling and being devoured, that I returned to my hellions in good temper."

I talked on because afraid Don Firmín Sanhudo would absent-mindedly say something he might regret and I suffer for his folly. These rich men do not greatly value our lives, and I had no will to pay for his mistakes.

"This man Sturgo Nacimbin"—he spoke to himself as never before had I known him to do, and yet I dared not go away—"I respected more than any other, and ever since have hated him. Yet I saw him only once. General Viconte said to me about him: 'He has insight. He knows that a beautiful woman can control me, and that a doubloon for me hides the Cross. But he merely pities me. Not that he told me so, for he is a gentleman; but I knew it. Beware of him, my good friend Don Firmín. Should he become fanatic, there will be no place in New Spain for us, who now rule.'

"Sturgo Nacimbin lived in misery," continued Don Firmín, "to lose all he valued, and died of the only horror which destroyed his self-control; yet I envied him his life. Were he alive he might bring peace to Doña Ysabel's mind. But what is religion to a woman?

Chapter 13

A bishop to marry her, an archbishop to christen her children, and the cardinal to lounge about her drawing-room fingering a baretta as if it were some female's flesh! If this Nacimbin had convinced her or me, we would have followed him. That was why I hated him: from fear. We, who are too long civilized, fly to fanaticism for relief. Fanaticism is an unsatisfactory life without friends and with power and wealth and the Church against you."

He woke suddenly from deep thought and his hand went automatically to his dagger-hilt, but he hesitated, not knowing how much he had said aloud. We Spaniards are all alike. Once, being very lonely, I sat and thought aloud before my pet hog at San José del Arroyo and, suddenly remembering I was not alone, nearly stabbed her from fear she might have understood my mind.

Don Firmín, looking at me, found me glancing impatiently at my hinny, and with one leg raised as if to steal away. With a sigh his hand dropped to his side and he motioned me away. That training one gets from Mission fathers is most admirable for a boy. It prepares one for every emergency. Where else could I have learned that when a man of power speaks his thoughts aloud, one must show no interest and seem impatient to be away?

With pleasure I started alone, southwest over twenty desert miles, toward the water-tank of *El Diablo Te Espera*. Inocente was no fool, but a child; and at thirteen years of age, as I should soon be, one looked at life from a different viewpoint. Also, he had father and mother and family, whereas I must carve my own path, striking down those who opposed me and treading upon such as blocked my way. There were, therefore, always grave matters to be considered when I was alone, and Inocente was perhaps a dangerous companion for this.

To think seriously while with others was dangerous, since who knew how much tongue or face or intuition might reveal to him who later might wish to stop my advancement? Beyond this, I went to see the bones of Don Sturgo Nacimbin, and I knew waves of emotion would surge over me; and being governed by feeling, not by reason, I might do or say that which would not fit with life as I must lead it.

I will tell you about him, for at one time all the Californias waited breathlessly for his Revelation; and had he raised a finger, who can tell what might have happened? No one knew exactly what he hoped, nor why Nacimbin seemed to be our only escape from utter despondency. This country was misgoverned. So greatly that when Luis Lopez was appointed Governor, the written official order to him was: "Observe the decencies, or at least pretend so to do."

I knew Lopez, and he made no pretenses. Our Missions, robbed by Franciscans to found Alta California, were in quick decay, and Indians were perishing by tens of thousands. They had forgotten how to live their old, wild life, and yet had been turned away from their Missions without supervision to support themselves. Padre Serra himself, on his way north to San Diego, met at Santa María of the Angels a priest so nearly insane from grief at seeing his congregation perishing of starvation that he had to be sent elsewhere. Serra said to the man with whom I talked there that the mountain caves and cañons, as he passed, were full of starving children, and Christian Indians sent from Missions to live on roots and bugs: all perishing from hunger.

This Sturgo Nacimbin, who so strongly influenced those he met, was, as all the south knows, son of a rich man owning five hundred cows. While young, he gambled and drank, and did all those things young men with money do. Even he went to Sinaloa and there spent more cows than was seemly; but his father only laughed, saying:

"So also did I when hot-blooded with youth: but a season or two of prolific calving will restore my herds. When my son is older, he will tell me good stories of his youth, as I will tell him of mine. Thus we shall grow into age contentedly together, and increase our cattle, so that his boys may also scatter cows over gambling-tables and in liquor shops. Youth is sparkling wine which must explode in foam before it is consumed and passes away. To know women as my son has learned to know them is worth a diminishing herd."

Don Sturgo Nacimbin married, after many adventures with girls who held out to him the left hand. A good woman was she he married;

and adoring him, she gave him two sons. The old man, his father, set his grandsons upon horses before they could walk, and talked foolishly about them as grandfathers will.

Then there came to their Mission a monk whose eyes were fire and his tongue a scourge. Those who loitered within the church laughed and whispered, and were glad when their riding horses fought without, and it was necessary to go out and quiet them; but Don Sturgo Nacimbin listened. When the monk had finished, he left the church so deep in thought that he forgot his wife and children.

"That which you say is true?" Nacimbin asked the monk, who answered, "It is all here," and opened a New Testament. Which Don Sturgo Nacimbin took, and when the monk wished it back, answered: "Who knows but my soul is therein? By what right have you so long concealed my soul from me in this book?" And when the monk replied: "Heaven cannot be had by theft of my Bible," Don Sturgo Nacimbin merely laughed and turned away: for all his life he had done that which seemed to him best.

I was too young to know all this, for he died when I was a child; but his life was everywhere talked of, and often my grandfather discussed him, saying one could tell where he went by the expectancy in people's faces. Even the Indians, who think of naught but food, ceased to eat where he came, and went about in thought, wondering and troubled. The Church hated him, but Jesuits are wise and wily. They were not ones to set a spark to tinder, knowing too well where its flame might spread. Lonely priests welcomed him secretly; Mission guards followed him, asking but a word from him. Our Governor, seeing him, went away in deep thought and sought service elsewhere, saying: "*Ojala!* But I must be elsewhere when it happens. For such as we Governors are, there is no place in this new order."

Days and weeks and months Don Sturgo Nacimbin sat in the sunlight by day and firelight by night, learning those letters which form words; for at that time few were taught to read. But he in time mastered the alphabet as he had mastered horses and men, and could read as well as any padre. Never once did he ask a question, nor permit help, saying always: "This affair is between God and myself: He who gave the soul, and he who has it."

His father had now grown old and enfeebled by anxiety regarding his son and fears for his grandsons. He looked after their cattle as Don Sturgo Nacimbin had before done: and overtired in a wet season, the old man fell violently ill.

"Thy father would see thee," his wife said to Nacimbin, when the old man lay dying, and he answered only, "My Father is in Heaven."

When she came again to him urgently, he exclaimed loudly: "This book commands me to leave father and mother and to follow after Him. Leave me, woman, my soul trembles in the balance; and shall I lose it because a worm dies?" At which the old man within, hearing his son's speech, turned his face toward the adobe wall and died. There had been great love between these two men, and the father was a Spaniard from Spain, proud of his ancient family, and like so many of us, wishful to found in New Spain a stronger and ever-enduring race.

When his father's funeral passed from the Nacimbin ranch-house, the son sat deep in thought by an open door with the Bible upon his knees. A coffin-bearer touched him with one corner of the wooden box, thinking to rouse him, but Don Sturgo Nacimbin only drew his dagger, and, placing it across the Bible, dropped his head. They buried the old man, his father, without him; and all wondered and gossiped. His wife's brothers took charge of their cattle, saying: "This man is loco. To read is dangerous. See what it has made of our sister's husband! A man he was, too."

Thus it went on for a year, or perhaps two, for it was before my time, and all men talked of him, but years have little meaning to us.

Suddenly, one day, Don Sturgo Nacimbin stood up, saying aloud, but not addressing anyone: "I must now go into the wilderness and live alone until I know what work God prepares for me."

His wife, La Paloma,[1] hearing him speak, fell on her knees before him, and he stroked her hair, saying, "Work in God's Vineyard is

[1] *La Paloma:* the dove.

hard, and tests my soul." When he left her she lay upon the ground weeping, but content; saying to everyone that her husband became more sane, since he had gone to plant *paras*.[1]

He was long in the wilderness, passing from one Mission station to another, and listening to lonely priests who saw white men but once a year. To them he said not a word, for a vow of silence was upon him; but he left them comforted and lifted above all those things which fret the souls of pious men living with careless heathen.

To Nacimbin's silent influence over such as these, many said it was due that, when the King ordered all Jesuits from California, they left without protest. These Jesuit priests endured frightful hardships in their hurried trip on foot across Mexico, and died by scores in Vera Cruz and Cuba, but without complaint, as if on God's service.

How Don Sturgo Nacimbin lived in our deserts, the Mother of God alone knows. Some said the heathen Indians went hungry themselves that they might leave in his way such food as deserts provide. Others claimed birds brought seed to him, and that natives had seen *nopales*[2] bend themselves toward him, that he might eat fruit from the *tunales*.[2] However it was, I have heard he returned gaunt and scarred, but with a light in his face which made life more easy for all those who met him. To all who begged, he gave of what he had. If he ate, and any asked, he would part his food with them. If they complained, he gave them all he had. His clothing he divided among the poor, until he wandered in a breech-clout only, and when one in joke asked him for this, he answered, "This is Caesar's," meaning, my grandfather said, that he must obey the law regarding decency.

[1] *Paras:* grapevines.

[2] *Nopales and tunales: Cactus opuntia;* the edible cactus, so much planted around old Missions of the southwest. The fruit is the size of a turkey's egg and filled with a sweet juice and many seeds. It is harvested by means of a stick with a fork at the end, and the fruit then dropped in fire for a moment to sear off the many very small spines. A joke of the early days was to carry ripe grapes in a sack with the unseated Tuna de Castillo, and thus fill, from the grapeskins, the mouths of grape-eaters with these small and painful prickles. Don Juan Obrigón here uses the terms in accord with local custom in his district, *nopales* meaning single plants, *tunales* rather the cluster of plants, or mass of plants. *Nopal* sometimes means the great leaf alone.—*A. de F. B.*

About that time there came into this district the ex-Admiral of Pearl-Divers, Sotelo Sebastiani, a man without morals or breeding, but fearless as a manta, and of great strength. He sought the left hand of La Paloma, Don Sturgo Nacimbin's wife: but she, though fearing the Admiral greatly, yet held him away, saying: "Not until my husband casts me off. Go find him and learn his wishes." For thus she hoped to bring back her beloved.

Sotelo Sebastiani sought Don Sturgo Nacimbin, and when he found him, called, "Come," and Nacimbin followed him; for it was in his mind, so people said, that he awaited a sign from God, and knew not who the messenger might be. At his house, and standing before La Paloma, as Nacimbin's wife was called, Sotelo Sebastiani demanded, "Give her to me!"

The wife, looking at this unclothed man who had been her husband, asked, trembling, "What shall I do, Sturgo?"

And he answered only, "Obey thy conscience, woman."

So she spat at him and lived with Sotelo Sebastiani.

To fear a rattlesnake is no disgrace, for it carries death in its fangs, but Don Sturgo Nacimbin felt for them a horror which is unusual among us. Boys, knowing this, would call "loco" after him, and when he turned to win their love—for who could resist his voice?—they would throw down a garter snake to see him tremble all over. Then, stooping slowly as if attempting to touch the harmless reptile, he would shrink from it and go silently again into the desert, there to regain his peace of mind.

Mexicans observe closely and, having many idle moments, deduce from what they see. Therefore, it began to be said the Devil had again taken a snake's form to defeat Nacimbin, and that, when without thought or fear he could lift a serpent from the ground, the New Era had come. People, watching anxiously, therefore laid harmless snakes in his path with high hopes; but always they were disappointed.

Sotelo Sabastiani, having his wife, now wanted the Nacimbin property, but in Mexico there was no divorce. Here among heretics,[1]

[1] *Heretics:* literally, in this Country of the Damned.

now that I am old, even Mexicans are not married by priests, and are divorced with pictures in that great bulk of ink-spoiled paper my people get on Tuesday. But there were then no divorces in Mexico. Therefore, Sotelo Sebastiani followed Nacimbin as he walked in the desert, and when he was more than a day's journey from any water except the tank of *El Diablo Te Espera,* caught up with him and called, "Give me a drink from thy water-bladder." For, like the Indians among whom he lived, Don Sturgo Nacimbin carried water for journeys in a deer's bladder.

When he received the water-bag, Sotelo Sebastiani jabbed it with the point of his knife and rode off without looking back. Whatever his crimes, this Admiral of Pearl-Divers was no coward; for he turned his face away from a man who, for the moment, had lost faith in God. Nacimbin's determination to be godlike had changed him from one ever too quick with his knife's point to the meekest of men. But for that second, when he lost his faith in God, his hand hovered about his knife-hilt. Then he threw the knife from him as a temptation of Satan. Casting himself upon the broiling sand, Don Sturgo Nacimbin cried out in anguish to the Lord of Hosts, for he knew why Sotelo Sebastiani had chosen this locality to deprive him of water.

In our deserts one does not live long without water, and after a moment's thought Nacimbin set his feet toward the great water-tank, called by all "Hell Awaits Thee!" This is a rounded cleft in high granite walls. Below lies a pool with ten thousand barrels of clear water; and on each side and at the upper end, walls of smooth, vertical rock. Its only approach is from the west, where through clear sand one may enter, if so minded, and drink. Within is no spring, but only what water each rain, running from mountains long devoid of soil, may carry to this tank.

But rattlesnakes must also drink, and are cleanly brutes, devoted to bathing in clear, cool water. Moreover, for twenty miles in all directions there is no other bath, and nothing else with which to stop thirst. Therefore, from leagues around, these squirming serpents come to luxuriate in cool liquid, to breed, to be born, and also to die.

For a mile in all directions the air is fetid, and he is brave who, passing among unnumbered waiting fangs, reaches this tank's polished rock sides to look into the hell of snakes below. But he who imagines it possible to pick his way across sand littered with deadly snakes stretched at length, or coiled, or in squirming masses, and drink, is no longer sane.

To this place Don Sturgo Nacimbin came before sunset, and by his tracks, which those who sought him found, he halted and moved restlessly about as if he doubted God and his mission. After dark, as those who sought him could tell by his careless footprints, Don Sturgo Nacimbin went in to drink and there he died.

Half trust is lack of faith, and God deserted him. Had he boldly gone in by day!—but who knows? Had he lived to return from drinking at this snake-inhabited tank of *El Diablo Te Espera*, he could never more have feared. Certain of his calling, he would have led the way, and all New Spain would have followed.

His wife, who had been known as La Paloma because of her purity and beauty, but was now called Doña Pepa, drank each day more and more. When drunk she would sit, backed against the door frame of her house, looking, always looking, along that road by which her first husband had last left her; so that, being polite, we said, "Doña Pepa seeks the north early this morning," meaning she had drunk herself off her feet before noon. But when Doña Pepa was sober, she never even glanced out of her house.

While Sotelo Sebastiani was away, seeking Don Sturgo Nacimbin and his water-bladder, Doña Pepa was sober all one day, and all her neighbors remarked it. Throughout the whole of that day she sat on a bench with her elbows on the table and her head held tightly in both hands. At dusk she rose suddenly, shrieking wildly, "Sturgo! Sturgo Nacimbin! Save yourself, loved one!" and died.

Doña Pepa's two sons by Sturgo Nacimbin were hanged by order of our Governor, who said shooting was too good for them. Sotelo Sebastiani pleaded for them, saying their assault on a girl was drunkenness, not vice. But both Government and Church feared all the Nacimbins, whispering among themselves, "Who can tell what fool may give these boys a Bible?" And also it was not considered seemly that a man so highly respected as Don Sotelo Sebastiani should be further disgraced by two such stepsons.

Some said Sotelo Sebastiani had winked at the witnesses, each wink being worth a hundred silver pesos. Others claimed the assaulted girl was hired to swear falsely against the two Nacimbin boys. Certain it was that the girl, who swore these boys' lives away, had been unrestrained when younger. Afterward this girl, being drunk, offered to have Saint Anthony of Padua hanged as a bigamist, if these *sinverguenzas*[1] so wished.

The two Nacimbin boys perished silently, refusing the Sacraments of our Church, and spitting at the Governor and their stepfather when asked to justify themselves. Before they died, Indians from every Mission on our coast came to Loreto, and it was said these two boys had but to raise a hand and every official and priest in the Californias would have died by Indian hands. To all such offers the boys merely replied, "When the whole tree is rotten, what good would it do to lop off a few decayed limbs?"

The night the boys were hanged, their bodies were carried off by Indians into the hills; the rope with which they had been hanged also, which caused much uneasiness among officials in Loreto, since it is an old Indian justice to use the weapon with which a crime has been committed to avenge it.

All that night, from our hilltops, came sounds of the greatest Indian incantation ever known in the Californias. *"Hu! hu hu!"* they sang wildly while darkness lasted, in attempts to raise the dead, or divine from spirits their wishes; but fruitlessly. Thereafter our Indians died like sheep with the rot, since they had no more hope.

Next morning the Governor of Lower California rose from a sleepless bed, saying, "If there were more of these Nacimbins, God knows what might happen."

[1] *Sinverguenzas:* shameless ones.

And Sotelo Sebastiani replied to him, laughing and winking, with his usual jovial ways, "Wash thy hands, Pilate!"

Then they drank steadily for a week, and Sebastiani lost a thousand silver pesos at cards to our Governor.

Señor Don Sotelo Sebastiani of the Thousand Virgins' *Rancho* was a great man, though he would explain his *rancho* name to you if you asked and were not too prudish. He died at perhaps eighty or perhaps ninety, for men of his origin do not know their ages with any certainty. Rich and influential, without an ache or an ail, his eyes full of guile and his hands ever gainful. To the Church he gave much, and his sons inherit the Nacimbin lands.

Now I have told you why as a boy I felt I must look upon Nacimbin's bones and the place where Don Sturgo Nacimbin died.

A league from this water-tank of "Hell Awaits You" my hinny began to sniff the air and glanced back at me doubtfully, as if distrusting my common sense or her own nose. A mile from this tank I left her loose, that she might find her way to camp if I died on my trip. Wrapping my legs to the knees with repeated folds of buckskin, I went my way, a long stick in each hand; and killing rattlesnakes on each side and all around me. At last I stood on a slippery cliff sloping toward the pool, and looked down upon Nacimbin's skeleton stretched upon the sand, but not near water.

"He died without drinking," I said to myself, and as I spoke his head turned its eye sockets toward me and an arm bone twitched as a serpent crawled over it. It was only playful snakelets inside his skull which caused empty eye sockets to glare at me, but nearly the shock cost my life. I stepped backward too near a great rattler and then fell, rolling toward the sloping cliff's polished edge to avoid merciless fangs. Just in time I saved myself by grasping the snake's tail and flinging it over the cliff toward which I slipped. That I did not follow the snake into the pool below was due to Saint Apollinario, to whom that morning I had vowed a pearl for cure of my toothache. Not only did the broken tooth cease paining, but fortunately he had me otherwise in his care as well.

Don Firmín Sanhudo looked at me when I returned, but said nothing. Doña Ysabel called me to her, and gave me of a strong cordial she carried, saying, "Inocente sleeps in my room tonight." At which I was glad, for the day had wearied me. I feared I might terrify the boy by turning and twitching in my sleep, or even by calling out, as may happen when one is young and not yet hardened to this world.

All that night I struggled with Sotelo Sebastiani, or dreamed I did, urging La Paloma, Don Sturgo Nacimbin's wife, to trust him; trying to snatch Nacimbin's deer bladder away from him before he could hand it to Sotelo Sebastiani for destruction; making ropes of my clothing, and a bucket of my hat, in order to draw up water for Don Sturgo Nacimbin from the water-tank of *El Diablo Te Espera*, and thus save him from serpents. Worse still, for hours stabbing with both my daggers at Sotelo Sebastiani, who always evaded my knives, and who, laughing, threw live rattlesnakes by their tails at Don Sturgo. When finally the sun in my face woke me, I felt upon my chest, holding me down, the heavy hand of Heraclio.

"Holy Saint Benedict! What poison hast thou eaten, child," he asked me as he saw my eyes open, "that this Saint has no antidote for it? He and I have been wrestling with thee all night. If that Saint slept as little as I, either his reputation for curing the poisoned is undeserved or he is one of those indolent pieties who cure the sick only when priests light candles and make prayers in Church.

"Had I three wives and from each a son each year, and were all these boys for ten years as restless in bed as thou, I might forget how to sleep. Not that I need more sleep than a mule, for an hour suffices me; but often last night I wished for thy mother."

"Why only three wives? Art thou ageing on this trip?" I asked him, for he was the ugliest man in our party, but the greatest favorite with women, because flattery was his mother tongue.

He winked at me, saying: "One from San José, from La Paz a second, and Loreto as well. At San Antonio we stayed but few hours, and time was too short to accumulate a fourth. Alas! this is a difficult world, Red Head. If Don Firmín refuses my boat passage to Mexico,

I must stay in the chilly north all my life to avoid my three wives of the south. Wilt thou remain under thy blanket while I cut a string of dried bull's beef and fill my cup with coffee? If not, I'll sit upon thy legs the rest of this idle day."

He soon came back with Doña Ysabel and the priest, and I, trying to greet them by rising, fell backward as a stricken enemy does when a careless fighting man drives his knife into him with too great force. A knife thus driven with overstrength against a man's ribs carries him backward, and that which killed is carried with him in his fall. It is skill, not strength, which makes a knife dangerous. This, in my age, I have often said. If the dead man carries the dagger with him in his fall, wherewith shall the live man defend himself from others? Or, if an assassin, how can he prove himself guiltless, since his knife, being known, as are all good knives, proves his guilt? Rather, one who knows his profession should strike gently and, pulling his enemy toward him in the fall, thus easily extract his blade.

"Pick the boy up," ordered Doña Ysabel, "and lay him in my house." And to the priest: "I would bleed him in the old way and that would relieve his fever, but also weaken him unduly. For a fevered part bleeding is necessary, but to take blood from the whole body, we in my family for a hundred years have hesitated to do."

"Each barber uses a different-sized basin," quoted the priest.

I found, when later I asked, that barbers are surgeons in Spain and do the bleeding. Here in my country, where every man carries two knives, we have little need for haircutters to lose our blood. In fact, we cut even our own hair.

They went off discoursing on medicine and surgery, in which Doña Ysabel, like all great ladies of her time, was deeply skilled. She carried in her head and hands the knowledge of her ancestors, as well as her own experience. Now, women gabble of dress as they sit on the floor sewing, but in olden times costume was by caste, and all women when they met gossiped concerning cures of wounds and disease. In those days women were respected, now they are looked at.

When Heraclio dropped me on the bed, it was so comfortable that I closed my eyes to rest, but when he went out, I felt with my hands to see how it was made. I found below rawhide strings laced, while wet, around stout poles, with a cross-piece at head and foot. As the hide dried and contracted, it formed a springy support, on which one could turn over without having to pick bits of stone or wood from one's hips each morning. Over this was a mattress of short lamb's wool picked apart, and fluffy as down from a cotton-wood tree. Hearing Doña Ysabel come into the house, I closed my eyes and lay quiet, as I had no wish to trouble her.

"He sleeps," she said to Don Firmín Sanhudo as she went out. "There is naught the matter with the boy except a fevered brain, over-excited by what he has been through. Consider, *esposo mio*, he is but a child. Praise him a little and show confidence in him, for one made so suspicious as he by too early knowledge of life craves trust more than all else. I have absolute faith in him, and shall even today send our little girls with Inocente to play in his room. A child demands children as playmates. Remember that in these desert trips thou also art subject to accident, and then I have only this boy to bring us safely to the north. The rest of the men are faithful servants, but that is all."

As she talked, I fell soundly and quietly asleep. In my life up to then I had faith only in Don Sturgo Nacimbin, and no one had ever trusted me, since it is universally believed that red hair lacks stability and is too easily angered. Now, having one person I could confide in and who relied upon me, a great load was taken off my heart. It is difficult to pass one's life with only a pet hog at San José del Arroyo as confidant.

Even the best mother can never know all one's secrets. I could now ask advice and discuss my plans, and yet repay these obligations. On our long trip to Monterey and the north there was much my foresight and knowledge of Indians could do for this Spaniard and his wife. My acquaintance with Indian languages ensured that.

Besides, I carried, hidden away, a package of pearls of great size and unusual in colors. One of these, wrapped in mescal fibre, and given to each of the Sanhudo children at the last moment as they embarked at Monterey Bay, would acquit me of accepting from Don Firmín Sanhudo too freely.

I was waked next morning by my hinny, which, with her head through the window of my room, brayed into my left ear all those melancholic fears of a friendless mule which has lost father and mother and food at the same moment. Before itself expiring, it therefore sounds one last hopeless appeal to a deaf God.

"By our Holy Lady of Sorrows," swore Heraclio, "if I ever catch that tuneless brute of thine alone, I'll make guitar strings of her entrails."

Lying on the hard dirt floor beside my bed, Heraclio had kept awake all night to watch me; and, falling asleep at daybreak, was roused by this deafening bray just over his head and full into both ears. Moreover, being startled, he had bounced up as if built of springs, with a knife in each hand. I laughed at him, and then at my surprised hinny which, having caught Heraclio's head on her nose, had lost the pleasure of completely emptying her mouthful of misery.

"Never again will I sleep in a house," vowed Heraclio. "This floor is harder than the stones with which Saint Stephen was killed, and more lumpy than a gravel desert. Where else than in a house could a sleepy man be waked by such Devil's discord as thy hinny's bray within a foot of his ears? To prevent her from waking thee during thy twenty-hour sleep has kept me more busy than a hairless dog in mosquito time."

"Get thee hence, *mula*," I ordered, and, though tears ran down her nose, she went slowly and with many a reproachful backward glance toward me.

"Hold on," I said, "let me up for a moment. I have a charm to use on that hinny. Turn thy back, Heraclio, and I'll show thee a miracle."

Into the hinny's mouth I crammed a double handful of tobacco, and she went off in silence and bliss, with jaws mumbling silent prayers for my recovery, as I pointed out to Heraclio.

"Teach thy brute to pray alone in our deserts as other Saints do," Heraclio grumbled. "Between the two of you I am more dead than alive."

Doña Ysabel came and, placing her hand on my head and on my heart, and counting my pulse, which never before had I known existed, ordered me out to console my mule. I was well, and for seventy years never again was ill.

Then in old age came a disease from Spain, and I tried to die, but could not, being too weak to be properly dressed for burial. Of which I was afterward glad, though it took me a month to feel gratitude, or do more than curse all who asked me a question. Why a Spanish cold should be so much worse than any other, God alone knows. Perhaps it is an *empleados'* disease, and therefore *apestosa*[1] like any Spanish official.

[1] *Apestosa:* infected with pestilence. A reference to officials, who are called "the worst pest of God."

CHAPTER 14. *Winter at the Mission La Purísima*
Concepción de Cadegoma—A Conversation Between
God and the Devil—Albondigas de Abalone—How
Female Saints Should be Selected— "Remember, a Nose
Cost Spain One Great Colony"—Slapping His Thighs
and Laughing as a Mule Brays—A Ship Loaded with
Pearls—The Misfortune of that Great Pilot Iturbe

FROM SAN JOSÉ COMONDU, we traveled forty miles to La Purísima Concepción de Cadegoma. I was glad to see the last of that narrow lava cañon, at least a hundred feet deep, near Comondu, which is so closely associated in all minds with Don Sturgo Nacimbin, our only modern Saint.

Because of its mild and pleasant climate, abundant water (this stream which flows past the Purísima is next largest in Lower California to the Colorado River), and the profusion of fruit and food, Don Firmín Sanhudo determined to spend at the Purísima two months of winter. Nothing renders pack-train travel so difficult as short days, and this effect of decreasing light we had already felt. Men and mules both work badly and are irritable in darkness.

A mule, for example, is unloaded too quickly on its left side by one man. Owing to the packer's inability to see what his helper is doing on the other side, the animal staggers toward the heavy right side, not yet unloaded, and thus steps upon the other *arriero*'s toes.

He kicks the beast, which harbors a grudge, and whales both hoofs into the belly of whoever next passes him. Thus come endless squabbles, and occasionally a man or a mule is crippled. All this applies especially to shortening days; but when sunlight each day lasts longer than the previous one, all are encouraged, and from day to day call to each other:

"Did that clumsy brute step on thy foot, Benjamin? *No le hace!*[1] Tomorrow with more light thou canst tread on his tail." Or when an *arriero* is kicked: "What one does not see does not matter, *amigo;* but tomorrow beware, for daylight is longer, and then thou canst both see and feel that she-devil's hoofs in thy belly."

La Purísima was the most prosperous of all the Missions we had so far seen because it traded with whaling vessels for all its needs and gave in return dried fruit. This Mission dried, they claimed, in good years twenty-five thousand pounds of fruit, chiefly black figs. Also jerked beef was sold to vessels, and fish, mutton, and pork, with all grains, including *garbanzos;*[2] besides excellent wine and brandy, though few except sailors could drink such heady stuff.

Below the ten-foot waterfall of their river the Jesuits had built a mill, still running and grinding good flour. Here Padre Ugarte, who was forever experimenting, attempted to make cloth by help of the mill wheel, but failed; as may such attempts always fail. If women are not kept busy with the loom in order to clothe their nakedness, with what shall their time be occupied? God gave them their extravagant love for fine dresses simply that their supple tongues might be hampered during their manufacture of raiment.

When Adam's rib was extracted for the making of Eve, they say God stood on one side of our Ancestor and Satan on the other, taking turns to endow Eve with those qualities each approved. God, being more a gentleman than His rival, bowed to him and gave Satan first choice.

"Her tongue shall be bitter and always flapping," he said, and the Lord added, "But her heart shall be tender."

[1] *No le hace:* Never mind!   [2] *Garbanzos:* chick peas.

"Until her brain is developed," chipped in the Devil.

"She shall adore children."

"But dresses still more," added Satan.

"She shall be beautiful."

"And therefore idle and useless," consented the Devil.

"She shall make her own clothes, and thus have little time for mischief," and God winked at Satan, thinking He had him floored.

"Until foolish man provides a mill wheel to make them for her," and the Devil put his thumb to his nose and wiggled his fingers.

"Get thee gone to thy Hell, Foul Fiend!" roared our Lord. "Men shall call her an angel."

"And when she is bad, she shall fill all Hell with envy!" shouted Satan, flipping up his tail and diving under a cloud in time to avoid being burned by lightning from God's eyes.

Thus it is due, they say, to this quarrel between those who endowed Eve, that either forgot to grant her good judgment and honor.

One thing which caused us to winter at La Purísima Mission was that the church, while partly of adobe and with only a tule roof, contained a library of two hundred books uninjured by rain. Doña Ysabel would thus be able to occupy herself during long winter evenings. Also five hundred cattle and a thousand sheep would furnish us fresh meat and renew our stock of *carne seco,*[1] while their three hundred horses and mules would enable us to rest our travel-worn stock without forcing us to remain on foot all winter. As Don Firmín Sanhudo had power to take from all Missions what he might need, our long stay was at first not approved by the hundred souls here. When he offered to pay for what we used, they overwhelmed us with courtesy.

In the past this Purísima was very rich in all goods. Captain Portola took from here, to found Serra's Franciscan Missions in Alta California—so the priest said, sighing—eight mule-loads of rawhide, which represented many dead steers; four mule-loads of wheat biscuits; one mule-load of sugar; and two mule-loads of dried

[1] *Carne seco:* dried meat.

black figs, besides flour, corn meal, seed wheat, and such else as pleased him.

One anxiety all have, in these winter camps, is that idleness produces quarrels; which cause trouble later, and at times even prevent completion of such journeys as ours. Therefore, I watched with curiosity Don Firmín Sanhudo's system.

His Mayas guarded him and his family day and night, in camp or in travel, and had little enough time to rest. The *soldados de cuero* he now divided into three watches also; and day and night, fully dressed for war, they patrolled around our camp as the Mayas did about the Sanhudo tent. The *arrieros* he divided into three parts, and each took eight hours' work daily in watching and guarding our mules.

There were left only *muleros,* and of these a part were used in breaking a score of five-year-old *bronco* mules, bought to replace those killed or dead on our trip; or those which, by defect of temper, muscles, or training, were considered unfit for the harder journeys ahead of us. Other *muleros* were employed to bring daily, from nearby ocean bays, ducks, geese, fish, lobsters, and abalones, so that all of us varied our diet from time to time.

Our supple-tongued Cabeza de Vaca was here useful to us. Within half-hearing of him, Don Firmín Sanhudo said to me, "When we leave here, I shall give to whoever has been most useful to us those mules we are discarding." Cabeza de Vaca, having set his wide ear-flaps in our direction, overheard enough to spread this news widely that night, and added thereto that women also would receive their share.

Thoroughly gentled mules being in demand, especially among women, there was great excitement and much competition as to serving us. Soon I was forced to decline more than one meal a day from those many cooks who desired my influence regarding these mules, and who by their cooking contested for my favor. These women fed me so well that, had I eaten thrice daily, our *soldados de cuero,* who are rough jokers, would have been pinching me at intervals, as we do a pig to find out whether he is fat enough to kill.

Of all those things they cooked for me, whether with olives, or raisins, *garbanzos,* lard, or *chilli,* far the best was abalone force-meat balls. Of abalones there are three breeds—red, black, and yellow— of which the last is best, but also most difficult to find. To obtain them, men seek a rocky coast and, waiting for low tide, scramble down steep cliffs to the ocean edge. There below water, clinging to vast stones, abalones live in such multitudes that one could feed a hundred hogs daily on them and yet never miss what were thus consumed. They have but one shell and must secrete some strong glue with which they paste themselves to the rocks, for a muscular man using an iron bar is needed to pry them loose. The very ancient ones are covered with seaweed and their shells are pitted like the wrinkles on a century-old man; but as these are as large as a hat, and very tough, one does not eat them.

Having chosen those one needs, they are cut out of their shell, with belly slashed off; and their meat, being spread at once on a smooth stone, is pounded with a cobble. On this depends its tenderness, for leave them out of their shell unhammered for ten minutes and no stone can tender them nor any teeth chew them. Then the abalone meat, being well softened, will keep for days and is the most delicate of food. It is, our padres say, that manna with which God fed His people in the Red Sea country. Probably this is true, for abalones are also the strongest food known, and may have helped Jews to subdue the Egyptians. He who eats a meal of abalone in the morning can work all day untired and, returning home, wait without anger for his evening fare.

This meat is good in all ways: fried in steaks it is delicious; stewed with milk it is still better; but ground finely on a *metate*[1] and with fat and corn flour made into balls and boiled with *garbanzos,* it is so good that nothing is better. After my first meal of such—for this sea food we did not have at San José del Arroyo—I was shamed to have eaten so much. Yet I drank of the soup in which these force-meat balls had been boiled until I felt like Padre Salvatierra's gulls after

[1] *Metate:* stone hand mill.

their feast on grasshoppers. Also, I feared illness that night; but slept without dreams, except regrets, when half awake, that I had not eaten more.

Next night I took Inocente to my cook, and had to carry him back to his mother in my arms, for he could not walk, nor could I without exertion. While I carried him, I warned him that to attempt to pry off abalones with his fingers would be worse than putting them in a rattler's mouth; for the shell, being opened to absorb food, closes on a man's fingers and holds him despite all struggles until the rising tide drowns him.

In this way, natives of these parts said, an Indian revenged himself on those *pecho-lengua*[1] pirates, who were such a pest on our coasts for fifty years.[2] Afterward, the Dutch disappeared so utterly from our seas that in my time we laughed when our oldest men repeated stories they had heard concerning them. Three of these *pecho-lenguas* found an Indian and his wife, a girl of twelve, cooking abalones by the seacoast: and first maltreating the woman, sent her aboard their vessel. Then, tempted by smell of the steaming shellfish, they sat down and ate all there was.

Seeing them eat, the Indian thought out his vengeance and, as if by accident, crushed his fingers on a rock so he could not be set at getting more abalones. When they asked for more, he showed them by signs how to get this fresh food, by prying off shells with their fingers; but warned them to go silently, and one at a place only. The abalone, he explained, was shy and swam away into deep water at any noise. Thus each pirate was caught by a shell, which took care to hold him until he drowned; and, as the man who told me this story said, "Three dead men for one wife is not so bad, and a new wife easily gotten in those days, since women were plentiful."

I have seen this place and it is still called "Pirates' Fingers."

These meals on abalone force-meat balls set me to thinking of the injustice of life. Had I my way, our female Saints would be selected yearly from our best cooks, and all such, as chosen, be allowed to

[1] *Pecho-lengua:* throat, or deep voice—Dutch pirates.   [2] From 1615 to 1665.

wear a crown or assorted haloes while still alive. Thus, by encouraging their love of dress and of approbation, and securing them against hell fires, such fashion might be given to cooking as would make it the worthiest pursuit of woman.

Had Satan been the All-Wise our monks claim for him, he had endowed Eve with the art of cookery. Then old women could have led men as young ones now do, and all mankind would have landed in Hell with absolute certainty. As for me, neither then when young nor now when I am old, have I been an admirer of women; though a perfect cook, loving her art as I love my work, could have led me anywhere and, if using tact in threatening me with hunger, might even have married me.

As for those female Saints who live with lions or talk abusively to Governors, possibly they have their uses in other countries, but on our deserts would be little thought of, and by frequent beatings perhaps converted into reasonable cooks. Though to cook really well cannot be taught by abuse. I have known men who try it and fail.

Having arranged all things for our two months' stay at the Purísima Mission, Don Firmín Sanhudo called his men before him and warned them, against neglect or carelessness, ending with: "Remember, a nose cost Spain one great colony for a hundred years! Be careful!" At which all laughed, for it is the story of Vizcaino's *soldado de cuero*,[1] who, being hit on the nose by an Indian arrow, upset his boat, drowning fifteen soldiers; and so discouraged the rest that for a century the settlement of California was abandoned.

Those were the times when it often took eighteen days to cross my Vermilion Sea from the mainland to La Paz, and when Vizcaino, exploring Alta California, could not drop anchor from his ship because so many seamen were dead or unable to stand up after violent scurvy. My grandfather gossiped so much of those old days and their heroism that some laughed; but not I, nor they, if they were boys of my size.

[1] In 1596.

Talking so much of cookery reminds me that, at the Purísima Mission, I listened to an Indian for whose father Salvatierra had prepared a dinner. In those old days[1] our greatest man, Fraile José María Salvatierra, just landed near Loreto, was governor of all the Californias. He was also priest, officer in command of the King's garrison, judge, *fiscal, escribante,* cook, and at night sergeant of the guard, since he had but six soldiers for his garrison. Yet he found time to hold religious services and to learn Indian languages.

It was to induce this Indian's father to teach him a dialect that our famous sainted padre cooked him a meal of *peʒole.* Perhaps from hunger, or because Salvatierra did all things well, this old native talked all his life of this dinner of corn. So much, indeed, that he was exiled from Loreto to the Purísima in order to still his tongue, since he scurrilously compared all Mission food to that incomparable hominy he had received from his priestly cook.

There came to me soon after we arrived at the Purísima an Indian who whispered to me in his own language, "One of your men just hiccoughed," and while I struggled not to laugh, for this is a deadly offense and stops all flow of information from natives, he repeated, "He hiccoughed."

"He has eaten too much," I answered, for the man he spoke of was a gross feeder.

"It is not 'The Disease' then?" he questioned, much relieved: and I found that in this vicinity, years before, there had been an epidemic of hiccoughs which had utterly destroyed whole villages, so that not even a child remained alive. Since then their terror of this painful death has been so great that strangers who overate from that plenty which exists here have been secretly killed and buried lest they infect this Mission with the hiccoughs.

In truth, these natives were not without reason in their fears, since they had no resistance to those infections we Spaniards felt only slightly. When Padre Serra took charge[2] a thousand Indians died

[1] In 1697. [2] In 1769.

of measles, brought by his soldiers from Sinaloa, and other thousands the same year from the Black Death and the fever.

Under Ugarte[1] one tenth of all our natives perished of dysentery, and under the Dominicans[2] pulmonary consumption destroyed three thousand of those few remaining. All this I have frequently heard discussed, since no one knows why Indians die so easily. I can remember, at San José del Arroyo, our fear of smallpox; which, when my mother was a girl[3] lasted a year, destroying whole tribes, and not sparing *gentes de razón.*[4] I warned Don Firmín of their anxiety whenever anyone hiccoughed, and he took such precautions as saved us possible trouble.

In contrast to this easy yielding to death from new diseases was the ability of those desert Indians to withstand wounds and loss of blood. Once on this trip I followed an aged *Guaicura* chief into a cavern. Why, I have forgotten. An uninvited lion attacked him ahead of me in a narrow passage. Until I smelled this beast's foul breath, I thought the battle just beyond me merely a test of my valor, and therefore let my leader attend to his own affairs.

"You are brave—but slow," gasped the old fellow as I dragged him out. The quickness with which wounds healed on him was beyond imagination. I had thought my *Guaicura* mangled beyond possibility of life, but a little melted gum from *taytay* bark, mixed half and half with tallow, and complete avoidance of wash water—which was easy for him—cured him before we were ready to move on to the next Mission.

Only one trouble I had. Tallow is a luxury, and the old man insisted on eating it before I could mix it with the gum. Fortunately, I had more fat and blended my balm out of his reach. As for endurance of pain, were I half the man these Indians are, I would be twice as brave as I am. Not a groan nor a complaint did I hear from this old *Guaicura,* though it seemed to me he had no skin left on his whole body and not much blood within it.

[1] In 1723. [2] 1791 to 1800. [3] In 1781. [4] *Gentes de razón:* Spaniards.

Chapter 14

When we were well settled in camp, Don Firmín Sanhudo sent me to the coast, that I might report to him on his arrangements for sea food. I found abalones so abundant that the three men who supplied us with this fresh meat could also easily dry these shellfish for our journey. In two months we thus secured five mule-loads (fifteen hundred pounds) of dried sea flesh, which we preferred to beef; so that all regretted it when a small part of these cargoes was traded for other foods.

Turtles filled this great bay in endless profusion, but men soon tired of this meat. Even when it was made into soup with proper spices, they grumbled and gnawed dried bull's beef instead. By suggestion of a half-breed, I had a mule-load of this flesh dried— secretly, to prevent complaint—and on our journey fed it to these grumblers. They ate it willingly and craved more when it was gone. Thus dried, it was like meat from a fat yearling steer, tender and luscious, but not tasting of turtle. Of turtle eggs we got few, and these were for the Sanhudos' table. Whether it was too early or our men lazy, or whether those we hired ate all they dug up from sand beaches, I do not know.

Regarding ducks, our method of hunting was new to me, being brought by Don Firmín Sanhudo from the south. All our Indians were fearless in water, being accustomed to swim off to whaling vessels; and when a ship departed, to go with it for a distance. Then, jumping overboard, they made land without trouble. Also, they were great divers and able to catch before it reached bottom a silver peso thrown from a ship's deck.

Therefore, they were ready to accept with glee Don Firmín's suggestion that, with seaweed on their heads and some cork-tree wood tied under each arm, they float with the tide and wind among those great flocks of birds which covered these bay waters. Then, with a hand outstretched on each side, they would quietly pull under water such ducks as pleased them, and so continued to gather ducks as one might pick figs from a tree. They held them under water until they drowned, and the flock, supposing them to have dived for food, did not miss them at all. In this way, with no expenditure except for men's wages, our whole party was easily fed on this delicious flesh; but I shook my head as I watched these Indians. It is one thing to swim and another to float motionless in our shark-infested waters.

Going home that night, I met Heraclio outside our camp, and he was slapping his thighs and laughing as a mule brays. Usually I paid no attention to his jokes, which were not to my taste; for like all men who easily control women, he was a great gossip and continually interested in petty affairs. Men over-favored by women may be brave, as was Heraclio, and may have certain manly qualities; but also they must be more woman than man, or they could not so easily understand and profit by the weaknesses of women. Therefore I knew, even in my youth, that they must have many petty and contemptible qualities, love gossip, keep their tongues constantly in motion, and be able to retain few secrets. While, for their purposes, they hunt females as if they were wild game, nevertheless they prefer their society to that of men. If they marry—which is seldom, and then only because they cannot otherwise secure the person of the girl they seek—the wife quickly discovers them to be incapable of love, and is unhappy. She appreciates what her husband is, and either by a scourging tongue controls him or leaves him.

This time, however, Heraclio would not let me pass, but called to me, "Our patron, Don Firmín, is the wisest man I have ever known."

Naturally I stopped at once and waited to learn his mind.

"You have seen those natives he selected to furnish us duck meat?" he went on. "By Santa María de la Luz, they are well chosen! Do you know their local nicknames? *Bribón, Chambón, Chismón,* and *Bajón!*"[1] and he roared with amusement again. "Every old man in this village goes around laughing into his hand and casting dogs' eyes of admiration at our Patron. Our very priest giggled during Mass at the acuteness of this choice. The sharks will get all these miscreants before we leave the Purísima, and rid this Mission of as

[1] Various kinds of petty rascals.

troublesome a lot of worthless *rateros*[1] as ever worried decent people. The best of it is, their laziness adores their job, and their wages, while high, will not trouble our King, since sharks are never idle. My guess is, Don Firmín Sanhudo has ordered up a lot of man-eaters from the south lest those sharks now here lack appetite. He is always forehanded."

After this explanation, I ate with better appetite duck's breast stewed in *garbanzos* and *masa*,[2] flavored abundantly with *chilli*, and just a touch of garlic. I still was loyal to force-meat balls of abalone, and could I have located her I would have given my largest Loreto pearl to the woman who first added onion to that delectable nourishment.

To be in camp meant more or less idleness, and that brought out stories of past adventure; for all of our men had spent their lives as guards or packers for Spanish explorers, and were full to their necks with truths, *chismes*,[3] and imaginations.

One of them, Tiburcio Manquerna, took me apart with much secrecy to relate a tale concerning our celebrated pilot Iturbe, who was first to sail along our California Gulf Coast,[4] fishing vast quantities of pearls; also buying many other bushels of these jewels from natives for old clothes and wormy ship's biscuit. This hard bread was especially valued by the Indians and brought a higher price in jewels if the biscuits were so full of maggots that they could run about the ship's deck on their own legs; since it was then esteemed as fresh meat.

Señor Iturbe, being explorer for our King and pearler on his own account, first loaded his fifty-ton ship with a sufficiently great fortune in pearls and then sailed on past San Felipe; but found no Colorado River mouth, as later our padres, Kino and Ugarte, in their ship *Triumph of the Cross*, mapped this gulf. Instead of a river mouth, Iturbe saw a vast sea extending far inland,[5] and with high mountains on each side. Iturbe was certain he had found the Straits

---

[1] *Rateros:* petty thieves. [2] *Masa:* corn dough. [3] *Chismes:* wild stories.
[4] In 1615. [5] Imperial Valley.

of Anian, long sought, often found, and as often again lost, and by which he could pass his ship from the Pacific to the Atlantic Ocean. Iturbe sailed on and on up this vast sea, but slowly, as there was little wind and intense heat. A month he spent aground on a sandbar, when a great cloudburst, rushing down from high mountains, filled a part of this inland sea with its debris and created such vast waves that his vessel became unmanageable. Two months he passed on land where the water ended, attempting to locate any continuation of this supposed Straits of Anian, and seeing from the highest mountain-top a vast body of water winding toward the northeast,[1] but the entrance to which he could not find.

Then other weeks he occupied in drying flesh from antelope and wild sheep, since they were nearly out of provisions. Still dreaming that each of his crew would be ennobled *(Hijosdalgos)* by the King for his great discovery, and that he might ask what he would, since there was fame and fortune for any discoverer of these Straits, Señor Iturbe sailed south, only to find arid sand where he had entered this inland sea from the Gulf of Cortés, as now they call our Vermilion Sea.

Cursing that sorcerer who had lured them into his trap, he attempted again to sail around this landlocked ocean, looking for an entrance to the Vermilion Sea, or perhaps to that continuation of the Straits of Anian he had seen from a mountain-top. His voyage ended when his ship grounded, and the water, receding as if by enchantment, stranded them on soft and boggy ground from which with difficulty they escaped alive. They left their ship and its vast treasure of pearls upright as though sailing, but with its keel buried in sand.

All this Manquerna told me fluently, as of a story often heard or oft repeated, and later I learned from Don Firmín Sanhudo that in 1615, Iturbe had made such a pearling trip and lost his vessel. Now came Manquerna's personal narrative, and he almost wept lest I doubt his truth.

"As a boy," said Manquerna, "I went from Sinaloa to drive mules for Juan Bautista de Anza, whom the King had sent to discover a

[1] The Colorado River.

land route from Sonora to Alta California. After we had with difficulty traveled through *Pimaría Alta,*[1] we came to sandy wastes and crossed a great river with still more sterile deserts beyond it. Being the lightest in weight, I was sent to the right of our course, on our best remaining mule, seeking a road to the ocean.

"Traveling by night because of the heat, I stumbled upon an ancient ship and in its hold so many pearls as is beyond imagination. Fevered by this wealth, I abandoned my comrades and, riding toward the ocean as far as my mule could carry me, I climbed the precipitous western mountains on foot. Fed by Indians, I at last reached San Luis Rey Mission. Since then I have spent my life searching for this ship. Help me, or speak to Don Firmín Sanhudo for me, and a half of what we find shall be yours."

I was polite, and promised such aid as I could give, but warned Don Firmín; since a man is but a boy grown up. If he abandons his comrades in a pathless, waterless desert before his beard grows, he will do the same later when his hair is gray.

Finding no other way in which I could hear Don Firmín Sanhudo and the Purísima priest converse, I learned to control *(manejar)* Doña Ysabel's shawl. When taught by her that two corners must cover each other, like clashing bulls' horns when they fight, I practiced with a blanket on an Indian girl until I could drop it about her neck without sweating all over from shame at my clumsiness.

Though I had bribed this girl not to mention my method of learning, I soon saw that women tell each other all things; for it was plain by Doña Ysabel's smile when I first folded her shawl neatly about her that she knew of my days spent in learning this trick. To be clumsy with a woman's dress, I thought, was not as if knives did not follow my will or wild horses could tumble me. Therefore, after the first shame a boy feels at any laughter against him, I handled her *bronco* shawl perfectly and without difficulties. One good thing came of my care; for Doña Ysabel, seeing me eager to learn, showed her kindness by calling me when there was any discourse of interest to me.

[1] *Pimaría Alta:* Sonora or Arizona.

In this way one day I learned much about our *Indiada*. As we sat warming ourselves upon the ground on the sunny side of his house, the priest told us that the greatest holidays these Indians had, before Jesuit times, were when dead whales floated ashore; and that such were not hard to find, since their great oily bulks, rotting in desert sun, tainted the air for miles around.

Clothing these Indians considered unmanly; and after seventy years of Jesuit teaching, Padre Serra, on his trip to Alta California, found them "unclothed, and the women great talkers."

The males were provided by our Mission fathers with trousers and jackets; the women with skirts and jackets; but they wore them only at night about their Mission. By day they hid all their clothing in bushes and worked in nakedness. Salvatierra himself dressed two boys to accustom the others, but their clothing caused such indecent mirth everywhere that this effort was abandoned.

The Indians of Lower California, the priest said, were tall and robust, with splendid white teeth, always perfect. Even when over a hundred years old, they seldom had gray hair. Their features were heavy, with narrow foreheads and thick noses, but their eye-corners round, not pointed. They had no idols and used no strong liquor of any kind. To offset these excellent qualities, they made no clay vessels of any kind and were superstitious in many ways, fearing ravens more even than lions.

For the padres they worked six hours in winter and eight daily in summer; but toiled less in this time than one could think possible for anyone awake. Nevertheless, they were so enduring that their only word for sickness was "to lie down," and their only pleasures dancing and wrestling. This Purísima priest called them the most musical people in our world, as with trifling instruction each Mission, soon after being established, had a complete and musical Indian band.

Also, he thought them most imaginative, saying that our law, which requires as witnesses six Indians giving separate identical testimony in court to obtain the same credibility as one Spaniard, is just and necessary. Once, this priest told us, a whole Indian family had sworn in court that they had seen their Mission priest kill with a club King David, the Jewish ruler of Israel, in their house and in their presence. They invented much detail concerning David's pearl crown and clothes, and the filthy language both had used, and which had led to their fatal quarrel. They even produced that bloody club with which this ancient Israelite King was killed.

Concerning their imagination, I think them to have been like ourselves, but less controlled. I have known, as a boy, natives from every tribe on the Peninsula, and they taught me much of great value; but never did one lie to me. Some of their stories I did not then believe, but each as tested proved to be true in all parts. Of course, self-interest controls all, and knowing little of oaths they would forswear themselves more readily in court than *gentes de razón*; but were they sworn "By the Ravens of Mulege," their testimony could be accepted as truthful.

CHAPTER 15. *Winter Amusements at the Mission La Purísima Concepción de Cadegoma— "Let Us Roast a Mescal for Lunch"— "Teach a Banker's Son to Steal and an Official's Boy to Lie"—The Marquis of Sonora Brought Six Hundred Monkeys from Guatemala to Till California*

AT THE PURÍSIMA, having time for idle amusements, I taught Inocente to inflate those food pouches which desert rats have under their ears and which are their storehouses for uneaten food. These pouches open into the rat's mouth, and in some unknown way the food thus stored can be extracted for eating or for hoarding in their earth dens. Nothing more amuses a child than forcing these little animals to show an egg-sized air bag protruding at the side of each ear.

Also, we lay quiet on desert sand to fool the *zopilotes*[1] which watched from high in the sky, suspiciously at first. Finally, being satisfied we were dead, they settled in great flocks all about us and slowly waddled toward us to peck out our eyes. Eyes, whether human or of animals, they consider great delicacies. Then, having collected buzzards all around us, we jumped up both at once; and they, being large and heavy birds, slow to rise from the ground, became greatly excited as we rushed among them, pulling out their

[1] *Zopilotes:* buzzards.

tail feathers or pushing them over as, running along the ground, they attempted to ascend.

Because of these games, Doña Ysabel called me to her one day and said:

"Inocente remembers every word you say. Not a thing is forgotten, but when I teach him the child forgets. Therefore, you must impart useful knowledge to him."

And I answered, ashamed:

"But Madame, I know nothing. At San José del Arroyo there are no teachers, and knowledge is little considered in my country. Whether the world is round or flat does not help us to more or better food and is, therefore, of no importance to us."

"Sometimes I so think myself," she replied, sighing, "but I want Inocente to learn from you of desert plants and animals."

This I promised her willingly, and the boy had from me all I knew; though a child must be taught with tact, as he learned from me, or through hunger, as I myself learned.

"Let us roast a mescal for lunch," I would say to him; and taught him to cut off the mescal stalk when its leaves began to separate, in order to preserve the sweet juice within. Then, in that fire where cobbles were heating for the *tatema*,[1] to sear the selected mescal so that, as it roasted in a pit with red-hot stones under eighteen inches of dirt, no sweetness was lost.

Sitting about the barbecue pit while the mescal roasted, I made thread from mescal leaf fiber and wove this into a carrying-bag such as Indians use. *Madre de Dios!* With what eagerness the child followed my fingers and, aided by his mother, improved on my methods, until one day he showed me with pride a hot-weather shirt he had made for one of his sisters!

When I found a tall fifteen-foot mescal stalk in full bloom, we chopped it down and tasted the sweet but unpleasant liquor in its flowers. I called my hinny, and she ate, but without much good will. I showed Inocente that what a mule despises, cows so love that they

[1] *Tatema:* barbecue.

have learned to use crooked horns to hook down these tall stalks. A cow with incurved horns thus is often fat in rainless years when there is little grass; whereas, a straight-horned beast dies. Also, it occasionally happens that those fortunate cows with crooked horns, rearing to hook down a stalk, fall over upon the stiff sharp mescal spines and are killed.

Upon these mescal plants all Indian life on the California Peninsula depended until the Jesuits came. Moreover, were it not that God had forbidden locust armies to eat mescal, Salvatierra would have found no human beings alive here.

Having *pita*[1] from mescal, we hunted a *viznaga* stem, and from the hooked thorn at its top made a needle such as all used in my country. Finding other thorns, we also made toothpicks. While he was interested in desert plants, I found for him a *nombo* shrub, which has so accustomed itself to our sterile deserts that, after a rain, leaves sprout from its dry stalk, but drop again if no more water reaches its roots within a month. Thus, after each rainfall come new leaves, for this plant cannot be discouraged by arid years nor killed by too often producing leaves. Its value lies in the sap, which is blood red and indelibly marks all clothes which touch it.

Pitahaya candles Inocente had seen everywhere, for they were almost our only indoor light; but I showed him how to select dry stems and clean them. There is so much fat in the pith of this wood that it can be fried out, but this Indians never discovered, nor did we use it. *Uña de gato*,[2] with its vicious curved thorns, nevertheless yields a fruit in pods; while the *cardón*, which grows forty feet high, gives a seed excellent after roasting. Its branches, boiled and skimmed, furnish a cure for wounds and ulcers; though for burns the *taytay* gum from a bark incision, mixed half and half with tallow, is, to my mind, better.

To show Doña Ysabel that our time was well spent, we hunted on level ground near the hills for cork trees, and brought her their beautiful purple flowers. The wood from this tree is the lightest

[1] *Pita:* thread.   [2] *Uña de gato:* cat's claws.

known to us, and from it rafts are made and stoppers for wine-flasks. Then, to convince Inocente that everywhere God provides all essentials, I took him to a pitch tree, and we gathered from it a glue which exudes from any bark cut. This gum is perfect for cementing earthen vessels, or for pitching the bottoms of boats, or for fastening arrow-heads.

From *jojoba*[1] beans we made an excellent chocolate and even pressed out an oil which is used to replace olive oil. The *jojoba* has these peculiarities: that it bears only on ground underlain by an impervious stratum of clay, and asks that this top soil be not over two feet thick. Though it will grow on deeper earth, it will not then bear its beans in quantity. It demands also one light shower at least each year, or it will not bear fruit; but does not fruit in rainy years.

Of poisons we also have our share, and lest the boy investigate for himself, I pointed out the black pea, which, when eaten, has no effect for several days, but then kills. Also poison ivy, which swells the whole body but is not dangerous to life unless used for firewood, when breathing its smoke is to breathe in death. *Palo de flecha*[2] we found in abundance. From this the *Seri* cannibals make their poison arrows, and those deadly bits of sharp wood which, set in the ground after being steeped in poison, cause insanity if stepped on. Our kindly natives used neither. *Tobacco coyote* grew wild. This was formerly much smoked by the natives and drove them temporarily crazy. Our native fig *(anaba)* is called "infernal" because, if eaten, it is so violent a purgative. From it, however, comes a burning oil for those too proud to use pitahaya stems for light at night. Our native plum tree is scarcely worth mention, since only its pit is edible.

After I had shown Inocente all these things and more, I said to him:

"Nothing angers me more than to be told that people starve on our deserts; for on them we have all that man needs for food, clothing, and light. Truly a great city could not be supported in any one

---

[1] *Palo de flecha:* arrow wood.

[2] The *jojoba* is cultivated in South America and there grafted to obtain the best varieties for commercial use.

place, but when a man goes hungry or naked in my country, it is only ignorance or laziness which causes his trouble, since here God has provided for all human needs. Where there is naught else grows mesquite, the bean of which, in its season, fattens Indians and animals until they resemble hogs fed on black figs. Bread made from mesquite beans is also excellent and used by Indians everywhere. Edible fruit palms and cabbage palms, with cone-bearers full of seed, and the *guacamote* with its deliciously flavored root, furnish vegetables and nuts. Truly, that man is ungracious who calls our deserts inhospitable, for their grass seed alone has supported tribes of natives for thousands of years."

Notice also that, since Inocente was too young to hunt, I said nothing to him of wild meat, which was everywhere: antelope, deer, and desert sheep, for those too delicate to eat rats and snakes. Moreover, ocean shores supplied such a profusion of food that he who starved must have been blind, deaf, and dumb, and have lost the use of both legs and arms.

To live well on these deserts was far easier than in populations, but required youthful training enforced by hunger. In my youth with Don Firmín Sanhudo, as in my age seated in my own house and relating my youth to those who honor me with their presence at my hundredth birthday, I have considered this matter of training children. Had I my way, each child would be educated according to his place in life: such as Inocente, in languages and politeness, and how to manage ladies' shawls; officials' sons, in less crude methods of robbery than they now practice; but children of the poor, by hand labor and privations as I myself was taught. I am convinced that had some kind lady fed me well and taught me writing and figures I could never have been more than a pen-pusher in some official's office. What an ending that would have been for a man like me!

Teach a banker's son to steal and an official's boy to lie, and, being interested in their fathers' pursuits, they will learn quickly and do well. But give to the poor desert-knowledge. Teach them to manage cattle and to irrigate crops and care for trees. Barefooted children must labor early in life and need instruction by work.

Where there is an upper class which, by knowledge and craft, lives upon those below, a few may be idle all their lives; but if every child is educated not to labor with his hands, who will then produce that corn and beef needed for their existence? Belief in equality, which now causes all boys to turn from hand labor, is merely a disease born of vanity.

With Inocente's opportunities I would have controlled millions of men instead of thousands of cattle. Perhaps I might have become King of Spain, in fact if not in form. But I did not have Inocente's opportunities of birth. Therefore I am not Inocente's equal. Nor is the hoe-handler my equal. In my old age I speak of this now, because today on my hundredth birthday there has been here a man who teaches school and who seeks Heraclio's grandchildren under pretense that education means success in life to others as well as to himself. At what school was Don Jesús? The carpenter's bench! From what books did God learn how to create this world? Our Lord's Church was founded upon Peter, not upon Paul learned in written things!

Parasites will always exist in this dying world, but do not imagine they are parasitic merely because they are educated. Perhaps such lying teachers hope their pupils may succeed where our *Visitador-General* Galvez, Marquis of Sonora, failed: and bring six thousand monkeys from Guatemala with which to till Alta California! But this highly educated Galvez also began a ship canal extending from Guaymas to the City of Mexico, disregarding seven-thousand-foot mountains; and when listening to his engineer's plans for a river bridge, rebuked him for not explaining whether this bridge would extend across or lengthwise of the river. Doubtless God had stricken his brain for destruction of Jesuit Missions in Lower California; though, if so, what must happen to teachers who with books destroy the working capacity of children born with souls? At worst Galvez only injured Indians. But I am growing old, and mix present with past events. When I traveled with Don Firmín Sanhudo for a thousand miles, there was no thought of equality; and, therefore, no feeling regarding inequality.

To return to the story of my youth, Don Firmín Sanhudo remained at the Purísima Mission for a month. Then, finding all in perfect order, with every objectionable man employed a desert day's journey away at the ocean, and the kindliest feelings existing between those at this Mission and our party, he felt safe in leaving his wife and children here while he traveled. He carried me with him on a rapid survey of our ocean coasts. For this we took newly broken mules, and each of his guard led a spare mount, so that with good luck and light packs we could make forty miles a day. Eight of his Mayas remained to guard Doña Ysabel, and by their faces as we left, I knew no one of them would be alive if any injury came to those they protected.

CHAPTER 16. *Indian Justice Destroys by Flame—Unimaginable Quantities of Sea Life in Lagoons and Bays—Three Gulls Support an Indian Family—Point Open-Your-Eyes—The Ituma Bird Which Tradition Says Once Spoke Several Indian Languages*

ABOUT SIXTY MILES from La Purísima Mission, Don Firmín motioned me to the left, where in a grass-covered valley were a few "houses"[1] of *gentile*[2] Indians, among whom something created great excitement. As I reached this village, a man darted out as if toward the sea, but, noticing my approach, bolted up the valley. A native girl savagely yelled, "Justice! Justice!" after him as he ran.

I waited with curiosity, since these people have a well-defined code controlled by their *guamas*. A very old Indian rose slowly and took from his fire a burning brand. Holding a wetted finger in the wind to locate exactly its direction, he walked toward the right and, waiting for a purpose I could not guess, finally scattered sparks among bunches of tall, dry grass. The wind was not faster than an antelope running, but gusty; and the *guama* had started his fire just as a little whirlwind, such as raise dust columns in our desiccated deserts, approached him. This caught up and spread the flame with a rapidity which surprised me. Before I could change my glance from the wizard to the running man, a wall of fire roared up the

[1] *"Houses"*: families.   [2] *Gentile:* wild.

valley, continually widening from both ends until it covered the narrowing bottom and hills on both sides.

The half-breed, who was running away from a murder he had committed, looked back and soon saw he could not outrun his fate. He stopped on a little knoll to curse those he had injured, though what he howled was drowned by hissing of crackling grass and continual explosions from brush as intense heat split open every branch it passed over. For a moment he was outlined against a six-foot bank of crimson flame, which roared as do those *cordonazos de San Francisco*[1] which in December devastate our southern seas. Then he lay hairless, eyeless, and without skin, but alive, in a cloud of gray ashes, which that wind following the conflagration carried behind the blaze as it galloped up hill.

A twelve-year-old Indian girl who had flirted with both half-breed and Indian, but lost by murder the man she had meant to live with, left the dying native she had been tending and, knife in hand, leaped up the valley.

"Fool!" called a shrill-voiced old woman. "Why kill him? Rather sit near and taunt him while his soul quivers on the edge of Hell."

"Why set your fire so slowly?" I asked the aged wizard, who had recognized me at once; but he answered only,

"Cannot a Red Head think, Juanito of the Flaming Hair?"

And I sat by him until I understood that such a grass fire, if too soon set, could be leaped over safely by an active man as it began to burn. Also that a wizard must not fail, so that time and distance must all be correct when he destroyed a tribal enemy.

"Patient Jesus, I thank Thee!" I exclaimed aloud, taking off my hat and crossing myself. "By chance and Thy good will I have today learned something of great value." And so it was. Not many years later I was chased by a tribe of mounted wild Indians, until I wearied of their presence and of those insults they continually hurled at me. Therefore, I led them at a gallop until I faced the wind, on a steep descent with much grass and brush. When they were too near

[1] *Cordonazos de San Francisco:* cyclones.

me to escape fire and too far away to ride through it unhurt, I set my *incendio*. The flame I started by dragging lighted grass at a canter behind me across the hillside; which quickly made a blazing trap impossible for the fleetest horse to escape.

I am known in my age as *Juan Colorado*,[1] from my hair, but Indians also call me "The Flame," not from my head color, but because I have at times thus used fire against those enemies who trust rather to numbers than to valor.

Never in all my life had I imagined such vast quantities of animal life as we saw in those ocean inlets, which I reached with Don Firmín that afternoon. Whales crowded the bays so that it seemed possible to step from one to the other for miles; and when one rose suddenly from the depths, it shed from its exposed back a multitude of lesser life: fish, birds, and all those things which swim; besides being itself covered with barnacles and lice big enough to consume anything except these giants.

Low islands, studding the lagoons, were covered with turtles, sea otters, and seals, while other huge turtles lay asleep upon the water, as if space were lacking on land. Cow fish and porpoises gamboled in their ungainly way, yet never striking those innumerable whales amongst which they swam.

Shoals of hundreds of acres, left bare at low tide, were covered densely by millions of geese, ducks, and snipes, with other water-fowl unknown to me. Pelicans and cormorants filled the air as if neither land nor water had room for them; and, circling amongst them, vast flocks of *gaviotas* shaded these lagoons like rapidly moving clouds, as in their flight they hid the sun.

Here also were many *empleados*, as, in compliment to their skill as thieves, we called those fast-flying hawks which took their toll from all these multitudes of sea birds and fish. As we rode past, we saw many of them building their nests of sticks, in which to raise new broods of thieving *empleados* to continue their life of robbery.

Some of these lagoons extended twenty miles inland and were

[1] *Juan Colorado:* Red John.

shaded by evergreen mangrove trees, to the trunks of which the
sweetest of oysters clung. Through their over-hanging branches the
hollow sound of whales spouting filled the air. Here in these secluded
nooks, whales taught their newly born calves to swim, while vapor
from their blowing rose in clouds above tree-tops. Every flat was
covered with clams of such size that he who ate one had begun an
ample meal. Mussels and abalones densely covered all rocks along
this seacoast, and small shellfish, like cockles, filled each mud
flat. At low tide, as I ran barefoot, playing along the harder flats to
scare up those multitudes of slothful fowls which covered them, I
soon found that stepping everywhere on shells wounded even my
hardened feet.

Wherever the bottom was stony and covered with seaweed, lobsters lay. At times two and three deep, so that though we each ate
several of these shellfish at every meal, nevertheless in five minutes
one man with a pronged stick could throw out all we needed for a
day. Our cook then stood ready with his pail of boiling water; and,
still dripping with salt, a lobster was caught, boiled, and eaten before
it had time to grow angry and secrete that poison its rage causes.
Thus treated, this shellfish nearly equals *albondigas de abalone,* and
anyone may eat what he wills without anxiety for his night's rest.

At certain tides, all sandy beaches were hidden under infinite
quantities of sardines left there by retreating waves. Perhaps
because there was less water in these estuaries at low tide than at
high, these fish had overflowed onto the land as a brimming bucket
sheds its burden. These sardines had an exquisite flavor, and we ate
until we were completely full; but nevertheless envied whales those
vast bellies which daily they filled with this delightful fish. So also
their weaned calves ate, yet every tide again covered these beaches
with new thousands for our use.

Regarding larger fish, the whole sea teemed with them: ruffles,
corrundas, sea bass, sturgeon, porgy, dogfish, *esmirigales,* salmon,
tunny, *chucas,* sea horse, gilthead, muttonfish, newts, *tirgueros,* and a
hundred other kinds better or worse than these, but less familiar and

therefore forgotten. On this coast one might have eaten a new variety of fish daily, until one grew fins and longed for salt water to drink. How God created and fed these incredible multitudes of sea creatures not even Jesuits could explain, for my grandfather told me our learned priests marveled when they saw these lagoons even as I myself now wondered at their contents.

Being then only a boy, I watched with delight pelicans catch fish, and then, settling in the water of the bay, prepare to swallow their kill. A pelican, holding in its bill the fish, would throw it a trifle into the air in order to pouch it lengthwise. Meanwhile, an alert gull would hover above the big bird. As the fish was tossed slightly above the pelican's beak, this gull would swoop down and carry off its meal. The poor pelican's puzzlement and the way it looked about on all sides, thinking some lagoon current had carried off its dinner, kept me laughing until the hungry bird rose heavily from the bay and dove for another fish. Perhaps also it lost its new catch to a second hungry gull, which like our rich men paid no attention to the late owner.

Afterward I pitied these poor pelicans which, being dull-witted, were slaves to active-brained gulls. Therefore, I was pleased when on this bay I found a tribe of Indians who in turn cheated these robber gulls. These Indians would snare a gull and, breaking one of its wings, stake it out near the lagoon. When hungry, this bird would call to passing chums, which, stealing fish from pelicans, would drop them before the starving gull. An Indian seated in a hole dug in the sand near the staked bird would seize such fish as the gulls dropped, while other winged friends brought more fish to their wounded mate. Thus a few captive gulls supported a whole tribe of Indians.

Mangrove grew only where there was no sand, and its hardwood branches, growing horizontally and therefore straight, were most useful for oars. The leaves were small and a light green, which differed so much from desert growth as to rest the eyes pleasantly. The local Indians made rafts, and with mangrove oars rowed out to sleeping turtles, which they turned over in the water and towed ashore. More than one showed me scars left by turtle bites, which are dangerous at times, since the mouth is large and never releases its hold on whatever it once seizes.

This fertile plain pleased me more than aught else I had seen since leaving San José del Arroyo, for it was of enormous size, with good soil, and water only ten feet below surface. Its climate, too, was perfect, and had neither rainfall nor frost.

My idea of cultivating this land was to dig a long trench sixteen feet in depth, through which Indians would walk chin deep, filling leather back-bags with a hundred pounds of water as they trotted along. When again at ground level, they would empty these pouches of water into an earth ditch. In this way a score of Indians persistently working, as they would work for me, could irrigate a sizable acreage of land, and, though continually wet, few would die. Windmills, such as Inocente told me he had seen used in Spain, might have been used, but these would have implied money, iron, and oil, which were not to be had in my country.

On this bay were deposits of fossils, but seeing the first one, a stone oyster shell two feet long by nine inches wide and four inches thick, weighing an *arroba,* I begged Don Firmín Sanhudo to permit me to go elsewhere and wait for him. It was bad enough to have seen those horrid monstrosities of beasts in the Loreto Cavern. Nor could I understand how those beasts could have opened such oysters as this with their tusks.

Some things I noticed on this trip concerning which I gossiped to Inocente: first, an ash-colored bird, beautifully tufted on its head and with a tail like a peacock's. This was the *ituma* which Indian gods thus decorated for its services to those starving natives who first landed at Magdalena Bay. Coming from some unknown land from which a great catastrophe had driven them, a whole tribe of Indians traveled seated on the back of an enormous bird. This bird must have flown a very long distance, for it dropped dead in the surf at Magdalena Bay. Its passengers landed with difficulty, and were both starving and perishing of thirst, for it is impossible to drink salt ocean water.

The *ituma* showed these shipwrecked Indians how to catch abalones by dropping a stone into the abalone's shell while it was open to feed, thus forcing it to remain ajar. So far as I know, the *ituma* is the only bird which thus lives on abalone meat and secures it easily without risk. It has only to wait until the shell opens, after the abalone dies, to eat its fill. Having thus fed these starving Indians, the *ituma* flew slowly before them to the only spring of good water nearby. At that time this bird spoke the native dialect plainly, but now neither *guamas* nor *hechiseros* pretend to understand its language.

Wasps I also saw, which made mud cells with glue from their mouths; and having placed eggs within, they filled the remainder with spiders so their young might eat. Had my father been as wise as these wasps when he abandoned us, what suffering would have been spared my mother! The third notable thing was Point *Abreojos*,[1] which made me glad I had sworn never to enter a boat.

If a horse by mischance bucks you off, there is at least firm ground below on which to drop, but when a vessel is ill-tempered and unmanageable, Satanna alone knows where you land should you fall from it. I have seen a small boat off Open-Your-Eyes Point stand on its nose, and then suddenly rear back on its tail until the wild mule I then rode nearly perished of envy. Buck as he might, he could never hope to toss me about as this boat would have done.

[1] *Abreojos:* open-your-eyes.

CHAPTER 17. *The Mission of Santa Rosalía de Mulege and Its Good Wine—The Mission of Nuestra Señora de Guadalupe del Norte—"There is Nothing I More Detest than an Unnecessary Lie" —At Three Years Old is Bug Age; at Four, Mouse Age; at Six, Snake Age—"Why do You Bob Your Hair?" I Asked an Indian Woman*

THE WINTER OF SHORT DAYS being over, we went, soon after our return from this trip, from La Purísima Mission to Santa Rosalía de Mulege. Thence to the deserted Mission of Nuestra Señora de Guadalupe del Norte. Between here and Comondu, Padre Serra, on his way north[1] to establish Missions in Alta California, encountered everywhere Indians and their children starving to death for lack of those provisions his three pack-trains had carried from their farms. Don Firmín Sanhudo and Doña Ysabel talked much of Serra, but without praise, except that they said he was fanatically religious and told the truth always except regarding his miracles. I regard it as greatly in Serra's favor that he was truthful regarding our Lower California Indians. They were sacrificed to starvation in order to convert to Christianity the *Indiada* of Alta California. He acknowledged this, though it hurt both his feelings and his reputation. Many a religious would not have told the truth so plainly.

[1] In 1769.

There is nothing I detest more than an unnecessary lie; perhaps because as a child they called me inquisitive, and babbled many fables the truth of which I could not then test, and thus sullied my memory. Some also said I was acquisitive, but being now, as I talk to you, my guests, over a hundred, I have never yet taken anything I did not need, nor of food more than I could eat at once. Who does not do the same? Were Saint Peter the Apostle sufficiently impolite[1] to question a man of my age, I would answer him the same at Heaven's gate, and perhaps crow[2] three times to remind him we are all human. Saint Peter, as all know, is not in the best repute in Heaven. Therefore, he was made doorkeeper, since in that position he must meet many disreputable souls, and those in authority considered it best to risk a Saint already somewhat tainted.

This Saint's mother hangs suspended, they say, over the Bottomless Pit by a single thread of God's mercy. If Saint Peter can find in his books anyone to whom, in her lifetime, she did a single kindly action, she will be hauled up to Heaven. So far, it is said, no such record of a single good action done by her to others exists; but Saint Peter is so much occupied in receiving dead souls, and there were so many people alive while this Saint's mother lived, that he may yet find testimony in his mother's favor. Having red hair myself and having been lied about by some, I have always hoped Saint Peter might release his mother, even though so to do he must falsify his books. But I must tell you of my boyhood and not wander so far as Saint Peter's family.

My way during life has been, when questioning a man, to ask first concerning things I know; and if he answer correctly or with only reasonable deviation from fact, I retain what he has related until I can further test his knowledge. Thus, meeting at Guadalupe del Norte, on my trip with Don Firmín Sanhudo, a Mission guard who had spent all his life among Indians, I found him truthful when he

[1] *Impolite:* literally, "American," i.e., brutal.

[2] *Crow:* Peter remembered the word of the Lord: "Before the cock crow, thou shall deny me thrice."

said that our natives built no houses because they must so continually change their villages as water dried up or food became scarce. Their word for "week" means also "home," indicating necessarily temporary occupation. Scarcity of food and water accounted as well for our many small Missions, since a large population could not be supported in any one place.

Also, I knew that Indian children did not number their years, but at three years old were "bug age" because they could then catch bugs to eat. At four they were "mouse age," and at six, "snake age." Being then old enough to support themselves, they separated from their mothers and no longer named their years until adroit enough to kill deer, when they were "deer age." They were sought then in marriage by clamorous girls of twelve, who demanded a good provider and had little hesitation in using their charms to their best advantage.

How Indian babies ever grew up puzzled me always. The mother, seeking food, left them alone for hours, only returning to them when her over-full breasts became too painful. As soon as they could sit up, they traveled all day astride their mother's necks, holding by her bobbed hair; or when she ran after a snake for food, being grasped by their legs which hung across her bosom.

Nevertheless, all Indians, even at great ages, were erect, and seldom had gray hair. If so many of their women had not been barren and others with only one child, our Indian tribes would have peopled the earth; but as it was, one could traverse these deserts for a hundred leagues and meet no one. Because of this scanty population, it happened that each little bunch of isolated natives had a different language. They retained no knowledge of their origin, some even claiming descent from a great white ocean bird; though which bird none knew.

Hearing this Guadalupe del Norte Mission guard call an Indian "*Toro,*"[1] I asked why, and was told this man had seen their Mission father bring the Sacraments to a dying penitent. Carefully considering this method of obtaining bread and wine, the *Toro* announced

[1] *Toro:* bull.

himself sick to death; but never having seen a human die, since Indians left their sick to perish alone in the deserts, he did not know how to act. Therefore, he copied carefully the death of a bull, which he had often watched; bellowing as when the knife parted its neck, lolling out his tongue and licking his lips. All of which caused great laughter, but brought no food, and left him nicknamed *"El Toro"* for life.

That they will do anything for food I know, for at San José del Arroyo, Indians stole consecrated wafers from our sacristy; and once a servant, boiling beef for his padres, was seen to take out each piece from the pot and bite off a chunk, thinking a little would not be missed.

They are a simple people in spite of their cunning. One, being sent sixty miles with two loaves of bread and a letter to a neighboring Mission, hid this letter under a stone so it could not see him eat one loaf. He was confident, therefore, the letter could not tell tales on him, since it had seen nothing. Having finished eating the loaf, he took up the billet again and continued his journey, certain he would not be punished.

Father Ugarte, who understood these natives better than any other, once hung a hind quarter of deer about his neck while he taught his Indian penitents, knowing that only thus could he concentrate their attention upon him. But his audience smacked their lips so loudly as they watched the meat that he could not be heard. Whereupon, striking the loudest smacker violently across his mouth with an open palm, the father announced, "He who smacks his mouth does not eat." This, in an altered form, is still a proverb with us. "They would rather see a piece of meat than my most splendid vestments," I heard one padre lament.

This guard told me, what I have myself seen, that at baptism Indian babies were white as Spaniards from Spain but slowly took the chestnut bronze of their parents. It is true that grasshoppers alter their color five times before maturity, but why humans, even though but Indians, should also change color, puzzled me. The padres said it was sin which darkened them, and that a sinless Indian would be white until death. *Ojala!* but a sinless Indian would be more strange than a white one.

I have seen a fat Indian, squatted by a deer I had killed, eat an *arroba* of meat before morning. His family meanwhile starved at home. His father, a blind man of great age, was pounding up an old pair of sandals between two cobbles, for soup, when I passed their hut next morning. Nor was this gourmand blacker than the rest of his tribe. However, it is true they never ate human flesh, which is the more to their credit, since there was no other meat they did not consume.

Grasshoppers they ate fresh or dried as might happen, and in locust years they dried multitudes of them in the sun and, grinding them to flour, made bread. Deerskin or leather they milled between cobbles, and thus drank with water as *atoli*.[1] They did not boil or roast, saying this was a waste of time, but stuck all food in their fires, and when charred devoured it uncleaned. All ages and both sexes cooked, and food was eaten as soon as received, seldom being kept overnight. A dozen and a half watermelons to a man contented him.

At Pitahaya Time, by reason of continual food, they became so fat that it was impossible to recognize them, and even their Mission fathers then failed to know them by name. So important was eating to them that when appetite ceased in illness they considered the patient dead and, wrapping him in deerskin, buried him at once. This guard told me that recently, finding a girl wrapped for burial, his padre had unrolled her despite angry protests from the family. He found her living and to live. Some broke the backbone of their dead to prevent them rising as ghosts, and others put new sandals on the dead feet; but that was a very old custom and they had forgotten why they so did.

That afternoon, as we rode at a gallop into Guadalupe, we passed a "house" of Indians bound for Kadakaaman Mission, naked as when born. They carried their clothes, of blue cloth for men and white wool veils for women, in nets of string made from aloe fiber, and swung on their backs.

[1] *Atoli:* mush.

Besides these bags they carried only a knife of flint, a bone or flint root-digger, and a deer's bladder full of water; with, of course, curved bows about six feet long made from roots of willow, and flint-headed arrows. The bowstrings made of deer intestines were curious, but otherwise all was crude. Doña Ysabel, seeing them thus with all their possessions so easily carried, called me to her and said:

"Ride for a time with these Indians and teach my son how admirable is their simplicity. Without envy, jealousy, or slander, and no luxurious habits, they must be happy beyond all peoples of this world. Padre Francisco tells me he wearies sooner of riding than they of running, and that to go on foot sixty miles in a day, carrying letters, and return by the next afternoon with answers is not tiresome for them. Besides, they never have gray hair. I would that my boy could live so unhampered a life, full of realities and without thought."

Therefore, I waited for these Indians so that Inocente might observe them. But without disrespect to Doña Ysabel, it seemed to me that, having been rich and well cared for all her life, she little understood what hunger, cold, and foot travel meant to those who so lived.

To abandon sick or motherless children as they journey because of their weight, to carry no salt because too heavy; to marry at twelve years old and separate at the church door since they must procure that day's food; to have no jealousy, so that their word "husband" means to live with women generally—all these things would little have suited her. She came of a fighting family, and as castellan of a besieged fortress would have controlled and cheered all in it; but in idleness too much thought heated her brain because she lacked necessary work. Simplicity for her was but an added weary thought.

We found that band of Indians was a part of those who each quarter returned to San Ygnacio Kadakaaman Mission for training and work. As usual in all missions, the *Indiada* were here divided into four parts, and to each section a month of teaching and of food was given. The next division then replaced them.

They walked slowly because disliking return to school, and talked among themselves:

"I'll bite Padre Whipmuch if he strikes my child," whined a woman.

"You beat it yourself; and it is no good," sneered her husband.

"You whip me when you are angry, and I beat my child; but it is my own, and no one else shall hit it. He is not a bad boy," she flared up angrily; and kicking a prickly *cholla* spur from the trail, cried out in pain and hopped along on one leg, extracting thorns from her foot.

"The last child you left to die at the *Tunal*," continued her husband. "Drop this one behind some bush and its trouble is over."

"That was a bad one. When he fell off my neck, his arm was hurt and hung limp. If I ran after a mouse or a snake, he yelled so loudly I could catch nothing. Besides, he would eat only when I brushed from his food the ashes and charred part, and that is too much labor. If our padre whips this one, I'll bite him, I know I will."

"Lie on the ground kicking and screaming all you will, even tear your hair; but do not bite him or I shall be whipped," remonstrated the man. "Remember what happened to my last woman. There are several pretty girls just turning twelve who have glanced my way."

"I know I'll bite our padre, I know I will," moaned the woman.

"Why do you bob your hair?" I asked her. "Does it not hurt to cut your hair with sharp flints?"

"Does one cut hair for amusement?" she answered contemptuously. "At haircutting time we battle with each other as *correr caminos*[1] fight rattlesnakes, but it is the custom. What would you? One must be like the rest."

"And your ears?" I asked the man, pointing to ear lobes which had been cut and weighted with stones until they touched his shoulders. "Must they match your very long hair?"

"What girl of twelve would look my way otherwise?" he answered, shrugging his shoulders.

---

[1] *Correr caminos:* the birds named road-runners.

"Your mother-in-law?" I continued, well knowing they could not even glance at this relation.

"Where?" he asked anxiously, covering his eyes.

"Nay! She is not here. I asked only about the custom."

"Why trouble me, then? How can one get a girl without a mother, since motherless girls all starve to death?"

Inocente, who was young but no fool since he had begun to learn from me, had had enough of simplicity, and touched my arm as a sign; and we trotted on toward camp.

"These Indians are like the rest of us," I told him. "They are enduring, for they stay out all day in our torrid sun without head covering, even after our padres have taught them to weave grass hats. In coldest weather they wear at most a deerskin. The women perhaps wear a belly cover of vertical strings of white aloe fiber, through which wind sweeps as through a hut of mescal stalks. They are fearless, for they climb forty-foot swaying *cardones* looking for game, and in building our Missions they work on the weakest scaffolds.

"They are polite, for when one asks a question they wait to reply until they know the questioner's desire. If in doubt of your wishes, they answer 'yes' and 'no' in the same breath, so that all may be pleased. Yet see what they are! Thus it is not to have a soul: but even that does not free them from styles and customs."

That evening at Guadalupe Mission, by command of the Dominican padre, Indians roasted mescal for us. First cutting plants at the right stage and, by some system I could never learn, selecting those which were sweet in taste, though most mescal remains bitter even after roasting; then starting fire by twirling a stick in their palms against a hollow in one below. When the roots had been seared sufficiently in an open fire to prevent the juice escaping, they were buried with red-hat cobbles in a hole and there left twelve or fourteen hours. We ate of them for breakfast next morning, and found them tender and palatable, though roughening our throats a little from some astringent acid therein. In color they were yellow like cane shoots when cooked.

Sitting around our open fire while mescal roots cooked, I learned much of this *Indiada* while they sang for us. Doña Ysabel, who sat near me, shuddered and whispered that it was the baying of witch-dogs at a waning moon; but she waited till the last wailing note was finished, and at the next Mission had its Indians sing again, saying:

"It is a dying nation in a dead country which originates such music, and it is worthy of them. Gracious God! Have they never known a joy? Nor even release from pain? I shall not sleep for a week from thinking how many joyless centuries must have been needed to extract all except misery from such plaintive melody. Yet I cannot leave them while they sing. It must be that Devils from the Bottomless Pit were their teachers."

For my part I liked their songs. Youth demands thrills, and their music caused gooseflesh to come out on me. At times I shuddered as when filmy ghosts, shining dimly, moved about our graveyard at San José, and I, afraid to stay, yet from curiosity could not run away. Partly, perhaps, I thrilled because I came from our beautiful south-land where emerald verdure began in every valley and covered every mountain-side; whereas these desiccated deserts through which we had traveled for weeks oppressed me, as though inhabited by ghosts which had taught these Indians their songs. Or as if Death, contracting grimly around every little Mission oasis, gradu-ally pushed life into smaller and smaller compass in order finally to destroy it.

Each morning I woke almost expecting the desert to have cov-ered what few struggling remnants of green growth remained from modern neglect. The very coyotes there had a starving tone in their yap-yap howl which was different from that of our hearty, well-fed beasts, but made an excellent chorus for Indian music. The desert was death, and the oppression of its silence and decay was upon all people and animals near it. To hear our mules bray as we neared a Mission made clear their thoughts.

What was still more saddening was that each Mission, as we came to it on our way north, was more neglected than the last. Padre Serra may have done much for Alta California, but when he took from our Missions thousands of cattle, horses, and sheep, with countless *fanegas* of wheat, barley, and dried fruit, and even dried hides, wine, and brandy, he ruined us. Those spots which, founded by Padre Salvatierra, would have sustained and civilized our *Indiada* were now merely their burial-places. Starving Indians, having through Mission training lost in part their hardihood, perished so fast that often only the very old remained.

CHAPTER 18. *The Dead Jesuit's Curse—The Door is the Mouth of the House, Because All Who Enter It are Swallowed up—If a Man's Tongue is Split Lengthwise, Can He Talk Twice as Much as Before?—Rain from a Cloudless Sky—The King's Mail Passes —Arrival at the Mission of San Ygnacio Kadakaaman*

T HAT EVENING, after listening to the Guadalupe Indians singing, I lay long awake. It seemed to me that the dead were all around me, as decay certainly was. Thus there came into my mind the legend of the Dead Jesuit's Curse, known to all in Lower California, but of which none dared even confess knowledge. One would have been brave, indeed, in those days, to listen to, much more to relate, this story as I now tell it.

An aged Mission priest lay dead in that hour when the political authorities seized all our Jesuit priests, and, *incomunicado,* took them as prisoners on foot to Vera Cruz. Half of them died upon the road from hardships and quick travel. The rest were set down moneyless and foodless on a desert Italian coast, with only those clothes in which they had crossed a continent, an ocean, and a sea.

When all our priests had embarked on the Vermilion Sea, and this dead *fraile* was the only Jesuit left in the Californias, he rose from his bier, clothed in his shroud; and with eyes closed, and motionless face and figure, he stood in the street and cursed the Franciscans.

"By lies to the King of Spain ye have replaced those who, with countless hardships, have civilized and adorned with churches this new world of California. By jealousy, deceit, and fraud, ye Franciscans have driven us out," he intoned, as if it were a church service. "We built of hewn stone as everlasting as the souls of those we saved. Ye shall build of mud and slime like your own minds. One church of stone ye shall construct in imitation of our glorious work, and God shall so destroy it that for a century its very location shall be unknown. For three months the solid earth below it shall quiver and, shuddering, struggle to repudiate your fraud. Those poor souls ye have deluded, flying to this church for protection, shall perish in it.

"The damned shall pay to repair your mud wrecks, and for a rial scoffers may enter and laugh at your religion. Evil houses shall be built about them, and the cornerstone of your greatest temple shall be found by the damned in a house of bad repute, where the evil spit at it, saying: 'If there were a God, it would not be here!'"

So ending, the holy priest fell forward without a tremor, and none dared pick him up, lest the Spirit of God so manifest in him should injure others.

I lay sleepless, dreaming of this Jesuit curse and wondering regarding San Juan Capistrano,[1] which was a Franciscan Mission built of stone and one we should pass in our Alta California travels. At that time it stood uninjured, so that Serra, I thought, must be more favored in Heaven than Padre Salvatierra; though perhaps these feuds between Jesuits, Franciscans, and Dominicans were not carried on so bitterly in Heaven as in the Californias.

I could not make up my mind whether Doña Ysabel should be allowed to enter this church at San Juan Capistrano, nor how to prevent her; since women are not reasonable in questions of religion, and she frequented all churches without regard to orders or curses.

[1] San Juan Capistrano was destroyed in 1812, with great loss of life, by that earthquake which seemed to select Missions for ruin. The widely separated churches of Capistrano, Ventura, Santa Barbara, Santa Ynez, and the Purísima (Lompoc Valley) were either destroyed or seriously damaged, while towns around or near them were little injured.

A Mission guard interrupted the thoughts caused me by my memories of this curse.

"Do you know what these Indians call a house door?" he asked me, laughing. His tongue was like a creaking ox-cart wheel, never still. "'The mouth of the house,' because it swallows all who enter; and wine is 'bad water,' though the natives like it well enough. They have no word for month, but a year is 'pitahaya,' because this fruit ripens once in twelve months, and while they have ten fingers and ten toes they can count only to six. Beyond that is 'much.'

"I have lived long among them," the guard continued, "but have yet to find out why their men sit cross-legged, while women extend their limbs. Did you notice their Song of the Dead? It was the last one, where they shouted *'Hu-hu—Hu-hu.'* Had our padre not been here, they would have cut their heads with sharp flints till blood ran in streams. Their great conjurer is just dead and they sang to his ghost, but I did not tell our Old Man, or you would have lost that song. Let these poor creatures have their fun, I say, but all the same it makes my blood run cold when ghosts answer their call.

"You were all too thrilled by their singing to notice the dead conjurer's head begin to form in fire-smoke. Could I have got our padre away, you would have seen this wizard's whole figure; but one unsympathetic person prevents this. I attend all their pow-wows 'as guard,' you know"—he winked at me—"and I have seen forms of dead devils emerge scowling and threatening from the smoke, while all Indians went into convulsions of fear.

"This living long months alone makes one forget how to talk," he continued. "When I say but a word to our padre, he closes my mouth with 'Silence, fool!' You did not ask me why our coyotes yelp with their noses turned toward their tails, or I would have told you a pretty jest; but all those who come from San José del Arroyo have no humor. That is why we of Miraflores are silent when with you glum people.

"A man from your little village spent a week with me once, and each day tried to get away, but was too weak. He claimed his illness required silence for cure, but that is nonsense. What else is there here but silence? When he insisted on going, I walked two days with him to entertain him on his road, which is all anyone could do; but after I left him, he lay down quickly to die. Later we found his bones. Silence killed him, as I knew it would.

"When I get my discharge and return to Miraflores, I shall have to teach myself to speak as if I were a baby. Perhaps I had better stop at Loreto on the way, to limber my tongue, or my old friends at home may think me insane. Come, thou silent one, and sleep in my hut, and we will converse a little."

The Mission guard at Guadalupe came of a mother whose tongue was hung in the middle and worked sideways as well as up and down. But for my excuse that I must lie by Inocente, who of late had refused to sleep in his mother's tent, I also might have left my bones on this desert in welcome silence.

When leaving the Guadalupe Mission I spoke to Don Firmín Sanhudo, telling him that this Mission guard would probably be killed if he followed us to San Ygnacio Kadakaaman. Already he had been thrice silenced with a bare knife at his throat, by men little accustomed to sheathing a dry blade.

He had completely deafened our greatest talker, Heraclio, within an hour. Heraclio, irritated at being talked down, planned, if this guard came with us, to slit his tongue in half lengthwise. Already every *mulero* and *arriero* in our company had betted wildly on one side or the other of this question: whether such tongue-slitting would silence this guard or enable him to talk twice as much. I heard Heraclio discoursing on a parrot he had so treated, proving by it that a slit-tongued man would be able to talk as fast with each half of his tongue as before with the whole, thus doubling the quantity of his words.

It was a week at least before our men ceased to argue this problem, and never have I known anyone so regretted as was this guard, when they found he had remained at Guadalupe.

On our way to San Ygnacio Kadakaaman,[1] the Dominican and Don Firmín talked much of Indians, but I listened with irritation, as I knew more of the subject than either, yet could not correct their errors. A boy, from politeness, can only assent to what his elders say.

One thing which mystified them, as it does me, was that under Indian polygamy, during many centuries before the Jesuit conquest of Lower California, and when life was so terribly hard for all Indians, more girls were born than boys; whereas, when Indians were restricted to one wife, and food became abundant, many more boys were born than girls. Already in Salvatierra's time and equally since then, Yaqui girls were brought from *Pimaría Alta* as wives for Lower California Indians.

Another matter much discussed by Don Firmín and the Dominican friar was the few obstacles placed by nature in the way of Salvatierra and Ugarte, whereas every effort of the Franciscans was opposed by all those forces called natural. Salvatierra landed at San Dionisio Bay, so the Dominican said, after a quick and quiet trip across the Gulf; and though he greatly feared Indians, since he had but six soldiers with him, the natives knelt when they saw him land and helped him as best they could. There was only occasional trouble with our Indians because of careless and cruel soldiers, and only one rebellion of Indians, which came because Padre Tamarel chose our coldest winter to preach of the intense heat of Hell. The padre refused his flock's demand for immediate entrance into Hell; and with Boton as leader they then destroyed our four southern Missions.

Thereafter, eight thousand converts in fourteen Missions, with as many more wild natives, were easily controlled by one or two soldiers at each Mission. I listened to all our Dominican padre said, but remembered that Dominicans hated the Franciscans.

The first year Salvatierra landed in Lower California was the most rainy ever known in my country. This was especially favorable to Jesuits' projects, as for a score of years previously the sky had

---

[1] *Kadakaaman:* Land of the Sedgebrooks.

rained grasshoppers rather than water. From the landing of Salvatierra[1] to his departure,[2] not a tornado nor a waterspout troubled Christian or native; but as soon as Salvatierra had crossed our Vermilion Sea on his way to the City of Mexico, all of Lower California was devastated by great hurricanes and irresistible cloudbursts. When this great man Salvatierra left us, he promised Ugarte five years with this same extraordinary freedom from grasshopper armies, which under him this country had enjoyed for twenty years; and so it was. Five years later[3] came the first locust damage during Jesuit times.

To all of their conversation I listened with great interest, and especially when their talk turned to Padre Serra, since I would soon be in Alta California, which is Serra's country.

"This Franciscan Saint," mused the Dominican padre, "arrived in Lower California on the ship *Purísima Concepción de María Santísima*, and was twenty days crossing our Vermilion Sea in a Gulf storm so terrible that all were nearly lost. Our Indians, therefore, avoided him as a bearer of ill luck. This was true in a way, since his troops carried measles, the Black Death, and an unknown pestilential fever which, spreading from Mission to Mission as he walked amongst them, caused many thousands to perish miserably.

"'Death precedes and follows him,' those poor creatures in their superstitious ignorance said. Smallpox followed; and Nature, disturbed in some manner, devastated our whole peninsula with great whirlwinds, tremendous hurricanes, and innumerable waterspouts, which tore up and destroyed many of those trails the Jesuits had built.

"Serra's *Visitador-General*, Galvez, who prepared this trip to Alta California for him, was forty days in crossing our Gulf; and Serra's supply vessel, the *San Carlos*, arrived at San Diego after having been a hundred and eight days in making less than five hundred miles. It reached San Diego with only two men on board able to stand up. The rest were so ill with scurvy that an anchor could not be dropped, nor sails taken in, until help came from shore.

[1] In 1697. [2] In 1717. [3] In 1722.

"His second supply ship, the *San Antonio,* was only fifty-four days from its Sinaloa port when it sailed past Serra at San Diego in a heavy fog, before Serra's first supply ship, the *San Carlos,* had arrived. Had the *San Antonio* been a day later in arriving at San Diego from the north, where it had been seeking the San Diego harbor, starvation would have forced abandonment of Serra's settlement of Alta California. Famine, drought, and earthquakes pursued all Serra's work.[1]

"I can understand," continued the Dominican friar, "that superseded Indian gods may by their sorceries have caused much of Serra's troubles in both Lower and Alta California, but at times I wonder whether Jesuit control of Nature, as shown by Salvatierra's freedom from locust flights, had to do with Franciscan troubles. We know Franciscans complained to the King that Jesuits were working gold mines without paying to the King of Spain his tenth. This, of course, poisoned the King's mind."

Both Don Firmín Sanhudo and the Dominican knew how Padre Kino[2] explained the resurrection of men's souls to the Indians. Padre Kino drowned flies until they lay apparently dead. Then, placing them in the sun and blowing upon them, as he said the Holy Ghost treats our souls, the flies came to life again and flew upward in a sunbeam as our souls fly to Heaven.

I carried Padre Kino's story farther for Don Firmín Sanhudo. The revival of the Kino flies made a vast sensation among our Indians, and for years I had heard old servants discuss this miracle. At a great pow-wow of which ancient Indians have often gossiped to me, three old native women were drowned. The Indian magicians were then ordered to restore these women to life as Padre Kino had given new life to the flies. If not all, then at least one woman must be restored to life, if wizards and sorcerers were to be longer respected. As all these women perversely remained dead, multitudes of our *Indiada* worshiped Padre Kino and his Cross, and thus made

[1] In a single year—1812—scarcely a Mission church in Southern California was left standing.

[2] In 1683.

Salvatierra's work among them easier. Don Firmín laughed at this, as I have always done; but Doña Ysabel flushed with anger that women could be so treated, and the Dominican friar crossed himself, saying: "How wonderful are Thy ways, O Lord!"

When nearing San Ygnacio, two events fastened themselves in my memory. We had heavy rain falling sudden from a cloudless sky. This drenched every one of us to the bone but did no damage to Doña Ysabel and the little girls since a torrid sun shone even while it rained, and dried us off almost as fast as we were wetted. Don Firmín explained this as water from a distant cloudburst, carried by violent winds which dropped it on us at such an angle as left the sun still shining over us. But Doña Ysabel sniffed, saying: "Another time warn me beforehand, rather than afterward explain why. A butterfly and a woman need shelter from rain, not reasons for having been drenched!"

Inocente smothered his face in his hands, but finally laughed shrilly through his fingers.

"See, Mamma!" he called. "You and Juanito's hinny are acting in the same way." For my hinny, having set her ears forward to hear the coming storm, had been surprised by sunny rain. Now at every step she shook her head violently to expel water from her ears. Doña Ysabel also tossed her head to throw off those raindrops which dripped continually from her hair. Fortunately, she had recovered her temper and laughed with Inocente, shaking herself violently until he, who rode beside her, thought himself in another rainstorm. At this we all felt free to laugh, and Don Firmín called, "These desert rains are full of sun and of sunny people." At which reproof she blushed and sat her saddle quietly; but by and by, leaning from her mule toward Inocente, she pinched him until his mouth opened widely as if ready to howl with pain. She shook a finger at him, and they rode hand in hand, laughing each time their eyes met.

The second event of our trip, and one which lingered long in my mind, occurred as we neared the Arroyo Carrisal in which was the Mission of San Ygnacio Kadakaaman. While still a few miles distant, we were met by a gaunt, sun-baked man riding at a fast gallop, who looked neither to right nor to left as he passed us. This was the monthly mail carrier who bore the King's letters.

For a thousand miles from Monterey to San José del Arroyo he had right of way; right of food; and right to horse or mule over all humans in the Californias. Often as a child I had dreamed concerning these men, for they were more sacred even than priests or governors. In Boton's rebellion, four Missions were burned and three priests killed, but our Governor did nothing. Then a mail carrier, ignoring rebellions and contemptuous of tumults, rode at a gallop through a band of those rebels, and that poisonous half-breed, Chicori, dared to kill him.

At once five hundred Yaqui Indians were brought from Sonora, and of four thousand natives soon only four hundred survived. The orders were to kill all who could have been within forty miles of this dead mail carrier. Not being slothful, these Yaquis exterminated all natives within sixty miles of this mail carrier's grave.

"House with lions or sleep with rattlesnakes," we said, "but never delay our King's letters."

One man delivered mail from Monterey to Todos Santos del Sur, five hundred and sixty leagues in fifty days. From the City of Mexico to Monterey, Don Firmín's letters were carried in ninety days, of which thirty was the time allowance from Loreto to Monterey.

These men were not allowed to leave the main road nor to lay aside their arms, nor even dismount unless essential. They ate on horseback and slept when they must with the mail-bag under their bellies. At each presidio four horses by day and eight at night stood saddled for their selection, and every Mission must have ready its best stock when the mail carrier was expected. If his horse fell or his mule died, he ran on foot with his letter-bag, and from the first he met— were that one official, priest, or rich man—he took his mount, and galloped on without even a backward glance at him thus left on foot.

Justo Roverto, carrying this mail from Monterey, was caught in a cloudburst at the *Malpaso del Infierno*,[1] north of San Ygnacio, and lost both horse and mail-bag. Running like a madman he reported his loss to the padre in charge at Kadakaaman Mission, then cut his own throat, standing at salute before the King's picture. For this reason, when mail carriers (on furlough) drank, they raised their glasses and called loudly, "To Justo." In the year 1900—for being born in 1798, I have passed the eighteen hundreds and reached the nineteens with better sight and hearing than when I began life in the seventeens—I heard a tipsy Mexican say, "To Justo," as he drank, but not knowing why. Thus do great reputations become merely exclamations.

Had it not been for the Sanhudos' kindness to me and Hidalgo's rebellion, I would have become a mail carrier. They were built of fine steel, needing neither rest, sleep, nor food, when at work. He who offered them drink while they were riding the mail risked his life from them or from our Governor. When their trip was done, they had twenty-four hours' rest with pay for each day they had ridden, which made a pleasant life.

When we arrived at the high cliff which overlooks San Ygnacio Kadakaaman, the Dominican *fraile* halted for a moment, and, pointing toward our zigzag road leading downward through many turns and twists to the Mission, said:

"See for yourselves what glorious work one devoted man can do. Padre Juan Bautista Luyando found here wild heathen without souls. They lived naked, and with no shelter from sun, wind, or rain except dry[2] stone walls, five feet high, roofless and doorless.

"Using only his own fortune and his own time, he left behind him Christianized Indians devoted to him. When he set one tribe at work building the road by which we are now descending, and another constructing that by which we shall travel north, competition to please him by quick completion of their work became intense. It is said that our Indians were lazy, but they needed only a leader loved

---

[1] *Malpaso del Infierno:* Hell's back door.   [2] Made without mortar.

and respected. Those two tribes of *Chokimas* worked early and late without wages: poorly fed, lacking proper tools, and in a soil which makes road-building difficult and laborious. Their only pay was approbation of Father Luyando, who would praise both parties of workers, but chiefly those who first completed their task. Therefore, the southern tribe, which was being beaten in its *takio*,[1] stole from Padre Luyando a piece of his writing paper. Making on this paper some scribbling marks, they forced a house servant to take it to the northern road-builders as orders from Padre Luyando that they stop work at once, thus allowing the southern tribe to finish their road first.

"Is not that true devotion? How many of us would attempt such hard labor for God as this road shows? And much less for any man!"

For my part I listened with difficulty to the Dominican's sermon, for my eyes and mind were fixed on our volcano of Las Virgenes, then in sight. I thought only of all the traditions and superstitions which centered there. It was this volcano, all Indian wizards and sorcerers insisted, which, bursting into rage at some unknown insult from ravens which were also gods, bellowed and spouted flame until that pleasant Gulfland, which then connected Lower California with Sinaloa, sank, and salt water for the first time flowed in and formed my Vermilion Sea.

It was a pleasant country of fertile, rolling hills, tradition states, and inhabited by those strange beasts I saw in the Loreto Pearl Cave. Or, rather, it was the heads of these beasts turned into stone I there saw. Of these animals even I could never make the Indians talk. Into that fertile Gulfland our grasshoppers flew for so many centuries, seeking their food, that this flight became their habit. Now these locusts perish in the waters of that Gulf where formerly they fed.

"Why do you worship *chimbecas*,[2] which are cowardly brutes?" I asked the natives.

"It is an oath," Indians answered.

[1] *Takio:* work allotted to a man or tribe for completion by an allotted time.

[2] *Chimbecas:* mountain lions.

"Oaths are easily broken," I retorted.

But the Indians only trembled and stopped my mouth with their hands, saying: "Not this oath. It is true these lions hunt us as they do deer, and we avoid killing them, but how many of us do they eat in a year? Very few. Whereas, the father of these lions was brave and killed us for mere pleasure of slaughter. If we break our oath this father will return," and their teeth chattered with fear.

"And these ravens?" I asked. "You catch a fish and they take it from your very hands and eat it, sitting within a foot of you. Not until these birds are full fed can you also satisfy your hunger."

But they only answered: "Juanito of the Volcano Hair, even your red head would not save us if we broke our oath to the ancestors of these ravens. Greedy and lazy these birds are, but not so were their fathers, who did not eat fish. Rather they then preferred to eat us. You have seen buzzards swallow the eyes of half-dead cows; and we know that which happened in our past."

Here at San Ygnacio Kadakaaman, José Robea dug from a cliff the bones and skull of a stone man eleven feet high. Here there was a river which emptied into San Rafael Bay, and along its banks were many caves and boiling springs, which covered the lagoon water with red and blue patches of color. No one knew where this color came from, nor what it meant. Possibly, therefore, it was well to propitiate ravens, since it was little trouble to feed them a few fish.

On our arrival at San Ygnacio Kadakaaman, Doña Ysabel went at once to pray at the church, which was called the most elaborate in California, and was of hewn stone four feet thick. Inocente, by guile, escaped being taken with his sisters to this shrine, and together we waded the stream and played with rafts upon a lake six miles long and which was praised everywhere as the largest in Lower California. With all this water there was little soil for cultivation, since those floods which followed the Franciscans into my country had washed away all irrigated land at this Mission.

[1] In 1770.

San Ygnacio was near a long lagoon and was, therefore, rich in sea food, as also in dates; but best of all, I found there many sea-otter skins. With a few pesos those Loreto officials had paid me for my advice regarding the *empleado* who lost his teeth, I bought many of these beautiful pelts and gave them to the little Sanhudo girls.

For them we also invented a story which Inocente told them. He whispered to them that these furs had been cast off by beautiful princesses, turned into seals long ago by Indian enchanters; but that the princesses were now, by Don Firmín's coming, released from their enchantments and restored to their kingdoms. Probably Inocente added that I had myself had something to do with freeing these princesses, for when I next saw his little sisters they looked at me with wondering, widely opened eyes, which caused a longing within me for real enchanters that I might vanquish. But one who begins life barefoot has no time to seek adventures with sorcerers.

That night a half-breed, who had the day before killed a lion, received from the padre of San Ygnacio Kadakaaman a bull; a live bull for a dead lion's hide being there the customary exchange. So great was the festival which followed that before morning even its bones had been pounded into soup. I heard this padre tell Doña Ysabel that, because of the howling of lions, he had not slept for four nights. But now he hoped that one killed would prevent the rest from coming so close to his Mission.

CHAPTER 19. *We Said Our Prayers to Satan at Hell's Back Door—The Mission of Santa Gertrudis—The First Wine Made in the Californias—Padre Serra's Kindly Action*

O UR ROAD NORTHWARD from the Mission of San Ygnacio Kadakaaman was over steep, barren ridges, separated by sandy *arroyos;* but to them we paid little attention, since all knew the *Malpaso* lay ahead of us. He is, indeed, foolish who worries over small troubles when great tribulations await him. Even our mules must have heard those of San Ygnacio discuss this *Infierno,* for they twitched their ears and clung timidly close together as they did at smell of a bear. When a pack needed arranging, all that mule's chums hung about, crowding the *arrieros:* brushing against them with their packs, and if kicked, clumsily stepping upon some other packer's foot. Therefore, I did what I could to hurry the Sanhudos ahead so *arrieros* could swear their troubles away.

It is always better to curse a mule than to kick him; and when these animals are nervous, as they were that day, their drivers must either curse or kick. To my mind, it heartens a mule to hear good swearing, whereas silence terrifies him.

I remember, years later, a grizzly bear suddenly crossed the trail ahead of my pack-train, and being then a full grown man, I said my prayers to Satan so resolutely that my mules crouched and quivered, whispering among themselves their certainty, through my oaths, that I was more to be feared than any bear. As for the bear, he slouched along scratching his left ear,[1] into which my language flowed, and each moment less inclined to eat mule meat.

Not that I hold with those who habitually praise Satan by curses. There is a time for all things except getting drunk; and some say that, had I married, I would make no exception.

This *Malpaso del Infierno* was high and steep enough on the southern side, though passable; but on the north only birds climbed it without fear, and they looked down with wonder at the endurance and courage of those wingless human beings who risked such a passage.

The bottom of this great cañon contained only a dry *pedregal*[2] deposited by that last cloudburst which had torn through this gash in towering cliffs at lightning speed. This rain wave must have been at least sixty feet deep, since it had left behind it a thick pine-tree trunk balanced on a projecting pinnacle of at least that height. Some later flood would in its turn tear out all those vast boulders over which, with difficulty and danger, we now must clamber, and leave behind it new difficulties for the next unfortunates. Like ourselves, they would shudder each moment they were detained here, since no day and no hour could be counted safe from those enormous cloudbursts, which came without warning and left nothing behind them which had been there when they arrived.

One could measure the height of each inundation by long gashes worn into the cliff's faces by boulders borne too swiftly to sink. At bends in this cañon the hard rock had been so deeply cut by these rough graving tools as to leave a perpetual memorial; unless some later flood reached the same height and thus obliterated old scorings by making new ones.

At the southern edge of this *Malpaso* our whole party halted, while half of our Mayas on foot advanced to the *pedregal*, examining

1 *Left ear:* The truth, justifiable praise, and good advice, we believe, enter the right ear. Curses, flattery, and bad advice enter the left ear.—*A de F. B.*

2 *Pedregal:* mass of jagged rocks.

every foot of soil for tracks which might indicate enemies awaiting us; then, up and down the *arroyo,* until certain no ambush had been set for us. While unChristianized natives hereabouts were reputed gentle, yet at this spot more lives had been lost within two hundred years than at any other place in California. Worn by frightful heat, due to a torrid sun untempered by clouds and reflected from polished stone in this box cañon, even the most cautious travelers became careless, and therefore lost their lives.

The Mayas having satisfied themselves that no one lurked in this cañon, it was then occupied by half of our *soldados de cuero* as foot soldiers, while Mayas ran up the northern trail, tracing every side *arroyo* to its source, and with noses almost to the rock watching for tracks or sweat drops of any who might have preceded us. Once on top of the northern cliff, they spread about looking for warm ashes or bits of food, by which careless enemies might have betrayed their presence. As I watched them, they seemed to me more like very alert dogs tracking hares than men. I greatly admired them, because no matter how steep or slippery the trail, their hands never left their dagger-hilts. More than one man has lost his life by the time needed to raise his fingers to a knife-handle.

All being thought secure, two Mayas advanced, and, with hats off in apology, each took one of Doña Ysabel's elbows; and almost raising her from the ground, hurried like cats treading on wet grass down the trail, across the *pedregal* and up the northern side. Don Firmín Sanhudo with two Mayas had preceded Doña Ysabel, and following her came the little girls, each carried. Half of our *soldados de cuero* followed on foot, of course, while Doña Ysabel's women servants scattered themselves as best they might between these escorts.

Muleros had already begun carrying stone to a *brincón*[1] on the northern side, too high for our *mulada* to ascend. *Arrieros,* meanwhile, packed dirt from the southern cliff-top on our spare mules, and this, dumped over the stone filling, left this *brincón* so that the

[1] *Brincón:* a low cliff.

forelegs of an animal could reach over its top. This smooth stone top had been roughened as much as possible by our only two picks. So scarce were tools in my country that even Don Firmín Sanhudo could obtain only two picks for his trip.

"Your hinny was born of a cat and sired by a bird," said the foreman of *arrieros* politely to me, and I was, therefore, compelled to let her be the first to make this dangerous ascent; since one must either accept a compliment or deny its truth. *Madre de Dios!* How I sweated blood while leading my poor brute! She, snorting, picked her way across this *pedregal,* smelling before she set down a hoof, testing each foothold, and at chasms leaping like a goat and landing with her four hoofs together on the very center of a boulder, lest her weight on either edge cause it to shift.

At the *brincón,* first smelling with extended neck all about its top, she threw her forelegs over, and by a tremendous upward heave of hindquarters landed on its polished, sloping surface, snorting and trembling, but safe.

Thence to the top this trail was a succession of rapidly rising shelves of smooth rock, slippery like that ice I saw years after on top of San Pedro Martyr Mountains. On this stiffened water in a basin left half-full overnight, my cook, who had never even heard of ice, at earliest dawn bruised his nose when attempting to dip his face in the basin.

Every foot of this path up the *Malpaso del Infierno* was so narrow that my stirrups must be tied over my saddle, lest on the ascent they strike against the inner vertical cliff and thus perhaps push my hinny over and down a hundred or five hundred feet, as Satan had arranged these precipices. For most of the ascent, this trail sloped not only steeply upward, but also slanted so sharply sidewise, toward the abyss, that mules instinctively leaned toward the vertical cliff rising beside them on the inside of the trail. Crowding thus against this cliff, they were sometimes pushed over at sharp turns, where less fear on their parts would have taken them safely past the dangerously narrow points. These turns, which should have been curves, were usually sharp right angles, which were hard upon the backbone of a mule. I know my hinny several times expected to break in half in the middle, and looked at me so piteously that I would have turned back had that not been more dangerous than continuing upward.

At the top of this infernal ascent, I was so wet through with sweat, half caused by the long, hard climb and half by anxiety regarding my hinny, that the little Sanhudo girls, seeing perspiration falling from my face, came to me running, and calling: "Mama! Mama! Juanito is crying. His mule must be hurt." But my hinny answered them by such a loud and prolonged bray of triumph over the cliff's edge, at having won the ascent, that they ran back to hide themselves in their mother's skirts. Every *mulero* and *arriero* in our outfit gave my pet a piece of *panocha* that night, for the triumph in her bray saved many a mule which, disheartened by dangers of this *Malpaso*, might otherwise have lost confidence and fallen into the abyss. Already buzzards had gathered there, well knowing no pack-train ever passed without leaving them food, whether with four legs or two.

Where a mule has recently passed, other mules follow with little difficulty, stepping in his footprints and jumping where he jumped; so that our only real trouble came at those places where some careless mule of ours had fallen over the cliff. The next behind him on this trail, seeing the mule fall, or smelling traces of his struggles where he had lost his balance, stopped dead and began to tremble like an aspen leaf. The mule would have brayed to warn and discourage the other mules behind it had not an *arriero,* life in hand, climbed under or around those terrified animals and with his club driven the balky one onward or over the cliff. This destruction of panic-stricken mules was essential, since once these terrified animals began to crowd each other on a narrow ledge, a whole pack-train might be lost over such cliffs.

"Kill one rather than lose all" was a motto well known to packers.

Following me, after my ascent, came our old gray mare; fat, because she did no work, troublesome, because all mules deferred to her, and careless, as knowing herself of vast importance to us. Two *arrieros* led her, one by a long rope halter and the other with a riata about her belly, while two more followed, ready, by pushing at risk of their lives, to save her from a slip, or recover her if half-fallen.

This mare was indispensable; since thus is a mule born, that he must have a friend or a mother: and losing this friend, he goes crazy. Then, unless caught at once, he will gallop about, braying perpetually, until, worn out by travel, thirst, and starvation, he falls dead. To eat, drink, or sleep without a friend or a mother is impossible.

Once "lost," he will gallop madly through a herd of those animals he has been with for months, without recognition of them; and unless yoked to another mule for a day or two, he is incapable of recovery. Therefore, as on a trip like ours many mules must perish and their inseparable mates become a nuisance, all pack-trains take an old gray mare, which from the first day is a mother to every mule in the train.

For horses mules care little, and for mares of other colors scarcely more, but for a dapple-gray mare they have an attachment so passionate that they yield to tyranny from her which they accept from no other animal. With teeth and legs such an aged mare will drive all the hungry young *mulada* from hay or grain, even though herself already full fed. They accept with humility the grossest forms of abuse. If a lion or a bear cross their trail, they crowd about their adopted mother to protect her; though otherwise, fear would drive them insane. Where she goes, they follow or perish.

At this *Malpaso* which I have just described, Tempis Gerónimo, with twenty mules, bound to claim a land grant in Alta California, allowed his dapple mare to slip over the cliff. Caught on a pinnacle, she unluckily had life enough in her to whinny once, and therefore every one of his riding- and pack-mules, whether by accident or intention, followed their "mother" to death, taking several of his *arrieros* with them.

Don Tempis Gerónimo and his family nearly died of thirst and hunger before they reached San Ygnacio Kadakaaman on foot, and he was ruined by this catastrophe. Becoming insane through this misfortune, he later, when money was earned by him or his boys, spent it in buying gray mares. These he killed, claiming that he thus destroyed female devils, and that if he had enough gold he might thus depopulate Hell. With all their females dead, devils could no longer breed and their race must perish, he thought.

Following our dapple mare came all our riding- and pack-mules, but the latter without *aparejos*, as these leather pack-bags were so bulky as possibly to catch on projecting rocks or at sharp turns on this narrow trail. They would thus force a mule into the abyss. Where four-footed animals must place one hoof directly in front of the other, because of a narrow trail, or at places jump from such a pinched track across a gulf and land on another ledge equally constricted, the least side resistance or push tumbles them to death.

Between each four mules on the ascent of the *Malpaso* came an *arriero* or *mulero,* as it was essential to stop crowding, and especially to prevent some scared animal turning around at a gulf it feared to jump across. These men faced dangers for which I had little stomach. They must in such cases crawl under terrified mules balanced on cliff edges. Or, if this proved to be impossible, then they must mount the animals' backs and jump from one to another of these swaying, frightened brutes, until they reached the balky one. This one must be immediately driven onward or else forced over the cliffs. Then it was no trifling job for such a man to resume his proper place, by passing again over or under animals wild with terror at what they had seen him do to one of their own kind.

At the top of the *Malpaso*, I stood near the trail's mouth, holding our old mare where all mules could see her as they reached the last ascent. Thus no crazy mule would think of returning to seek a lost mate, and so block the way for those still climbing the trail. Others of our party stood in a half-circle from cliff to cliff, holding back from further travel all mules as they arrived.

We lost few animals in this ascent, though many were scratched and bleeding, so that for a week we had our troubles to prevent maggots from breeding on such raw flesh. Powdered oak bark, of which we had much, is the only remedy, as it hardens their flesh; whereas grease, such as the ignorant use, softens new skin and continues the danger.

Then came that endless carrying of our mule cargoes which, when finished, left our *arrieros* and *muleros* mere wrecks of men. Had they not been selected from those who had worked with mules from generation to generation, they would have died from their first trip. Six *arrobas* are more than a man's proper load on level ground. Add an ascent too steep in places to stand upright on, and slippery footing sloping steeply to vertical cliffs, and one wondered that man could do what these men did.

Yet up this same trail Father Salvatierra climbed, taking that part of the load which belonged to him, and among Indians who did not always hold him in respect. These old *frailes* were better than we who followed them. When I remember that Salvatierra made this four-hundred-mile desert trip, inspecting his Missions, I regret at times those torments I devised for his successors at San José del Arroyo.

In all this exhausting work of carrying pack-outfits and pack-cargoes across the *pedregal* and up the northern side of this *Malpaso del Infierno,* neither I nor our *soldados de cuero* nor the Mayas helped in any way. In fighting, agility and quickness as well as strength are needed; and while a laborer may have more strength, he is slow in thought and action. In all my life I have never seen a hoe-handler kill a knife-man, unless he struck from behind. As our old proverb says, "One must choose between hoe and dagger."

We reached Santa Gertrudis worn out by our trip from San Ygnacio. Though this Mission was in a deep and gloomy *cañada,* so narrow that room for the church could only be made by shelving out one rocky side, we were forced to spend a week there to rest and cure our mules. Here were only a few peach and olive trees, though grapevines did so well that Padre Retz,[1] so the Dominican priest told us, fermented in these stone cisterns the first wine ever made in any of the Three Californias.

[1] About 1755.

In one of these tanks cut out of solid rock and covered with stone slabs, they kept part of this first wine crop, and annually refilled it, though never more than half-emptied. To each of us was given a small cup of it, that we might boast we had drunk of wine which was parent of all wine since made in the Californias.

At this Mission of Santa Gertrudis, Padre Retz at one time had fourteen-hundred Indian learners. He was greatly helped by our most famous Indian, a blind man named Comanji, who began his work by wandering for two months in these steep mountains until God led him to a spring. This water the blind man inspired his tribe to carry to Santa Gertrudis, through an aqueduct cut out of solid stone in order that not a drop of water might be lost. Then the Indians formed land by carrying dirt in baskets, which they spread on rock cut into terraces, and planted with orchards and gardens. The church in which this blind Indian taught as native assistant to Padre Retz was of stone, but all other buildings were of adobe and small stones, roofed with tules.

This Mission was helpful to us, since they had here a carpenter shop and smithy; which was unusual in my country, and still more uncommon in Alta California as I first saw it. Here I bought an *almud* of dried fruit for distribution among those who had praised my hinny for her encouraging bray at the *Malpaso*.

One of those kindly actions which made the Franciscan Padre Serra so loved occurred here, if the Dominican who journeyed with us spoke truly. Padre Serra was traveling hurriedly north to join Captain Portola, who had preceded him, and who was so anxious to continue his way to Alta California that he threatened to leave Serra behind. Stopping for one night at Santa Gertrudis, this padre found there a young Franciscan missionary, merely a boy, just graduated from the College of San Fernando in Mexico, and almost insane from loneliness. Only ignorant Indians were about him. There were no Mission guards with whom he might speak, and leagues of desert separated him from the nearest white man.

Three days Serra spent here, praying with and teaching this poor boy, and he left him so uplifted in soul that five years later the boy wept when, for the first time, he left this Mission. Serra then continued his way to Santa Maria of the Angels, hurrying to make up for lost time in spite of a foot ulcer and an open leg sore which threatened his life, but which were cured by an Indian wizard, who wished him no good, but desired him to leave his tribal territory.

Leaving Santa Gertrudis and on our way to San Francisco Borja, we were tried by a dazzling white soil which so reflected the sun's rays that we were all half-blind by the second day, and mules stumbled against mules, biting and kicking to show they also were ill-tempered from dazed eyes. Quicksand in *arroyos,* and some springs and streams, poisoned by Satan, troubled us little, since, when a mule drowned or a thirsty man could not drink from a spring because his mule refused the water as poisoned, we said only, "The *Malpaso* is behind us," and were so cheered by this thought that all annoyance passed away from us.

CHAPTER 20. *Gossip Regarding Maria Borgia,
Duchess of Gandia—She Sent That Brilliant Jesuit,
Winceslao Link, to This Desolation of San Francisco
Borja to Save Her Own Soul—Don Firmín Compares
Padre Lasuén and Padre Serra—The Mission of San
Francisco Borja—Doña Ysabel Asks that the Trails
North of This Mission Shall be Included in the List
of California Pests Her Little Girl is Keeping—
The Mission of San Fernando Velicata—The Lost
Mission of Santa Ysabel and Its Treasure*

DOÑA ISABEL STOPPED on a ridge overlooking the broad
arroyo of San Francisco Borja, and examined that Mission
with greater curiosity than I had seen her show regarding any of our
settlements.

"Maria Borgia, Duchess of Gandia, obtained, in heavenly credits
for her soul, a golden peso[1] for every silver peso of the sixty thousand expended for her on this Mission of San Francisco Borja,"
Doña Ysabel said. "That was what this Duchess always demanded;
but God's mercy! What a place to send a brilliant Jesuit like
Winceslao Link!" She half-laughed, half-sighed as she looked down
upon the church and buildings, all showing that desolation which
came to our Missions when their Jesuit builders were exiled from
them. Yet this Mission was in better condition, I thought, than most.

[1] A golden peso is of the value of $11.28, and a silver peso, fifty cents.

Then, in answer to a glance from Don Firmín Sanhudo, Doña Ysabel went on:

"She was my grandmother's friend, and there was gossip about her all over Spain, because she felt so shamed by her name of Borgia that she founded this Mission on condition that San Francisco 'Borgia' should thereafter be called San Francisco 'Borja,' which is the ancient Spanish name of all the Borgias.

"She was descended from Saint Francis Borgia, who was grandson of Pope Alexander VI, and nephew of Caesar and Lucretia Borgia. Caesar killed his brother, the Saint's father, because Pope Alexander favored him too much. It is a curious family, always eccentric, whether for vice or religion; but always brilliant and cultivating the arts and literature. Caesar Borgia claimed, so Doña María, the Duchess of Gandia, said, that he did more for the Italian language than any other patron of letters, since authors must praise him if they valued their lives; and that thus they acquired a finesse and control of the Italian language not previously known.

"As for Saint Francis, God's justice! How he would have adored this place! Desolate mountains towering to the sky; no grass; cactus covering the ground; and everywhere half-starved hares and rabbits relentlessly pursued by famished coyotes! To drink—only vile-smelling sulphur water which must cool before one, shuddering, swallows it, because thirst forces. A soil so sterile that even our pitahaya, which loathes rain, will not fruit there. To eat—mescal which must be roasted twelve hours while one waits and starves. At times a few tasteless dates. No pasture land, and from scarcity of water only the smallest garden. Padre Link planted the first garden with his own hands, and, when it was just ready to furnish him food, it was pulled up by stupid Indians, who mistook his orders as to greens for Palm Sunday.

"Then the Holy Spirit led Padre Link to a pasture for his cattle, but fifty-four miles away! Think of driving your milch cows fifty-four miles to be milked twice a day! Or was it only once? I know it all!" Doña Ysabel shuddered. "Maria Borgia explained it thoroughly to my grandmother, who adored her and me; and I, when a child, often wondered why the Holy Spirit had not placed a pasture for eight hundred cattle nearer to this Mission.

"Saint Francis of Borgia was always my ideal, and as a girl I vowed myself a halo and canonization if I could ever find such perfection to lead me to Heaven. The handsomest man in Spain or Italy, and one of the richest; Duke of Gandia, which is not a bad title, and Prince of Benevento, if he chose to claim it. A Borgia, which meant great ability and the world at his feet. An admirable courtier and a perfect lover. Yet all things with dignity and grace. Then he saw a dead Queen in her coffin; and waiting calmly until his wife died and his dozen children were safely grown, he, because of this dead Queen, renounced this world and became General of the Jesuits; thus ruling the world he had abandoned. He died, exclaiming to priests about him:

"'God pardon my life! But to enter His presence after signing an appointment to office for this ungodly man, as you request, would be impossible!'

"That was a Saint for you, but I think I like the wicked Borgias better than the fanatic ones. Besides, Doña María de Borgia was always in my old nurse's mouth, and therefore bored me even as a child. She insisted that, if one desired to live a luxurious life, it was necessary to save one's soul by paying some priest to exist in privation and misery."

Doña Ysabel touched her mount with a spur and trotted down the almost vertical declivity toward the Mission at a pace which caused anxiety to every mule in the outfit. Not because of the risk she ran, but lest they be asked to do the same.

Don Firmín Sanhudo was equally interested in this Mission for another reason—because Padre Lasuén, the ablest of the Franciscans, had remained here alone for five years, daily dreading insanity because of loneliness, and wearing for sixty months the only suit of clothes he possessed.

"The Indians," Lasuén wrote to a friend, "get on so well with me because I am nearly as naked as they."

"There have been only three great priests in the Californias," gossiped Don Firmín, talking to his wife as we rode to the Mission of San Francisco Borja. "Salvatierra, Ugarte, and Lasuén, and this last was not the least. He received the Presidency of Alta California Missions when there were but eight hundred *gentes de razón* in all of Alta California. Of these most were children and practically all half-breeds. In 1797, when seventy-eight years old, he himself founded four great Missions—San José del Norte, San Juan Bautista, San Fernando Rey, and San Miguel—in one year, which is more work than any predecessor had ever accomplished. At eighty-three he died, leaving twenty thousand Christianized Indians in his Missions.

"Compare Lasuén's results, in saving souls, with those of Serra, who is so greatly praised by priests. Having begun his missionary work in 1769, Serra's Missions—San Diego, San Gabriel, San Luis Obispo, San Antonio, and San Carlos—had in 1773 only sixty-two baptized Indians—scarcely more than a single convert for each of Serra's priests in four years! *Madre de Dios!* From how little can a great reputation be made! The King asked me to kneel at Serra's grave because he thought him to have been our wisest man in California!

"Yet, but for Governor Fages' famous grizzly bear hunt at San Luis Obispo,[1] California would have been abandoned to Russians or to the English.

"Serra was a man of boundless energy," continued Don Firmín Sanhudo. "Starting from Loreto he walked fifty-four miles to Comondu before midday. Thence thirty miles to the Purísima: and sleeping alone upon the ground for two nights, one hundred and eleven miles to Guadalupe. His pack-mules arrived three days later. On he went, seventy-five miles to San Ygnacio Kadakaaman Mission, with one night's sleep upon the ground, and living upon raisins and figs carried in his pockets. Thus he went on to Alta California in spite of ulcers upon his leg and foot which a black-smith, with a wizard's salve, cured. What an admirable walker! But

[1] In 1772.

a leader works with his brain, not with his legs; and no man can labor hard with both.

When we left San Francisco Borja, the Dominican priest in charge walked with us, reluctant to remain alone again. Overcome by pity for him, Doña Ysabel exerted herself to charm him, which no one knew better than she how to accomplish. As we looked eastward from a hilltop, Angel's Island, with its streams and pasture lands, beautified my Vermilion Sea and made us regret excessively those arid wastes and ruined Missions which lay ahead of us.

Near this place, north of San Francisco Borja, its Indians told me, is that famous spot called "The Arrow's Flight." When their ancestors came to this country, carried by a great white bird, their Indian chief, standing in Philippine (Pacific) ocean surf, shot an arrow which killed an antelope drinking from the Vermilion Sea, then fresh water, they say. Thus an arrow's flight was the width of Lower California at that time. As this antelope furnished the first meat they had eaten for so many weeks that starvation and a leg illness was upon them, the site of its death became sacred; and while an Indian lives it will be remembered. This spot is still the narrowest place on the Peninsula of Lower California, being only thirty-five miles across, but much stone and many high mountains must have been cast up by the sea since an arrow flew across it.

I asked these Indians why they so greatly feared lions, as without resistance to allow themselves, their women, and their children, to be hunted by lions as deer are stalked and eaten.

They answered: "These lions were enchanted by our wizards, but on condition that we feed them. If we resisted, they would break through all enchantments and again become what they once were." Beyond convulsions of fear at this thought, I could get nothing more.

After we had passed this Mission of San Francisco Borja, our trails become so bad that Doña Ysabel asked that they be included in that list of California pests which one of the little girls was keeping in her diary.

"Cholera or Black Death," she exclaimed, "may kill more certainly and more quickly than these trails, but one does not watch those forms of death approaching a hundred times a day and trust a mule's legs to carry one away safely!"

We passed up and down the sides of steep cañons, which had a hard stone above and soft below, so that not a mule dared to bray lest insecurely balanced tons of this hat rock might be disturbed and roll down upon us.

At the *Paraiso*,[1] twelve hundred feet deep, every man out of hearing of the Sanhudos swore violently at that angel or devil which, flying over this death-trap, had so named it as a jest upon all traveling humans who must later pass that way.

North of San Fernando Velicata were the *India Flaca*[2] plains, with bitter water and all discomfort; so you can think of our expedition as plodding through deep sand and sweating from intense heat, with only bitter alkaline water to drink, while I tell you of a conversation between Don Firmín and Doña Ysabel which will interest each one of you who has vainly hunted for the lost Jesuit Mission of Santa Ysabel.

They spoke in Spanish, so that I listened without hesitation; since for private matters they used French or Italian. French, I recognized because it is spoken through the nose, and I memorized a sentence of what Don Firmín had said in French to his wife, not knowing its meaning.

Repeating this sentence one day to Doña Ysabel very clearly through my nose, when we were alone, she at first was astounded, then puzzled, and finally laughed so long and with such hearty good will that I was delighted to have pleased her.

"Yes," she acknowledged, "that is French, and what a Frenchman would say to me if he dared." And laughed again until Don Firmín rode up to ask the cause.

As for Italian, it is like the cooing of doves, and you move your arms while speaking as a cock flaps its wings while crowing. He who

1 *Paraiso:* Paradise. 2 *India Flaca:* Starving Natives.

fights must keep silent in Italy, or his knives would be merely gestures, explaining his hate, but not satisfying his lust for blood.

"Listen, *esposa mia*," Don Firmín Sanhudo said to Doña Ysabel. "If I go to seek those great treasures left by the Jesuits at their deserted Mission of Santa Ysabel, I must go alone. I will leave with you all my men except six Mayas. They belong to me, and will not gossip regarding my find. A certain risk there is for me, as for you, but that risk is trifling.

"Here is the history. Remember it and decide, when you have heard it all.

"For ten years before the Jesuit expulsion from all Spanish domains, there had been much gossip in Spain regarding the Jesuit desire to establish in the Californias a pure theocracy, governed by them without regard to Spain or our King.

"Again tongues vibrated in Spain because the Jesuits had established in San Bartolo that *caballero* with whom we there stayed. All Spain thought that gentleman the true heir to the Spanish crown. They imagined him to be one falsely reported dead but saved by Jesuit guile for its own purposes. That he had been settled in the wilds of Lower California seemed wise to all, since he was safe there. Spain's local officials paid him high honors, and so gossiped, in their letters home, that this gentleman's right to rule Spain became every year more discussed.

"Also it was freely said in Madrid that our late King was illegitimate, being really the Queen's son by Alberoni, her favorite. Also that the Jesuits possessed, or had forged, proof that Charles III was a bastard. All gossip went to the King, and he, in listening to it, wasted his time which was needed for government and to prevent official corruption.

"The King expelled the Jesuits," continued Don Firmín. "The Franciscans have been accused as the cause of this expulsion. They profited by it, but did not cause it.

"When I was a child like Inocente, my father in Spain and his brothers in Mexico became uneasy. Something was in the air and all about them, but not even their best spies could piece together a cause for nervousness.

"Finally my father wrote to his brothers and cousins in Mexico: 'Something is about to happen, and Jesuits only could keep a secret which every leaf whispers, but no human understands.'

"His correspondents answered: 'So it is also in Mexico. This is the place to seek an answer to your question.'

"My father, therefore, went to Mexico, and placed in each Mission a confidential man, who was already an initiate. From each spy so placed by my father came reports that Jesuit shrines everywhere were being stripped by the Society of Jesus of all votive offerings and adornments of jewelry and gold, but that silver was left untouched. Finally, from a northern spy, my father located a boat which made repeated trips across the Vermilion Sea, but its port in Lower California was unknown. The treasure thus transported from all the richest shrines in Mexico was later to be used by the Jesuits in retaking the Californias when Spanish official corruption had driven Spain from the Americas.

"One of my father's trusted men was on this treasure boat, and from him came a map showing where, at the Mission of Santa Ysabel, all this vast treasure from Mexican shrines was being buried. This was the accumulation of two hundred years from the then richest country in the world: and not only the richest, but that land most loyal to our Church.

"Then all his spies disappeared, and my father prepared for death, thinking the Jesuits had discovered his efforts to locate their treasure; but it was only that those who handle secret wealth for others have short lives.

"Later, within an hour, every Jesuit in Mexico was arrested, imprisoned, or deported in such haste that a third of them died on the road to Italy. At once my father understood Jesuit efforts to save their wealth; but being a cautious man, indisposed to risks, he left this secret for me, saying: "In your time perhaps you can make this treasure available, but not in mine."

"Therefore, when the King offered me this post in Mexico, I willingly accepted. The more readily because, having supreme authority in all the Californias, it would be possible for me to obtain and remove all this treasure, provided there were no gossip.

"With the money thus provided by Jesuit hoards, this California colony can perhaps be retained for Spain. Without it, revolution will take the Californias from Spain, as it will all of South America. I shall need a month for my trip, for this lost Mission of Santa Ysabel is at the base of an impassable cliff seven thousand feet high. Its desert entrance was purposely blocked by a great landslide when Jesuit priests, abandoning it, retired to Sonora. There they awaited news of that expulsion from California and Mexico, of which all Jesuits knew months in advance, but of which no word was said outside their Order."

Don Firmín Sanhudo sighed at this evidence of silence and obedience, saying: "If in government the King could obtain such loyalty as these Jesuits showed, with what ease could I retain the Spanish colonies for him!

"My map," he continued, "shows a mountain sheep's trail passable for laden mules, and by this I can secure from the deserted Mission of Santa Ysabel that which I seek. Santa Ysabel is your own name Saint, and she should aid us."

They sat then long silent, and finally Doña Ysabel, with her head upon his shoulder, refused to permit him to leave her.

"I will go where you go," she exclaimed, "but to be left alone in these vast, silent deserts would drive me mad. I know your name protects us, and that your brothers would sail a ship over these mountains on blood alone, were we injured; but I had rather live than be amply avenged when dead."

Don Firmín sighed, and they walked on. Therefore, this great treasure of the long-lost Mission of Santa Ysabel still awaits a finder.

At first I was greatly pleased that Don Firmín Sanhudo trusted my silence concerning this great affair. Later, I was less pleased, for I had seen no map, nor heard any location discussed except that the lost Mission with its great treasure lay on the desert side of San Pedro Martyr. This is a great range of mountains nine thousand feet high, and a hundred and fifty miles long. Had I desired to search for this Mission, it would have been like seeking some special fish in that bay of fishes I saw near Comondu.

CHAPTER 21. *I Am Ordered by Don Firmín Sanhudo to Stay Within Our Circle of Fighting Men in Event of Battle—A Tidal Wave of San Vicente Indians Rose from an Arroyo in the Plains of the Cross—Doña Ysabel Draws from Her Breast a Tiny Stiletto with Its Handle a Serpent's Head—The Battle Won, Our Mayas are Calmed with a Word—With Tears I Say Good-bye as a Great Ship Takes the Sanhudos from Monterey*

I OMIT ALL THAT OCCURRED until we came to the Mission of Rosario. Nothing happened, and the rest was too unpleasant to remember. We endured such desert travel as those before us had endured it, and as after us many others would doubtless suffer it through.

The Mission of Rosario marked for me the final break with my own land. To the pitahaya and many southern cacti I had already said good-bye, and now the last *cardón* moved me almost to tears. The finest specimens of all vegetation are always at the extreme northern limit of their growth, and this last *cardón* proved the rule. It was over forty feet high, erect, gaunt and forbidding, like a great giant barring the north to those from the south. Forbidding equally the south to those ignorant water-guzzlers who exist in the north, but who lack foresight, strength, and endurance for my own delight-ful country. In later years, when, overcome by homesickness, I rode three hundred miles merely to salute this great *cardón* and the tall date palms near it, I turned back refreshed in soul, since I had seen something at which my own people daily gazed.

At Rosario we camped for a week in a charming valley with a spring of pure water, from which all drank as if it were the finest wine, since we were weary of alkali water. From an ocean inlet two miles away came sea food of all kinds, and the Mission with its two hundred souls furnished us milk, fresh meat, and all else one could expect. Here we began to meet live-oak trees, and Mission herds being small, burr clover and alfilaria covered the ground, and were eaten by our *mulada* without hesitation. Had we remained a week more, all would have fattened as did my hinny, which demanded two inches longer latigo straps for her saddle *cincho*.

We were in our second year of travel, for Don Firmín Sanhudo had taken time to examine all Missions and all land through which we passed. At Rosario friendly Indians had warned me regarding the San Vicente Bravos. These were Indians who talked little, but struck hard when they were so minded. Therefore I warned Don Firmín, and he called me to him just before we crossed the great wooded plain of Colnet, saying:

"In event of trouble with these San Vicente Indians, stay thou always within our circle formed by my Mayas. If danger becomes great peril, fling my older boy across your saddle, so he be little exposed to arrows, and fly with him. You are the lightest and your mule the swiftest in my outfit."

I looked toward Doña Ysabel, but he shook his head impatiently and went on:

"We are no concern of thine. I have brothers who will fill every *arroyo* in this desert with corpses if we fall, but Inocente must live to continue my line."

La Señora Doña Ysabel de la Cerda Sanhudo traveled in a com-plexion mask, as do some of our greatest ladies to this day, and with her hands in gauntlet gloves. Because of the battle of San Vicente, occurring sixteen months after we left San José del Arroyo, I think of her always as one of a trinity with my mother and that girl at San José who wept for me as I left home.

Such as Doña Ysabel are not for such as I, but with one of her breeding and courage and a dozen sons from her, I could have founded a great family. That which caused me to adore her was her calmness, when even I cried out. Being now a hundred years old, I must tell of this battle in my own way, and if there be those who do not understand me, let them go elsewhere and talk to themselves.

Beyond Colnet we left the ocean, and turning inland by the Salada Pass came upon those great Plains of the Cross which are almost level, but intersected by sunken water-courses, worn deep into fertile soil by floods from dimly distant mountains. It was a country delightful in springtime of rainy years, when alfilaria and burr clover covered the ground like a mattress two feet thick. Had it possessed an ever-flowing river for irrigation, I would not have blamed these Indians for defending it against the Sanhudos. In fact, until an arrow struck my hinny's flank, I respected them for battling to preserve such a land.

Overflowing from one of these deep *arroyos* in the Plains of the Cross, twenty miles north of the Salada, compact masses of San Vicente Indians fell upon us suddenly like an overwhelming tidal wave. According to my orders, I stood within our circle of Wild Men, holding my mule with one hand and Inocente with the other.

Our Mayas fought in a circle about us to protect us, and, as was their way, with a knife in each hand. When not in use these knives dangled from their wrists by leathern thongs. When too closely pressed for knife-work, they would seize an Indian and, swinging him about their heads, thus clear space around them. Or perhaps jumping their height in the air, to clear themselves, would strike with both feet and knives as they came down.

When one fell beneath a crush of attackers and rose again, having slit the throats of those who would have tied him, I yelled with excitement. While our Wild Men were so garbed in leather as to be impervious to arrows or knives, their faces were open to any chance thrust.

"Silence, fool!" whispered Don Firmín to me, knowing that to attract attention of the Indians to us within the circle was bad policy. While evidently they wished us prisoners rather than dead, the rage of battle might easily make them disobey their chief's orders. My hinny just then tried to kick loose an arrow which dangled from her flank, and I did my best to say "Quiet, fool" in the same low, calm tones my patron had used to me.

All these Indians fought on foot except one great chief who, saddleless but with a rope around his horse's belly to hold his knees, rode about encouraging his people. Doña Ysabel stood beside us and watched it all, as if it were without personal interest to her. For this I adored her, but I noticed her right glove dangled loosely behind her hand from its gauntlet, leaving her free to grasp her dagger firmly, if so happened it should be needed for her death. Where the Sanhudos obtained such women, God alone knows.

Her children looked on with great eyes wide open; but not even the boy in arms, who, when cow's milk failed, whined at night, made a sound showing fear.

When the worse came to the worst, and I had Inocente in my arms ready to seek safety in flight, Doña Ysabel drew from her breast a tiny stiletto with its handle a serpent's head, fangs open. I have seen many a man's knife-point describe a circle from fear as he drew it from its sheath, but this woman's *misericordia* was as steady as my own, when I see before me a man waiting for death. Its thin blade would have been in her heart with no trembling of her hand; but as she paused, her husband whispered to her: *"Un momentito, querida mia."*[1]

Seizing the heavy hat from his head, he skimmed it through the air so that its brim struck the Indian chief below his chin. Then, while this man was momentarily stunned—for the hat was no light missile, being loaded with silver as became its owner's rank—Don

---

[1] *Un momentito, querida mia:* wait but a little moment, dear one.

Firmín leaped upon the shoulders of an Indian before him, and treading on the closely packed heads of those who attacked our circle, or supported by his guardian angel, reached to the chief he sought. With his right hand he gave that Blow of The Assassin, which with sufficient strength almost severs head from body, and with his left plunged a small dagger into the Indian chief's horse.

The beast, frantic with pain, plowed a way through hordes of natives, with their chief lolling almost headless upon its neck but held to his horse by that rope about its belly through which his knees were passed. Don Firmín Sanhudo returned as he had gone, and stood beside his wife. As the Indians hesitated whether to fly with their dead leader or avenge him, our heavily armed fighting men galloped up from the rear. Their mules, trained for warfare, rushed headlong into the press of struggling men, striking with their fore legs. Also with their teeth they tore away the faces of those Indians within reach, so that scores of faceless, sightless natives staggered over the plain, or falling, waited for some merciful knife to end their misery.

Nor were their riders less useful. With heavy swords, which they swung in circles about them on each side, and always at naked necks, they soon cleared the ground near us, and passed on, seeking any group of Indians which held together; and at last following even single men. Always with fierce competition between rider and mule as to whether the beast's teeth should first reach the foe's face or the rider's saber the necks of those who fled.

Of all things to be feared, the worst is a horse's teeth—nor are a mule's better. Twenty years after this trip with the Sanhudos, I once faced a *mesteño* mule mad with hydrophobia; my two knives against thirty-six teeth and four flail-like hoofs. Though I am built of Toledo steel and nerveless, I lay down beside the beast for an hour after I had killed it. Therefore, this onslaught of trained mules and saber-armed *soldados de cuero* remains in my mind as the most gruesome feat of war ever known to me.

We, who had been encircled by Maya guards, remained within a ring of dead, while all, even our *arrieros*, spread over the plain, killing those who had not the speed of deer. Inocente clasped my hand as an abalone grasps its sea rock. It would have needed a crowbar to pry us apart, but his color had not forsaken him, and with his eyes he eagerly followed all that went on. His left hand he held negligently on the handle of a wooden sword I had made for him, in imitation of his father; thus standing ready to meet any Indian who, rising from heaps of slain, might wish to sell his life dearly.

The two girls now had their faces hidden in their mother's skirt, but of fear there was no sign. Doña Ysabel held her hand upon her husband's as he clasped his dagger, and with clear eyes watched the slaughter.

"Not too many," she begged of him, sighing; for to her breed the butchery of flying foes has no charm. Reluctantly Don Firmín raised a silver whistle, carried to give orders, and recalled his men. Our heavily armed fighting men lumbered back at a gallop, eager to protect pack-train and cattle from any surprise; but the Wild Men returned slowly and sullenly, showing their teeth and acting like hounds called back from a cat chase.

To them Don Firmín said but a single word in their own language, and at once they smiled and, sitting down, whetted their knives on such leather as was least bloody, whether their own boots or a neighbor's back. Again they looked at their patron with a proud, wolfish respect. The Mayas are a race which cannot understand an enemy being left alive except from fear.

What that word was which Don Firmín used to content them, I learned only long after, by payment of a pearl—from those I took at the Loreto wizard's cavern—to his chief packer, who also came from southern Mexico. It is not that I am curious, nor fond of gossip, but a mystery spurs me on until I solve it. The word with which he so changed Maya faces was "Later."

This I did not understand until we reached San Diego, when Don Firmín returned with a hundred *soldados de cuero* to San Vicente and exterminated every male Indian who had returned alive from their battle with us. On his return northward he also hanged a dozen

Indians from Santo Tomás Mission, who on his first trip had been surly. From courtesy to their padres he hanged them not near their Mission but at the Chocolate, farther south; which has since been considered haunted, and no man lives there. To me this is ridiculous. It is conceded by all that an Indian is without reason and has no soul. How, therefore, can such have a ghost?

Of all Indians I have known, those of San Vicente Ferrer were the most unquiet, proud, and disdainful of danger. Those of Santo Tomás truly were treacherous and quick-tempered, but they lacked sustained effort in war. Among Indians each little tribe differs from the next, and one must learn their ways to be safe among them.

Those of Comondu, Loreto, and the Purísima Concepción, I found false, melancholy, and filthy beyond words. To eat what they prepared was impossible. But natives of San Fernando and Rosario were pacific and easily managed, being by nature talkative, jolly, and usually of large size and great strength. Perhaps it is soil which determines these temperaments, for in my age I find Mexicans from these parts not unlike what their Indians were.

It was no slight task for our *arrieros* to cleanse a path and so cover it with dust that we might pass dry shod over what our battle left; but that night we camped at San Vicente and received submission from a dozen chiefs. To them Don Firmín Sanhudo, smiling, forgave all, and even parted a crate of *panocha* among them. It is a tribute to this great man that not the most suspicious of them, nor any of his own party except the Mayas, knew the deserved slaughter he planned for these Indians as soon as he could return from San Diego with his *soldados de cuero*.

All this I have told lest, being old, I might die before explaining what manner of great lady Doña Ysabel was. God rest her in the hereafter, for she withstood danger and hardship as none other I have ever known.

I was so riven by the certainty of losing Inocente and Doña Ysabel at Monterey that life lost all its savor and food all its taste. I felt that could I die for Doña Ysabel before we reached their seaport, it would make me happier than I ever again could hope to be. That great lady was the only person, except my mother, who had ever trusted me. And who properly values his mother's confidence or deserves it? At San José del Arroyo, when I was but four years old, the baby of one of the women fell into an open fire. Its whole face was so scarred that to look at it terrified me. Yet its mother always called that over-hideous child "my beautiful one." Such an example of a mother's love made me cynical regarding all mothers, even my own.

Beyond having confidence in me, Doña Ysabel had caused all others to trust me. Thus she had made a man of me. At San José del Arroyo, had a single person called me aught but "Hellion," I would have died a dozen deaths for him.

Beyond San Vicente lay Santo Tomás Mission, in a wide and beautiful valley. They have above their Mission buildings the largest spring of cool water I have ever seen, and their bands of sheep were larger in number than we had met on our trip. Between Santo Tomás and San Diego, along the coast, were several small Missions or per- haps, rather, *Asistancías*, divided between the Dominicans on the south and Franciscans on the north; for the Alta California line lay far south of San Diego. We did not go to the inland Mission of Guadalupe, as Don Firmín was depressed by all he saw and anxious to reach Monterey and receive his letters and news from Spain.

Regarding Alta California all is now so well known that I will tell you only a few incidents I myself saw, or that were reported to me by those I trust; and I trust the truth of few men.

Where we crossed a great river (Soledad?) with difficulty and danger, we came to a little Mission, and the Indians asked me con- cerning a great event which had happened to them there. At the ded- ication of their Mission, their padre had suddenly gone crazy and stood upon his head in the Sanctuary, waving his legs and braying like a donkey. Also he had performed various other amusing tricks, such as drawing a picture of the Devil in red ocher, and worshiping him while standing on one leg and flapping both arms as a crane does in rising from the ground. His companion priest fled in horror, believing fire from Heaven would consume all who witnessed this sacrilege.

These Indians begged me to tell them why their services could not always be so interesting. They said that to the next services in this Mission, Indians, both baptized and unbaptized, had come from all parts, but uselessly.

At Monterey we arrived, travel-worn but unharmed by our eighteen-months' trip. Here a house had been provided for the Sanhudos, with servants and all manner of things I had never seen before. Therefore, I was glad when Don Firmín Sanhudo took me with him to the extreme north.

At the Mission of San Francisco, near a great bay, I saw only hillocks of sand and hills of rock, with much marshland. The Indians there had one custom new to me. In cold weather they clothed themselves with layers of thick mud, and thus slept warmly. These Indians said that their long and wide bay was very new and had been formed by a great earthquake. Many of their tribe, who had lived in the green meadows now below this bay, were drowned when a river and the ocean covered them. To prove their truth, they took me out on the bay in their fishing boats and tied them, while they fished, to the tops of tall trees formerly growing in these submerged meadows. These trees were so far below salt water that to touch even their tops one must reach down from the boats.

When we returned to Monterey, a vast ship lay in the harbor, and many guns sounded when Don Firmín Sanhudo entered the presidio. I was terrified, thinking a great war begun; but Inocente told me it was only a royal salute, since his father represented the King of Spain in person.

That afternoon Don Firmín took me to the corral where his men were being paid off, and ordered me to select for myself the six best mules *aparejado*[1] and two riding mules with saddles. This I did so well that the men, clustered around us to bid a respectful farewell to

[1] With all their pack-outfits.

Don Firmín Sanhudo, yelled approval; and he a little ruefully laughed, saying he would sometime have me brought to Spain to choose the King's horses.

I placed all my beasts in charge of Heraclio, except my hinny, which I kept always near me, since she mourned and lost flesh if she could not occasionally nuzzle my hand at night. Also, from fear of this hinny, no man could rob me at night, and Monterey was not Paradise nor guarded by angels.

In the morning I moped about Doña Ysabel and Inocente, until she, guessing what troubled me, got me an order to visit the ship on which they were to sail that evening. I was rowed out to this ship in Don Firmín's own boat, and a little officer received me as if so ordered. He wore more gold braid than our Admiral of Pearl-Divers, and treated me as if the Governor were behind me.

"You wish first to see?" he asked politely, lifting his hand in salute, to which, of course, I removed my hat, now covered with many silver ornaments Inocente had given me.

"The drinking water," I replied, which astonished him. Water was that which most troubled me for Doña Ysabel's trip, since I had dreamed of her lying under a sail drip, lapping fog as Don Felipe Romero of San Luis Gonzaga Mission had told me he was forced to do on his trip from Manila.

The water supply was so ample that even the sailors washed their hands once a day, the young officer told me. As for provisions, never had I seen more. A milch cow for the children, and hens to lay eggs; so that I went ashore happier than I had been for many a day. To bid Doña Ysabel good-bye was bad, but to have had her sail short of water and food would have been more than I could have endured.

On saying good-bye and thanks to the young officer, he gossiped to me: "I hear you are a great landowner."

To which I replied: "Somewhere I own a plot of ground, six-by-four; or if I die young, perhaps only five-by-three," alluding to my grave.

But he laughed as if I were a great wit, for he knew what I had not yet learned.

When I went ashore I was so changed that Doña Ysabel smiled at me, saying: "Inocente told me of your fears, but did you imagine that Don Firmín would care for me less well on sea than on land?"

That afternoon I walked behind them with Inocente, and therefore heard only part of their conversation.

"I could hold these Californias for the King and force honesty," Don Firmín confided to Doña Ysabel.

"But the Council of the Indies?" scoffed Doña Ysabel; at which Don Firmín raised his left hand, while the right hand went to his knife-handle; as if he would grasp the beards of these old men with one hand, while with the other he cut their throats. That showed my master not to have been born, as we say, with a knife in each hand. If one of your hands is occupied with a man's beard and the other in cutting his throat, your enemy must be a fool not to rip up your belly with one or both of his knives.

"If the King would but give the Californias to me and to my brothers for a hundred years, it would then go back to Spain a greater Empire than is Spain," sighed Don Firmín.

"A dream, Firmín," replied Doña Ysabel. "Such a dream as the De la Cerdas dreamed in their day, yet where are they now?" And she in her turn sighed deeply.

"Revered by us," he replied gallantly, "and their memory respected by all Spain. Did not the King himself remove his cap when he spoke to you as we left Spain, out of respect for those you represent?"

"Still, it was a dream," she replied; and woman-like, by her tone, she demanded accomplished dreams of her ancestors.

For a moment I doubted Doña Ysabel's wisdom, for I also was a dreamer. Then I remembered that if, as a small boy at San José del Arroyo, I dreamed at night of a fat shoat roasting itself before a fire of hot coals and grunting to be to be eaten by me, I took great care to realize my dream before noon next day. Dreams by men become facts. Dreams which remain dreams debase the will.

Before sundown that day they sailed away, and Inocente, at parting, gave me a packet, saying: "A letter from my mother, Doña Ysabel."

One of the little girls called me to her, suggesting: "Lean over, Don Juanito." And when I did so, she whispered, "Look in your *aparejos* when you are alone, kind boy."

To Doña Ysabel I gave the *machete* with a great pearl in its handle, with which by my side I had cut such a figure at San Buena Ventura. This she took almost in tears, whether at parting from me or at parting me from my *machete* I do not know. To each of the children I gave one of those great pearls I had taken from the Wizards' Cave at Loreto. Even to their baby boy I sent such a pearl; but all so wrapped that none saw these pearls until aboard their ship.

While the small boat waited, with sailors in the water on each side holding it level, Doña Ysabel de la Cerda Sanhudo curtsied deeply to that half-circle of all the best in Monterey which surrounded her on the beach.

The officials, in more gold braid and gold lace than there is gold in my country, bowed with hats off, while their ladies bent until noses and the ground met. But to me alone, who stood within the circle about her, she extended her hand. Taught by Inocente, I dropped on one knee and kissed her hand. Never before had I touched even the hem of her garments, and I then made that vow I have since kept.

When they had sailed away I called to Heraclio, who stood with all of Monterey, far on the outskirts of the officials. With him, in a quiet corner of my corral, I sat down, while my hinny looked inquisitively over my shoulder.

Heraclio had been trained as a priest, though by his too open vices he had lost his chance; but he could read Spanish. I held Doña Ysabel's letter before him, for I would not allow him even to touch it, and he exclaimed so loudly that I said: "Silence, fool," and touched my knife-hilt.

The letter from Doña Ysabel, which I had so longed for, was merely titles to land from the King of Spain, signed by Don Firmín and God knows what other officials. By their great seals with letters I knew they were real. Also I knew why the little officer of their ship had thought it my jest when I spoke of the six-by-four plot of land I would sometime own.

"Patron!" said Heraclio, speaking the word slowly, for he was a clever man and knew I would never forget the first time that word was spoken to me. Between the *P* of *P-a-t-r-o-n* and the *n* at its end, I grew a foot, and ceased forever to be a boy.

I had money, for Don Firmín Sanhudo had paid me ten silver pesos a month. This is far more than a boy is worth, but I took it, feeling that, while he might not know it, I had been useful to him on our long trip. Having money and titles to land by the courtesy of Don Firmín Sanhudo—though to him land in the Californias meant nothing—I selected four of our best *arrieros*. When I had given Heraclio opportunity to explain regarding my land, they willingly agreed to serve me and with a deference which charmed me. This assured me we would long be friends.

Taking Heraclio aside I said to him, "Were it not for thy lewd tongue we could work long years together."

"Patron," he answered me, "my tongue is well trained."

Thereafter he never troubled me, though at times I heard circles of my men cackle at his jokes. When I ceased to be young, say at about sixty, it made me lonely to have men's voices hushed as I passed. "Better would it be," I thought, "to be always twelve years old, even though thus forced to listen to lewdness and foolish jokes." But loneliness is the penalty of age and of much land and wealth. Heraclio lived his life with me, and his children and grandchildren as well, whether legitimate or otherwise.

Next morning we started south, though with a short day's journey, as I remembered what the little Sanhudo girl had said to me while we stood in the half-circle, as the Sanhudos made their adieus to all the officials of Monterey. I was curious to know what the *aparejos* might contain. A child makes much of a secret, yet there was that in her voice which seemed real to me.

At the first ranch to the east of Monterey, we stopped for the night, and, with the mules' *aparejos* arranged in a circle about me, I lay down, telling my men that sorrow for the Sanhudos' departure prevented my eating. While they ate and played their mouth-organs within this ranch house, I examined the insides of those leathern bags used for packing on mules.

Within each *aparejo*, to one side of that hand-hole through which we rearrange the hay stuffing, I found a small package of gold money. Gold I had never seen before, except such as Don Firmín had paid on our trip for supplies. So much gold as I now owned would make me a rich man even in Heaven.

Within one package was a letter from Doña Ysabel, and, as I could not read it, nor permit any others to read it to me, I have treasured it all my life, like nothing else I have ever had. There is one grandchild of Heraclio's who seems to me clean inside and out. If she learns to read Spanish well, and at sixteen seems to be what she now is, I may trust her to read this letter of Doña Ysabel's to me; though not to touch it.

Of the rest of California del Norte I saw nothing because of my tears at leaving Inocente and Doña Ysabel. Below San Luis Obispo we met everywhere the ruins of that great earthquake[1] which destroyed or greatly damaged every Mission south of the broad valley of Santa Maria. I gave thanks daily that Doña Ysabel and her children had not been in one of these fallen churches.

Now all is gone. These Southern California Missions, built of adobe, when once unroofed melt away in the rains as quickly as Christianized Indians also disappear. I have lived to ride past San Miguel on the coast north of Todos Santos Bay, and ask myself: "In God's truth! Which, then, of these heaps of broken-down adobe bricks was Padre Valdellon's house?" Or to stand near the great

[1] October 1812.

spring at Santo Tomás de Aquino, and say: "Here it must have been that his Indian pets killed Fraile Rudoldo Surroca in his bed[2] before I came from the south; but by the Blind Man Whom Christ Healed, I am not certain. It may be that the poor padre's bed was not in this mud-pile here, but rather in that roofless, melted-down ruin yonder between the two bushes." And so at San Vicente Ferrer, and at Santo Domingo on San Simón Bay, and at how many other places I do not like to think. All fades and disappears, vanishing forever with that past I knew.

So must I also disappear. Having now passed my hundredth birthday, and today having been honored by those not born barefoot, as was I, what remains for me but that piece of ground, six-by-four, of which I spoke to the young ship's officer at Monterey?

At least in life I have gained that increased size of permanent abiding-place, from the five-by-three which would have been mine had the church-robber killed me, to six-by-four. If aught else is permanent with me, it must be pride that so many good friends have honored this my hundredth birthday by their presence.

[1] In 1813.

OTHER CALIFORNIA LEGACY BOOKS

One Day on Beetle Rock
By Sally Carrighar, foreword by David Rains Wallace,
illustrations by Carl Dennis Buell
Written with exquisite detail, Carrighar brings readers to an exhilarating
consciousness of the skills, intelligence, and adaptations of Sierra wildlife.

Death Valley in '49
By William Lewis Manly, edited by LeRoy and Jean Johnson,
introduction by Patricia Nelson Limerick
This California classic provides a rare and personal glimpse into westward migration
and the struggle to survive the desert crossing.

Eldorado: Adventures in the Path of Empire
By Bayard Taylor, introduction by James D. Houston, afterword by Roger Kahn
A quintessential recounting of the California gold rush, as seen through the eyes
of a New York reporter.

Fool's Paradise: A Carey McWilliams Reader
Foreword by Wilson Carey McWilliams, introduction by Gray Brechin
This collection examines some of historian/journalist Carey McWilliams's most
incisive writing on California and Los Angeles.

November Grass
By Judy Van der Veer, foreword by Ursula K. Le Guin
This novel transports readers to the coastal hills of San Diego County and brings
clarity to questions of birth, death, and love.

Lands of Promise and Despair:
Chronicles of Early California, 1535–1846
Edited by Rose Marie Beebe and Robert M. Senkewicz
This groundbreaking collection presents an insider's view of Spanish and Mexican
California from the writings of early explorers and residents.

The Shirley Letters: From the California Mines, 1851–1852
By Louise Amelia Knapp Smith Clappe, introduction by Marlene Smith-Baranzini
With the grandeur of the Sierra Nevada as background, this collection presents an engaging, humorous, and empathetic picture of the gold rush.

Unfinished Message: Selected Works of Toshio Mori
Introduction by Lawson Fusao Inada
This collection features short stories, a never-before-published novella, and letters from a pioneer Japanese American author.

Unfolding Beauty: Celebrating California's Landscapes
Edited by Terry Beers
The beauty of California is reflected in this collection of pieces by John Muir, John Steinbeck, Wallace Stegner, Jack Kerouac, Joan Didion, and sixty-four other writers.

If you would like to be added to the California Legacy mailing list, please send your name, address, phone number, and email address to:

California Legacy Project
English Department
Santa Clara University
Santa Clara, CA 95053

For more on California Legacy titles, events, or other information, please visit www.californialegacy.org.

A CALIFORNIA LEGACY BOOK

S ANTA CLARA UNIVERSITY—founded in 1851 on the site of the eighth of California's original 21 missions—is the oldest institution of higher learning in the state. A Jesuit institution, it is particularly aware of its contribution to California's cultural heritage and its responsibility to preserve and celebrate that heritage.

Heyday Books, founded in 1974, specializes in critically acclaimed books on California literature, history, natural history, and ethnic studies.

Books in the California Legacy series appear as anthologies, single author collections, reprints of important books, and original works. Taken together, these volumes bring readers a new perspective on California's cultural life, a perspective that honors diversity and finds great pleasure in the eloquence of human expression.

Series editor: Terry Beers
Publisher: Malcolm Margolin
Advisory committee: Stephen Becker, William Deverell, Charles Faulhaber, David Fine, Steven Gilbar, Dana Gioia, Ron Hansen, Gerald Haslam, Robert Hass, Jack Hicks, Timothy Hodson, James Houston, Jeanne Wakatsuki Houston, Maxine Hong Kingston, Frank LaPena, Ursula K. Le Guin, Jeff Lustig, Tillie Olsen, Ishmael Reed, Alan Rosenus, Robert Senkewicz, Gary Snyder, Kevin Starr, Richard Walker, Alice Waters, Jennifer Watts, Al Young.

Thanks to the English Department at Santa Clara University and to Regis McKenna for their support of the California Legacy series.